DRAGONKIN

BOOK TWO: TALISMAN

DRAGONKIN

BOOK TWO: TALISMAN

ROBIN WAYNE BAILEY

ibooks

NEW YORK
www.ibooks.net

DISTRIBUTED BY SIMON & SCHUSTER, INC.

Some say that we are gone—
It is not so.
Some say that we are dead,
Or passed on long ago—
But, no.
In the golden sunset,
Or in the dark of night,
Sometimes in the silver glow
Of full moonlight,
We ride the currents of the stars—
Look and see!
For there we are
On the borderland 'tween
Dusk and dawn—
Dragons all in graceful flight!
Some say that we are gone.
Ah, but others know
It is not so,
That the world still is full of
Wondrous things—
So pause and listen
For the whisper of our wings!

—A Song from
The Great Book of Stormfire

PROLOGUE

THE DRAGON MARINA WAITED AT THE DOOR to her cave as the last faint rays of the sun faded in the cloudy west and the darkness of night slowly settled over the world. A soft snow had begun to fall, and the air sparkled as the intricate flakes caught the final light. The fine, white powder already outlined the leafless branches of the trees as it accumulated on the bark, and a frosty blanket was spreading upon the grass.

A covey of honking geese winged southward across the sky. She watched them go past and listened to their noisy cries.

"Fly on, heralds of winter," Marina murmured. She smiled and waved a wingtip to speed them on their way. She was glad that they weren't stopping to visit. It wasn't that she didn't like geese, but she had too much on her mind and wasn't in the mood for company.

She glanced back inside her cave and fought down the impulse to sweep and dust it again. She'd already done so three times today, and shaken all the carpets. After that, she'd cleaned out the fireplace and built a new fire, too. The flames crackled merrily, and a pot of sweet-smelling potpourri simmered on the hearth. For the past hour she'd tried to distract herself with reading, but the red ribbon marker between the pages of the book near the hearthplace revealed how little progress she'd made.

Outside, the snow continued to fall with an almost lazy grace. There was no wind to drive it, to make it swirl or dance. Unfolding one wing,

Marina extended a silver-scaled paw and caught a flake on the tip of an ivory claw. She barely had time to admire the snowflake's ephemeral symetry before it melted away.

Her ears pricked up suddenly as the soft beat of leathery wings caught her attention. The worried look on her face became a stern frown as young Puck sailed around the hillside. He skimmed the tops of the trees in a smooth glide, his golden wings widespread and tail lashing behind, then swooped upward and backward in a playful loop-the-loop before he turned toward the cave.

Marina drummed the claws of one paw against her chest and thumped her tail on the cave floor as she watched his antics. She thought of calling to him and decided against it. Indeed, her impatient anger melted like the snowflake as she noted the sure, strong control of her son's flight and admired his sleekly powerful form.

She leaned against the door and sighed. It didn't seem so long ago that she had stood on this same spot and held Puck in her arms, cuddled him, tickled him, and told him stories as they watched the sun go down and the stars come out together. She'd loved those storytimes, and she missed them. Puck was growing up so fast. He didn't show much interest in stories anymore. It wouldn't be long before he'd find his own cave or dig a new one for himself. Maybe he'd go to Stronghold.

As Puck flew nearer, he noticed her standing at the door. He seemed to hesitate, hovering briefly in mid-air, before he folded his wings and landed. "I'm home!" he announced too brightly.

Marina smiled a secret smile. Puck thought he was in trouble, and by rights, he should be. He'd been gone all day, but this was the first time he'd stayed out after dark. She knew by the uncertain look in his eyes that he expected to be scolded, but she only turned away, went back to the hearth, settled down, and picked up her book.

Puck stared at her from the threshold, then followed her inside. "Aren't you mad at me for being late?" he asked.

She moved the red ribbon marker and turned a page. Without looking up, she answered her son. "I'm never mad at you, dear," she said in a calm voice. "I was worried about you, but you're home safe, and this really is a very good book." She gestured for him to step back a little. "If you don't mind, please, you're blocking my light. You know my eyes aren't what they used to be."

Puck moved to the opposite side of the hearth and leaned on the mantel. Tilting his head, he narrowed his eyes to wary slits and thumped his tail in a slow rhythm on the carpeted floor. "Don't you want to know where I've been?" he asked after a few nervous moments.

Feigning disinterest, Marina shrugged as she turned another page.

Puck frowned and fell quiet again. Then he turned away from the mantel and studied a shelf of books that stood against the far wall. His gaze roamed along the titles while his mother watched him slyly over the top of the volume she held. When he glanced back at her again, she quickly returned her gaze to the open page before her and pretended not to notice.

"I chased a pair of leopards," he told her. "I found them prowling at the edge of the woods on the shore of the Windy Sea." He waited for a response, and when Marina gave none, he added, "I think they came up from Degarm."

Marina turned another page, although she hadn't really seen half the words on the previous page. "That's nice, dear," she answered.

He took a book from the shelf, then set it back without opening it, and began to pace the floor. The tip of his tail brushed a vase full of pussy willow branches that stood on a pedestal near the bookcase, but he caught it before it could fall and set it upright. He shot a hasty look at his mother to see if she'd noticed, but Marina kept her nose in her book—and waited.

Puck wanted to tell her something, she felt sure. His demeanor and his pacing gave that much away. Yet, he seemed reluctant to do so, and she was certain his small adventure with the leopards was just part of it. But Marina wasn't going to chide or berate him to get his story, though he'd plainly expected her to do just that.

Her dragon-son curled up on the floor and turned his gaze on her once more. A certain puzzlement that bordered on hurt burned in his blue eyes. "Don't you care what I've been doing?" he said suddenly. "Or where I've been? I figured you'd be chewing me out by now, but this is almost worse!"

Marina sighed as she carefully marked her place with the ribbon and closed her book. "Of course I care," she answered as she met Puck's gaze evenly. "But you're not a child anymore. I have to remind myself of that sometimes, and maybe I need to remind you, too." She leaned forward and affectionately brushed the top of his scaled head with one paw. "You've got your wings now, Puck. You can fly, and the whole wide world is out there for you. You're growing up, and you're bound to get into some mischief. I expect that." She smiled at him with a mother's smile. It was still so easy to think of Puck as her little dragon-baby, her hatchling. Indeed, she knew a part of her would always see him that way. Yet, she spoke from her heart and knew that the words were meant for herself as much as for her son. "I have to trust your common sense," she continued, "and hope that you know that when you have something to tell me, you can, and that I won't get angry with you."

Puck closed his eyes, laid his head on his crossed forepaws, and swallowed. "I flew farther today than I've ever gone," he confessed. "All the way to Thursis."

A chill rippled up Marina's spine, but she did her best to hide her reaction. Carefully, she set her book aside and leaned back in her corner as she watched her son. Without lifting his head, he opened his eyes again and stared into the fireplace flames. His golden scales shimmered redly in their light.

"It was just like in the stories," Puck continued. "Scorched and fire-blasted and barren. No grass, no trees." He swallowed again. "No life at all. It was horrible."

Marina reached out and touched her son's head again; she felt the slight shivering that ran through him. No one ever went to Thursis any-more. Once, it had been a paradise, an island garden, and the home of the last Merfolk. But that had been long before the Great War. Now the paradise was only a big, charred rock in the Windy Sea—and a profound memorial to foolishness.

"Why?" Marina whispered as she stroked her son's head.

"I had to see it," Puck replied without looking at her. "I wanted to know if all the stories were true."

Marina didn't know quite what to say. It frightened her more than she wanted to admit that her son had flown so far from home and to such a terrible place. And yet, Thursis was a part of Wyvernwood's history, and there were lessons to learn among the blasted rocks and in the ashen dust of that unfortunate place.

A coyote's lonely howl drew Marina's attention, and she looked away from the fire toward the entrance to her cave. The snowflakes that fell outside were larger now, and the ground glistened with a thin, white blanket. Easing away from her son, Marina rose to shut the door. There still wasn't much wind, but the temperature had dropped. She pushed the door softly closed and turned toward the fireplace again.

Puck had picked up her book.

"*TALISMAN*," he read, running one claw carefully over the lettering on the spine. "We haven't read this in years. You used to tell me the story when I was too little to read."

"I remember," Marina answered, settling beside the hearth again. "I used to love to read to you and tell you the old stories." She forced a smile as she ran her gaze over the many shelves of books around her domicile. "But then you decided you were too big to let your mother read to you."

Puck studied the book's spine for another moment, then opened it to the place marked by the red ribbon and scanned a few lines. He closed the book with a snap, hesitated, then passed it to his mother.

"I'm not too big tonight," he said. He laid his head once more on crossed paws and regarded his mother. "Would you read it to me?"

"Are you sure?" Marina asked. She removed the red ribbon and turned back to the very first page. The title and words were written in a rich, black ink, and in a flowing script that was easy to read even by firelight. Still, she moved closer to the hearth and curled up on the floor. An even greater surge of warmth filled her when Puck curled up next to her.

There was still something he wasn't telling her, Marina realized with a mother's instinct. He was too pensive, too quiet. She wanted to ask him what was troubling him, but she resisted that impulse. She had to trust his common sense, she reminded herself. Puck would talk to her when he was ready.

"The title of our tale is *TALISMAN*," she said in a gentle voice. She hesitated for a moment, almost overcome by emotion as Puck began to purr against her side. This was how it used to be when he was a baby and she read to him by the door or by this very hearth. She draped her tail over her son and snuggled closer to him. Yet even as she did so she knew this might be the last time he ever asked her to read to him again. "It begins with a poem." She recited:

All the dragons are gone, my love,
And all the griffins fly above
The realms of mortal men

No more to come.
Yet leave me some
Last dream by which to weigh
The passing of my days.
Sprites and fairies all have fled;
The last remaining elves have shed
This world to search the moon,
And I am left alone, bereft
Of all my gallantry.
Unicorns have hidden in the wood,
Afraid for life that they should
Be discovered true and real and fair.
If only I could share their
Airy wanderings
And leave behind the common world.

1

JAKE WHOOPED AND YELLED as he flew above the green treetops of Wyvernwood on the neck of the great dragon, Chan. His newly designed saddle held him securely in place. The straps and buckles around his ankles, calves, and thighs left his hands free, and he held his arms straight out to his sides to feel the pressure of the wind.

He'd never known such an exhilarating sensation! Once before he'd ridden on Chan's neck, but then he'd been tied in place with uncomfortable ropes and large, tight knots. Oh, that had been exciting, too, but he'd borne the itchy marks and rope-burns for weeks afterward. This saddle was perfect!

He grasped the saddle horn between his legs. "Higher!" he shouted to Chan. "Loop-the-loop!"

Chan seemed to hesitate for a moment. He was a cautious dragon, but even he trusted the new saddle, and more, he trusted Jake. Boy and dragon had formed a bond over the past month, a unique friendship. Chan lifted his head and angled his wings. He climbed slowly at first, sloping upward, gaining gradual altitude. "What did you have for breakfast?" he called back over his massive shoulder.

"Maybe I'll show you in a moment!" Jake answered with a laugh.

"That's what I'm afraid of," the dragon replied. "Hold on!"

Spreading his wings to their fullest, arching his great scaled body,

Chan soared sharply toward the sun. Jake groaned deep in his gut and clenched his teeth as he clutched the saddle horn with all his strength. Forest and sky, treetops and clouds all merged into one vertiginous swirl. For an instant, Jake saw the top of Chan's flame-colored head and the tip of his tail at the same time as the two nearly touched.

Then Jake screamed. Upside-down, he felt his weight strain against the straps around his legs. Brief panic stabbed through him. His stomach churned, and his senses tumbled. Despite himself, he squeezed his eyes shut.

"Want to do it again?" Chan asked in a teasing voice. He finished the loop and resumed a straight, smooth flight above the trees.

Jake tried to sound nonchalant, though he thought he'd sprained every one of his fingers gripping the saddle horn so tightly. "That was nothing," he answered.

"I still don't know what you had for breakfast," Chan reminded him, laughing. "Let's try it a second time, and see if I can find out!"

"Oh! Noooooooooo!" Jake made a desperate grab for the saddle horn again. Once more earth and sky pinwheeled crazily. The wind whipped around Jake. His long brown hair streamed straight back, and the sleeves of his linen shirt snapped. He clenched his teeth, but this time to stifle the scream that threatened to rip from his throat.

Without warning, Chan twisted at the apex of his loop, rolling from left to right, wingtip over wingtip. Caught off-guard by the unexpected maneuver, Jake let go the scream he'd tried to hold back. He felt like he was sliding through the center of a kaleidoscope with pieces of earth and sky fragmenting and jumbling in dizzying sequence before his eyes. The pressure of the straps and buckles against his legs became briefly painful, but his faith in them didn't waver.

Nor did his faith in Chan or himself. Through the entire maneuver, Jake never lost his sense of balance, never yielded to the confusing dizziness. On the ground, he was an acrobat and a tumbler, one of the best ever trained in the carnivals of Degarm, his homeland. He could perform long combinations of flips and handsprings and arials without breaking a sweat, without so much as breathing hard.

But that was on the ground. Height added a grand new dimension. As the sky spiraled around him, his heart pounded and the breath caught in his throat. His scream was not the sound of fear, but a cry of pure adrenaline-inspired excitement! He felt the sleek power of Chan's body through the saddle, the throb of the dragon's powerful muscles, the rhythmic beat of his wings, and these only intensified his thrill as his own reflexes worked in harmony with Chan.

The ground raced suddenly upward at them. Jake leaned as far back in his saddle as he could until he nearly lay flat and felt the heat of Chan's body through his shirt. With stiffened arms, he braced himself on the saddle horn, and his lips curled back from his teeth.

At the last possible moment, Chan pulled out of his dive. His tail brushed the treetops, ripping leaves from the branches as he leveled out. A family of startled turtledoves flashed into the air, abandoning their nests in a flurry of wings and feathers, voicing indignant and chirping insults. Their vocal outrage alerted a host of crows that flew up in black panic directly in Chan's path. The dragon rolled sharply aside to avoid them, and Jake felt the muscles in his neck pop.

"Miserable sky-hog!" the crow-leader cried after them. "You think your size gives you a right to the airways? You smug, up-sized viper!"

"Sorry!" Chan called back to the crows as he raced onward. Then, to Jake, he gave a low laugh. "Crows are such complainers. I missed them all by a wide margin." He chuckled again. "You still with me, Jake?"

Jake sputtered and spat crow-down from his mouth and picked a black feather from the neck of his shirt. "You were so worried about my breakfast," he shouted over the wind. "Well, I just nearly had my lunch!"

With a graceful beat of his wings, Chan climbed a little higher, putting some altitude between them and the trees. "How did it taste?" he asked, grinning as he looked back over his shoulder.

Jake held up the black feather and let the wind snatch it from his fingers. "Fowl," he answered with an exaggerated frown.

Chan turned his nose to the east. Neither he nor Jake had any particular destination in mind. They were only out for fun, enjoying the open sky and practicing Jake's riding skills while they tested the new saddle. For a while, with the turtledoves and crows far behind, they flew without speaking, not in silence exactly, for the wind rushed past Jake's ears, but with a warm and growing contentment in each other's company.

The deep green of Wyvernwood gave way abruptly to the broad white-sand shores and blue expanse of the Windy Sea. Jake breathed deeply of the rich, salt-scented air and smiled. He couldn't be sure, but as he looked down he thought he noted something familiar about the curve of the beach and the spur of forest that jutted out over it almost to the water's edge.

"This is the spot where you rescued me, isn't it?" he said with renewed excitement.

Chan raised his head slightly and gazed over the water. "Well, to be accurate it was Luna who rescued you, and you were way off-shore and going down for the third time."

Jake slowly nodded his head. "Yeah, and a bunch of sharks were swimming around with bibs and knives and forks and very expectant looks on their faces." He chewed his lower lip, feeling strange and slightly sick as he remembered. He tried not to think much about his life before Wyvernwood, and he never told anyone about the nightmares that continued to haunt him.

But as he gazed at the beach below, it wasn't Degarm or kidnapping and slavery that he remembered. Instead, he thought of Stormfire, immense and golden and gleaming with the sun on his scales and wings. Over the rush of the wind, Jake could still hear the great dragon's thunderous voice warning the slavers away. They had run as quickly as they could.

"Why did we come here?" Jake asked.

"Call me sentimental," Chan answered as he flew northward along the shore.

Jake twisted in the saddle to stare back at the spot on the beach where he'd first been brought ashore along with his four friends, Trevor and Markam and Ariel and little Pear. It was the same spot where he'd first seen Chan.

"I thought you were a monster," Jake murmured half to himself.

"You were afraid," Chan answered with the slightest shrug of his wings. "But you rose above that fear, and that's called courage." Chan circled outward over the water, dipping so low that he cut the waves with one wingtip and threw up a sparkling curtain of droplets. Jake felt the cold, fine spray on his face. "That's called a shower," he added with a dragon-smirk.

Jake wiped his face with a sleeve; for once, he didn't have a clever response. The wind would dry him quickly enough. But Chan seemed to be headed back to that same stretch of beach, and for some reason Jake didn't understand, that made him shiver. "Let's head back to Stronghold," he suggested. But Chan stretched out his neck, folded his wings, and settled down on the shimmering sand.

Jake watched as the advancing surf teased a few strands of seaweed and shifted the sand around an old piece of bleached driftwood that stuck up like a half-buried bone. He stared across the waves. Somewhere at the bottom of the sea, far offshore, lay the wreckage of the ship that had brought him here. The sharks hadn't gone completely hungry that day.

Leaning over the saddle horn, he ran his hand along Chan's neck. A fine, silken oiliness coated the dragon's scales, making them moist and supple, lending them a sheen that caught both sunlight and moonlight. Chan's scales were red and orange and gold, tinged sometimes with white and even blue. On earth or in the sky, he looked like fire, a living flame, and Jake thought he'd never seen any creature so magnificently beautiful.

He trembled with sudden emotion as he stroked the dragon, and thought of how lucky he was to have Chan for his friend. No other man or boy had ever ridden a dragon. It was more than just an honor that Chan was willing to carry him, teach him, and train him. It was a sign of their friendship—perhaps even an act of love.

Jake didn't want to be here on this particular stretch of shore, but plainly Chan did. The dragon lowered himself until he lay full-length upon the sand. With his wings compressed against his body and his tail curled close, he shut his golden eyes and began to purr like a cat.

"No, don't dismount," Chan said in a quiet voice when Jake began to unfasten one of the buckles on the saddle. "We won't be here very long, but the sand is warm, and the memories are warmer." He drew a deep breath, and his purring grew louder. A smile turned up the corners of his dragon-mouth. "I come here sometimes to be alone . . . and to remember my father."

Jake tilted his head and frowned, then leaned forward to stroke Chan's neck again. He didn't want to be here, didn't want to be reminded of the sunken ship offshore, didn't want even to gaze across the waves to the place where it went down. Yet Chan's presence and the soft vibration of his purr calmed Jake a little.

"You're not alone this time," the boy whispered. He wondered what it was like to lose a father; he'd never known his. He asked again, "Why did you bring me here?"

"Because it's time," Chan answered without opening his large eyes.

"You pride yourself on your balance, Jake, as if it was only a physical skill. But do you understand that *everything* is always in balance? The land is balanced by the sea; the earth by the sky." He fell silent for a moment, and the only sound was the soft rush of the surf.

The frown on Jake's face deepened, yet suddenly he closed his eyes, too. He'd listened to Chan talk before, and old Ramoses, too, and usually their strange dragon philosophies flew right over his head. He was only a boy, after all, an acrobat and a tumbler.

Still, with his eyes squeezed shut, a bare glimmer of understanding flashed through his mind. "Silence," he murmured, then hearing the surf, "balances sound." With his eyes still closed, he could almost see the water as it retreated, followed by the wave of silence that rolled in to take its place.

"A few months ago I lost my father," Chan continued. "Yet even in that there's balance, because I've gained a little brother. This is why I brought you here, Jake, to the place where you came out of the sea—because it was time for me to say that, and for you to hear it."

Jake's mouth went dry as Chan's words sank in. Opening his eyes, he once more stared seaward. Chan's declaration filled him with pride, with more joy than he'd ever known. Yet, a vague chill crawled along his spine, and he shivered in his damp clothes.

"Who told you?" he said finally, barely able to get the words out.

Chan twisted his long neck until he looked at Jake. Though his eyes looked like discs of shining metal, they were filled with gentleness and concern. "Little Pear let it slip a few nights ago," he answered. "But I'd already guessed. You were out of balance. Trevor and Markam are twins; they work and perform together in perfect harmony as if they were one. Ariel and Pear are different, yet much the same—not sisters and not the same ages, yet they complement each other."

"Pear shouldn't have told," Jake whispered. "We all swore never to talk about it!"

"They look to you, the oldest, as their leader," Chan pressed, "and you all work together like a perfectly trained team. Yet within your team, they function as smaller teams." The dragon paused and slowly blinked his eyes.

"His name was Keven!" Jake blurted. He gripped the saddle horn with both hands and squeezed until his knuckles cracked. "He was my partner, and my team-mate! And they killed him! They all got drunk on the deck, and they made us perform for them." Tears began to spill down Jake's cheeks as he stared outward. But it wasn't the blue, sun-sparkled sea he saw—it was darkness and stars and a ship lit only with lanterns, and Keven falling, falling and screaming, before he struck the deck.

Sound. Then silence. The thought hit Jake like the point of a knife.

"They knew that Keven walked the high wires, so they ordered him up into the ship's rigging to walk a line for their entertainment. All the sailors said the wind and the waves were responsible—but *they* were responsible! They killed him! That's why we five made a break for it the next morning, before they killed another one of us!" He slammed an angry fist down on Chan's scales. *"Why did you bring me here?"*

He didn't wait for an answer. His hands flew over the buckles and straps with manic determination; in no time, he had freed himself from the saddle. Headfirst, he dived from Chan's neck, jack-knifed in mid-air, and landed on his feet. Without looking back, he ran down the shoreline almost to the water's edge. There, he stopped and kicked sand, then picked up a handful and flung it at the advancing waves.

Then his legs seemed to lose strength. Losing his balance, he plopped down to sit with his hands folded limply in his lap. The sun burned his face, and the Windy Sea still rolled inexorably before him, but he hardly noticed, barely cared.

There was more to tell about that night. He hadn't revealed how the sailors had ordered him, not Keven, into the rigging first. Or how Keven, knowing the danger, had leaped to take his place, virtually sacrificing himself so that Jake would live.

He gripped twin handfuls of sand and watched the grains slip through his fingers. Chan had come here to remember his father, the Dragon Stormfire. But Jake's people, the people of Degarm far to the south of Wyvernwood, didn't cling to memories of the dead. They never spoke of the dead, and tried to forget so that the ghosts of those they loved wouldn't follow and haunt the living.

For a long time Jake sat still, no longer crying, breathing softly. In the gentle rush of the surf, he thought he could hear Keven's voice. His friend's body had gone down with the ship into the sea. Keven was part of it now.

After awhile, Jake got up and walked back to Chan. He felt slightly embarrassed, but he also felt unburdened. "You brought me here to say goodbye to my friend, didn't you?"

Chan was gazing out to sea. Slowly, he turned his head and looked at Jake with those large golden eyes. "I brought you here to say hello."

Puzzled, Jake tilted his head and frowned again. Why didn't dragons ever just say what they meant? Why did they have to be so cryptic? He threw up his hands, then slapped his sides in exasperation. "I don't understand!"

With a blink of his eyes, Chan interrupted him. "I lost a father," he reminded Jake. "I found a brother."

Jake thought about that. Sometimes he felt so small and stupid when he listened to dragons talk. "I lost my teammate here," he said carefully, groping for the words. Then he looked up at Chan. "But I've also found a teammate. A partner. A . . . brother?"

The dragon blinked again and grinned. "Now get back in the saddle. It's time we headed for home."

Jake liked the way Chan said *home*. He bounded onto the tip of the dragon's tail. With the merest flick, Chan propelled him upward as they'd practiced, and he caught the horn. A moment later, he swung into the seat and fastened the straps securely around his legs. "Does this mean I get to call Luna *Sis*?" Jake asked as he worked the last buckle into place.

Chan gave a low chuckle. "Not where she can hear you," he answered. "And she can hear a bee on the far side of the forest."

"What about Harrow?" Jake persisted innocently.

Chan spread his wings and with a powerful beat, caught the air and rose into the sky. "I *definitely* wouldn't call him *Sis*."

Laughing, they turned their backs to the Windy Sea and flew over the forest toward the south and west. The sun slid past zenith. Most of the clouds had vanished from the sky, leaving only a few wispy strands of whiteness on the horizon. For a time, they followed a creek. Jake didn't know which one; he still wasn't familiar with a lot of Wyvernwood this far north of Stronghold. He was learning though, learning so many things!

There were times when he could barely remember his old life, the carnivals and the circuses, the crowds. He didn't miss Degarm at all. His people—he hardly considered them *his people* anymore—thought Wyvernwood was full of monsters and horrible creatures, but he had come to think they, along with the men of Angmar in the far north, were the real monsters. In Wyvernwood he'd found kindness and caring such as he'd never known among men.

Yet, Wyvernwood held its dangers, too.

As he glanced down at the creek, he spied four shadows reflected on the dappled water. Twisting, he stared back over his shoulder. "Griffins!" he cried. "Coming fast!"

Chan bent his neck around to see, and let go a roar. He was flying low, close to the treetops with little room to maneuver. Above them, the four griffins dropped swiftly out of the sun with razor-sharp claws extended.

Chan let go a blast of fire to warn their attackers off. A flickering barrier of flame hung briefly in the air. Undeterred, the griffins scattered, taking four divergent paths around the blast, and still they came on. Their eagle-like wings, though smaller and feathered, were as powerful as a dragon's leather pinions, and the griffins themselves were far stronger.

Jake corrected himself. There *were* a few monsters in Wyvernwood.

With the advantages of surprise and position, the four griffins surrounded them. No longer silent, the griffins roared and screamed and made menacing gestures. They snapped their beaks, raked the air with their talons. One swerved suddenly and darted at Jake's head. He ducked, flattening himself as much as he could over the saddle horn. At the same moment, Chan swooped even lower, shattering branches and raising a flurry of leaves.

"You should have let me bring my bow!" Jake shouted nervously as he watched the griffins on either side. They seemed to be staring particularly at him. Indeed, one tried to lock gazes with him!

"No weapons!" Chan called back.

Overhearing, the keen-eared griffins seemed to smile as if they knew that Chan wouldn't roast them. "Give us the Man-child!" one of them cried, swooping close to Chan's left wing. "Give us the murderer of the griffin-leader, Gaunt!"

"Go back to Redclaw!" Chan answered angrily. "There are dragons in these skies who aren't as tolerant of your kind as I am!"

There weren't any other dragons close. Both Jake and Chan knew it— and from their higher vantage in the sky, the griffins knew it, too. Jake reached into a pouch on his belt and extracted a slim strip of leather and a smooth stone. Chan had forbidden him to bring his bow and arrows, but he wasn't completely unarmed. Placing the stone in the center of the leather strip, he whipped it around his head and let fly.

The nearest griffin screamed and veered sideways. Chan took the opening and swooped higher. At the same time, he lashed out with his tail, batting the wounded griffin from the air, knocking him into the trees below. With another roar, he twisted and rolled. Jake lurched in his saddle and grabbed for the horn as the world spun around him.

Suddenly, Chan was above the three remaining griffins. He blasted fire again, not to burn their attackers, but to force them into the trees.

"You can't protect him forever!" one of the griffins shouted before he plunged into the branches of a red oak. "He's raw meat!"

Chan didn't waste time. He raced on, leaving the four griffins behind, flying as swiftly as he could for the safety of Stronghold. "What did you hit that griffin with?" he demanded as he flew. "What have you got, Jake?"

Jake wrapped the leather strip around his hand and stared grimly ahead. "It's called a sling," he answered stubbornly. He knew what was coming.

"Another weapon? We're surrounded by Man's wars, Jake! You know how I feel about such things!"

Jake fought to control his temper. He'd had this argument before with Chan. "You have your claws and your fire," he said. "The griffins have their talons and their strength!"

"Throw it away, Jake!" Chan demanded.

"I will not!"

"Throw it away!"

Jake's eyes narrowed to angry slits. Then he drew a deep breath. Chan didn't understand, but now wasn't the time for debate. He didn't wish to upset Chan today of all days, not after what they had just shared on the beach. The dragon was his teammate, his brother. With a sigh, he unwrapped the sling, held it up, and tossed it into the trees below.

When the need arose, he had another sling coiled in the same pouch. *Life balances death,* he thought to himself, considering his lesson. *War balances peace.*

He bit his lip and hoped that he'd gotten the lesson wrong.

AN UNSETTLING QUIET HUNG OVER THE WHISPERING HILLS. No breeze rustled the summer leaves. The birds sat nervously in their nests, not singing. The fireflies that should have filled the dusky evening with their twinkling instead hid in the grass. Even the crickets and cicadas were silent.

The Dragon Ronaldo stood outside his cave with his gray wings wrapped closely around his body, his eyes narrowed to stern slits. He listened for the sounds that should have stirred in the forest but weren't there, and he watched the sky. He didn't know exactly what had drawn him outside away from his paints and canvasses—perhaps another bout of the restlessness that seemed to plague him these days, or some deeper sensation he couldn't explain.

Low in the west, the sun burned like dying fire through the trees, and the black branches shattered its weakening light into myriad glistening needles and spears that stabbed through to the mossy earth. In the east, the purple clouds of night had begun to gather. A three-quarter moon floated on the edge of the darkness, pale as a ghost, not yet very bright. A covey of geese, little more than black and distant dots, flew across its face in regimental formation. Something else drifted there, too; something wispy and tenuous.

Smoke.

Ronaldo displayed his wings in sudden agitation. The smoke was too diffuse to be close. Creeping farther from his threshold, he craned his long neck upward for a better view of the sky. The geese were barely visible as they slipped lower and lower through the twilight and wheeled in a graceful arc toward the horizon. Ronaldo gazed back toward the moon and watched as a second gray tendril wafted through its light. His dragon's heart quickened. With a frown, he left his cave behind and started upward toward the crest of the hill where he made his home.

Before he took ten paces, the hum of tiny wings sounded softly in his right ear. "Hey, watch where you're going!" a small voice shouted. "You're gonna crush my favorite eucalyptus bushes!"

Ronaldo stopped immediately. He'd been gazing at the moon so intently, he hadn't paid any attention to where he was placing his sizable feet. A small, greenish blur darted back and forth before his eyes, then perched on the scaly tip of his nose.

"Oh, forgive me, Bumble," Ronaldo said to the diminutive hummingbird, his frown abruptly fading. Bumble was Ronaldo's dear friend. They shared his cave and kept each other company. Ronaldo had planted his hillside with eucalyptus and lantana, nasturtiums, ocatillo, and lemon bottlebrush—all Bumble's favorite flowers. The rich perfumes of the different blossoms infused the air, and indeed he loved the garden his hillside had become. The flowers were a smorgasbord for Bumble, and for Ronaldo an inspiring source of beauty. "You know I wouldn't hurt a leaf or bloom on purpose." He glanced toward the wisp of smoke again. "My mind is elsewhere this evening."

Bumble folded his wings and puffed out his chest. "Well, strolling through my scarlet sage isn't going to satisfy your curiosity." He hopped lightly from one taloned foot to the other and shook his tail feathers, then continued in a high-pitched, singsong little voice, "I know what's caught your interest."

With a sudden shake of his head, Ronaldo dislodged the humming-bird. Caught off-guard, Bumble spun upward, head over talons, until he spread his wings and righted himself in mid-air. For a brief instant, his tiny black eyes filled with fright, but then he flew down again to hover before his dragon friend.

"Sorry," Ronaldo apologized. "Your tail feathers tickled my nose, and I thought I was going to sneeze. Just a little bit of flame and . . ."

Bumble's eyes widened as he considered his narrow escape. "And you might have roasted me!" He clapped a wingtip to his forehead as he land-ed on Ronaldo's nose again. "The horror! Roasted Bumble! Barbecued Bumble! Fricasseed Bumble! I'm too young to fry!"

"It's allergy season," Ronaldo explained with a shrug. "I don't usually snort fire when I sneeze. It's such a disgusting habit. Still, I thought it best to get you out of the way, just in case. Oh, and don't forget 'broiled Bum-ble.' Yum!" He licked his lips in an exaggerated fashion.

Bumble fluttered his wings, then grew still and put on a serious look. "I don't really care about the sage," he said with an uncharacteristic edge in his voice. "Or the thyme, or the rosemary, or the honeysuckle for that matter. What are we waiting for, Ronaldo? Let's go see what's really burn-ing!"

Ronaldo hesitated. The idea of leaving his cave unsettled him. He hadn't been away from the Whispering Hills for weeks, maybe not for months. He couldn't remember precisely how long it had been. He found a sheltering comfort in the familiar, forested peaks and the gentle valleys. The thought of leaving them made him shiver.

Bumble flew up into the air, but he didn't go far. An instant later, he perched in Ronaldo's right ear. "A great many adventures begin with a distant wisp of smoke," he said in a conspiratorial whisper.

Ronaldo gazed toward the moon again. Another shadowy tendril crossed its face, born by a faroff wind. The tenuous vapor seemed almost to paint a smile on the moon as it drifted passed.

Bumble flew over the dragon's head and landed in his left ear. "But home is so safe and cozy," the hummingbird whispered in a sweeter voice. "There's no danger here. Let's just stay content and roll in the monkey flowers."

Ronaldo frowned. His gaze wandered over the horizon. There were other wisps of smoke that hadn't yet reached the moonlight.

The little hummingbird flew over Ronaldo's head again and resumed his perch in the dragon's right ear, and his voice became harsh. "Someone could be in trouble," he said. "Someone could need help."

Ronaldo shivered again and thought of Ranock and Beatrice, his minotaur neighbors. Their home had burned last year in the middle of the night and caused untold grief. This smoke was much farther away, but he wondered if it was someone else's home burning.

Bumble flew around to Ronaldo's left ear. "It's no skin off our noses. We're artists, not adventurers!"

The dragon squeezed his eyes shut. Uncertainty gripped his heart, but Bumble's words stung! How was it that with but a few choice phrases a hummingbird could make him feel so small?

Bumble flew around to his right ear again. "Adventurers?" he cried. "Of course we're not adventurers! We're heroes!"

"Stop it!" Ronaldo shouted. He clapped one massive paw to the side of his head, and Bumble darted into the air barely in time to avoid being squashed. "You little imp!"

Bumble made a greenish blur as he flew three swift circles around the dragon's head. Then he landed on the tip of Ronaldo's tail.

Ronaldo's heart raced, but slowly he calmed himself. The thought of leaving his home was almost too much for him to bear. His claws dug into the earth, as if by doing so he might root himself to the spot. And yet, he spread his wings.

His wings. How long was it since he'd actually flown? He couldn't quite remember. He'd taken to strolling among his beloved hills, never taking to the sky. Why was that? He stared yet again toward the smoky moon and let his gaze follow the way the geese had gone.

Carefully he curled his tail, bringing the tip and Bumble up to meet his eyes. "My paints are unsealed," he said quietly.

Bumble inclined his small head and answered in a whisper. "The imp says forget them."

Great gray wings flexed almost of their own accord, testing long unused muscles. "The front door is still open," Ronaldo said.

"Leave it," Bumble said.

The moon continued to rise. The shadow of the hillside began to grow and stretch and elongate until it touched the black edge of the forest. Again, Ronaldo listened and noted the absence of the usual night-sounds. The smoke was not the only thing amiss. He'd felt it before—something not yet seen, stirring and slouching through the woods—but each time he'd only closed his door and curled up by his hearth with his paints or his books.

"I suppose you think you're coming, too?" he said to Bumble as he swept his gaze around. It was hard to leave his beloved cave, his home. He'd tasted adventure before, and it had left a bitter, sad taste in his mouth. Then, as now, Bumble had been at his side.

"Now and forever," the little hummingbird affirmed, "Bumble is your fearless protector."

At first reluctantly, then with a swelling sense of excitement, Ronaldo spread his wings and glided quietly into the sky. Bumble flashed upward on diminutive wings, passing the dragon, leading the way as he set a course for the moon.

The warm summer air kissed Ronaldo's face, and he rejoiced in the exhilarating sensation of wind rushing under and over his leather wings. All his doubts and fears fell away. His heart swelled as he soared higher and higher. Wyvernwood stretched out beneath him in all directions like a glimmering sea as the moon's brightness silvered the leaves and tree-tops, the peaks of far-off hills. For a brief moment, lost in its beauty, he forgot about smoke and danger.

Bumble darted back to Ronaldo and settled in the gray dragon's left ear. The tiny hummingbird was fast, almost too fast for the eye to follow, but only for short distances. For longer excursions, either by land or by air, he often rode thus, in one ear or the other, and Ronaldo never objected.

Without warning, Bumble began to sing in a soft, high voice.

> *"Oh, the sky is wide and far,*
> *But the way is lit by moon and star!*
> *I feel the wind upon my face*
> *And yield to the unknown embrace*
> *Of things I have not seen,*
> *Places where I have not been!"*

The dragon smiled. The gentle melody of Bumble's song soothed him, and his apprehensions became as thin as the smoke he chased. Directing his gaze straight ahead, he flew eastward with a newfound determination.

Behind them, the last traces of sunset faded away, and night closed about the world. One by one, the first-magnitude stars appeared, twinkling like rare jewels in the firmament. Soon, the lesser stars followed until they peppered the blackness. The moon made its way slowly among them.

The smoke was nearly invisible now, but Ronaldo had fixed his attention on a spot on the horizon from where he thought the smoke originated. The Whispering Hills were far behind, but even in the dark he knew Wyvernwood, and he knew his way.

Bumble had been quiet for some time, a rare thing for the hummingbird. He had sung his little song four or five times, once directly into Ronaldo's eardrum, and then settled back in the leathery folds of the dragon's ear to enjoy the flight. But suddenly he fluttered his tiny wings.

"That tickles!" Ronaldo warned as Bumble's feathers brushed his sensitive lobes.

The hummingbird became still again. Grimly, he spoke one word. "Fire."

Barely visible above the trees, a dim reddish glow pulsed, no more than a bubble of color on the horizon. Ronaldo dipped his left wing slightly and flew toward it. At least one of his fears was allayed—the glow was too contained to be a forest fire. He knew of no settlement or homesteads in this part of Wyvernwood, either.

What, then, could be burning?

His answer came a few moments later as he swept low over the edge of the forest and past a high clifftop. The Windy Sea tossed and turned, stretching as far as his eye could see until its dark waters seemed to merge with the star-flecked sky. But far off the coast, he spied a terrible sight: six sailing ships, all on fire!

For an instant, Ronaldo felt sick. He gyred higher in the sky, then turned back toward the cliff and landed on its rocky pinnacle to study the dire scene through narrowed, disapproving eyes. Where there were sailing ships, there were Men, and Ronaldo wanted nothing to do with those miserable creatures!

Scarlet flames crackled along the decks and up the masts. Fiery rigging and tattered pieces of burning sail whipped and snapped on the wind. The sea reflected the glow of the fires, and the water gleamed with a horrible redness.

Bumble flew a circle around Ronaldo's head and perched on his nose. "Bumble doesn't understand war," the little hummingbird said softly as he stared toward the burning ships. "What is it good for?"

Ronaldo slowly shook his head. As he watched, one of the ships slipped over on its port side. He could hear the boards straining and cracking, the angry hiss of steam as the sea swept over the blazing decks, the shattering of the fire-weakened mast as it struck the churning waves.

"Absolutely nothing," Ronaldo answered in a coldly distracted voice. He didn't understand it, either. There was no understanding the madness of Men. But the artist in him wouldn't let him look away from the destruction. He found himself stirred by a strange, stark beauty that seized his imagination. It was a scene of chiaroscuros, myriad contrasts and contradictions, unlikely motions, all of it subtly distorted by veils of smoke and shadow.

A voice spoke from the concealment of some nearby trees. "I suppose you're going to paint it."

Ronaldo turned his head so quickly that Bumble lost his balance on the dragon's nose and tumbled through the air. The last unicorn in the world emerged from the foliage near the cliff's edge. Her white mane was tangled, full of burrs, pieces of leaves, and small twigs, and her forelock hung over one golden eye. Her hide was dirty, and her tail was as matted as her mane.

"Marian!" With a sharp hum of tiny wings, Bumble flew straight for the newcomer and perched on the tip of her horn. With frenzied energy, he darted to Ronaldo's nose, then back to Marian's horn, back and forth, as if he couldn't choose between them, couldn't decide upon whom to settle. Finally, panting with his exertions, he landed on the low branch of a tree and folded his wings. His minute eyes glazed over and gleamed like fine, black beads as he declared, "Bumble is dizzy with happiness!"

Ronaldo turned his gaze seaward again. "Painting it would be a challenge," he admitted. "The glow of firelight on the water, the sheen of wet, charred wood, the intricate shadings—and there's some element missing that I haven't yet put my paw on." He shook his head once again and looked back to the unicorn. "How long have you been hiding there?"

"A lot longer than you, my Dragon-come-lately friend," Marian answered with an indignant snort. "I was down on the shoreline among the rocks when ships from Angmar attacked and set fire to the nine Degarm vessels."

Ronaldo frowned. "I only count six."

The unicorn shook her head. "Three have already sunk beneath the waves."

The gray dragon scowled as he looked out toward the burning ships. He didn't understand war, and he understood Men even less. They were vain little creatures full of jealousies and greeds. He studied the chaotic panorama and almost sighed.

Instead, he gave a sharp, low roar. The missing element in his envisioned painting—he realized with a start what it was. "Where are the Degarm sailors?" His voice was the barest whisper, for he feared he already knew.

Marian supplied the unpleasant answer. "At the bottom of the sea with their ships. The Angmarans weighted them with stones and cast them overboard."

Ronaldo squeezed his eyes shut, but his mind too quickly applied that final detail to the mural taking shape in his head. Trembling with outrage, he cursed himself for leaving his cave and his lovely garden in the Whispering Hills. Had he remained there, he'd be curled up snugly by his hearth with a good book, or daubing perhaps at a still life or floral. But there was no turning away now, no forgetting what his eyes had seen, and whether he wished to or not he would paint this conflagration in all its beauty and all its obscenity. It would take time, and he would live with the vision night and day until he'd finished it.

"Where are the Angmaran attackers?" he asked in an icy voice.

Marian lowered her head until her mane almost touched the ground, and pointed southward with her horn. "They sail on for Degarm's coast," she informed him. "Twenty ships and well-armed, under black sails that will make them hard to spot as they make their way."

Ronaldo's gaze turned baleful. "I won't have any trouble spotting them."

The last unicorn snorted and stomped the earth with golden hooves. "Dragon!" she cried. "Do you think it's wise to interfere? This is Man's war!"

Ronaldo lifted his head and blew a narrow stream of fire at the three-quarter moon. "It stopped being Man's war when they seized the island of Thursis and killed the Merfolk," he answered sharply as another burning ship broke apart on the sea. "I'll remember this sight for a long time to come. Now I'll give Angmar something to remember!"

Spreading his wings, Ronaldo leaped from the edge of the cliff. He swooped low over the water, cleaving the burgeoning waves with the slashing tip of his tail, then with a powerful beat of leathery pinions, he climbed higher and flew toward the burning ships.

It took only a few moments of circling to be certain there were no survivors. Despite his animosity for Men as a race, he would have done what he could to haul drowning sailors ashore. Cursing and scowling, he made a final pass above the wreckage.

A soft weight struck him in the right ear, and Bumble's tiny claws took a firm, familiar grip. The little hummingbird coughed and wheezed.

"Smoke!" he managed between coughs. "I got a lungful!"

"You should have stayed with Marian," Ronaldo said sternly.

Dipping a wing, he turned and raced southward after Angmar's fleet. It didn't require any guesswork to find them. Navigation was still a primitive art where Men were concerned, and he knew they'd be following the coastline. Black sails and nighttime might keep them safe from the eyes of their enemies, but not from a dragon.

It didn't take long at all to catch up with the Angmarans. A few dim lanterns glowed along the rails of each of the twenty ships, else they might have drifted away from each other in the darkness. Ronaldo soared a little higher, making certain that he cast no moon-shadow on the surface of the sea.

Bumble looked down carefully from inside the dragon's ear and waved one wingtip. "Yoo hoo, sailors!" he called, knowing there wasn't a chance he would be heard. Then, in his best pirate voice he said to Ronaldo, "Sink 'em! Sink 'em everyone, I say! Yo ho!"

Ronaldo glanced toward the coast and the wilds of Wyvernwood. Even with their lanterns to reassure them, the vessels were hugging the shoreline. Bumble wasn't serious about sinking the ships, of course, nor was that Ronaldo's plan. Down on the decks, he could see scores of tiny figures stirring listlessly under blankets, or moving about in sleepless anticipation with their crude weapons.

Such fierce little monsters, he thought. *Cowards and sneaks!*

He surged far ahead of the leading vessel, then dropping low, turned back and made straight for it. A breath of red fire announced his coming. It lit the night with a horrible glow, reflecting on the water, startling the unsuspecting sailors. Screaming, they cast off their blankets, snatched up their weapons. The deck quickly turned to chaos, but some ran to the bow rail to see the dragon that raced over the water toward them.

It seemed that Ronaldo intended to ram the leading ship head-on, but at the last minute, he drew up, snapped his wings sharply and hovered in the air above the bow. He could see the fear-filled faces of the sailors and laughed to himself as a few struggled to fit arrows to bowstrings.

"You burned those ships!" he shouted at them. "But you're not the masters of fire! Let me show you real fire!" Stretching his long neck upward, he blew a blast of flame that seemed to ignite the sky.

The other ships couldn't fail to notice the display. More shouting and screaming filled the night. A small rain of arrows shattered harmlessly on Ronaldo's chest. Those tiny shafts had no hope of penetrating his scaled hide!

"Turn back for Angmar!" he warned them. "You go no farther!"

Another rain of arrows flew through the air. Ronaldo glared at the archers and exhaled a controlled breath. Fire blossomed in the air, engulfing the shafts before they could reach him, singeing the beards and eyebrows and mustaches of the men behind the bows.

On the leading ship, a red-bearded man pressed forward against the bow rail and brandished a sword. "We have no quarrel with you, Drag-on!"

Ronaldo glared at the speaker. "But I have a quarrel with you!" he answered. "Your battle interrupted my peaceful evening. Now I'm interrupting your little war!"

The speaker, apparently some kind of leader to judge by the way the other sailors rallied around him, shouted back, "I have twenty ships—"

Ronaldo blew flame into the black sails of the ship. The men aboard shouted and scurried about the deck like panicked mice. The red-bearded leader stared upward in disbelief and rage as the flames swiftly spread into the rigging and flickered along the mast.

"In a few moments you'll only have nineteen," Ronaldo shouted over the crackling heat. "If you're quick, Redbeard, you can all swim to other ships! But you go no farther!"

The screaming grew louder, more desperate. Redbeard shouted orders and threw himself overboard. His men wasted no time following his example. Ronaldo flew higher, skimming the masts of other vessels. He saved his fire, but the wind generated by his wings filled their sails, rocked them, knocked them from their courses. Two ships scraped carelessly against each others' wooden hulls, then side by side, they collided with yet another. Timbers shattered and crashed with a sound that was almost as terrible as the screams and cries.

But no one drowned. Ronaldo watched carefully to make sure that each man in the water reached another ship and was taken aboard. Slowly, ponderously, the nineteen ships turned and steered a course away from the coastline and northward for their homeland, leaving one vessel to burn and sink.

Ronaldo gave a sigh as he measured their retreat. Bumble stirred lightly in his ear. He'd been awfully quiet for a long time. Too quiet. "Well?" Ronaldo said as he followed the fleet at a distance. He'd go at least as far as the clifftop where he'd left Marian.

The hummingbird fluttered his wings and settled down again. "Bumble didn't say anything. Nothing at all. Nope, not me." He grew silent, but a moment later, he added in a strained tone, "We left the door open, didn't we? You said we left the door open."

Ronaldo nodded. "And my paints are unsealed."

Bumble swallowed in Ronaldo's ear. "We probably should go home," he said. "The mark of a successful adventure is always going home."

3

PHOEBE, THE LAST PHOENIX IN THE WORLD, glided low between the towering canyon walls of Stronghold, as was her habit at the end of each day. Her plumage shimmered like fire in the red rays of the setting sun, and she sang out a high, sweet cry that echoed from one side of the canyon to the other. In her talons she carried bunches of wild-flowers she'd gathered from the forest, and as she dipped and soared loose blossoms fell like soft snow into the waters of the Echo Rush below.

Along the stony rims of the canyon, the citizens of Stronghold turned out to witness her flight. Dragons and minotaurs, satyrs and Fomorians, bears and rabbits and foxes and squirrels, all manner of creatures stood in quiet reverence. Like the Phoenix, a few held handfuls of flowers, which they cast after her as she flew past.

At the far eastern end of the canyon, a tall, flat-topped spire of stone rose up from the river's edge. Known as Stormfire's Point, the last Phoenix sailed straight for it. Three times she circled the Point, releasing her bouquets upon its summit before she finally landed there. Then, folding her wings and facing west, she waited for the last rays of the sun to fade.

On the northern rim, the Dragon Ramoses watched quietly apart from the other citizens of Stronghold. His thoughts were not on the

Phoenix or his gathered friends and neighbors. He stared toward the Point, as he often did, and remembered Stormfire, the great golden dragon for whom the stony pinnacle was named. Whether awake or dreaming in his sleep, he still saw the flames and smelled the smoke from his old friend's funeral pyre, though months had gone by. Stormfire's memory haunted him. He felt old and alone.

But most of all, Ramoses worried. The Age of the Dragons was passing, giving way to the Age of Man. Wyvernwood, so long the home and haven of the Dragonkin, was no longer a safe place. The war between Angmar and Degarm threatened them all. Both sides coveted the lands and the resources of the great forest. Worse, the warlike ambitions of those nations had infected the Griffinkin, who once had been good friends and allies.

While Phoebe kept her watch, other dragons took to the sky. Ramoses' daughter, Diana, her cobalt wings and scales glimmering, circled high above the Point, with emerald Fleer flying at her side. Below, the orphan Snowsong, white as the powder for which she was named, skimmed the Echo Rush. At the western end of the canyon, the amber twins, Sakima and Kaos, sailed from one rim to the other, looking lost and restless. The eagle, Skymarin, followed them with two of his brothers.

Stormfire's death had touched everyone. Uncertainty hung like a chill fog over Stronghold. Everyone went about their daily tasks, but with a sense of wariness, one eye always on the sky in anticipation of another griffin attack or on the woods itself. From dawn until dusk, the sounds of industry, conversations, and even laughter filled the air, but when the sun went down Stronghold grew quiet. When darkness closed in, its citizens huddled on their doorsteps or inside their homes. It made him sad. He remembered when the evenings were filled with music and dancing, or with quiet walks in the forest, or playful flights high among the clouds and the stars.

A sudden rush of blackbirds from the treetops interrupted Ramoses' thoughts. Rising to his full height, he craned his neck and stared toward the disturbance, his heart hammering. Off to his left, Diana and Fleer veered away from Stormfire's Point and raced northward. With a shrill screech, Phoebe spread her wings and rose into the air.

An instant later, alerted by the Phoenix's cry, an ivory shape emerged from a dark cave mouth far down on the southern wall of the canyon. The Dragon Luna, only daughter of Stormfire, displayed sleek wings and, hesitating only a moment to guage the situation, soared into the sky to join Phoebe above the Point. There, seeing something from a higher vantage that Ramoses still could not see, she flexed her wings and chased after Diana and Fleer.

A loud, ursine growl sounded near Ramoses's right foot. The blue dragon glanced down. A large and agitated brown bear glared back at him, its dark eyes burning. The bear clutched an expertly made spear in one paw. "What's all the commotion, Ramoses?" the bear demanded as it rose on its hind legs in a useless effort to see beyond the treetops. "'Tis another attack, eh? An' we all knew it would come!"

"Be calm, Byron," Ramoses counciled in soothing tones. Still others were gathering closer. Ramoses spread his wings to shelter as many as he could. They were all his friends and neighbors, and no matter the danger he would protect them all—he had sworn an oath. Stronghold would never again suffer a sneak attack like the one that had killed his leader and his friend, Stormfire.

Four more small figures raced out from between a pair of houses. Like diminutive soldiers, gripping spears, they took ready positions in front of Ramoses and the rest. Ramoses couldn't help but smile at the grim expressions on the faces of the only human children in all of Wyvernwood.

"Trevor! Markam!" Ramoses called down in a stern voice to the bare-chested twin boys. "Get back here with the rest of us! You can protect us better at closer range!" He looked to the two girls. "You, too, Ariel and Pear!"

Pear, the youngest, immediately shouldered her weapon and ran back to stand at the blue dragon's feet. With a little more reluctance, the twins joined her. Yet, Ariel obstinately turned her back to Ramoses and stood her ground while she aimed a watchful gaze at the sky.

The treetops rippled suddenly. A collective gasp went up from Stronghold's residents as leaves tore from their branches and limbs cracked. Alone at the fore, Ariel felt the full force of the wind. Her blond hair streamed away from her face as it blew her over. A brief, startled scream, and she landed hard on her backside.

Skimming the uppermost branches, the Dragon Chan sailed over the village with his sister, Luna close on his tail. Dust rose in a wake after them and swirled around Ramoses as the pair flew out past the canyon rim, circled back, and landed on the village perimeter.

Angry and embarrassed, Ariel leaped to her feet, cast down her weapon, and brushed herself off. Pear ran to help her, while Trevor and Marham laughed and pointed and clapped each other on the back.

Ramoses's voice boomed as he called to Chan. "You've excited and frightened everyone, young dragon!" Though he tried to conceal the fact, he felt more than a little afraid himself. His heart still raced, and his tone was scolding as he wrapped his wings more protectively around those gathered near his feet. He turned his gaze on the human boy named Jake, who sat saddled on Chan's neck. He wasn't sure he approved of the relationship between Chan and the boy. "You'd better have a good reason!"

"Griffins!" Jake shouted as he clung to his saddle horn. He looked flushed and out of breath.

"They attacked us twice," Chan answered in a restrained voice. "First, out by the coast. We fought them away, but we found a second flight waiting for us as we made our way home to Stronghold."

Luna fluttered her pale wings and then folded them against her body. "Diana and Fleer will chase them back to Redclaw," she said. "Griffins are cowards at heart. If they can't sneak up on you, they turn tail and fly away."

"Not all griffins are cowards," Ramoses answered. He cast a glance over his shoulder toward Stormfire's Point. Phoebe the Phoenix had settled back down on the pinnacle to watch the last of the fading sun. To the old blue Dragon, that was the surest sign that the danger had passed. He folded his wings as his neighbors began to drift away. They'd had enough excitement for the day and were returning to their homes. Only a few lingered: the four human children at his feet, Bear Byron, and the owl-man Fomorian named Gregor.

"The saddle worked great!" Jake called to Gregor as the Fomorian walked to Chan's side. Chan stretched his long, flame-colored neck down to the ground.

"Lucky for you that I'm the best craftsman in Wyvernwood!" Gregor answered as he reached up and unfastened the buckles around the boy's legs. He fluffed and fluttered his small, downy wings as he worked, and turned owl-ears this way and that. "The way Chan was flying, you'd be a dull red stain on a dark piece of tree bark right now!" Freed from the saddle restraints, Jake jumped down. Gregor shot out a feathered hand to steady the boy.

"I guess his knees are a little wobbly," Gregor said, grinning up at Chan.

"Yer knees might be a bit wobbly, too," Bear Byron said as he stood behind Gregor, "if the hosts of Redclaw wanted yer innards!" The bear shot a hard look at Chan as he put a paw on Jake's shoulder. "I tell ye, Minhep an' his monsters are out fer this boy!"

"You always manage to be the center of attention, don't you?" Ariel accused Jake as she walked up with her hands braced on her hips. She wore an angry look on her face, and the other three children followed her at a safe distance. "You're always grabbing the stage!" For a moment, she glowered at the older boy; then her expression melted, and she flung her arms around him. "Idiot!" she whispered. "What are we supposed to do if anything happens to you? I should kick your butt!"

"Better wait," Jake answered. He winked at the other children as he rubbed the seat of his trousers. "It's a little numb back there right now."

Ramoses turned his head toward the darkening sky. The sun had gone down at last, and Phoebe was departing the Point to seek her nest in the forest for the night. "Byron," he said to the brown bear, "why don't you see the children home, and stay with them for awhile. I'm sure Carolla won't mind another mouth to feed, and I know you like her cooking."

"Best wife a fellow ever had!" Gregor said proudly. Carolla was a Fomorian like her husband, but while he was half man and half owl, his wife was half cat. A generous and loving couple with no young ones of their own, Gregor and Carolla had taken the five human children into their home.

"You get that collar off Chan," Ramoses told Gregor.

Chan frowned. "It's not a collar . . ."

Ramoses deflected Chan's protest before the younger dragon could finish it. "Your brother and mother are somewhere in the forest," he said to Luna. "Find them and bring them back before the moon rises at the east end of the canyon. Then I want to see all of you—indeed, all of the Dragonkin—on the shore of the Echo Rush where the shadow of Stormfire's Point stretches across the sand."

Luna shot the great blue dragon a questioning look, then turned to her brother. An uncertain frown flickered over Chan's red-scaled face as he drummed the tip of his tail softly on the ground around his clawed feet.

With a stern expression, Ramoses looked from one to the other as he informed them, "I'm calling a formal council."

It was close to midnight when the moon began to rise above the eastern horizon. At the bottom of the canyon the swiftly flowing waters of the Echo Rush glimmered under its pure effulgence. On the river's wide, sandy shoreline, Ramoses gazed upward—first at the moon, then at the twinkling band of stars visible overhead.

He drew a slow breath, feeling his age like a heavy weight on his shoulders. With Stormfire gone, he was the oldest of the Dragonkin now. The fact brought him no joy. The world had changed too much since his hatchling days. It was still changing, and it would continue to do so. He wondered how much more he could endure.

Licking his lips, he glanced toward Stormfire's Point. Under the rising moon, its shadow stretched down the length of the canyon. Sometimes Ramoses felt angry at his dear friend for dying so unexpectedly, without even the opportunity to say goodbye or the chance to offer some last word of advice. What was Ramoses supposed to do? He was no leader. He was only a librarian and the chronicler of the Dragonkin.

In the crook of his right forepaw he held a large hand-bound book. He tapped a claw lightly on the Dragon-hide cover, and tears of grief welled in his eyes. It still smelled faintly of Stormfire, from whose golden sloughings the book had been made. Ramoses knew every word written on its pages. He'd read them many times, and over the last few days he'd reread them yet again.

He closed his eyes tightly before the tears could fall, and steeled himself. The time for mourning had passed. *Change is the essential nature of life,* he reminded himself. Pressing the book to his heart, he invoked Stormfire's spirit.

Forgive me if I'm wrong, old friend, he prayed, *but the Dragonkin stand at a fork in the road, and you aren't here to guide us.*

Without moving from the place where he stood, Ramoses opened his eyes again and gazed around. For just a moment he thought he'd felt a touch at his elbow, and his instincts tingled with an overwhelming sense of Stormfire's presence as real and powerful as it had ever been in life. He forced a weak smile. It had only been his imagination, fueled no doubt by the book he carried and the scent of his friend that clung to it.

On the canyon rim far above, his sharp ears heard an increasing stir and shuffle. He could feel the nervous gazes of Stronghold's citizens gathering at the edge, all staring down at him, waiting.

There was no reason to delay longer.

Ramoses turned his head to the right and breathed a bright stream of fire onto a tall pile of wood. It burst into flame. On the other side of the river stood another pile of wood. With one powerful exhalation, Ramoses ignited it, too. Twin pillars of crackling fire shot upward, spilling an orange light over the rushing waters and on the canyon walls.

On the rim, a group of minotaurs hunched over log drums and established a slow, ominous rhythm that pulsed through the darkness, penetrated the forest depths, and spread over the wide gorge.

In twos and threes, Dragons on both sides of the canyon rose into the air and gyred downward toward the shore. Silver-scaled Paraclion and ruby Tiamat landed first beside Ramoses. Diana and Fleer arrived next, not from the rim, but out of the western dark, gliding low between the rocky walls. Ramoses nodded to them. His daughter had been spending a lot of time lately with Fleer.

Kaos, Maximor, and Starfinder landed on the opposite shore. A moment later, Snowsong and Sakima, who was twin to Kaos, landed behind them. Still more dragons sailed down to the river's edge. Their shadows rose huge and majestic on the canyon stone.

On the southern rim, Luna emerged from her cave and spread her wings. Her ivory scales caught the moonlight and reflected it. She shone like a pale, falling star as she descended and took a place beside Tiamat. Luna's gaze fell instantly on the book in Ramoses arm, and her eyes narrowed to suspicious slits.

A soft glow in the west drew everyone's attention. Side by side, Chan and Phoebe swooped low and sailed down the center of the canyon. When Chan landed beside his sister, the Phoenix continued on alone. Climbing again, she settled on her now familiar perch atop the Point. There, folding her wings, she gave a cry and turned her back to the council gathering.

"I asked her to keep watch," Chan said to Ramoses. "It isn't wise to leave Stronghold unguarded while we stand around flexing our wings and beating our tails on the sand."

The old blue dragon gave an approving nod while silently chiding himself for not thinking of it himself. But, as he had told himself before, he was only a librarian, not a true Dragonkin leader.

Chan turned to his sister. "Did you find Mother?"

"She won't attend," Luna answered stiffly. "Harrow still can't fly, and he's too proud to walk down, so Sabu intends to stay with him on the rim. I hate the way she dotes on him lately."

Chan only shrugged, but Ramoses couldn't hide a frown of disappointment. Black-scaled Harrow, the first-hatched of Stormfire's triplet offspring, had suffered severe trauma to his wings in a vengeful attack on the griffins' Redclaw Fortress at the northern edge of Wyvernwood. He'd nearly been killed, and most of Stronghold regarded him as a hero, but since returning home he'd kept mostly to himself in the deep woods with only his mother to attend him while he recovered from his wounds.

Still, Ramoses had hoped for the presence of all Stormfire's children.

The council was not restricted to dragons, and the other residents of Stronghold filed carefully down a steep stairway that had been cut into the rock. They assembled quietly among the dragons on both sides of the river. The drums fell silent as even the drummers descended to join the crowd.

"I have no tongue for long speeches . . ." Ramoses began as he gazed around at the questioning faces.

A powerful blast of fire from the canyon rim above their heads interrupted the old dragon. All eyes turned upward, and a second blast followed the first. Poised on the rocky edge, Harrow spread his ebon wings and fell forward into space. A chorus of gasps and shrieks went up from villagers. Ramoses stared gape-jawed.

Then, with a strong downbeat of his wings, Harrow soared upward again, banked, and descended into their midst, landing finally in the middle of the Echo Rush. He waded ashore to stand with his siblings.

Luna shook her head. Sounding much like the Human child, Ariel, she snapped at Harrow. "You always have to make an entrance!"

"Look!" A minotaur in the assembly thrust a finger toward the rim again, and again everyone gazed upward.

The Dragon Sabu, Stormfire's mate, soared over the rim and circled downward. One of the oldest dragons, she was huge, immense as Stormfire had been, and as black as her son, Harrow. For years, she had not flown at all, and most had thought her too weak. But the murder of Stormfire and Harrow's nearly fatal injuries had reinvigorated her. Beloved by all the Dragonkin and villagers, they moved back, making room for her to join them.

"That was a stupid stunt!" she said to Harrow. "You'll walk back up!"

Harrow's eyes flashed defiantly, but then he hung his head. The scars on his wings still showed plainly, and the leather membranes had not yet fully thickened. The griffins at Redclaw had pinned him like an insect to the earth—but with tree trunks instead of pins.

Sabu turned to Ramoses as she folded her wings, and her voice turned sweetly sarcastic. "I assume you haven't called us here to tell ghost stories and recite poetry."

Unnoticed by many, another shape glided down from the rim on soundless, feathered wings. Landing at a distance from the assembly, the only griffin in Stronghold sat back on powerful haunches to observe with a leonine gaze.

Ramoses watched Morkir over the heads of the others, hesitating long enough to allow the griffin to join them, but the brother of Stormfire's murderer remained apart. Under Morkir's intent gaze, Ramoses felt uncomfortable and uncertain of his words.

He turned toward Chan. "This is about the boy, Jake," he said finally. He looked down nervously, then back up again. "But only in part. You have to take him away from Wyvernwood. He's no longer safe here."

Chan nodded. "I've had the same thought," he said. "The griffins that attacked us today were after him, not me."

"Jake delivered the wound that eventually killed Gaunt," Harrow explained. "Minhep leads the griffins now, but he was Gaunt's friend, and he's sworn the boy's death."

"That was a lucky blow in the middle of a battle!" Chan answered. He raised his paws in exasperation and thumped his tail on the sand. "Where can we take him? There's no place where he'll be safe except here with us!"

"We can't return him to Degarm," Luna said in support of her brother. "He won't go, and I don't think any of the other man-children will, either."

Ramoses nodded. "No, we can't send them to Degarm or Angmar." He turned to Chan again. "Still, for his sake you must take him away. Let animosities cool down. Events will change."

He raised the book for everyone to see. "Indeed, changing events are the reason I called this council. None of us are safe anymore. Wyvernwood is no longer a refuge for us. The world of Man is pressing ever closer. They threaten our homes and our families! Their wars spread into our forest, and they fight to claim our lands for themselves!"

Luna leaned toward Chan and touched his shoulder. "He has no tongue for long speeches," she said in a caustic whisper.

Ramoses overheard and glowered at her. "You are Stormfire's children!" he said with sudden bitterness. "One of you should be leading us, seeing to the safety of Stronghold, and looking to the future of the Dragonkin!" He waved the volume under Luna's nose. "I've shown you the *Books of Stormfire*—not just this one volume, but all the books—and you've read your father's words. You know he foresaw a haven beyond Wyvernwood, a place to which one of you would lead us!"

Harrow flexed his wings in indignation and drew himself erect. "Unlike you, old Dragon," he answered, "I don't believe any longer in the infallible wisdom of the great Stormfire."

Ramoses shot a pained look at Sabu, but he found no support in her silence. Though he'd known her most of his life, he understood her least of all. She had been Stormfire's mate, had done the impossible by bearing him a clutch of three eggs. She knew the prophecy that one of her triplets would save the Dragonkin. Yet, she stood as aloof as the griffin, Morkir, with an unreadable fire in her Dragon eyes.

Once again, he felt the weight of his years. But at the same time he felt his strength. He surveyed the faces of Stronghold's assembled citizens— Dragons, minotaurs, satyrs, even a griffin. And in other parts of Wyvernwood, Wyrms and merfolk, and even stranger creatures. Stormfire had gathered them all, their parents and their grandparents, rescued them from the encroachments and cruelties of the race called Man, and led them to the safety of this forest.

Ramoses remembered that Great Migration as if it were yesterday. He had journeyed from the beginning at Stormfire's side and recorded it all in the books.

"Well, *I* believe," he answered. Rising on his hind legs, he drew himself to his full, imposing height as Harrow had done, but like Sabu, he was one of the old dragons and much taller. "I've told you before," turning his sad and angry gaze each of the triplets, "that your sire created three talismans and hid them along the way. Into each of those objects he poured the last of his magic—the last vestiges of magic in the world, and there is no more of it."

"The Diamond Dragon," Chan interrupted thoughtfully, "the Glass Dragon, and the Heart of All Dragons. Yes, we know the stories. Stormfire thought that, at a critical time, they would show the way to a new homeland."

Bear Byron had stood by silently, but now he spoke in a growly voice from behind the ring of dragons. "Did Stormfire think to ask our lowly opinions?" he demanded. "What if'n we don't want to be leavin' this Wyvernwood?"

"This is our home, Ramoses." Diana pressed forward to look up at her father, and though the love in her eyes was plain, she spoke with firmness. "I won't abandon these beautiful woods. Come what may, my heart is here."

Ramoses put a paw on his daughter's shoulder.

"We should find these talismans." Chan spoke in little more than a whisper. He raised his head toward the star-flecked sky, though his eyes were closed. "I doubt the tales of magic. But if my father made these things, then we should find them. They're part of our history, and they belong with the Dragonkin."

A flood of emotion surged through Ramoses. In many ways, he had regarded the children of his old friend as his own. They had played and studied in his cave, learned to read at his hearth. Sometimes they made him proud, and sometimes they disappointed him, but always he loved them. "Your eyes may be closed," he said to Chan, "but you're beginning to see."

"I've seen very little of the world beyond Wyvernwood," Luna said. Her eyes were riveted on the book, and they gleamed with uncharacteristic eagerness. She thrust out a paw. "Give it to me, Ramoses. I can fly faster and farther than any of the Dragonkin. I'll scour the world and retrace the routes that brought us here and come back with all three talismans!"

Chan bit his lip, and his nostrils flared. "No, I'll go," he said, interrupting his sister. "And I'll take Jake with me. That will get him out of Wyvernwood and away from Minhep's grasp. I don't think the other man-children are in any immediate danger."

Harrow embraced him with one wing. "I'm coming with you, Brother," he said. "I've stood on the highest peaks of the Imagination Mountains and glimpsed the lands beyond, and I hunger to know more." He looked from Chan to Luna and back again, and his eyes were full of fire and excitement. "Three talisman—and three of us! Maybe Father really did plan it all!"

Sabu gave a vigorous shake of her head. "You managed a short flight from the rim, and you were barely ready for that. Have you already forgotten Redclaw? Your senseless heroics almost cost you your life once, Harrow! Maybe I can't stop Chan—"

"I wish you could," Chan said. He looked around the canyon as he spoke. "I don't really have the heart to leave Wyvernwood. I'm not an adventurer like my brother." He thumped his tail on the ground, and his wings visibly shivered. "But it's the safest thing for the boy."

"Is that your only justification for this insane journey?" Sabu demanded.

Chan met his mother's angry gaze with a cool look. "I don't need a better one." He extended one paw.

Solemnly, and with reluctance, avoiding a withering glare from Sabu, Ramoses placed the *Book of Stormfire* on it. "Put out the fires," he told the assembly. "The council is over."

STRONGHOLD BARELY SLEPT THAT NIGHT. After the council, many returned home and put out their candles and lanterns and went to their beds as they did every night. But this night was not like any other, and everyone knew it. Most of those who tried to sleep only tossed and turned. They beat their pillows and tangled themselves in their bedsheets, got up to pace their rooms, and lay down to try to sleep again.

Some, knowing that sleep would never come that night, lay quietly on their backs in darkness with their windows open so that they could listen to the flower-scented breeze that rustled through the trees and whispered across the canyon. When the breeze paused, they turned over on their sides and folded an arm under their heads to listen to the crickets and cicadas softly singing. When they heard the occasional restless footstep or muttering of some neighbor ambling about, they sat up and hugged their knees and hoped that no family member noticed their trembling.

A very few sat outside on their doorsteps and watched the moon crawl across the star-flecked heavens. They counted down the hours and minutes as they remembered old stories and dreamed old dreams and wondered what the future held for Wyvernwood and for themselves.

As the moon disappeared below the western treetops, a Fomorian female walked with a soundless, soft-pawed tread into the village square. Wearing an expression of serene composure on her cat-face, she folded golden-furred legs, curled a slender tail around her feet, and sat down on her haunches in the dust to wait. The breeze stirred her silver whiskers, teased the ruff on her neck. She closed her eyes briefly to savor the sensation. Her nose twitched as she sampled and sorted the myriad scents on the night. No sound escaped her ears.

After a few moments, she began to purr.

On the canyon rim where he sat alone in the darkness, Chan heard her faint vibration.

For half the night, with Ramoses and Luna at his side, he'd poured over the many dusty volumes collectively known as the *Book of Stormfire* in the old blue dragon's cave. Together, they'd read and researched the most important passages, gleaned the most promising clues, and planned. After a while, Luna had returned to her cave and to her mate, Tiamat.

Chan had come to meditate on this singular place on the rim. No matter if it was day or night, he loved the view, and the muted rush of the river far below soothed him. Stronghold was as much the canyon as it was the village, and it was all his home. The panorama of striated stone conveyed an inexplicable sense of comfort as well as wonder. Like so many of the Dragonkin, he had learned to fly between its towering walls. The canyon had been his playground.

The sounds of familiar laughter rose up from the windy depths. It was only his imagination. Through half-closed eyes, smiling faintly, he watched the shadows of childhood—his brother and sister chasing each other, skimming the foam-flecked water in a reckless game of chase-and-tag, spiraling and rolling between the walls, climbing above the forest into the broad sky. He saw his younger self as they chased him, too.

He smiled, remembering those happy days. He had not spent much time with his brother and sister lately. He regretted that.

With a glance at the stars overhead, he turned away from the rim and walked slowly toward the square. The Fomorian cat-girl sat still with her eyes closed, continuing to purr as he approached, but making no other movement. Stretching his neck down close to the ground, he greeted her in a whisper.

"Katrina, Katrina, little ball of fur,

How I wonder when you purr

Why you sit and never stir?"

Katrina opened one green eye. "Don't try to charm me with your sweet tongue, you great scaly bird," she answered. "You're not so big that I can't use your leg for a scratching post."

Chan gave a low chuckle and curled up around her until the tip of his tail nearly touched his nose. For long moments, neither spoke. They listened to the sounds of the night together, felt the wind shift, and waited for dawn to break. When Chan began to purr, Katrina opened her other eye to regard him with a look of amusement.

"That's a truly horrid sound," she murmured with a mock-shiver as she brushed her whiskers. "As bad as a human trying to sing."

"Your ears are too small to appreciate good music," Chan replied with a lift of his nose. "Dragons invented the purr, you know. We were purring before the feline species coughed up its first hairball."

"A pity that after so much time you still can't get it right," Katrina shot back. The tip of her tail rose and fell in a smoothly rhythmic motion. "You may have had it first, but we perfected it." As if to demonstrate her claim, she began to purr more loudly.

With ivory wings outspread, Luna soared over the canyon rim and settled down on the square beside her brother. Even in the pre-dawn darkness, her scales held a shimmer, and she seemed to glow. Looking from

Chan to Katrina, she raised one pale pinion as if it were a shield against their noise.

"Neither of you could carry a tune to the river and back," she said, grimacing as she peered around her wingtip. "Why, the battlecries of Degarm's soldiers are not so blood-curdling! Pay attention now, for this is how it's done!" Folding her wings close to her body, and draping her tail over her brother's, she lifted her face to the lingering stars and commenced a high, sweet-sounding purr of her own

"Sing it, sister!" Gliding softly up from the Echo Rush, the Dragon Diana landed beside her best friend. Putting her head close to Luna's, she, too, gave out with a raw vibration.

At the far end of the village square stood a longhouse made of logs. It was in this house, not in a cave, that the Dragon Sabu lived. She didn't live there alone, however. The Griffin, Morkir lived with her as friend and guardian—a strange relationship, but one the Dragonkin had come to accept. The longhouse's door opened a crack. Morkir peered out suspiciously, and the starlight glinted on his golden eagle-beak. A moment's pause as he looked all around, then, with his gaze settling on Katrina, he padded toward the group and sat down next to the cat-girl.

"I'm half-lion," he announced in a gruff voice. He held up one paw and flexed the joints to extend his claws. "If this is some contest I guess I should do my part to uphold the honor of our feline lineage." Closing his eyes, he began his own deep-chested rumbling.

Chan stared at him with surprise. The spectacle of a purring Griffin was enough to make him fall silent. Was this really Morkir—whom the Dragonkin used to call *Mad Morkir*—sitting before him? Chan had never heard a griffin make such a soothing sound. No one had ever told him that they were capable of it!

He glanced back toward the longhouse where his mother, Sabu, lay listening at the doorway with her long neck stretched just across the threshold and her jaw resting on the grass. Her eyes were closed, but he knew that she could feel their vibration through the ground and that she was also purring.

Drawn by the sound, other Dragons gathered on the edge of the square and joined in. Some stretched out where they could while others, sitting on their haunches, closed their eyes and swayed to the perceptible rhythm as the volume rose. The gentle swell of it spread over Stronghold on the warm air through the open windows to the citizens sleepless in their beds or pacing in the darkness. It was a reassuring sound, and it drew everyone together. It brought calm and promised peace.

Gregor appeared at the edge of the square and walked with solemn dignity toward Chan. Between his white-feathered arms he carried the saddle he'd designed as if it were a crown of jewels. The Son of Stormfire bent his neck and allowed the owl-man to fasten the straps and buckles.

Luna ceased her purring long enough to lean her head close to her brother. "Is it uncomfortable?" she whispered.

Chan didn't answer. He held still for Gregor, and he didn't want to interrupt the delicate group harmonic, but he smiled a soft dragon-smile and hoped that Luna would understand. The saddle wasn't uncomfortable at all. It was made of his own sloughing. More, it was the physical expression of the bond he'd found with the boy, Jake.

With the saddle in place, Chan lifted his head. His heart quickened, and he quivered with so many emotions as he looked at the faces of his friends and family. Stronghold was his home, and Wyvernwood was his world. Only once in his entire life had he ventured beyond the boundaries of the forest. The world was bigger than he knew.

And yet . . .

He looked to the west where the night was still blackest. He was not as tall as his father Stormfire had been, and the trees were too thick and close. He couldn't see the ominous lofty peaks of the Imagination Mountains, but now, like a different kind of vibration on his skin, he thought he could hear the wind rattling over them.

To fly beyond the Imagination Mountains. Among the Dragonkin, that was a euphemism for death.

And yet, that was exactly where he was about to go.

He looked down again, and Jake stood at his feet between Gregor and Katrina. He wore a plain brown trousers and boots, but Carola had made him a new shirt from white dragon-hide. No, not white, but ivory, and it shimmered. Chan glanced at his sister. The shirt bore Luna's scent.

Luna blinked her eyes and shrugged. "You can't drop a scale around here without one of the Fomorians recycling it," she murmured.

Jake wore his brown hair bound back with the same leather thong he'd worn before, but though it was actually a clever weapon this time Chan didn't object. Nor did he object to the leather pouch the boy wore over one shoulder, which he suspected contained stones as well as the sandwiches and cookies he could smell.

"Carola's outfitted you well," Chan said to the boy. As he spoke, the chorus of purring ceased. Chan felt a pang, missing the sound instantly, but he resisted the impulse to look around.

There was no fear on Jake's face, though he tried to conceal a look of worry. "Gregor says we're going on a journey," he said with controlled calm. "I know you're keeping stuff from me, just like grownups always did before we came here. I thought we trusted each other more than that." He clutched the sleeve of the dragon-hide shirt and frowned. "Well, wherever we're going, we'd better go now before Ariel wakes up."

Gregor nodded his agreement. "Carola's with the other children," he said. "But Ariel was quite distraught. She finally fell asleep a little while ago."

Chan looked from Gregor to Jake, but Jake seized the saddle grips and began fastening himself into place. "It doesn't seem right for her to wake up and find you gone," Chan said. "Wouldn't it be better to tell her good-bye?"

"I know Ariel better than you do, and I didn't tell any of them good-bye," Jake answered stiffly. "I'm coming back."

Chan looked at his sister as she folded her wings around herself. The other dragons were all watching him now, and Katrina and Morkir were, too. His mother, Sabu, looked asleep on her threshold, but he knew she wasn't. More of Stronghold's residents were gathering near the square, and dawn was breaking in the east.

Chan wrestled briefly with his conscience. He looked for a long moment at Morkir, and then made a decision. "Minhep has put a price on your head," he told the boy. "He blames you for the death of Morkir's brother, Gaunt."

"So we're getting out of town?" Jake said in a dubious tone.

Morkir snorted. "If you call this a town, boy."

Jake let go a sigh, and Chan felt some tension ease from the boy's body as he settled into the saddle. "You explain this to Ariel, too," he called down to Gregor, "and Trevor and Markam and Pear. Don't keep secrets from them." He sighed again, then took hold of the saddlehorn. "All right," he said to Chan, "where are we going?"

"Westward," Chan answered as he spread his wings and rose into the air. Though the sun was just rising in the east over the Windy Sea, it was still dark over the mountains. "We follow the night."

But they didn't depart alone. Luna and Diana took wing together and flew in close escort. The eagle, Skymarin, and a host of his brothers also rose from the treetops and gave chase. Mingled among the eagles were a host of hawks and ravens and owls. Far off to the right and keeping an easy pace, Chan spied the sleekly golden shape of Morkir.

The dark green leaves rippled and shivered as they flew past. Chan angled his wings and climbed higher into the sky. Half the pursuing birds dropped back into the trees, but the rest, led by the eagles, continued to follow in respectful silence. Diana surged up on his left; Luna did the same on his right and brushed the very tip of her wing against his in a gesture of affection.

"May the sun and moon light your way, Brother," she called as they flew side by side, "and let my heart be the beacon that guides you home."

Chan turned his head and gazed into his sister's warm, blue eyes. He and Luna had always been close, had always flown side by side as they were now. It felt strange to be leaving her behind. "Guard the forest well, Sister," he answered, "so that we have a home to return to."

Luna nodded and brushed his wingtip once more before she veered away.

Chan turned toward Diana. "Be sure that you guard Luna," he said to his sister's best friend. "But I know I don't have to tell you that."

"My father," Diana said, inclining her head toward the pinnacle of a hill that rose directly in their path. The old dragon stood at attention, still as stone upon the rocky summit, his great wings displayed in dramatic fashion. Clutched in both paws, he held before him the *Book of Stormfire*. He had urged Chan to take it along, had even prepared a leather backpack so the boy, Jake, could wear it on his back. But the book belonged with the Dragonkin; it was a piece of their history, and Chan would not risk its loss. It was enough that he had committed to memory every word of it.

There will come years of fear.

Chan swallowed, choking up unexpectedly as he flew closer and closer to the hill where Ramoses waited, and he wondered why that particular poem from the book had crept into his thoughts. The blue dragon had been more than just his father's friend. Ramoses had been uncle to the children of Stormfire, tutor and teacher, confidant and confessor. Chan realized that Ramoses was paying him honor by standing alone, apart from all others, to witness the beginning of his quest.

> *There will come years of fear*
> *When a raindrop and a tear*
> *Cannot be told apart.*
> *Then hold fast and trust your dragon heart,*
> *And dream of those you hold most dear.*
> *No matter where upon this sphere*
> *You wander, love will steer*
> *You home.*

They were Stormfire's words—his father, the secret poet who never in life shared his verses with anyone except Ramoses, who had written them in the books he so faithfully kept. Was it odd that as Chan remembered those lines he heard them, not in Stormfire's, but in Ramoses' voice?

"Farewell, old Teacher!" Chan shouted as he flew above the hilltop. He rolled from left to right, dipping his wings as he passed above Ramoses. It was his way of saying goodbye. "Fly well!" Ramoses lifted his noble head and let out a roar in reply. Then Chan was beyond the hill.

"And you," Diana said, brushing his wingtip as Luna had done. She winked at Jake in the saddle on Chan's neck. "Both of you fly well." With that, she turned back and settled on the hilltop with her father.

An icy cold gripped Chan's heart. He was truly underway, his quest begun. The forest swept by, turning a deeper green as the sky brightened with morning. Wyvernwood—his home! Almost before he realized it, he crossed the broad Blackwater River. The cold he felt gave way to an unexpected excitement. He climbed higher in the sky, the better to see ahead.

With the sharp vision of a dragon, he spied the distant peaks of the Imagination Mountains. Snow-capped, they shimmered in the first rays of daylight. He wished that Jake could see them, too. The boy had been quiet for a long time.

"We're on our own now, Jake!" he called back over his shoulder. "It's just you and me on the verge of a great adventure!"

"I think we'd better fit you for glasses!" Jake shouted back. "Really big glasses!" He tapped the scaly side of Chan's neck and pointed. Far off to the north and lingering back, barely a golden speck against wispy clouds, Morkir still followed.

"He's not the only one, either!" Jake extended an arm. Opening his mouth, he gave a shrill cry, an excellent impression of an eagle's call. A feathered bolt shot down from above, and Skymarin locked talons around the boy's dragon-hide sleeve.

Chan smiled slowly.

Dragon, griffin, eagle, and boy. He didn't know what lay on the other side of the mountains ahead. But he wondered if the world was ready for them.

5

WITH DRIED TEARS STICKY ON HER FACE, Ariel pretended to be asleep on her soft bed, her thin coverlet pulled up almost to her nose. But she wasn't asleep at all. She lay in the darkness of her room, listening to the faint sounds from the rest of the house, watching the shadowy movements that sometimes eclipsed the narrow band of light at the bottom of her door—Gregor, Carolla, and Jake moving around.

Things grew quiet after a while. She heard Jake and Gregor go out, heard the soft closing of the outside door behind them. She turned over on her stomach and pressed her pillow to her face so no one would hear her cry again, and when Carolla cracked open the bedroom door and peeked in, Ariel fell silent and again feigned sleep.

When Carolla went away, Ariel rose up on one elbow and peered into the bed next to hers. Little Pear remained fast asleep, a sweet smile on her tiny face. Pear liked living in Stronghold. She loved talking with all the fantastic creatures and playing with the animals. And they loved Pear.

I love you, too, Ariel thought. She resisted an urge to reach out and stroke Pear's silken hair for fear she would wake the little girl. *Everybody loves you.*

Glancing toward the door, Ariel eased back her coverlet and swung her feet over the side of her bed. She paused for a moment and listened, wondering if Carolla had gone out, too, or if she'd maybe fallen asleep in her favorite chair. When no sounds came from the outer rooms, she stood up and reached for her clothes.

Moving quietly, but wasting no time, she pulled on the close-fitting trousers of green cloth, brown socks, and the soft brown boots that Carolla had made for her. She particularly loved the boots, for they were supple, yet sturdy with a low flat heel, and they rose nearly to her knees, offering both comfort and protection in the rugged forest. Then she slipped her white linen tunic over her head and laced a brown leather vest over that. Lastly, she tied her blond mane back with a fancy braided cord with beaded ends that trailed over her right shoulder.

When she had dressed, Ariel glanced down at Pear again. The little girl had turned over on her side and lay as if she were watching Ariel, but her eyes were closed. For a moment, Ariel sat down on her bed again and looked at Pear's sweet face shining in the faint starlight that spilled through the window. Ariel's shoulders slumped, and she pursed her lips. Her empty hands hung down between her thighs. A dull pain throbbed in her chest, and she thought her heart was breaking.

All she'd ever known was abandonment. Sitting in the darkness, she tried to remember her parents, but their faces were only indistinct blurs to her. She tried to remember Keven, whom she'd loved and looked up to like a big brother, but he'd sacrificed himself saving Jake. At that memory, Ariel clapped a hand to her mouth to stifle a sob.

Now Jake was leaving, going somewhere far off with the Dragon Chan.

And Ariel was leaving, too. She hoped Pear would forgive her, but Pear liked it in Stronghold. Even with monsters for parents and beasts for playmates, she liked it better than the carnival in which they'd all been raised. Trevor and Markam seemed to like it, too. She didn't think any of them would miss her.

There were a few more things she needed. Slipping a hand under her pillow, she drew out the sling Jake had made for her and tied it around her right wrist. She remembered smiling when he gave it to her, thinking that maybe it meant something, that at the very least he felt concerned about her safety. She wasn't sure about that any longer, but she wasn't leaving it behind.

Getting down on her knees, she felt under her bed for her old slippers and pulled them out. From inside the left one, she extracted a kitchen knife that she'd hidden there. It gleamed as she turned it in her hands, and for the first time, she realized that she'd actually been contemplating this moment for some time and preparing for it.

Slipping the knife into her left boot, she crept between the beds to the window. "Goodbye, Little Pear," she whispered, pausing at the sill for a final look back over her shoulder. She wiped a tear from the corner of one eye. Pear looked so small and innocent, barely the same age Ariel had been when her parents sold her to Master Grimm and his Carnival of the Grim. She wished she could remember their faces.

Would Pear remember hers? "Goodbye," she repeated. "Don't forget me, and don't hate me for leaving you, my tiny love!"

With that, Ariel climbed through the window and dropped to the ground. The other homes nearby were dark, but a few shapes stirred on the porches and stoops, or leaned in the doorways. She remained crouched beneath the window, half hidden in Carolla's bed of larkspur and bleeding hearts, until she felt sure that she hadn't been observed. At last, she sprang up and ran at lithe speed past Gregor's workshop, down a brief sidestreet, between a pair of houses, across a community garden, and into the black forest.

With one hand on the thick trunk of a moss-covered tree, she paused and looked back at the village, more than a little surprised that no one was following her and that she had actually made it. Biting her lip, she played idly with the beaded ends of her braided hair band. The night wind felt warm on her face. It smelled of honeysuckle and clover, and she tilted back her head to breathe deeply.

A sound from the direction of the canyon drew her attention, a vibration on the air that reminded her at first of a cat's purr. But it grew louder and louder, becoming a chorus with different pitches and odd musical rhythms, like nothing she'd ever heard before! Her curiosity piqued, she considered investigating, but she resisted the urge. With stubborn determination, she turned and set a course deeper into the woods.

Her heart hammered as she made her way, and soon the strange purr-vibrations faded in the distance. Another music, the music of the woods, closed around her. Cicadas and crickets sang their raspy summer-songs to a beat set by the burpings and croakings of tree frogs. Insects droned in the grasses, and the breeze rustled the leaves.

Yet the darkness unnerved her. She flinched each time an unseen limb brushed her face or snatched at her hair. With no warning at all, she walked right through a spiderweb. She danced a frantic jig, rubbing her cheeks, slapping her neck and throat to wipe away the creepy, sticky strands. But she didn't scream. She only prayed the disgruntled web-builder wasn't now lurking someone on her clothing!

"Sorry!" she whispered, hoping the spider would understand and forgive her as she hurried on.

A sudden gust shivered through the trees, and leaves fell like dark snow. Startled, Ariel stopped and stared around until the wind passed and the shivering limbs calmed. On a branch overhead, an owl suddenly hooted, and Ariel jumped with wide-eyed fright.

"Who-who-who are you, little Man-child?" it asked with a flutter of its wings. "Where-where-where are you going so late at night?"

"None of your business, you old hooty-bird!" Ariel answered sharply, recovering herself. "You've got a nerve scaring little girls like that! And don't you dare tell anyone you saw me, either!"

The owl blinked its bright-glowing eyes and hooted again. "How rude-rude-rude!"

Ariel increased her pace, afraid that the owl would fly back to Stronghold and give her away. Stealth was not as important to her now as putting distance between herself and the village. She headed west, intent on reaching the Blackwater River. Once there, she could decide where she really wanted to go. Stronghold was not the only community in Wyvernwood. She knew about the Wyrm-town, Grendleton, which was north of Stronghold. To the south, there were the Whispering Hills of which she'd heard some nice stories. And up north, near the border with Angmar, there was Redclaw, the griffin fortress.

She had no wish at all to go to Redclaw and end up as a griffin-slave. But if Wyvernwood contained such places as these, perhaps there were other communities, too, that she hadn't heard about. She only wanted to get away from Stronghold!

Hoping for a glimpse of the sky, she looked up. The trees and the leaves were so dense. Surely it was near dawn, and yet the woods were still so dark. The moon was already below the horizon, and the little starlight that penetrated the thick canopy offered no comfort.

Ariel hugged herself, slowing her pace again as she continued on. The owl was not the only one with whom she shared the night-woods. No other creature tried to speak to her. Yet cold eyes glittered in the tree limbs above or watched from behind the ancient bolls as she passed. Claws curled and scratched on bark. Teeth clicked.

"You can't scare me into going back!" Ariel muttered as she looked from side to side into the brush and undergrowth.

A wolf appeared directly in her path and glared at her with red, hungry eyes for a long moment before stepping aside. "Do you like my bigggg eyes, little ggggirrrrl!" it growled. Then it seemed to smile a terrible smile, showing its fangs. "Do you like my bigggg teeth?" It gave another low growl, sprang into the thicket, and vanished.

Frozen in place, Ariel stared after the wolf, her mouth dry and open, her fists clenched. But when the wolf didn't return, she relaxed and called after it. "I hope you get fleas!" She licked her lips and swallowed. It wasn't a very clever thing to say, and in a few moments she'd probably think up something better.

But she wasn't going to get the chance. A chill shot up Ariel's spine. A deep, almost instinctive fear turned her blood to ice water. She tried to look down, but couldn't, as something cool and slick and smooth coiled around her ankles.

A huge snake lifted its head as high as her waist and unhinged its jaws with a hiss. Its fangs dripped, and its eyes burned like tiny coals as they fixed on her. "Unwise to jjjjourney these woodsssss at night!" it whispered, rising still higher around her legs until they were face to face. It swayed back and forth in a sensuous motion as it spoke. "Dangerssss you know nothing offfffff! More there issss in Wyvernwood than niccccce dragon-ssss."

Ariel screamed, and the shrill sound echoed through the forest, shattering the quiet. Birds and bats shot up from their perches, filling the air with barely glimpsed shadows. The bushes came alive with scampering, half-glimpsed shapes. A leopard roared, wolves howled.

Then everything became quiet again, and the woods settled down.

Without another word, the snake uncoiled and slithered off into the underbrush.

Ariel shivered, then began to run. Branches slapped her face, caught her hair, scratched her hands. She tripped over a thick root and fell. Glancing back, she mistook the root for the snake, leaped up, and continued to run until her pounding heart began to ache inside her chest, and her breath turned ragged.

Finally, her rubbery legs gave out. She fell again, stretching out full-length upon a grassy patch. Her eyes stinging with sweat and tears, she covered her head with her hands and squeezed her eyes shut. She was too afraid to look around, too afraid even to get up.

Yet, little by little, as her heart calmed and her breathing eased, she discovered something—some pleasant smell that tickled her nose and soothed her fear. Slowly opening her eyes, she rolled over and raised up on one elbow. As she moved, the aroma wafted up around her even stronger. She squinted in the darkness and took note of the slender stems rising all around. Flowers! She gathered a handful, pressed them to her face, and inhaled their perfume.

Sweet williams. She'd fallen in a thick bed of the tiny blossoms. Wiping away her tears, she gave a soft chuckle and chided herself for giving in to fear. She raised her nosegay and breathed in the gentle fragrance again. In daylight, the delicate petals were rich purple in color. Now they seemed like small black stars in her hands.

She laughed softly to herself. There was nothing to fear in Wyvernwood. Well, nothing except the griffins, and they had no interest in her. The wolves and the snakes would not eat her, and the leopards kept their distance. All she had to do was keep her head and remember it would be dawn soon.

Clutching her bunch of sweet williams, she got to her feet and frowned. In her panic, she'd gotten herself hopelessly lost. Without sun or moon or visible stars to guide her, she wasn't even sure what direction she was going or how far from Stronghold she'd come.

The trees were still filled with ever-present eyes. She appealed to the creatures of Wyvernwood. "Won't someone please tell me the way to the river?" she pleaded in a calm voice.

A soft growl issued from behind her. "Every tree and creature shouts it, and still you refuse to listen!" it scolded. "Go back, you stubborn child!"

"They don't want me in Stronghold," she answered the unseen speaker. "It's not my home!"

"Foolishhhhhh!" another voice replied. "Foolishhhhh!"

But for a breeze that rattled the leaves, the woods fell suddenly silent. Not even the crickets and tree frogs made a noise. It felt as if everything living had abruptly turned their backs on her—everything except the myriad fireflies that wandered among the trees, and even they kept their distance.

Ariel shrugged, chose a direction, and started off on her own again. It would be dawn soon. It had to be. Even in Wyvernwood the night couldn't last forever.

Sometime later, however, she began to grow nervous again, and she wondered if she'd chosen the wrong direction. The woods became thicker, wilder. A bramble ripped her right sleeve from shoulder to elbow, leaving a bloody scratch on her arm. Her legs began to feel heavy and tired, too. The ground turned softer, almost spongy, making walking a chore. She slogged her way along, pushing through dense undergrowth, sometimes crouching to protect her face from low limbs.

Without warning, she found herself ankle-deep in a narrow stream of water. The muddy bottom sucked at her boot as she tugged her foot free, and she gave a little gasp, nearly losing her balance. She tried to step across to the opposite bank, and her other foot sank just as deeply into the grasping mud.

A terrible thought flashed through her mind. *Quicksand!*

She floundered and flailed, freeing her right foot, but her left foot only sank deeper, nearly up to her knee! Her struggles turned frantic. Planting her right foot on the opposite bank, she tried to pull herself free and nearly succeeded before she toppled backwards with a shriek! Her small bouquet flew up into the air. Her left arm sank in the mud up to her elbow, and the cool stream water splashed over her, drenching her, filling her eyes and blinding her. Like an afterthought, soft flower petals rained down upon her face.

Then powerful fingers closed around her right hand, and someone pulled her upright out of the water. With immense strength, they lifted her free of the treacherous, sucking mud, and set her on the bank.

"Thank you!" she sputtered, wiping her face with her tattered right sleeve. "I thought I was going to drown! I thought . . . !" She tried to pull her left hand free. The stranger kept his grip, and he was painfully strong!

Ariel wiped her face again and blinked the mud from her eyes. The darkness was playing tricks on her vision! She stared, and the joy of her rescue turned to horror as she looked at the thing that had saved her. A scream bubbled up in her throat, but she couldn't even voice it!

The creature was a man, or man-like, heavily muscled and strong with arms and legs that bulged, and covered with coarse, curly hair. But it had no head! It was only a torso with monstrously developed limbs!

Ariel writhed and fought, desperate to break free. She kicked its legs, beat at the hand and arm that held her, tried to pry its fingers back, all to no avail. It was too strong! When she tried to scream again, it clamped its other hand over her mouth, nearly smothering her as its immense long fingers wrapped around her head.

Finally it freed her captured hand. With both fists she pummeled the monster's chest and headless shoulders.

It was useless! The monster picked her up and held her at arm's length, shook her until she went limp and senseless, then turned and headed away from the stream, dragging her after it like an old doll. She kicked weakly at the spongy ground, tried to regain her footing, scratched the hand that gripped her head. Its thumb and fingers seemed almost to meet behind her head, such was the size and power of its hand!

Suddenly, she was drenched again. The monster dragged her through another muddy stream and then a third. The bark of a fallen tree scraped against her calves as he dragged her over it; her heels banged roughly on a half-rotted log.

Helpless, she stared upward, too tired and battered to fight anymore. A patch of stars mocked her through a gap in the leaves, and then were gone. A new jolt of panic shot through her. For an instant, she thought something was wrong with her eyes. No more stars, then no more leaves, no more trees!

The darkness became complete and total, as irresistible as the grip around her face. The spongy earth turned to stone, and the air took on a dampness and a chill. Her boot heels clattered. Through her terror, Ariel perceived that she was in a cave!

Deep into the earth, her captor dragged her. At last, it stopped. Briefly, she hung limp at the end of its arm, then it lifted her and flung her into a corner. Ariel's head struck a wall, but through the pain she laughed as she curled into a ball.

She'd been looking for the stars, and there they were dancing inside her skull!

After a while, though battered and bruised, she tried to rise, but wobbly knees refused to support her. She managed, however, to sit up. Drawing her feet close, she put her back to the wall and remembered the knife in her boot. It had slipped down deep, and she shoved her fingers inside the leather, fishing for it, and finally drew it out. It was only a kitchen knife, but it was better than nothing.

It wasn't her only weapon, either.

A crash in the darkness made her jump. She couldn't see anything, but she was sure the headless monster could see. How, she couldn't guess. She also knew by its footsteps and the sounds it was making that it was rummaging around.

She held her hand out, moved it closer, unable to see it at all. *So dark you can't see your hand in front of your face.* How many times had she heard that? Now she knew what it really meant. Careful to make no sound, she leaned forward and swept her other hand over the cave floor, exploring the space around her.

Her fingers brushed something. She picked it up.

The object was slender, smooth, and not too heavy. She ran her hands slowly along it, trying to visualize what she held. The ends were rougher. Lumpy. Knotted?

Gristled!

With a short gasp, she dropped the object and curled back into her corner.

A bone! She'd found a bone!

The sounds of rummaging ceased as the bone hit the floor. Ariel could almost feel the creature's gaze upon her. Shoving her knife out of sight, she squeezed her eyes shut, hugged her knees tightly, and tried to hide behind them. A wave of horror rushed over her again as she remembered her one good glimpse of her captor. She thought she'd seen every manner of creature in Wyvernwood, but she'd never seen a monster like this!

Out of the darkness came a soft chopping, and the odor of fresh, wild onions and radishes wafted through the cave. Ariel sniffed, then began to shiver. Was the monster going to eat her? It didn't have a mouth! Or did it? She thought about the bone on the floor as the chopping resumed.

A fat pair of tears rolled down her cheeks, but she brushed them away, and drew out her knife again. Steeling herself, she forced away her fear. She'd been in hot water plenty of times before—but she had no intention of becoming a stew meat to feed this creature!

Keeping one side of her body to the cave wall, she began to crawl quietly along the cave floor. She didn't get far before something small and invisible scurried across her hand. She froze, afraid to move, even to breathe. Whatever it was—a lizard maybe, or a mouse as afraid of her as she was of it—scuttled on. She let her breath out slowly and resumed her silent crawl. If she followed the wall and encountered no obstacles, maybe she could sneak past the monster and find the cave's entrance. It was a tiny hope, but her only one.

A moment later, that hope was dashed as her head bumped something. The chopping stopped again. This time, Ariel heard footsteps. Grasping her knife tightly, she reached out for whatever she'd bumped into. It made a wooden screech on the floor as she caught an edge and tried to rise. *A table with chairs,* she thought, too late.

The monster reached out for her. She couldn't see its hand, but by some instinct she felt it near an instant before it grabbed her. She slashed with her knife and kicked out with one booted foot, then groped her way to the far side of the table.

Without warning, the table upended and flew away. Wood crashed and shattered on the far side of the cave. The monster came at her again, shattering a chair in its path. The sound alerted Ariel. She lunged aside, slipping on a bit of debris, but getting quickly to her feet. Groping in the blackness, she nearly stumbled over another chair. It felt sturdy and well-made as she bent over it. With a fierce determination, she lifted it in both hands, careful not to drop her knife, and swung it in a wide arc. With a gratifying crash, it shattered against the monster's unseen form. She heard him fall in the darkness and let go a manic laugh.

The sound of her pulse made a loud hammering in her ears, but she wasted no time. She didn't know if she'd injured the monster or not, but she might not get a better chance to make her escape. With both arms stretched out before her, she made a break, chose a direction, and ran.

Straight into another wall. She spun about, nearly fell, but caught her balance with a gymnast's skill. Her elbow struck some kind of cabinet. She couldn't see what it contained, but the creature was getting up, coming for her again. Its harsh breathing and its footsteps gave away its location now.

She hesitated, all her senses urging her to scream, to run. Yet she had other plans. At the last instant, when she could smell the monster's breath and feel the heat of its body, she strained with all her strength and toppled the cabinet. The crashing and smashing echoed through the dark. Fragments of broken crockery scattered over the cave floor.

"Now, Mister Barefoot," she shouted in breathless defiance, emboldened by her success. "How do you like it when your dinner fights back?" She waved her knife, listening with a heart-pounding anger as she felt for the wall at her back. "My name is Ariel, and you'd better remember it the next time you think about dragging little girls around by their faces!"

Again, wood shattered as the monster rose to its feet. Splinters of the cabinet flew at Ariel. A larger piece struck her hand, knocking her knife from her grip. Pottery shards snapped and cracked.

At last, Ariel screamed. Yet, despite her panic, she knew better than to stand still. Dodging aside, she kicked at the creature's leg, and pain flashed through her foot. It was like kicking a tree trunk! She stumbled to the far side of the cave and bumped into a counter. The sting of onions brought tears to her eyes. With a sweep of her hand across the rough surface, she fumbled for the monster's chopping knife, but her terrified fingers sent it flying to the floor out of sight among all the other wreckage!

She had one hope left, one secret weapon that Jake had made for her. Not the sling that she wore around her wrist like a bracelet. That was useless in the dark and the closeness of the cave. Hastily, she unwound the length of braided leather with which she'd bound back her hair.

The Dragons didn't approve of weapons, especially, it seemed, in the hands of human children. So Jake had made some "adornments," unobtrusive and harmless looking pretties that few took notice of or objected to—like the band that tied back her hair and hung down over her shoulder. Unfolded, it was twice as long as her arm, and the beads at either end gave the lash extra weight and extra bite.

She spun the lash before her in defensive figure eights until it hummed like a bull-roar! Again and again it struck the monster, and it seemed to stagger back, stung by the force of the beads.

But if the monster hesitated at all, it wasn't because of her hair band! Too late, she smelled its breath close again and felt its heat. Huge hands closed on her neck and wrist. Ariel screamed in pain as tendons in her arm popped, and she dropped the weapon Jake had made for her.

The monster lifted her until her toes barely touched the ground. A wet tongue slathered slowly across her face, from what kind of mouth she mercifully couldn't see. Ariel cringed, yet still tried to be brave. "Ugh! Roach-breath!" she cried. "No wonder you live alone in this hole!"

The monster tightened its grip on her neck. Long fingers squeezed her windpipe. Ariel kicked and thrashed as the pressure increased and the blood began to pound in her head. *I guess I'm licked!* she thought, laughing inwardly. *Licked!* It would be her last little joke.

Little Pear flashed into her thoughts, and Trevor and Markam. She missed the laughter of her friends. And Jake, dear Jake—would he forgive her for running away and getting herself killed, for her jealousy?

Her eyes rolled sideways, but instead of mere darkness, she saw a soft light that seemed to swirl and coalesce out of the blackness. At first, she thought she was just imagining it. Yet the light grew brighter, shifting from an amber gold to an eerie wavering fireglow—and some figure stood at its center!

The grip on her neck and throat relaxed, unwillingly at first, then suddenly. Ariel collapsed to the floor, gasping for breath as the monster turned away. It no longer seemed interested in her. The firelight, so bright for an instant, receded into another part of the cave. The monster followed it as if entranced.

Ariel rubbed her throat as she stood up. Her senses reeled, but she had to follow that light, too! Where it came from, she didn't know, but without it she might never escape this place! Painfully, she stumbled after the monster, ignoring the broken crockery and the obstacles barely visible in the diminishing glow. Keeping her gaze on that light and on the monster's broad back, she moved across the cave.

Then the firelight winked out. Ariel felt a stab of panic. But as her eyes adjusted, another hazy light replaced it. Finding strength, she quickened her pace lest she lose that light, too. The monster still preceded her. It moved with slow, shambling steps, drawn or summoned by something she couldn't yet see.

Hope swelled within her. The hazy light came from the cave's entrance! It was the light of dawn filtering through the thick trees beyond! It was all Ariel could do to keep from running, yet she still feared the monster and dreaded passing within the reach. She hung back waiting for a chance to make a fast break.

But something strange began to happen to the monster. As it stepped from the cave's darkness into the blossoming daylight, it began to change. Its pale pink skin hardened, crusted, and turned gray. It faltered, but still it continued forward until it stood fully bathed in the light of dawn. Then it froze in mid-step.

Gathering her courage, Ariel crept up behind the monster. It didn't move or take any notice of her at all. Finally, drawing a deep breath, she raced out of the cave, ducked below one of its outstretched arms, and ran as fast as she could.

She wasn't sure why she stopped and turned around. Some fearful part of her still expected the monster to give chase. But it stood absolutely still, its gaze fixed on the rising sun. Then, some motion off to the side, barely glimpsed from the corner of her eye, drew her attention.

"Who's there?" she cried, staring into a thick copse of vine-dripping trees.

But no one answered, nor could she see anyone in the gloom that still lingered there. Yet she remembered a figure she had first seen at the heart of the light—a light someone had dared to carry into the cave's darkness. Someone had saved her life.

She looked back toward the monster. An incredible sight greeted her eyes. The creature had turned to stone, and it was cracked and discolored with age as if it had stood on that spot for ages like an ancient headless guardian, lost and forgotten in the forest.

Ariel let out a slow breath and felt her fear drain away. She looked toward the copse again. Someone was still there in the shadows. She could feel them watching. "What happened to it?" she asked quietly. "What was it?"

The voice that answered was old, gentle, and feminine. "A Night Troll," it said. "They cannot tolerate the touch of the sun, but neither can they resist it once they feel its rays. I lured it from its cave with this."

A small round mirror, a highly polished piece of silver about the size of Ariel's hand, landed in the grass at her feet. Ariel bent to pick it up. It was beautiful! The wooden frame around the mirror had been ornately carved to represent a snake with two heads. The two heads entertwined to form a brief handle for the mirror.

"What are you?" she asked uncertainly.

"Something old." There was just a hint of amusement in the answer. "As old as the Night Troll. There was an Age before the Age of Dragons, child, and there are things more ancient in Wyvernwood than even they know." A tangle of long vines stirred at the edge of the copse, and the speaker came half out of the shadows, but not so far as to show her face. She appeared to be tall and thin, and she wore threadbare robes of green and black that made her blend in with the foliage. "I am called Agriope."

Ariel took a step toward her, then stopped. This woman called Agriope may have saved her life, yet she suspicious. "Why don't you come out of there and let me see you better?"

"Because the daylight is no more my domain than the troll's," Agriope answered. "Tell your friends, child. They won't believe you, but tell them that things are awakening in the forest that have slept for a long time. The tides of war are disturbing our sleep." She held out a slim hand. "Walk with me, but promise not to look upon my face. I'll lead you back to Stronghold."

Ariel took Apriope's hand, and they began to walk, but always in the shadows of the trees or under the thickest leaves. Still, stray beams of sunlight touched Apriope's hand, and she didn't turn to stone like the Night Troll.

"Can't I go with you?" Ariel asked, as they walked. "They don't want me in Stronghold."

Agriope gave a soft laugh. "Are you so sure?" she said. "Would the young white one fly all the way to the Tangled Marsh in search of you if you were not dear to their dragon hearts?"

Ariel resisted the urge to look up at Agriope's face. The touch of the old woman's fingers in hers felt so gentle and inspired her trust. But she had promised. "No one's coming after me," she said sadly.

Agriope laughed again, and pointed up from under some willow branches where they stood near the edge of a small clearing toward the rising morning sun. White wings flashed in the brightness, and a sweeping tail lashed the treetops. The Dragon Luna sailed low overhead, as if searching for something. She glided past, then let out a cry and circled back.

There was just enough room in the clearing for her to fold her wings and settle to the ground. She stretched out her senuous neck until her nose parted the willows. "How ever did you get so far out here, child? We've been scouring the woods for you! The entire village is frantic!"

Agriope's voice issued from the shadows, no more than a whisper. "Are you so sure?"

Ariel whirled. When had she let go of Agriope's hand? A few willow branches in the deeper shadows stirred, then became still. The old woman was gone! Ariel spun toward Luna again, but Stormfire's daughter gave no indication that she'd heard anything.

She looked down at the mirror Agriope had left her. "There are older things in Wyvernwood than even the dragons know," Ariel said as she stared at her own bruised reflection. "Things are waking up." She gazed past Luna into the bright clearing, then turned and stared back into the Tangled Marsh. "You don't believe me, Luna."

Luna gave her a sympathetic look, then smiled a dragon smile. "I've watched you, Ariel," she admitted, "I've watched all you Man-children since the day we rescued you at sea and brought you to Wyvernwood, and I think I know your heart." She backed away from the willows into the clearing. Sunlight shimmered on her ivory scales. "I know you're every bit as agile as Jake," she said. "If we go very slowly and very low, would you like to fly back home?"

Ariel's eyes widened with sudden excitement. "You mean you'd let me ride you?"

Luna shook her great head. "I'm not a common beast to be ridden," she chided. "But we can fly together."

It was Ariel's dream to fly the skies as Jake flew with Chan! With an exuberant burst of energy, forgetting all her aches and bruises, she somersaulted through the air and executed a series of handsprings.

Then she turned back toward Luna and held out both hands. For just a moment, the sunlight danced off the mirror she still clutched in one fist, dazzling her. She thought of Agriope somewhere in the shadows—still watching, she felt sure.

"Thank you," she whispered. Then she turned her face toward the bright sun.

BUT THERE WAS NO GOING HOME for Ronaldo and Bumble. With one eye on the departing Angmaran vessels, the gray Dragon returned to the cliff edge above the Windy Sea where they had left Marian. There, with his wings in full display to slow his flight, Ronaldo extended his claws and landed on the very precipice. Bits of stone and rock cascaded to the shore far below as he took a step away from the edge.

As soon as they touched the ground, Bumble abandoned his perch in Ronaldo's ear and darted straight to a patch of fragrant asphodels to feast and replenish himself. His tiny wings hummed in the darkness as he sampled one rich blossom and then another, draining them of nectar until his belly began to bulge.

While his companion gorged himself, Ronaldo turned back to watch the burning flagship. The flames soared upward in the night. Fiery bits of sail, caught by the wind, blew like bright ribbons across the water. Sparks and ash swirled upward. Fire engulfed the deck and rails, climbed the mast, danced among the rigging.

Perhaps because the ship was built so well it burned for a long time. Through squinted eyes, Ronaldo watched it all. There was a terrible, violent beauty in the flames, in the way they reflected on the tossing water, in the harsh contrast they made against the velvet shimmer of the star-flecked horizon, in the veil-shifting smoke.

With a crackle and hissing that carried across the waves, the bow finally pitched forward and slipped below the surface. The stern rose out of the water. In one smooth, astonishingly graceful slide, the vessel dived under the waves.

An unsettling sense of satisfaction filled the Dragon Ronaldo, and he kept still until the ship vanished. The rolling smoke that lingered over the sea dispersed on the wind, and after a few moments not even the smell of it remained to taint the salt air.

"A good thing we've done, yes?" Bumble landed on the dragon's nose and hopped excitedly from one leg to the other. "We've stopped a war! We gave 'em what-for! And if they come back, we'll give 'em some more!" He sprang into the air in a somersaulting blur, then resumed his perch. "Bumble and Ronaldo—we're the team!"

The outrage Ronaldo had felt earlier had drained away. In its place was something more uncertain and troubling. His old, familiar self-doubts asserted themselves, but there was something else, too—something new.

A sense of power.

"Don't gloat, Bumble," he cautioned. "We didn't stop a war at all, only a battle."

Bumble stamped his foot. "There you go again!" he said. "You always take the fun out!"

Ronaldo thought for a moment. Without a doubt, lives on both sides had been spared tonight. And the look on the Redbeard's face as he dived over the side—that had been precious! Ronaldo slowly grinned. "It was fun, wasn't it?" Before he could say more, the dragon sneezed. A short burst of heat and smoke shot forth from his nostrils. Bumble sprang into flight, flurried about in a panic, then settled on a nearby tree limb to inspect his tail feathers.

"I'm very sorry." Ronaldo rubbed the tip of his nose with his right wingtip. "The asphodel pollen on your feet—I think I'm allergic!"

"I think I'm singed!" Bumble complained.

Ronaldo reached out with one paw to the limb upon which the hummingbird perched. With a mischievous wink, he bent the limb, released it, and launched his little friend into the air. "Maybe that'll put your fire out," he suggested.

Bumble flew three swift circles around Ronaldo's head, then returned to the same place on the same limb and stuck out his slender, thread-like tongue.

Ronaldo stretched his neck toward the sky, raised his head, and laughed. His bleak mood vanished, and his pulse began to quicken. He gazed at the sky, the stars, and the rolling sea, at the forest all around. This was his home. It was all his home. And tonight, he had acted to protect it. He puffed out his chest with new pride.

He gave his attention back to his companion, but suddenly he thought of Marian. "Indeed, we're a team," he said. "But we're a trio—and one of us is missing." Bending low, he turned and peered into the dark spaces between the trees, then sang softly. "Be you near, or be you far—come out, come out, wherever you are!"

Watching the shadows, Ronaldo waited for Marian to emerge from the woods, but nothing stirred among the foliage except the wind.

Bumble fluttered down and landed on Ronaldo's head. "Hey, hey! What do you say?" he called. "Join the fun! It's time to play!"

But Marian didn't answer.

"I thought she'd wait here for us," Ronaldo said with a hint of consternation. "It's rather late, though. Perhaps she grew tired of waiting and curled up somewhere for the night."

The hummingbird grew unusually still. "My Bumble-brain is small," he answered, "and it's hard sometimes to think back. But did Marian seem well? Dirty, I remember, and wild-looking." He fluttered off to another tree limb and turned to face the Gray Dragon.

"Of course she looked wild," Ronaldo said. "Whoever heard of a tame unicorn?" *Especially in Wyvernwood,* he thought to himself. Then he frowned and thumped the tip of his tail on the ground. In or out of Wyvernwood, there were no other unicorns except Marian. She was the last of her kind. He stooped low and peered among the surrounding trees again. Overhead, the moonlight threw wan shafts of illumination down through the branches, but that only made the shadows trickier and the woods more mysterious.

His frown deepened. What had Marian been doing all the way out here anyway? If the smoke of battle had drawn her, why hadn't she stayed to watch its finish? Why had she vanished so quickly without a parting word to her friends? The more he thought about it, the more it bothered him.

"You weren't really in a big hurry to go home, were you?" he said to Bumble.

Tiny wings blurred, then became still again. "You left all those paints unsealed," he answered. "And the door is still open."

Ronaldo growled as he heard his own words thrown back at him. "Nobody likes a smart-mouthed hummingbird," he warned.

Bumble darted from his branch and flew a circle around Ronaldo's head before settling in his right ear. "Nobody likes an indecisive dragon, either," he shot back. "Are we going to go look for Marian, or are you going to sit here and think about it some more?"

"I figured I'd follow you," Ronaldo answered with genuine surprise. "You can smell a daffodil on the far side of Wyvernwood. Can't you pick up her scent?"

Bumble flew around to perch on the dragon's nose. "Daffodils, asphodels, fuschia, lantana, honeysuckle. . . ." He sprang from Ronaldo's nose to land on a new branch. His small tail-feathers drooped as he spoke again. "Unfortunately, Marian smells like all of those and more."

"We'll just have to look for her the hard way then," Ronaldo said. Spreading his wings, he leaped from the edge of the cliff and sailed outward over the rocky shoreline.

Gliding just above the treetops, Ronaldo searched for a natural path that Marian might have taken. Dragons could see quite well in the darkness, and he hoped for some flash of mane or spark of moonlight on her golden horn. Unfortunately, he found no such path, and he began to search at random, flying southward, then northward, turning inland for a while, then returning to the coast.

As the moon sank lower in the west it played strange games with his shadow. Sometimes it preceded him like an eager guide, black and willowy and swift. At other times, it followed like a silent stalker, rippling and flowing over the quivering leaves. When he flew north or south it flew beside him, but then its wings were mismatched, one too short and one impossibly elongated. It startled him once as it seemed to tip its wings, to turn and take off on its own. But that was only an effect of a taller range of pines tilting his shadow back his way.

A tiny voice spoke inside his ear. "Do you know the three most important words in the world?"

Ronaldo thought for a moment. "I love you?" he answered.

"Bumble is starving!" A tiny kick tickled the inside of Ronaldo's ear. "The three most important words in the world! *Bumble-is-starving!* I can't continue all this arduous searching if my belly is rumbling!"

"Your belly?" Ronaldo couldn't resist sarcasm. The little Bumble-bird had been nestled quite comfortably in his ear while he'd been doing all the flying. "All I heard was the passage of wind."

"It was my belly!" Bumble insisted. "When I pass wind in your ear, you'll know it!"

The cliff where they had originally landed lay right below. Ronaldo had been using it as a hub as he patterned his searches. It seemed as good a place as any to rest for a few moments. Sailing outward over the shoreline, he banked and settled once more on the edge.

Bumble hesitated. "Asphodels? Again?" he said with obvious disdain. "Next time let's try to land near a nice patch of scarlet runner bean! I haven't had scarlet runner bean since yesterday!" He darted away and disappeared among the trees.

The surf boomed on the rocks below. Drawn by the sound, Ronaldo turned and stared outward toward the Windy Sea. There was no evidence at all of the battle or the violence that had taken place earlier. White-capped waves rolled in neat rows upon the glimmering surface and rushed to break upon the shore. He listened to the surge and roar the water made, finding a strange peacefulness in its inevitable rhythms.

Craning his neck, he glanced around for the moon, but it was too low to see through the trees. It seemed that he'd searched half the night, and still he hadn't found the unicorn. With a sigh, he curled up on the ground, folded his weary wings, and surrendered himself to the panorama of the sea's darkly glittering beauty. Bumble never took long to feed, and he was content to wait.

After a few moments, though, a thought whispered through his mind. *She's hiding.* Slowly, he flexed his claws and dug at the grass as he considered the idea that Marian might not want to be found. Wyvernwood offered countless tangles and copses and caves and places of concealment, and Marian knew the forest better than most creatures.

He hung his head over the edge of the cliff, and watched the waves smash on the rugged shore below as he wondered what to do. He loved the way the spray shot over the dark boulders, the patterns the white seafoam made as it swirled among the rocks.

Then a shiver passed through Ronaldo. He lifted his head and drew a sharp breath. "I'm an idiot!" he cried.

A much rounder Bumble landed on his nose. "Oh, I wouldn't go that far," the little hummingbird said. He touched his feathered chest with one wing and belched. "Pardon me!"

With a shake of his head, Ronaldo dislodged Bumble. "The asphodel pollen . . . !" He warned. "Don't make me sneeze!" But it was too late. The small, almost delicate explosion brought forth a marvelous burst of flame that withered the nearest leaves.

"Pardon me twice," the hummingbird said as he hovered safely behind the Gray Dragon. "Bumble is humbled."

"You Bumble-bird! I'm going to pluck your tail feathers and use them for paint brushes!" Ronaldo wiped at his nose with a paw. Bumble's eyes bulged with sudden fear, and Ronaldo winked. "But not right now. We're going down to the shore and see what we can see."

The hummingbird flew to the edge of the cliff. "Bumble's tail is grateful for the reprieve!" he answered, energized by his repast. "On danger I thrive! Into darkness I dive! No questions asked! No quarter given!" Without another word, he tilted his wings and darted straight downward.

Ronaldo stared at the empty space where Bumble had been and shook his head again. The impetuous nature of his little friend never ceased to amaze him, nor did the seemingly endless strings of rhymes and pronouncements that flowed from that narrow bill. By now, Bumble was already on the shore, perched on some dry spot, no doubt tapping an impatient foot.

"On danger I thrive," he muttered as he spread his own wings. "After one Bumble-brained hummingbird I dive."

The beach below the cliff was a narrow strip of rocks and sand. Seaweed and broken shells lay scattered about, and a few pieces of old driftwood stuck up like bony arms from old graves. The rush of the sea and the breaking waves sounded much louder as Ronaldo glided down through the salty spray and landed on an outcropping of rocks where the water didn't reach.

A greenish blur circled Ronaldo's head, then hovered right in front of him. "What took you so long?" Bumble said. "This is a bad place. No flowers! Just stinky dead sea-moss. Foul-tasting. Blechhh!"

Ronaldo blinked. "You actually tasted it?"

"Just put my tongue on it," Bumble answered defensively. "Just the tip. Just a little. Blechhh!"

Ronaldo stared toward the sea. The wind felt different down here, and the water looked blacker, angrier, as if a storm were coming. A white froth churned among the rocks and at the shore's edge. He'd noticed it before, and it had reminded him of something Marian had said. *I was down on the shoreline among the rocks. . . .*

His eyes narrowed as he turned toward the dark face of the cliff. It was cracked and rutted. Here and there, gnarly roots jutted out from the stone. Like the driftwood sticking up from the sand, they reminded him of bones, as if some creatures had been sealed up and had desperately tried to claw their way out before dying.

Ronaldo licked his dragon lips and shivered as he recoiled from the morbid imagery. He shot a glance toward the water again. Something about this shoreline bothered him. It triggered some dark place in his imagination. His senses seemed suddenly to sharpen. The waves boomed louder on the outer rocks. The air felt—no, tasted—not just of salt, but of *wrongness*!

He looked toward the cliff again. It seemed to loom outward, to reach toward him, and the jutting roots seemed impossibly to beckon. Folding his wings tightly, Ronaldo dropped to all four legs and crawled over the rocks and sand. His eyes narrowed to slits as he studied the darkness at the base of the cliff.

Caves!

In the rock face, half hidden beneath a sharp overhang, he spied a pair of openings, no doubt entrances to one large cavern beneath the cliff.

Dragons had no fear of caves. In fact, he lived in a cave. How, then, did he explain the chill that ran up and down his spine as he thrust his head inside the nearer opening?

Bumble landed on his shoulder. His wings hummed with excitement, then grew still. "Bad place," he said.

"Yes, I know," Ronaldo answered in mild annoyance at the distraction. "No flowers."

Bumble's wings hummed again as he flew into Ronaldo's ear. "Real bad place," he insisted. "Bad scent. It curls my feathers."

There was no denying the stench. It was a strange mixture of earth and seasalt. The way the breezes blew on this stretch of beach, it should have smelled fresh. But other odors corrupted the air, tainted it with vaguely fearsome perfumes that wafted up from the depths, from tunnels and chambers that he could sense, but could not yet see.

Ronaldo pulled back from the cave and shuddered. *The stink of death,* he realized. *But something more as well.* Backing up a few steps, he glanced toward the top of the cliff, then slowly turned and scanned the sky. *Not a bird in sight,* he thought to himself with growing unease. When was the last time he had seen a bird or a squirrel or a fox or any of the myriad common creatures that should be living in the forest above?

He turned toward the caves again. "Marian's here," he said to Bumble. "As sure as the dawn is coming, I feel it in my bones."

"Does Ronaldo want to know what I feel in *my* bones?" Bumble hummed inside the dragon's ear as he darted out, spiraled high into the sky, then settled again on Ronaldo's shoulder. "I feel we should shake a wing as fast as we can for the farthest corner of Wyvernwood." His small voice turned sarcastic. "But we're not going to do that, are we? No, because we're heroes!" His wings hummed again, but he kept his perch. "I know, I said it myself. But what I forgot to say is that heroes are innately stupid fellows! Always rushing in . . . !"

"I'm not rushing," Ronaldo whispered as he moved carefully toward the cave. "I'm sneaking on tiptoes, or I would be if you weren't running off at the beak. Stay here if you wish."

Bumble fluttered up into the air again and landed on Ronaldo's nose. His chest swelled out, and tiny black eyes glared into the Dragon's. "Hmmmph!" he said. "And have to dash in completely alone to save Ronaldo's gray butt when your tortured screams come echoing up from that blasphemous pit of despair?"

On the verge of thrusting his head back inside the cave, Ronaldo paused. His eyes crossed as he tried to focus on the feathered speck on the end of his nose. "Blasphemous pit," he murmured appreciatively. "I like that!" He nodded, as if savoring the words.

Bumble folded one wing across his plump stomach and made a curt bow. "Thank you," he said. "Now shake a tail, will you? If Marian's inside, why are you wasting time dawdling out here? Go! Move!"

The awful stench swirled into Ronaldo's nostrils as he hunched his shoulders and bent low to the ground. The entrances to the caves were narrow, a tight fit for any dragon, and he flattened his wings so closely against his sides they seemed to disappear. Like a giant worm, he crawled inside, keeping his head almost in the sandy soil to avoid the low ceiling. Off to his left, a faint gray light spilled in through the second entrance. As he had guessed, there were not two separate caves after all, but two narrow openings into the same cavern, a trick of erosion that did nothing to quell his apprehension as he pushed further inside.

Braving the blackness, Bumble flew forward, only to return a few moments later. "On danger I thrive," he muttered, shivering. He winked nervously at Ronaldo. "Just trying to convince myself." Drawing a deep breath, he posed on the dragon's nose like a springboard diver, then took off again.

Ronaldo slid forward. The ceiling slanted so low that he dragged his belly over the sand, making a soft slithering sound as he advanced. Even Marian would have had to duck and crouch to pass through here, he thought, hoping that things didn't get any tighter. Every few steps, he paused to look and listen. The cave was remarkably undistinguished, so far devoid of stalagmites or stalactites, flowstone, or crystal.

It was devoid of other things, too, like bats and lizards, snakes, or any of the scuttling life that should have made such a place their natural home.

Unexpectedly, another tunnel offered itself. The ceiling of the new passage seemed to slant upward, not high enough for him to stand erect, but enough for him to rise up on all fours and stretch his cramped legs a little. He paused again to listen, hoping for the hum of Bumble's wings, thinking that his diminuitive friend had been gone too long.

The peculiar odor grew stronger as he turned his nose into the new tunnel. Several odors, he reminded himself, none pleasant. Yet, among them one smell stood out sharper and more pungent than the rest. It was this odor, he realized as he inhaled it again, that sent the chills down his spine and set his heart to racing. Eyes wide and all his senses on edge, he stalked ahead.

Bumble came zigzagging back, darted into his ear, and there hunkered down into a feathered ball. His tiny heart beat so rapidly and so loudly that Ronaldo had no trouble hearing it. He tried to speak between gasping breaths. "Bumble's brain is too small!" he said, then paused. "No room for memories! But . . . ! But . . . !" He paused again and gulped. "Bumble has smelled this smell before! No flower! No blossom! Not nice!"

As Bumble trembled and gasped, the Gray Dragon felt his own fear subside and a grim anger take its place. Something had frightened Bumble badly, and that brought out his protective instincts. "It's all right, Bumble-bird," he said with cold calm. "Just stay with me now. We'll find Marian together."

"Dead fish!" Bumble said in a barely audible voice. Then, he tried again. "Dead fish-*men!*"

Ronaldo jerked his head around in surprise, forgetting that he couldn't see Bumble in his ear, and bumped his head on the cave wall with sufficient force to send a brief cascade of dirt and stone shuffling to the floor. A cloud of dust rose, and he blinked his eyes to clear them. "Mer-folk?" he said, making an effort to keep his voice low.

Bumble didn't answer. Ronaldo hesitated, his mind racing. None of the Mer-folk, not man or woman, had been seen since the Angmaran assault on their island home, Thursis. He sniffed the air again and stared ahead. The Mers were rare and precious creatures, few in number. The prospect of finding one dead in this place only made Ronaldo angrier. *Fish-men,* Bumble had said—more than one.

All his trepidation melted away. Casting stealth aside, Ronaldo moved as fast as the confined space allowed. In some places, his sides scraped the walls. In others, his head brushed the ceiling. It didn't matter. New tunnels offered themselves, a maze of mysterious opportunities. At each he paused and sniffed. His nose guided him now as much as his eyes as he chose his way, and he followed the distinctive smell that only grew stronger as he plunged deeper into the earth.

Then, without any warning at all, he emerged onto a ledge overlooking a vast chamber, the far side of which even he could not see. It was as if an immense bubble had formed at the heart of the earth. The stalagmites and stalactites that had been missing from the other tunnels grew in spectacular abundance here. Ronaldo stared in amazement, and unable to restrain himself, he exhaled a short burst of flame. For a brief instant, the cavern became a wonderland, glittering and sparkling with crystaline and flakes of mica.

But in the red light of his fire, he also saw horror. Three Mers, their scales and jewel-like fins shimmering, hung caught in a net directly above his head.

Only the net was an immense web!

A voice shouted from some unseen part of the chamber. "Ronaldo! Get out!"

It was Marian's voice, and his heart leaped. Yet he couldn't tear his gaze away from the Mers. They were dead, as Bumble had said, but their bodies were bloated almost to the point of rupture, and their green hair hung limp as seaweed rope from the pale silken strands that enwrapped them.

Ronaldo swallowed and shook his head to clear it. The Mers were not the only dead things to greet his sight. There were hundreds of webs draped among the stalactites and filling the dark corners. Cocooned in their elaborate geometries were the dessicated shapes of rabbits and squirrels, leopards and bears, and even an unfortunate satyr!

"It's a larder!" Bumble managed to whisper as he stirred and poked his head around Ronaldo's earlobe.

A white shape danced into view far below. A golden horn flashed in the darkness, and Marian tossed her tangled mane. "Ronaldo, get out!" she cried. Then, "Look out!"

A sticky white spray fell like soft lace over the Gray Dragon's head and forelegs. Just in time, Bumble launched himself into the air, avoiding the web. The strands clung to Ronaldo, wrapped around him, and began to harden almost instantly. He felt their strength. The sickly stink of them hit him like a blow, filling his head, choking him. Half-dizzy, he teetered on the ledge as he tried to stand erect.

A black, eight-legged shape covered with spiky hair and as large as any house in Whispering Hills descended in creepy silence on a single strand of webbing. Another silken spray fell over Ronaldo's face and shoulders, and he looked upward into a multitude of glimmering red eyes.

His senses reeled. He thought he might fall off the ledge and tumble to the bottom of the chamber, but something anchored him, a cord of silk that bound him to the wall.

The impossible spider spoke to him in a voice that was raspy with seductive power. "Pretty Dragon!" she said, dropping closer. "Precious and sweet! So long, so long since I've sucked the tasty meat of your kind!"

In some dim part of his mind, Ronaldo heard the distant clatter of hoofbeats on stone. The sound echoed weakly through the chamber, like the brittle snap of pebbles falling into a bottomless well. Breathless and desperate, Marian called his name.

Ronaldo blinked. As if awakening from some spell, he gazed around. The sight of the once-beautiful Mers greeted him, and he recoiled. Again, a spray of sticky silk settled about him, tightening, binding. The stench burned his throat.

"Become one with me!" the spider urged. Her voice was feminine, as silky as the webs she spun. "Slake my hunger, my need! My sweet pretty!"

Ronaldo squeezed his eyes shut. Her voice—so compelling! It tingled in his ears like music! And yet, burning behind his closed lids, was still the image of the Mers. And Marian, the last of her kind, so angry and calling his name.

His heart lurched. The strands of silk, no matter how strong, could not restrain him. Snapping his eyes open once more, he breathed a blast of flame straight at his mesmerizing captor. With startling speed she scuttled back toward the ceiling on her web, barely avoiding his fire.

"Evil lizard!" the spider hissed as it hurled another lace-work spray over the Gray Dragon. "Sinobarre is hungry! Sinobarre offers you the greatest gift—to be her food! Too long has the unicorn made me prisoner here! I starve!"

Ronaldo flexed his wings, straining with all his might, and felt the binding strands weaken and part. "You look fat enough to me," he answered. "Too fat and far too ugly!" With a powerful shrug, he freed his wings and flew from the ledge. The stalactites that speared down from the chamber's ceiling were dangerously sharp. He banked and rolled through the air to avoid them, searching for Marian among the needle-like stalagmites below and finally spying her.

"You shouldn't have tried to find me!" the unicorn shouted angrily as he beat his wings and hovered above her.

"Nice to see you, too," he answered. "Can't say much for the company you keep these days."

Bumble darted out of the darkness and perched on the tip of her horn. "Tag—you're it!" he cried. "Enough adventure! Let's go home!"

Marian tossed her mane and snorted. "I can't go home," she insisted with a stamp of her hoof. "I've got a job to do! I accidentally set her free from a circus in Degarm, and she followed me to Wyvernwood. I finally managed to trap her here some days ago, and I've got to make sure she stays trapped."

Ronaldo twisted his long neck toward the ceiling where Sinobarre clung at the center of a sprawling web. Even across the distance now separating them he could feel her malevolent power. "You should have told us," he said with unconcealed annoyance. "We would have helped." Using his wings and his forelegs, he brushed off the strands of webbing that still clung to him. "What is she?"

"Something older than you," Marian answered, her voice strained and weary. "Something as old as I am." She lowered her head so she could see Bumble. "No cracks out of you, you overgrown mosquito!"

Bumble flashed into the air and circled Marian. "An insult!" he shouted before he landed on her forelock. "You really *are* glad to see me!"

"I'm glad you're alive," the unicorn answered. She turned her gaze upward. "Sinobarre is a remorseless killer. She can't be allowed to roam Wyvernwood. I've kept her from leaving these tunnels, but I can't reach her as long as she stays up there on the ceiling."

Ronaldo thought of the three dead Mers enwebbed in the blackness overhead, and suddenly he realized he knew the nature of the foamy whiteness that lingered at the water's edge along the beach—webbing, half dissolved in the sea water. It was easy to imagine how Sinobarre had ensnared the Mers and dragged them inside to her—what was Bumble's word?—her *larder*.

"You can't reach her," he said tersely, "but I can."

Blasting flame, Ronaldo flew upward. But Sinobarre wasn't to be caught off-guard. As one web caught fire, she ran to another. Dodging stalactites, Ronaldo breathed another stream of fire. More webbing burned. Spinning a new strand, Sinobarre dropped swiftly toward the cave floor and out of sight.

As fire burned the heavy webbing above, the chamber glittered. Shadows and light danced around the cave, making movement hard to spot. "It's my turn to say it to you, Marian!" Ronaldo shouted. "Get out! Take Bumble and get out!"

Marian reared. "It's my fight!" she protested. "I set her free!"

Ronaldo shot a look around the hundreds of webs that still hung in the upper reaches of the chamber, each containing the enwrapped shapes of creatures Sinobarre must have killed before Marian trapped her. Breathing fire, he burned them all, cremated them. Sinobarre would not be dining on their remains!

Fiery pieces of webbing rained down throughout the chamber. Ronaldo turned toward the Mers. Even in death, their scaled forms and rainbow-colored fins sparkled like starlight on the sea. He hesitated less than a moment, then reduced them to ashes.

It's my fight now, he swore silently without bothering to answer Marian. As he had when he stopped the Angmaran battle fleet, he felt a sense of his own power, his own deadly strength. It frightened him, but only a little. He pushed the fear aside and soared to the ledge that led to the outside.

Bumble landed on his shoulder. "Some fun now!" the hummingbird sang. "Gonna be a hot time in the old cave tonight!"

Hoofbeats clattered in the dark. Mane flying, Marian raced upward along another slanting ledge. A strand of webbing shot out from the shadows, but the lithe unicorn moved too swiftly. A brief chasm separated the ledge upon which Marian ran from the place where Ronaldo stood like a guardian. Shaking Bumble away, he spread his wings and sailed across the chamber again to make room for her as she made a graceful leap from one stony point to the next.

At the tunnel mouth, Marian looked back. "Some things can live too long!" she shouted. Then, with Bumble flying ahead, she ran for the outside world.

Ronaldo shot an angry gaze around the chamber. He had never deliberately killed anything in his life, but the thought of Sinobarre loose in Wyvernwood—in his home—hardened him. It wasn't just the Mers. It was his friends and neighbors. It was Marian and Bumble.

"Pretty Sinobarre!" he called as he circled the chamber. The edge in his voice startled and disturbed him. It barely sounded like his own. "Come out and play. Tell me stories of the old days."

Emerging from the shadows, Sinobarre wrapped her eight legs around a soaring limestone column and strode boldly halfway up before she stopped and glared. "What would you like to hear, my pretty dragon?" she clacked her fangs. "Would you like to hear how my brothers and sisters feasted on the eggs of your kindred? How we ruled the forests of this world long before you blew your first puffs of smoke? You can't guess how long I've lived, Dragon. I can tell you many stories!"

The peculiar smell of her webbing intensified, though she spun no more webs. With only mild interest, Ronaldo realized it wasn't just her webbing, but a scent she could exude, a weapon to compel. He felt its attraction, but now that he knew its effect it had no hold upon him. He guessed it was the same for Marian.

He flew upward to the center of the chamber and hovered, making a display of his wings. "There's only one thing I want to hear," he answered.

Sinobarre fixed her unblinking eyes upon him, so many small red orbs, each gleaming with their own hungry light. "What is that, my precious, my tasty?" she said.

Ronaldo met her gaze unflinchingly. He felt her power reaching for him, trying to bend him, to ensnare him. He wondered if she could feel his. A thousand things flashed through his mind, a thousand images and memories. He was just an artist, a hermit and a recluse, actually, and he still wasn't sure exactly what had brought him to this moment. Yet he knew there was no backing away from it.

"I want to hear you sizzle," he said.

He exhaled a blast of fire that roiled across the cavern. Sinobarre screamed and leaped, but swift as she was, nothing could have outrun such a conflagration. Stalagmites exploded in the heat. The walls and floor and part of the ceiling scorched. Stone cracked.

Ronaldo retreated to the ledge at the tunnel mouth and looked down. At the base of the limestone column, Sinobarre's heat-shriveled body burned. He felt no satisfaction, and astonishingly no sense of power or strength. Nor did he feel sadness.

He wasn't sure he felt anything.

Back on the beach, his friends were waiting near the water's edge. They watched him carefully as he emerged into the daylight, the white unicorn and the tiny green-feathered hummingbird with his red throat and puffy chest, neither speaking. The sun rose behind them, a red ball climbing out of the sea. Pushing back the last vestiges of night, it stained the sky with an ominous hue.

He tried to find it within himself to smile as he looked at his friends, but he looked back at the murky colors of the sky, so like a canvass of spilled paints.

It promised storms.

7

THE WIND BLEW CRISP AND COOL OVER TRANQUILITY TOR. Far below, Wyvernwood stretched eastward like a leafy sea. To the west, the lands beyond the Imagination Mountains burned in the harsh, red glare of the setting sun. With his wings folded tightly, Chan turned his gaze away from the forest that was his home and toward those alien hills and plains where he had never been. The chill that crept up his spine had nothing to do with the thin air.

Tranquility Tor loomed high above all the other peaks in the mountain chain. His father, Stormfire, had often come here alone to meditate, he'd said, and to remember the old days before the Dragonkin had taken refuge in Wyvernwood. Chan thought of his sire standing exactly where he stood now. He closed his eyes. It was easy to imagine Stormfire's golden scales and immense wings burning in the sunset of a dying age—the Age of Dragons.

With a soft rustle and flutter, Skymarin landed atop a nearby rock. "Do you feel his ghost as I do?" he said to Chan. His eagle's voice contained an awed reverence as he directed a keen gaze outward. "I came here once with your father. Long ago, my ancestors ruled these mountaintops and valleys, but we abandoned them to join the Dragonkin, to follow him, and watch over the forest." He made a slow display of his wings before folding them again, and the wind whispered through his feathers. "Many are the ghosts here with us now, Chan, and they're watching us."

Chan didn't believe in ghosts, and yet he could hear his father's voice in every wind that brushed upon his ears, see him sailing on the dazzling spears of light against the red, setting sun. Stormfire's spirit permeated the very stones beneath Chan's feet, stirring a flow of memories and emotions Chan had no defense against.

"What is a ghost, Lord of Eagles?" Chan murmured. "I've never seen one."

Skymarin turned his gaze on Stormfire's son. "Pain and rage, grief and longing and emptiness," the eagle answered. "But sometimes joy and sweetness and echoes of laughter, all reverberating in the caverns of our hearts, never letting us forget the souls that came before us."

"Then your ghosts aren't physical," Chan said, trying to sound philosophical.

Skymarin blinked and looked away. "Do you feel a chill on your neck?" he asked. "Does your heart tremble as you stand here where your father stood and think of him? Does your pulse quicken? If only in your mind, do you not hear the voice of Stormfire cautioning and advising you? From this peak do you not see him, no matter where you turn, no matter where you look?" The breeze blew with a sudden, mournful sound. Spreading his impressive wings, Skymarin caught it and glided away, but his voice carried back to Chan. "That is physical enough for me."

Then this place is truly haunted, Chan thought as he watched the eagle gyre higher and higher into the sky. *Or I am._*

An unexpected sound startled Chan, causing him to turn around as Jake dropped an armload of kindling and dead wood on the ground. The boy had been foraging farther down the mountainside below the tree-line, scrounging bark and branches for a fire. The fact that Jake had been able to climb back up unnoticed caused Chan to frown. It made him realize how lost in thought he'd been and how much Tranquility Tor bothered him.

Still, they all needed rest. None of them knew what lay beyond these peaks, and a little sleep before plunging ahead would benefit everyone, even a dragon. Perhaps the unease he felt was just a symptom of weariness.

"I presume you found flint to start your fire?" he called to Jake.

Jake brushed dirt from his hands as he made a face. "I presume you're gonna drag your tail over here and start it for me!" He beat his arms and then rubbed them briskly. "This has to be the coldest place in Wyvernwood, and if I don't get a little warmth soon I'm going to be the stiffest human boy in Wyvernwood!"

"Then we could eat you without feeling guilty." Morkir lay curled up on the sunny side of a boulder. He licked his lips as he stared at Jake. For a brief moment, Chan's protective instincts surged. Without conscious thought, he flexed his claws. Then Morkir looked up and winked. "Just kidding," the griffin said. He rose and stretched, and his lion's tail swished lazily back and forth as he gazed down the westward slopes. "So these talismans are down there somewhere, eh?"

Chan moved closer to Jake's pile of wood and blew a thin stream of fire on it. A blaze sprang up, and the boy threw himself down on his knees and began to warm his hands. Chan smiled, then joined Morkir. "I think so," he said, following the griffin's gaze. "It's hard to be sure. Stormfire scattered them—hid them, actually—in separate locations."

"My father was right," Morkir replied. "Your father was insane. But then, so was my father, and my brother was worse." He shrugged as he turned away and moved closer to the fire. "Makes you wonder how I turned out so normal, doesn't it?"

"Indeed, griffin," Chan answered as he stretched out on the ground.

"That very thought fills my every waking moment." He drew his tail completely around the small camp until it touched his nose. As darkness came on the night would grow colder, but his bulk would provide a windbreak for Jake and for the warming fire.

Morkir yawned and stretched his wings. "I forgive your sarcasm," he murmured. He looked toward the boy, then clacked his beak softly. Jake lay unmoving as close to the fire as he dared on a blanket that Carola had given him. "He's had a long day," Morkir said with uncharacteristic concern. Then, as if taking a cue from Chan, he curled up next to the sleeping human, adding the extra warmth of his lion-furred form and sheltering him beneath a protecting wing.

Chan marveled at the sight as Morkir fell asleep. *Mad Morkir,* the creatures of Wyvernwood used to call the griffin when he flew the skies with his crazed father and brother. But Morkir had changed, and the proof lay on the ground before his dragon eyes. His unease melted suddenly away, and for the first time since landing on Tranquility Tor he felt a glimmer of hope.

He craned his neck and looked westward once more. The sun had finally vanished below the horizon, and the gray twilight grew steadily darker. Rono, the eternal dusk-time star, burned bright in the firmament. One by one, other stars appeared to keep it company.

"Father," Chan whispered, when he was sure both Jake and Morkir were asleep, "if your spirit really is here, then lend me your courage and guide me with your wisdom. I miss you, and I'm so uncertain." He paused and listened to the wind, hoping it would speak to him with Stormfire's voice, but he heard nothing. After a little while he turned his gaze back toward the campfire.

The flames crackled and popped among the bits of wood, and sparks of ash swirled upward on the breeze. He watched the flames for a long time, admiring the colors, the simple power and energy in the shifting reds and oranges and golds, as sleep gradually stole upon him.

A chill gust blew across the tor. The flames sputtered, choked, threatened to go out until Chan stretched out one immense, sheltering wing. The fire settled down again, and its light shimmered on the reds and oranges and golds of his scales. Chan studied his wing in the firelight for a long moment, then smiled. More than ever, he felt Stormfire's presence. A soft starlit shadow passed over the camp. "Thank you," he murmured to his father. "And thank you, too, Skymarin."

"You're welcome, Son of Stormfire," the Lord of Eagles answered as he settled on the boulder.

Chan closed his eyes and gave in to sleep.

He awoke with a start and shot to his feet. Forgetting his tail and the way he encircled the camp, he knocked Morkir over as the griffin also sprang awake. Sparks flew as Morkir rolled across what remained of the fire, but he barely seemed to notice. Skymarin, also awake, flapped his wings and soared into the air.

A fierce screeching and roaring filled the night. The moon had risen while they slept, and against its fulsome light a shadowy battle waged.

"Griffins!" Morkir snarled.

Skymarin let out a screech of his own. "Harpies!" he called back as he flew toward the fight.

"We've been followed, Chan!" Morkir said angrily. "One of us should have stayed on guard!" He gave a roar that echoed from the mountaintop, then, leaping into the air, he chased after Skymarin to join the fray.

Chan hesitated only for a moment as he studied the battle and counted the numbers. Eight griffins! Three harpies! Yet, the harpies fought with such savagery and determination that they seemed to hold the griffins back. Still, in an aerial combat they could only do so much, and even as he watched the battle drew closer to Tranquility Tor. One of the griffins broke suddenly past the harpies, only to be intercepted by Sky-marin. The fearless eagle hit it like a bolt, raking his talons across the griffin's face. An instant later, Morkir hit the same one from the side. Sky-marin darted away as the two griffins, entangled claw and wing, plum-meted earthward and smashed into the trees farther down the mountainside.

Chan gave a cry and waited no longer. Spreading his wings, he sailed toward the battle, announcing himself with a blast of fire that lit the landscape. His heart hammered at the thought of a fight, and he extend-ed his own claws. At sight of him, one of the griffins turned tail and flew away. It was one thing to attack a sleeping dragon; quite another to fight a roused one!

Chan plunged into the melee. Mindful of the harpies, he batted a grif-fin aside with one claw, then sent it tumbling toward the trees with a powerful sweep of his tail. Another flashed toward him. Talons slashed across his shoulder before he could twist away, but a harpy drove his attacker off with a vicious blow.

"Welcome, Chan! Son of Stormfire!" the harpy called. She locked her arms and legs around the griffin and pummeled him with her fists. Her hideous features, though scratched and bloody, were bright with the joy of battle.

Chan had no time to answer. Griffins were the strongest creatures in Wyvernwood and not to be trifled with. Fortunately, most of them were also cowards, as these had demonstrated by attacking at night. They fought now because they had the advantage of numbers. He blew anoth-er blast of fire toward the moon, hoping it would frighten them into retreat.

Instead, his fire seemed to drive both griffins and harpies into a fren-zy. With wings and talons they slashed at each other. Locked in combat, they tumbled through space, crashed to the earth, and sprang upward to fight again. Morkir, too, rose up from the mountainside to join the fight. One of the harpies straddled his back and raised a clawed fist to strike. Then, as if recognizing him, she flew away to attack an enemy griffin.

"Apologies, Ugly One!" the harpy called to Morkir.

Morkir snorted. "Look who's using the word *ugly!*"

Chan drew a breath, then spat out a mouthful of feathers and wiped his tongue with the back of one paw. The air was full of them—eagle, griffin, and harpy. With a small explosion of even more, one of the griffins knocked a harpy across the sky. In turn, Chan lashed out with a wing, bashing the griffin earthward, creating another small cloud of feathers where that griffin had been.

A powerful grip locked unexpectedly around his neck, and Chan felt pain. He hadn't even seen his griffin attacker! Its claws raked and stabbed at his scales, but the danger lay in the creature's incredible strength. Chan shook his head, trying to break the grip and dislodge the griffin, but it hung on. The pain increased, and his eyes began to throb in their sockets.

Chan grew desperate. Arching his back, he flew straight up as swiftly as he could. Still the griffin clung to him. He spiraled, bucked, and looped-the-loop to no avail. The throbbing in his head grew worse. He couldn't draw a breath—not even one full of feathers!

A deep voice grumbled in his ear. "I've got you now, young Dragon!"

The griffin's hold was too strong. Gasping, Chan dove toward the mountainside. In the air, he had no chance against the griffin. If he could save himself, it had to be on the ground. He hit the stony earth hard, hoping to throw the creature off. The impact shivered through his entire body, but still the griffin clung.

Chan's lungs began to ache and burn. Folding his wings tightly, he rolled, writhed, twisted. Finally, he launched himself down the slope, tumbling head over heels out of control. The griffin rode him mercilessly, taking every knock and bump, until they crashed into the line of trees.

Over the snaps of branches and bushes and saplings, came a different sound: the breaking of bone! His attacker screamed and fell off. But more than his grip had been broken. Freed at last from the stranglehold on his neck, Chan looked back toward his would-be killer. One of the griffin's wings jutted at strange angles in two places!

The griffin looked at Chan with panic in its eyes. "Don't fry me!" it begged, cringing as it backed away deeper into the trees. "Don't broil me, roast me, or otherwise cook me!"

"Then crawl away!" Chan shouted. "Crawl back to Redclaw and tell all your brothers that the next time they come after the human boy I'll not only fry, broil, roast and cook them, I'll grill and bake them, too! Now get out of here!"

Despite the damage to his wing, the griffin turned quickly and limped down the mountainside and into the woods. Chan watched until he couldn't see the creature anymore, then turned his gaze skyward. The battle above was nearly over, too. Only two griffins still remained. Morkir wrestled across the sky with one of them while the harpies gave zigzag chase to the last one.

Chan thought of Jake and gazed up toward the pinnacle of Tranquility Tor as he rubbed his sore throat with the tip of one leathery wing. He ached all over from his wild tumble down the mountainside, and though none of his bones were broken, he didn't trust himself to fly. Drawing a deep breath into his raw lungs, he began the climb back to camp.

"Well, that was definitely applause-worthy!" Furred paws slapped together, and razor-sharp claws gleamed redly in the shimmering light of the coals, all that remained of the campfire.

Chan bristled. Some figure stood on the far side of the glow. Jake lay stretched on the ground, unconscious at the figure's feet. "If you've harmed the boy . . . !"

The figure threw back its head and gave a tinkling laugh. "Oh, don't be such a great, moulting scale-brain! I didn't hurt your little pet! All that growling and snarling and screeching, and he never even woke up! Look!" The figure bent down and lifted a corner of the blanket that Jake still lay upon.

The coals lit up a familiar cat-face.

"Katrina!" Chan bent down for a closer look at his Fomorian friend, unable quite to believe his eyes. "What are you doing here? How did you . . . ?"

Katrina came around the bed of coals and reached up to scratch Chan's nose. "It appears that I'm guarding the human while you were playing pattycake with those eagle-beaked flying furballs!" She winked as she held up her claws. They were still red, but not from the coal light. "I hope you had as much fun as I did!"

The blood on her claws was still wet and fresh. "Griffin!" Chan muttered.

"One enterprising loner came sneaky-sneaking up the slope while his playmates suckered you away. But who, to his wondering eyes should appear, but cheetah-cat Katrina full of fun and good cheer!" With a look of innocent mischief, she swished her long tail, then draped it over one shoulder and stroked its tip.

Chan's jaw dropped. "You fought a griffin?" he said. "By yourself?"

She gave a demure shrug. "It wasn't much of a fight. The mangy bit of bad temper actually thought he could take me! Talk about overconfidence!"

Chan grew sober. The smell of blood still lingered in the air, and the stains on her claws didn't account for it. "Where?" he said, looking around.

"Back there by that boulder," she answered. "It's a little messy, though. Guess I got carried away. If you puke, I won't tell the others."

"You're the very definition of kindness and courtesy," Chan said sarcastically as he moved toward the boulder. The griffin lay where Katrina had indicated. She'd ripped out its throat and opened its belly. Its fur and the ground beneath it were saturated and stinking. Chan felt queasy.

"I've always wondered," Katrina murmured, her voice turning strange as she looked down at her handiwork. "Strength versus speedy-speed—in a real mix-up, which would triumph?" She nudged the carcass with one toe. "Now I know."

Chan quietly shivered. He was having some difficulty accepting the fact that Katrina—little Katrina, whom he'd watched grow from a kitten-girl into a strong, young Fomorian—had killed, and, to judge from the evidence, killed with ruthless vigor.

Katrina turned away from the boulder and gazed toward the coals and Jake. "I can't believe he slept through all that!" she exclaimed.

With a sad shake of his head, Chan also turned away from the boulder and the griffin corpse. He scanned the moonlit sky. Morkir, with the three harpies close behind, flew toward the Tor. Skymarin gave a soft screech as he approached from another direction, and an instant later he landed on the ground right beside the sleeping boy.

At last, Jake stirred and yawned. "Silly bird!" he grumbled to the Lord of Eagles. "If you crap on my blanket I'll pluck your pinfeathers." Then, rubbing a fist over one eye, he went back to sleep.

"He's had a long day," Chan explained. Of course, Katrina knew that. She'd been awake to see their departure from Stronghold. "We all have." He looked down at Katrina and smiled weakly, suddenly very weary. "And you the longest day of all," he continued. "You ran all the way, keeping up with us on the ground, didn't you, you little purr-box?"

She blinked her round cat-eyes and draped her tail over one arm. "Don't make such a big deal out of it," she said. "I'm modest, and you'll embarrass me."

Chan gave her a dubious look. "Nice to see you haven't lost your sense of humor."

Nodding to Skymarin, Katrina curled up on the ground beside the warm coals and close to Jake. "Oh, I lose it three or four times a day," she said. "But when I realize it's gone, I just think of your silly face and burst out laughing."

Morkir and the three harpies finally reached Tranquility Tor. With a flutter of wings, they settled to earth and regarded the Fomorian newcomer in their midst. Then Morkir turned his golden gaze on Jake. "Heavy sleeper, is he?"

"He had a hard day," Katrina explained with a roll of her eyes before Chan could comment.

"We all have," the griffin agreed, echoing Chan without realizing it. He turned to the son of Stormfire. "Our harpy friends have some information. I think you'd better listen."

Chan repressed a yawn and wondered if he'd get anymore sleep before the dawn rose.

Closing her eyes and resting her chin on folded paws, Katrina muttered quietly—but not so quietly the others couldn't hear.

> *"A lusty young dragon named Chan*
> *Went questing without a good plan,*
> *But he swallowed his pride*
> *When a cat saved his hide. . . . "*

Perched on the edge of Jake's blanket, Skymarin leaned over and nipped Katrina's tail before she could finish. She gave an indignant yelp. He completed the limerick for her. "It's wise to shut up while you can," he said and closed his small black eyes once more.

Chan sighed and beckoned the harpies closer.

8

WITH SLOW CAREFUL STEPS, KEEPING ONE HAND on the rough rock wall, Ariel descended the narrow stone stairs carved into the face of Stronghold's northern cliff. A low covering of gray clouds, all that remained of the night's storms, made a pale white ball of the afternoon sun, and a soft wind blew over the canyon. From above, she could hear the sounds of industry and activity, but her mind wasn't on the village. Pausing, she glanced toward Stormfire's Point and bit her lip.

A third of the way down the cliff, she came to a huge cave and peered inside. She'd expected darkness, but a flickering fireplace glow lit the vast interior. Instead of dampness, she felt a gentle welcoming rush of warmth. Stepping off the staircase, she hesitated on the cave's threshold.

"Ramoses?" Her voice trembled.

A shape stirred in the deepest shadows where the glow didn't reach, and a pair of large golden eyes blinked open. With a yawn, Ramoses rolled over onto all four of his legs and arched his back in a lazy stretch.

"Come in, child!" he called. "Come in! I'm surprised and pleased to see you! This is your first visit, isn't it?"

Ariel nodded as she accepted his invitation and entered his home. "I didn't mean to wake you," she apologized.

The old Dragon moved out of the gloom and into the light from his fireplace. His scales glittered with a sapphire sheen as he sat back on his haunches. "Nonsense!" he told Ariel. "Nothing to apologize for! Every now and then, I take a short nap. At my age, I find it a great comfort and benefit." He stretched his neck down, bringing his huge head closer to Ariel, then winked one eye as he made a sweeping gesture. "But my home is also Stronghold's library, and the library is always open."

Ariel swallowed, and her eyes widened as she glanced around. Inside the cave where the fireglow was brightest, the walls were lined from floor to ceiling with shelves full of books. Her heart quickened at the sight. At the same time, she felt a measure of despair, for some of those shelves were far too high for her to reach.

"I came to learn," she said in a quiet voice. She felt her cheeks redden with the flush of embarrassment. Would Ramoses understand what she was trying to say? Or was the knowledge of the Dragonkin reserved only for the Dragonkin? "Stronghold's my home now," she continued. "I know I ran away, but now I'm back. I need to contribute something more than a few flips and cartwheels, Ramoses."

The Dragon brought his sapphire head even closer to her, and Ariel took an involuntary step backward. But he calmed her at once. "Would you mind scratching my nose?" he said. "It's one of the few pleasures left to an old Dragon, to have a friend scratch his nose."

A slow smile spread across Ariel's face. Tentatively, she reached out with one finger, then two, and scratched the cool, leathery surface between the great dark nostrils. Not just in one spot; she moved her fingers back and forth over the broad area with increasing vigor until Ramoses began to purr and she began to chuckle and laugh.

"Oh, joy!" her host moaned. "Oh, bliss and rapture!" He settled down on the cave floor, then with his wings folded against his body until they were almost invisible, he twisted his immense bulk and rolled over on his back. His purring grew louder. "Oh! Oh! Oh, stop!" he insisted. But still he offered his nose for more attention. "Oh, stop before I embarrass myself!"

Rather than stopping, Ariel grew bolder and scratching turned to tickling. Ramoses's legs twitched and kicked, and she laughed harder at the sight. "You called me your friend!" she cried in delight.

"So I did!" Ramoses answered. Abruptly, he rolled over again, rose up, and sat back on his haunches as he'd done before. "And so you are," he added, turning serious. "But Ariel, entertainment is a fine and noble art. And making others laugh and forget their problems, even for a little while, is a wonderful gift." He lowered his head a little, fixing her with his golden gaze. "You have that gift, child. These are troubling times, and your ability to make others smile is better than any medicine. Never forget that."

He looked at her for a long moment as if to drive home his point. Then he reached for a slim volume and drew it down from the shelf. Like all the books in his library, it was bound in the sloughed-off hide of Dragons, and the old scales glimmered with a silveriness as he pressed it into her hands.

"However," he continued, "learning is a fine and noble endeavor, too." He nodded toward the book she now held. "That is an early summary of our journey to Wyvernwood. If you wish to learn about the Dragonkin, it's an excellent place to start. Take it with you, and return it whenever you're done."

Without opening the volume, Ariel ran one hand lightly over the cover and over the edges of the pages within. She quivered with a rush of excitement and anticipation. Then she frowned. "I . . . I haven't had a lot of practice reading."

Ramoses' Dragon lips curled upward in a semblance of a smile. "Just tell Carola," he said. "She'll be happy to help you." He winked again. "Or come see me again. My nose always needs a good scratching."

"I'll scratch it for you anytime you want!" she promised as she clutched the book to her chest. She shot another look around at all the books. So much to read! So much to learn! She twirled with sudden happiness.

Then, just as suddenly, she stopped, overcome with shame. She'd run away last night and worried everyone. Yet everyone was being so nice to her. Gregor and Carola had hugged and kissed her upon her return. The citizens of Stronghold had cheered when she rode in on Luna's back. Trevor, Markham, and Pear had seized her hands and made her dance in a circle with them.

"You're not mad at me?" she murmured, her cheeks reddening again.

The old Dragon shook his head. "We all run away sometimes," he answered. "I go to the ocean when I need to think, or hide out here among my books." He ran one paw across the spines of a row of volumes. "Even Stormfire ran away sometimes to a mountaintop in the west, and often without saying a word to anyone." He curled the tip of his tail and thumped it on the cave floor. "Stormfire was my friend and a great Dragon leader," he added in a confidential tone, "but he could be very annoying sometimes and very hardheaded."

Ariel's lips drew into a tight line. "Kind of like me, I guess," she admitted. She looked again at the book she held and opened it to the first page. She studied the title and the elaborate flowing handwriting in which it was written. *The Books of Stormfire: Homecoming.*

Homecoming. Ariel liked the sound of that. She'd never had a true home until she came to Stronghold, just carnival tents and circuses. She closed the book again, determined to read it all, to learn everything she could.

She looked from the book in her arms to Ramoses. "Is there anything in here about Agriope?"

Ramoses' claw caught on the top edge of a book as he turned and shot her a look. It fell from the shelf and hit the floor with a heavy thud, but the Dragon barely noticed. Ariel jumped back, her heart hammering as she shrank away from Ramoses' harsh gaze. "Where did you hear that name?" he demanded. "Tell me!"

Ariel trembled and clutched the silver-bound volume before her like a shield as she took another backward step. The anger in the old Dragon's eyes! All she'd done was mention a name! All she'd done was risk her life on those stupid stone stairs to come all the way down here to learn something, and now Ramoses looked like he might eat her!

Well, she'd had enough of that! She'd survived all night in the forest and fought a troll and ridden the Dragon Luna, and no old Dragon was going to frighten her! Fear turned to anger, and her trembling stopped. Tucking the history book under one arm, she walked up to Ramoses and kicked him.

"I just scratched your nose!" she shouted. "You've got a nerve, scaring me like that now! I might be just a little girl to you, but take that again!" She dealt him another kick, hard enough to feel the impact through all her toes. She ignored the pain, though, and glared up at him.

Even in the uncertain fireplace light, Ramoses' face appeared more blue than usual. Then it resumed its familiar shade. "My apologies, child," he said as his expression softened. "You startled me. No one has spoken that name in a long time—a very long time, indeed." He drew a deep breath and sighed before he bent, picked up the fallen book, and replaced it on the shelf. He sighed again, collecting himself before he spoke. "Now, Ariel, please tell me how you heard . . . that name." He seemed unwilling to speak it himself.

Ariel licked her lips. "I met her last night," she said in a quiet voice. Ramoses squeezed his eyes shut and pressed his front paws together. Ariel repressed another shiver. Somehow, this new reaction from her host frightened her more than his brief flash of anger. "She seemed nice." She paused to gauge the effect of her pronouncement, but Ramoses didn't stir. Ariel's voice dropped to a whisper. "She said that there were older things in Wyvernwood than the Dragons, and that the tides of war were disturbing their sleep."

For a moment she wondered if Ramoses had fallen asleep, but slowly he opened his eyes. "Is that all?" he asked.

Despite the warmth from the fireplace, Ariel felt a chill. She watched Ramoses carefully. He tried to conceal it, but he was afraid, and she didn't understand why. "She said the sunlight wasn't her domain," Ariel remembered.

Ramoses gazed into the heart of the fireplace as he nodded. The flames shimmered on his scales and lit up his golden eyes. He seemed to need the fire's warmth, to see something deep within the fire that Ariel couldn't see. She crept up beside him and touched the side of his neck.

"I'm sorry I kicked you," she murmured, gazing into the fire with him. "Are you all right?"

He lifted his head up from the floor. "I have some reading to do," he answered distantly. Then, in a firmer voice, as if to reassure her, he added, "I'm fine, child. Please, enjoy your book, and come back for another when you've finished it. You're welcome here anytime, Ariel."

She knew Ramoses wasn't fine. Something she'd said had deeply upset the Dragon. But she also knew a dismissal when she heard one, yet she wasn't offended. She'd already stayed longer than she'd planned. "My friends are waiting for me," she said. She turned and started back toward the mouth of the cave.

"Ariel," Ramoses called. At the threshold, she turned back toward him. "Don't forget that you've got another friend down here."

A smile spread across her face as she gave a vigorous nod. Then she stepped out onto the narrow stone stair. For a moment, she paused to breathe the warm, fresh air and let the breeze play over her face. The canyon view excited her as it never had before. She gazed down toward the gushing river, where a group of minotaur children played on the banks, then up at the sky as a pair of Dragons sailed overhead.

Home, she thought, and she smiled again. She'd never had a place to call home before, but that's what Stronghold had become. She realized that now.

She climbed the steps at a rapid pace, no longer afraid of their narrow construction. At the top of the cliff, she paused again and gazed around the village, observing as if for the first time the way the smoke curled gracefully up from the chimneys, savoring the rich smells of cooking and industry, marveling at the natural sounds of everyday life around her.

Hugging the silver history book to her chest, she headed for Gregor and Carola's cottage—for *home*—and on the way she smiled and said a cheerful, "Hello!" to everyone she met. It doubly pleased her when everyone returned her greeting.

When she arrived home, she saw Gregor working at his forge in the workshop beside the cottage. The large wooden doors were pushed wide to let out the heat and let in the cooling breeze, and Ariel stopped.

"Thank you!" she called to the owl-faced Fomorian.

Gregor ceased his work and set down the metal tongs he held. Wiping his face with the back of a feathered arm, he flexed the small wings on his shoulders as he turned her way. "What's that?" he replied? "Thanks for what?"

Ariel shrugged and danced away with a mischievous grin. "I just thought it was time I said it," she answered. "I haven't before. So, thank you!"

With a shake of his head, Gregor picked up his tongs again. "Strange child," he said as he resumed his work.

Deliciously happy, Ariel pushed open the cottage door. Carola heard and poked her head out of the kitchen. Her green cat-eyes lit up, and she pointed with a wooden spoon toward the silver book. "Looks like Ramoses has taken an interest in your education!" she said.

"He loaned me a book," Ariel answered with enthusiasm. "I can't wait to read it! He said you'd help me if I had trouble."

"Wait right there," Carola said, disappearing back into the kitchen. She emerged again a moment later with a tray in one clawed hand and popped a fresh, warm cookie into Ariel's mouth. "We can read it together by the fireplace after dinner tonight," Carola promised as Ariel chewed. "And we'll have the rest of these for treats."

Ariel looked at the pile of cookies on the tray, and her mouth watered. "We were never allowed to have cookies," she said, remembering her days in the carnivals and circuses. "Old Micah said they'd make us too fat to perform."

"Well, old Micah was a foolish human," Carola answered tartly. She selected a second cookie and offered it to Ariel. "And since you have some cookie-catching-up to do, take a second one. But no more until tonight!"

Ariel sputtered crumbs as she spoke. "Thank you, Carola!" Then, wiping her lips with one hand, she set the silver book down on the nearby dining table. "Humans *are* kind of foolish, I guess," she continued with a flush of embarrassment. "I know I am. I shouldn't have run away and worried you."

Carola set the tray of cookies beside the book and leaned down to smooth Ariel's hair into place. "We all run away sometimes," the cat-woman said. "It's part of growing up."

Ariel looked into Carola's deep green eyes. For all the Fomorian's orange fur and feline features, she thought she'd never seen a more beautiful woman, or a kinder one. It hadn't always been that way. When she first came to Stronghold, Carola and all the other Fomorians and minotaurs and satyrs and creatures had looked like monsters to her. Even the Dragons.

Yet now she saw them differently, and it had nothing to do with her running away. The change had begun before that. It was as if a new pair of eyes had finally opened. It wasn't just that they were beautiful inside because they were gentle and kind. They were beautiful on the outside, too. Different, perhaps, and sometimes unique, but beautiful.

Again, she thought back to her carnival days. She'd been a tumbler, an acrobat, always a pretty little girl doing pretty little tricks with Jake and Kevan and Trevor and Markham and Pear. But there had been others in the sideshows under the shadowy tents. *The freaks,* Micah had called them. *The abnormals and monstrosities.* Ariel had always shrunk away from them. She wished she'd treated them better now.

Reaching out, she smoothed back the cat hair on Carola's head and smiled at its incredible softness. "Ramoses said almost the same thing," she said.

Carola stood up. "Well, he's a very wise Dragon," she answered. Then she lowered her voice to a conspiratorial whisper. "Although, just between us, I find him a little bit smug sometimes. Don't ever tell anyone I said so." The cat-woman took a third cookie from the tray and pressed it into Ariel's hand. "Now you'd better hurry," she added. "Pear might wait for you, but you know the boys won't."

Ariel bit into the cookie and then sputtered more crumbs as she blurted, "I love you!" It surprised her as much as Carola when she flung her arms around the Fomorian. Then, blushing with happiness and embarrassment, her cookie still in hand, she dashed out the door and into the street.

How could she feel this happy? The sky was still gray from the night's storm, and yet to her it was a gorgeous, perfect day! She ran with boundless energy between the houses and shops, down the streets and through the village until she came to the square at the heart of Stronghold.

Throngs of onlookers were already gathered on the grassy expanse. Carola had been right—impatient as always, Trevor and Markham had started without her. Little Pear, too, for that matter. At the edge of the square, unnoticed, she stopped to watch and finish her cookie as, side-by-side, the boys executed a swift series of backflips in flawless unison, followed almost as swiftly by Pear. The crowd laughed and applauded.

It had become a ritual at the end of every afternoon when the days work ended and the sun had not yet gone down. The human children took over the lawn and did what they did best, what they had done in the carnivals and circuses, in the courts of ambassadors and kings: They performed. They entertained. It was their way of repaying Stronghold for taking them in.

"For giving us a *home*," Ariel said to herself. The word tickled her tongue and made her feel so good! But it wasn't in her nature to stay unseen on the edge of a crowd. It was time for her to do her part, and of course that required an *entrance!*

Scanning the throng, she spied a pair of stout minotaurs standing side by side, both of a similar height. Maneuvering quietly behind them and backing up, she took a few deep breaths and gathered her strength. Then, with her gaze locked on the minotaurs' broad, hairy backs, she launched herself forward at top speed, attacking the ground, devouring the distance.

The minotaurs shifted—but not enough to upset her plan. A few steps away, still unnoticed, she leaped forward and upward, planting her hands on their muscled shoulders and vaulting even higher into the air. "Surprise on you!" she cried as she tucked her legs tightly to her chest. Three times she turned head over heels, her hair whipping as she flew over the rest of the crowd. A gasp went up as all eyes turned to her. With a final full twist she hit the ground again, sticking her landing with perfect balance near the center of the square.

"Now that's an entrance!" she shouted, beaming as she flung out her arms to draw the applause.

Nearby, Trevor and Markham frowned and stuck out their tongues.

"Lady Late!" Pear sang out. Shouldering between the boys, she took their hands. "Lady Late! Lost her mate and gets no date! Never early—always surly! That's the fate for Lady Late!"

"I'm not late," Ariel said as she joined her friends. She rumpled little Pear's mop of hair. "I'm just . . ." She hesitated, then shrugged and grinned. "Grandstanding! Now let's put on a real show!"

With polished precision they worked the square, performing practiced routines, improvising at times, drawing audience members into the act at every opportunity. The crowd grew with the volume of cheers and applause. Dragons lined the cliff edge and craned their long necks to watch.

Suddenly, in mid-routine, Ariel stopped and held up her hand. Her friends stopped, too, and the crowd fell silent. "We've gone on too long," Ariel said softly. She pointed upward.

Phoebe, the last Phoenix, glided out of the west. The pale ball that was the sun already perched on the treetops, and in the east the darkness had begun to gather. The crowd, taking note of Phoebe's approach, turned away from the square and drifted toward the cliff edge to stand with the Dragons assembled there.

The human children drifted with them.

Yet, as Phoebe settled atop the stony spire, the villagers turned almost as one to watch another sight. Harrow, the black Dragon-son of Stormfire, strode out of the woods at the eastern edge of Stronghold and took his place among his neighbors and friends on the cliff. Since his injuries he'd been little seen, and the pale scars on the dark leather of his wings showed plainly to anyone that cared to look.

"Welcome home, Son of Stormfire," someone murmured.

If Harrow heard, he gave no indication of it. He fixed his gaze on Phoebe and on the spire that bore his father's name and stretched his sinuous neck outward over the rim. In a soft, deep voice he began to speak:

"Now when day is nearly through
I do not fail to think of you,
For in the fading light I see
Your graceful form, your symmetry.
And when at dawn the world is new
I cannot help but think of you."

Struck to the heart by Harrow's unexpected poem, Ariel repeated it over and over to herself and determined to remember it. But as she did so, it wasn't Stormfire she thought about. She'd barely known the great leader of the Dragonkin. No, she thought instead of her own lost friends, particularly Kevan, who had drowned at sea, but also Jake. Having lost one, she couldn't bear the thought of losing the other.

She wondered where Jake was and prayed that he was safe. Surely Chan would protect him. *I cannot help but think of you,* she thought.

She felt a small hand slip into hers and glanced down at Pear. The little girl smiled, but there was a gleam of worry in her eyes, too, as if she shared Ariel's concerns. Ariel reached out with her other hand and brushed Trevor's shoulder. He moved closer in response, slipping his arm around Ariel's waist as, in turn, he drew Markham nearer.

"I don't ever want to leave here," Pear said with stern seriousness.

Markham rumpled Pear's hair, then wrapped her in his arms and lifted her onto his shoulder. "Hush," he told her. "This is a time to remember others, not to think of ourselves."

Once again, silence spread among the citizens of Stronghold. The sun sank out of sight in the west, but a bright pink and orange glow yet colored the horizon, and streamers of color stretched across the cloudy sky.

The silence, however, proved short-lived. A screeching and cawing suddenly filled the air, and the branches of the trees that surrounded Stronghold rustled and rattled and came alive as black, winged shapes sprang upward and gathered in a dark mass.

"Crows!" Bear Byron called as he pointed. "Look at all the crows!"

"What is it?" a minotaur mother asked. She instinctively gathered her pair of bull-faced children closer. "What does it mean?"

There wasn't time to answer her questions. Without warning, the volume of screeching rose, and the crows plunged downward.

Barely in time, Ariel snatched Pear from Markham's shoulders and wrapped her little partner in a protective hug. As she did so, pain sheared across her scalp. Stars flashed behind her eyes as if she'd been hit with a rock, and her legs buckled. Trevor and Markham caught her. Then Trevor screamed and clutched his cheek.

His hand came away bloody.

A tall, goat-legged satyr bellowed in agony and flapped his arms in a desperate effort to dislodge a pair of crows that perched on his horns. The vicious birds pecked savagely at his face, tearing a score of lacerations before he managed to drive them away.

Like black knives, the crows flashed through the village. The air became thick with them; they seemed to be everywhere. The panicked villagers ran. Talons and beaks ripped at their hair, their shoulders. A young female Fomorian with dog-like features tripped and fell. Before she could rise, three crows fastened onto her back.

"Run!" Ariel shouted to the boys. "Get Pear inside and stay with her!" Without questioning, Trevor seized their youngest companion and took off for the nearest shop door with Markham fast behind.

Ariel whipped off her tunic and ran straight for the fallen Fomorian. Birds flashed at her face, and talons drew a red scratch across her arm, but she ignored them, determined to reach the screaming dog-girl. "Get off her!" Ariel shouted. "Leave her alone!" With her tunic as her only weapon, she beat at the crows, driving them away.

The Fomorian's back was a ruin, a patchwork of lacerations and bloody ribbons. Ariel stared in horror as she kneeled over the dog-girl. Then, a black dart flew straight for her face. All her fear dissolved in an instant. Without thinking, she lashed out with a fist. An explosion of feathers! Stunned, the crow crashed to the ground.

Another crow attacked her. Ariel swung her tunic around her head as she fought to protect herself and the dog-girl at her feet. When still another crow flew at her from the side, she dodged and caught the evil creature by one wing and slammed it into still another bird.

Then a shadow fell over her. Ariel drew back her fist again and prepared to strike. There were too many crows, but she would go down fighting! Spitting out a couple of feathers, she turned toward the shadow—and stopped.

Harrow stood just behind her. And as she gaped at the black Dragon, ivory Luna sailed up from the canyon rim and landed on her other side. Without speaking, they raised their great heads and blew bright steams of fire into the sky.

The crows screeched in terror. Scores of black shapes exploded in brilliant fireballs and plummeted earthward. Still, others came on in angry waves, attacking Stormfire's children with beak and claw. Ariel flung her tunic over her head and clutched it tight as a wildly flickering rain fell all around.

Harrow and Luna blew fire again, and more birds burst into flame. Some fell into the canyon and toward the Echo Rush below. Others dropped in the forest, and some fell on the rooftops of Stronghold. Ariel screamed and pointed as the roof of a home threatened to burn, but Sabu lunged toward it and beat the small fire out with one wing.

Bear Byron rose up on his hind legs in the center of the square. "Into the woods with buckets and shovels!" he called bravely. With a backhanded swipe, he knocked a charging crow from the air. "Don't let the forest burn! Hurry!"

A small number of Fomorians, minotaurs, and satyrs answered his call. While some brought shovels and buckets, others carried brooms or hastily dampened blankets to beat out the flames.

"They're only a bunch o' crows, boys!" the large brown bear shouted to the volunteers. "Let's show 'em what we're made of!"

"Grrr, they already know what I'm made of!" a minotaur snarled. He held up his arms to show deep cuts and tears in his flesh. "The little beggars already got a good taste of what's inside and out!" Before he spoke his last word, a beak-faced crow raced at him. The minotaur raised his shovel and swung it with all his strength. A nauseating *splat!* resulted. The minotaur frowned, shook his shovel, and then shook it again. Finally, he scraped the bird off with the edge of his foot. "Don't know my own strength," he muttered apologetically to the others.

Ariel watched Bear Byron and his fire brigade rush into the woods. She wanted very much to go with them and help, but she was afraid to leave the dog-girl unprotected. Most of Stronghold's citizens were safe behind closed doors and locked shutters, and the crows seemed fewer, less crazed in their attacks.

"We've won!" she called to Luna and Harrow. "They're retreating!"

The dog-girl groaned and rolled painfully over onto one bloody shoulder. With watery brown eyes, she stared at Ariel and clutched at the human girl's hand. "But why did they attack?" Her voice was raw from screaming, and tears and dirt streaked her face. "What did we do?"

Luna leaned close to the ground. "We don't have an answer, young one," she answered in a soothing voice. "But if we have to pluck the tail feathers from every crow in Wyvernwood, I promise you we'll find out."

Harrow spread his scarred wings and blew one more deadly stream of fire as a line of crows retreated over the canyon. "That will be your task, Sister," he said as he turned back toward Luna. His scaled face looked grim and angry. "Until I can fly again, mine will be to stay here and protect Stronghold from any further attacks."

Luna straightened up to meet her brother eye-to-eye. "You expect more?"

Harrow thumped his tail on the ground as he turned to look back at Stormfire's Point. Phoebe no longer perched there. "Griffins sneaked in here and killed our father. Now crows have terrorized and panicked us. That's two attacks too many. It's time we prepared to defend ourselves."

"He makes sense!" Ariel called up to the two Dragons. She wrapped her tunic around the dog-girl and helped her to stand. "We need to make some plans to protect our homes!"

Harrow leaned down and cocked a scaled eyebrow. "I don't recall asking your opinion, Man-child."

Ariel was in no mood for Harrow's reputed rudeness. Her heart still pounded with a furious rhythm, and her cuts and scratches stung. "I don't recall giving a fig if you asked for it or not," she snapped.

Harrow rose up and winked at his sister. "I like her," he said.

The Dragon Luna sighed as she flexed her wings. "She takes some getting used to," she answered, "but Ariel has her moments."

THE STORM HIT THE BEACH with astonishing swiftness, driving Ronaldo, Marian, and Bumble back into Sinnobarre's cave. Sheltered in the black mouth, they watched the sky darken and the sea begin to churn. A savage wind ripped along the beach and over the water, raising veils of sand, whipping the waves into a froth.

Lightning shattered the clouds. For a brief instant, the world seemed to burn with a white, blinding fire. Marian bellowed and, rearing, slammed her hooves against the stone wall. Her eyes flashed, reflecting the searing bolts as she stared into the maelstrom.

Half-maddened by the thunder and the blowing rain, Bumble darted from one side of the cave to the other. Sometimes his tiny talons found purchase in the uneven rock until the next blast of lightning sent him flying again. Back and forth he flew, bouncing off the walls, off Ronaldo's head, off Marian's horn or rump. His wings itched with the constant surges of electricity in the air, and his ears ached.

Only Ronaldo remained still. Staring into the storm with a narrowed gaze, he gave his restless friends as much room as he could while protecting them from the stinging sand and needle-sharp rain. He hated the cave and hated the smells of death that crept up from its depths. Had he been alone he'd have braved the storm and the lightning and flown away, but for the sakes of his friends he stayed.

Gradually, the rain ceased, and the wind grew calm. The lightning and thunder moved farther and farther out over the sea, leaving a slate gray sky. Ronaldo crawled out onto the beach. Marian, with Bumble perched on her horn, emerged from the second mouth. Bumble's tiny voice was a constant chirp. "Home! Home! There's no place like home!"

Marian paced to the edge of the water. The surf caressed her front hooves as she stared after the last flickers of lightning on the horizon and nickered softly. "Ronaldo's not thinking of home," she said with a glance toward the Gray Dragon. "He's much too quiet, and that's never a good sign."

Ronaldo watched the white-capped waves rolling toward the shore and thought of the pale-haired Mers he'd seen in Sinnobarre's webs. Each wavelet seemed to him a desperate face calling him, appealing for help. "Marian will take you home, Bumble-bird," he said, turning his nose northward as he stretched his wings. "I'm not returning to the Whispering Hills."

Marian kicked at the sand and tossed her mane, sending her hummingbird companion spinning into the air. "Who made you King of the Dragonkin?" came her sarcastic reply. "The last unicorn in the world goes where the last unicorn decides."

The Gray Dragon rose up on his hind legs and lashed his tail across the wet sand. "You'd need wings to follow where I'm going."

A green blur whirred around the Dragon's head. "I have wings!" Bumble cried as he landed on the tip of Ronaldo's nose. "Swift and fine, these wings of mine!"

Ronaldo shook his head. "Not for this journey, little friend," he said. "Your wings are too small."

The hummingbird stamped a taloned foot. "Size doesn't matter!"

"Length does," the Dragon replied. "And this will be a very long journey."

Marian walked a short distance up the beach before she turned back to Ronaldo. "Not so long ago, Dragon, we left home and Wyvernwood and traveled together deep into Degarm. More than once I saved your hide. You saved mine, too. And Bumble saved us both." Her eyes flashed as she reared and crashed her hooves on the sand. "If you think you're going somewhere without us, then you've been sniffing your paints."

"You're a fine one to preach," Ronaldo said. He folded his wings and started walking up the beach. "Or maybe I didn't get the invitation to Sinnobarre's roast."

"Roast?" Bumble's wings hummed as he sprang into the air. "I'm so offended, Ronaldo, that even my rumbling stomach is calling you names!" Without another word he flew toward the clifftops and disappeared.

Frowning and uncomfortable, Ronaldo stopped in his tracks and stared after the little hummingbird. He flicked his tongue over her Dragon lips, waiting to see if Bumble would return. "I didn't mean to hurt his feelings," he said to Marian. "Do you think he's going home, or just looking for a snack?"

Marian trotted ahead, then turned and blocked his path. In the misty, post-storm grayness she looked angry, even dangerous, and definitely stubborn. "Did lightning strike you in the head when I wasn't looking?" she demanded.

Spreading his wings, Ronaldo soared upward and over Marian. "It's not some quest that calls me this time, Marian!" he bellowed, becoming angry himself. "It's battle! I'm going to Thursis!"

Marian looked up with wide, startled eyes and flaring nostrils. She raised a hoof and set it softly down, then tossed her mane. "To liberate the Mers?" she asked in an awed whisper. "It's a large island! Angmar won't surrender it easily, not even to a Dragon!"

Ronaldo drew a deep breath and raked the sand with a swish of his tail. "That's why I'm going alone," he said. "Bumble's too small. And you . . ." He hesitated, then fixed his gaze upon her, and his heart softened as he settled to the beach again. "Well, you're the last of your kind, my friend. I won't risk you."

Marian moved closer to Ronaldo. "My neck is getting stiff from looking up at you," she informed him. Then, changing her emphasis, she added, "And from looking up *to* you, you silly creature." She spun about suddenly, churning the sand and flipping her white tail as she skipped further up the beach.

"You've always been a little stiff-necked," Ronaldo sighed, interrupting Marian before she could say anymore. "I should have kept my mouth shut and just flown away the moment the storm cleared." Bending low, he brought his face close to hers. "You're coming, aren't you, whether I want you along or not? And if I don't take you, you'll find a way to follow."

Marian nodded her head. "Where you go, I'll go," she answered. "Where you sleep, I'll sleep. Your friends are my friends, and your fights are my fights."

Ronaldo looked at the last unicorn for a long moment. He'd lived most of his life as a recluse and a hermit, painting his paintings and thinking little about Wyvernwood or the world. He had few friends, and none more dear to him than Marian and the Bumble-bird.

Everything was changing.

"You have a great heart, Marian," he said, standing erect again. His eyes misted as he gazed down upon her white form. Among all the inhabitants of the forest Marian was legend; no creature was more rare. Older than Stormfire, she had traveled to Wyvernwood with the Dragon leader. She knew and remembered things everyone else had forgotten.

"I can't stop you from following," he continued, swelling his chest with determination. "But maybe I can clear the battlefield before you arrive." Spreading leathery wings, he rose into the sky. Marian stamped and snorted indignantly and shook her tangled mane in anger as he climbed higher and turned toward the sea. "Farewell," he called, "dear friend!"

A loud drone sounded in Ronaldo's left ear as Bumble intercepted him in mid-flight and settled in his familiar perch. "When she catches up she's going to kick your tail," the hummingbird warned, "and many other tender parts of you, as well." His wings fluttered with furious speed, and tiny feathers tickled before Ronaldo felt a sharp sting inside his head.

"Ow! What are you doing, you Bumble-bird?" he demanded. "That's maddening!" Twisting his neck back over a shoulder, he could still see Marian on the beach. But she was no longer watching and stamping. With all her formidable speed, she was racing northward along the shoreline.

"Bumble is too small to kick Ronaldo's tail," the little fellow answered in a mocking tone. "So I'll just nestle here for a little while and rake my tiny claws against your eardrum." Another lancing pain shot through the Gray Dragon's ear, and his passenger continued, "Maybe then you won't forget me again and try to leave me behind!"

"Ow! Stop! Stop!" Ronaldo shouted again. He squeezed his eyes shut against a flash of surprising agony and veered momentarily off-course as Bumble stabbed him a third time. "You'll make me crash!"

The hummingbird fluttered his wings again and then became still. "Just remember," Bumble said sternly. "I raised you up, Ronaldo, and I can bring you down! 'Too little,' indeed! Hummmph! Did you think I wouldn't hear what you told Marian?"

"I'm sorry!" Ronaldo apologized. "I wasn't thinking!"

Bumble tapped his talons on Ronaldo's eardrum again, not hard enough to inflict discomfort, just enough to remind the Dragon that he could. "Obviously you weren't! Rushing off to war without your steed is one thing. Rushing off without your strategist is quite another!"

Ronaldo gave a low chuckle. "Marian will step on you if she ever hears you call her a *steed.*" Again, he glanced back at the now-distant shoreline. The Last Unicorn in the World was out of sight. Safe, he hoped. Without wings, how could she hope to cross the wide span of water that separated Thursis from the mainlaind?

With Wyvernwood's shore barely in sight, Ronaldo turned northward and flew at his greatest speed. A grim darkness that drowned Bumble's constant chatter crept upon him as he thought of the Merfolk and the Angmaran foe that waited ahead. Unconsciously, he flexed his claws and scraped them on his scaly hide. In his throat he felt the bubbling fire ready to explode.

The storm-gray clouds began to break up. The sky cleared, and the sun brightened. The blue sea below sparkled. A school of dolphins raced through the waves, keeping pace with Ronaldo for a little while before losing interest and turning coastward. An albatross tipped one wing in greeting, then caught an updraft and soared out of the way.

The island of Thursis rose on the horizon like an immense emerald floating up from the blue sea. A brief range of mountains jutted like sharp spines through its center, but the lowlands were lush with forests that rivaled Wyvernwood for beauty, if not for size.

Ronaldo spent little time admiring the geography. With a squinted gaze he studied the thirty black-hulled ships that dotted the water around the island and the twenty more at anchor right off shore. A plan took shape in his head, and he climbed higher and higher into the sky where the air became cold and thin and the winds buffeted him. Thursis became a small dot on the surface of the vast sea, and the ships no more than specks even to his sharp-sighted eyes.

So high up, he doubted the Angmarans would see him at all.

Looking further northward and westward, he spied several more small specks making for the island. The size of Angmar's fleet surprised him, but at the same time it hardened his resolve. All the ships were grouped on the western side of the island, for the ships of Man always sailed with the coast as their guide and never ventured out of sight of land. That left the eastern side of Thursis unprotected.

With the sun and the cold air crisp on his wings, Ronaldo glided far out to sea. When the spiny mountain range hid him from view, he dropped close to the water once more, turned back, and approached the island on its farthest side. The white sand beaches shimmered, but he skimmed over them, swept over the treetops, and headed for the mountain peaks.

A river cut suddenly through the forest. A graceful arching bridge of white mica-flaked stone spanned its banks, and at either end stood a number of colonaded, temple-like structures. But except for landscaped gardens of wildflowers filled with colonies of butterflies and clouds of flies, Ronaldo saw no signs of life.

Further upriver he found another cluster of the temple structures. Like the previous ones they were ringed with gardens. Awakened from his sleep in Ronaldo's ear by the sweet smells of the flowers' nectar, Bumble sprang upright.

"A breakfast buffet!" he cried, and dived toward a crop of honeysuckle that grew right at the water's edge.

"Bumble, come back!" Ronaldo beat his wings with furious power, hovering over the temples and the gardens as his hummingbird companion plunged bill-first into a juicy blossom. There was no stopping Bumble, though, when his voracious appetite and nearly constant hunger overpowered his small brain. With a frown of annoyance, the Gray Dragon waited.

Then something else caught Ronaldo's attention—some deeper green amid a copse of green reeds along the river's opposite bank. It floated and bobbed, seemingly tangled in the watery growth until the river's current set it free.

A dead Mer female. Her hair swirled around her like thick seaweed. Her scales had lost all their gleam and shimmer, and the dorsal fin that extended from the nape of her neck and down the length of her spine seemed decayed. Again, the river current played a trick with her body, turning her over onto her back so that her wide, vacant eyes gazed upward.

Ronaldo caught his breath as that dead-eyed gaze seemed to lock with his.

The reeds stirred again, and a second Mer body floated free. The corpses of two fat fish escorted it, and they all drifted slowly downstream. A cold chill touched the Dragon's heart. Mindful of the delicate temple structures, he landed in the middle of the river and brushed a wingtip over the reeds. More dead fish floated free, brushing his leg as they followed the Mers. Not far upstream still more dead fish dotted the banks. He also spied the dessicated form of a deer.

Ronaldo bent low to taste the water. Then, spitting, he let out an angry roar. "Bumble!" he called. "They poisoned the river!"

The little hummingbird raced up from the honeysuckle flowers to perch on Ronaldo's nose. "Yummy are the gardens far away from the water," he reported. "But the blooms on the bank are bad!" He grew still as another dead fish floated past. "Poor fellow! And flights of anglers sing thee to thy sleep!"

Ronaldo trembled with rage at such wanton murder. A bitter chemical taste still tingled on the tip of his Dragon tongue, and he'd barely tasted the water. "Come on, Bumble!" he hissed. "I want to check something!"

With the hummingbird riding passenger in his left ear again, Ronaldo rose into the sky and flew back toward the beach. He'd been flying so fast with his attention on the mountain peaks, he hadn't paid much attention to the sandy stretches. The bones of fishes and birds lay rotting in the sun, bleached nearly as white as the sand itself.

"I don't understand," Bumble whispered in Ronaldo's ear. The little bird shivered.

Ronaldo didn't answer. He was beyond speech as he raked his claws in the sand at the water's edge and raised them to his nose. They smelled faintly of the same potent substance he'd tasted.

He couldn't imagine how the Angmarans accomplished it. Sneaked onto the island under cover of darkness, perhaps, and spilled cargoes of poison into the water. The Mers must have suspected nothing. They and the mindless fish died first. Then any creature that drank from the rivers or any carrion creature that ate the fish.

He thought of the pair of Mer bodies suspended in Sinnobarre's web. Those two, at least, had made it to the mainland. Perhaps others had escaped, but if that were so, why had no one seen them?

With another roar, he spread his wings and flew toward the mountains in the center of the island. He no longer followed the river and disdained a stealthy approach. On the highest, storm-weathered peak he landed, and from his excellent vantage surveyed the scene below.

Twenty ships lay at close anchor, and more dotted the bright blue sea close by. On the sandy shore, a fortified encampment stood. A blight on the island, Ronaldo thought. How crude it looked compared to the Mers' graceful temples. The encampment wasn't the only blight, either. The forest below had been ravaged by axes and saws. Half-built docks extended from the beach over the sea surface. Crates and supplies littered the ground, and barrels, too, containing water for drinking, he suspected, until the rivers cleaned themselves.

He didn't bother counting the sailors and soldiers. They scurried like ants busy about their labors and their thoughtless destructions. The sounds of tree cutting and the crashing of timbers reached his Dragon ears even on his mountaintop, as did the banging of their hammers and the fiery hiss of their pitiful forges.

Ronaldo knew something of fire.

Displaying his powerful wings and rising to his full height, he let out a roar that carried down the mountainside, then craned his neck and exhaled a red blast that for an instant seemed to devour the sun itself.

On the beach and in the encampment all labor stopped, and the ants stared. In the surrounding forests the sounds of labor ceased. Men rushed to the rails on the nearby ships at sea and pointed.

"We're having some fun now!" Bumble muttered as he leaned from Ronaldo's ear for a look around. "Once more, dear friend, onto the beach!"

But Ronaldo waited. He thought of the Mers and the fear they must have felt as they died and saw their island taken. He wanted the Angmarans to feel fear, too. When he destroyed their few ships off the coast of Wyvernwood the day before, he showed them mercy.

He felt no mercy now.

Bumble kicked insistently at the inside of his ear. "Ronaldo?"

The Gray Dragon didn't answer. He wasn't sure he even was *Ronaldo* anymore. That name belonged to another creature, an artist and a recluse, a gentler Dragon that he'd once known long ago and someplace far away.

His claws flexed in the stony ground as he tore a chunk of the mountain away and sent it cascading downward. It fell, gathering momentum, taking more stone and earth with it, growing like something alive, deadly, and full of rage.

A section of the mountain below had already been stripped of trees. It stood out like a great brown, thoughtless hole in a green carpet. Yet, still the ants gnawed at its edges, cutting more trees, enlarging the hole.

In a great cloud of dust, the slide slammed downward to fill the hole. Men screamed, threw down their axes and saws, and ran. But they moved too slowly. The boulders and the stones overtook them, smashed them, and the earth swallowed them whole.

Bumble's voice dropped to a stunned whisper. "Ronaldo?" he said again.

Again, Ronaldo refused to answer. He stared at his handiwork with grim satisfaction. Yet it wasn't enough to repay the Mers and the creatures of Thursis. It wasn't enough to punish the Angmarans for their wanton destruction. It wasn't nearly enough.

Innocent Thursis!

Now he would speak to Angmar in a language they understood, and the art he painted would be in blood.

With a Dragon scream, he blew another blast of fire skyward. In the encampment, the ants began to scurry and run in all directions. He didn't know where they were going or what they were doing. He didn't care. Anger and fury consumed him, burned away all vestiges of his old self, and from its flames he rose reborn.

A third time he blasted fire, not as a warning or a threat, but as an introduction—to Rage.

The Dragon Rage.

10

THE HARPY LEADER STEPPED FORWARD, and Chan regarded her with interest. Her body was as much that of a hawk as it was of a woman. Her feathered arms and legs were heavily muscled, and hands and feet were sharply taloned and bird-like. Tangled hair framed a heart-shaped face with sharp black eyes that glittered with a diamond intensity and a nose that hung hard and curved like a beak over her mouth.

Her most striking features were the golden-feathered, white-tipped wings that sprouted from her shoulders. With an impressive span, they appeared strong, yet flexible, allowing for a startling maneuverability that few other avian creatures could match.

"Greetings, Chan, Son of Stormfire," the Harpy said. Her voice flowed like a high-pitched song, clear and musical, unlike any other voice Chan had ever heard. "Welcome to the Wall of the Worlds."

Chan inclined his head in a gesture of respect. "It's been too long, Electra," he said. "I thought that after my father's funeral we'd see more of you in Stronghold."

Electra flexed her wings as she shook her head. "For more than three hundred years my sisters and I have guarded these mountains and watched over the Wyvernwood," she answered. "Our homes are here, Chan. It would seem to be a good thing for you, too, because we saw those griffins before you did."

Chan turned his head upward to search the sky. There was no real chance that the griffins would return, but he couldn't resist the impulse. "They're after the boy," he said with a nod toward Jake. "Minhep blames him for Gaunt's death."

"Minhep should be grateful," Morkir grumbled from the far side of the fire. "With Gaunt dead, he moved up to the Griffinkin leadership." He spat into the flames. "He's always been an idiot. More cat-bird than griffin." He made sarcastic cawing sounds and sneered.

Electra grinned for the first time. "Good to see you've found a sense of humor, Son of Gorganar," she said to Morkir. She glanced at the others one by one. "I remember you well, Man-child," she said, greeting Jake with a nod. "And Skymarin, old friend." Her gaze lingered on Katrina. "I don't know you, child, but if you travel with Chan, then you keep good company."

Katrina chuckled. "You've sure got her charmed, Dragon."

The other Harpies fluttered their wings as if offended by Katrina's laughter, but Electra held up a hand, and they calmed. Electra looked Katrina up and down. "You've got blood on your claws, little cat," she said with frank appraisal. "I like you."

Katrina pretended to study her claws in the firelight. "It's just a little nail polish," she replied, inclining her furry head. "You wear the same shade, I see."

Morkir spat another stream in the fire. "Why don't the two of you trade grooming secrets sometime?" he suggested.

Jake put a hand on Morkir's shoulder and, urging silence, quietly shook his head. Chan noticed, and his admiration for the boy went up a notch. But there were other matters on his mind right now. He turned away from the fire and stared westward toward the dark lands below the mountains. He felt a tingling in his bones and in his wingtips that told him even though it was night it was time to go.

Electra moved closer, and her gaze followed his. "Valindar," she said with a sweeping gesture. "And beyond that, Asgalun, the Haunted Lands." She turned her hawk-like head to left and right, surveying the high peaks that rose on either side of them as a chilly wind rustled the feathers on her brow. "What you call the Imagination Mountains, we Harpies call the Wall of the Worlds." She continued after a pause. "This stony range has protected Wyvernwood and all the Dragonkin, and kept you safe. We Harpies have tried to insure that safety by never allowing any outsiders to cross these mountains."

Chan understood. His father had told him tales of Electra and her people, how they had chosen to remain in the mountains and live apart as sentinels and guardians. Even Stormfire had spoken of the Harpies in mysterious tones and with a sense of respect and awe. Looking down at her sleek and powerful form, Chan had a sudden flash of insight.

"The threats to Wyvernwood have not always come from Angmar and Degarm, have they?"

Electra looked up at him and folded her wings tightly against her shoulders before she pointed outward. "Those are the lands we came from, Son of Stormfire," she said in a grim voice. "Valindar, Asgalun, and places far beyond those whose names are mostly forgotten to all but a few. But never believe that the Men who rule those lands now have forgotten us. The Age of the Dragons has passed, and it's their world now. They mean to keep it, and they'll not look kindly upon your invasion."

Chan squeezed one eye shut, frowning as he regarded her. "Invasion?"

"That's how they'll regard your return," she answered. "They won't wave banners and smile when they look up and see you in their skies."

She glanced over her shoulder toward the campfire. "Nor will they welcome any of your companions, save maybe the boy. You were wise to bring him along."

The Dragon considered Electra's words, and his gaze fell upon Jake. Though the boy still kept silent, his ears had pricked up, and he'd moved ever so subtly closer to the nearer side of the campfire so that he could listen better to the conversation. Skymarin made a soft squawk and glided through the air to settle on Jake's shoulder. The boy barely flinched at all.

Electra turned her gaze westward once again. "Do you have any idea where you're going?" she asked.

"To the Haunted Lands," Chan answered. *Asgalun,* he thought. The name sent a shiver through him. It was an ancient word from an ancient time, a remnant of the original Dragon language, when such words actually contained magic. Even now, generations after most of the language had been forgotten, few spoke the name casually, preferring instead its literal translation—*the Haunted Lands.* "There I'll seek my father's birthplace."

"It's a long journey even for one with wings," Electra warned. She turned her face up toward his. Her dark eyes glittered with unexpected moistness, and, though she fought to mask it, sadness transformed her features. Yet through the sadness there also flashed a keen look of interest. Electra's gaze turned hard and penetrating. Then her eyes widened, and she caught her breath. "By the Fires!" she whispered, turning her back to the others so they wouldn't hear. "I know what you seek!"

Chan bent his neck and lowered his head as he faced her. "The First Talisman," he said in a normal tone. The Harpy's eyes shot even wider, but before she could speak, he continued. "There are no secrets among us, Electra. My friends are putting themselves at risk to travel with me, so I trust them."

Electra spun about in obvious agitation, fluttering her wings and darting glances not just at Chan's companions, but at her own as well. She clenched her taloned fists and folded her arms over her chest, then wrapped her wings around her arms. For a moment, she closed her eyes tightly and trembled. Finally, she seemed to relax.

"The talismans contain the last drops of Stormfire's magic," she told Chan as she looked up at him again. "The last magic in the world." The rising breeze stirred the feathers on her brow as she hung her head. Suddenly, all her strength seemed to fade, and her vast age became apparent on her shoulders. Chan wondered at the memories dancing through her mind and felt a surge of sympathy as he curled his tail around her to block the wind.

"I remember Asgalun," Electra explained in distant tones. "We fought a great battle there against the races of Men. Driving us from our homes into Wyvernwood wasn't enough. They wanted to destroy us." She shook her head as she looked around the campfire. "Many died on both sides—such is the way of war—and so we named it *the Haunted Lands*." She squeezed her eyes shut again as she hugged herself. "I remember it well, Son of Stormfire. Too well. Some memories refuse to fade."

Her Harpy companions had contented themselves to remain in the shadows at the edge of the fire, but now, observing their distraught leader, they moved to her side. Electra held up a hand to stop them, and stiffened her spine as she drew herself erect. When she spoke next, her voice was stronger. "Your father hid the First Talisman—the Glass Dragon—in Asgalun as a gesture to honor those dead. He went alone, Chan, leaving us for a time on the silent battlefield, and no one knew where he concealed it."

Chan nodded and started to answer. This much he'd read in *The Book of Stormfire* deep in Ramoses' cave before leaving Stronghold.

But Electra snapped her wings wide and sprang into the sky. With impressive effort, she hovered just above their heads. "But a Harpy has eyes like no other creature, Chan!" she called down in her high, musical voice. "And Stormfire wasn't so swift that vision couldn't follow!"

Her words hit Chan like a blow, and he reacted too quickly, alarming his comrades as he rose up on his hind legs and stretched himself to his full height. Skymarin screeched and took to the sky. Jake and Katrina both gave a shout and threw themselves around Morkir to hold him down as he flexed his wings.

"You saw?" Chan cried to Electra hovering above him. "You know where it is?"

The Harpy leader looked perplexed. "You mean you don't?"

Chan regarded her for a moment, then smacked his lips and looked embarrassed. "*The Book of Stormfire*," he said with a shrug in a calmer voice, "lacked, well, certain specifics."

"Certain specifics?" Electra blinked, incredulous, and landed at his feet. The others around the campfire relaxed, but watched wary and uncertain. The Harpy leader slowly smiled as she studied Chan with frank, new appraisal. "Stormfire foretold that his children would some-day search for the talismans and that with them one would rise to lead the Dragonkin in his place. But whether that would be you, your broth-er Harrow, or your sister Luna, even he didn't know."

She turned to her harpy followers and spoke in a sharp series of chirps and whistles that Chan couldn't even pretend to understand, but when the other harpies laughed, he knew that some joke had passed among them.

"Well, who am I to interfere with prophecy," Electra said, ignoring Morkir's growl, grim once again as she turned back to Chan. "My sight was half-blinded by crusted blood and dried sweat and the lingering daz-zle of fire and lightning that day," she continued. "But if you reach Asgalun then look for the Drake. I don't know if the First Talisman lies there or if it merely points the way. But look for the Drake."

With one hand on Morkir's back to calm him, Katrina spoke up. "The Drake?"

Electra looked from the Formorian to Chan. "One of those *certain specifics* not mentioned in your book," she explained. "It's a mountain— three mountains, actually. From a distance and from the right angle they resemble a Dragon and the tips of its wings." She paused, and that look of remembering stole upon her once more. "I stood on the battlefield that day, my claws still red and unwashed. The fight was over, but there were the dead and wounded to care for. As I lifted one of my fallen sisters, a great shadow passed overhead, and for just a moment I felt fear again. But it was only your father, and I watched him for a long time. He flew toward the Drake."

The wind surged and, howling, lifted hot ash and smoke from the fire. Sparks swirled across the Tor and spiraled into the westward darkness. Jake coughed as he caught a deep breath of the smoke, and Morkir extended a wing to shelter him.

"Not to nit-pick your entertaining tale," Katrina said with characteristic sarcasm, "but you said *if* we reach Asgalun . . ."

"To reach Asgalun," Electra reminded with a veiled stare, "you'll have to cross Valindar. And just as we Harpies have guarded this refuge of the Dragonkin from the races of Men, so Valindar has guarded the world of Men against the Day of our Return." She flashed a quick and nasty smile at Katrina. "Did you think we called these mountains *the Wall of the Worlds* because it sounded nice? Harpies make poor poets, kitten."

Morkir growled low in his throat. "Then we'll just fly over Valindar, and to the fires with these so-called guardians."

Katrina draped her slender tail over one arm and looked thoughtfully toward the west. "I don't have wings," she said.

The griffin clacked his beak and chuckled. ""You've proved your worth in a fight, Kitten." He put a teasing emphasis on the nickname, enjoying the expression of distaste that crossed her feline face. "If the Son of Stormfire can debase himself by carrying a Man-child on his back, I suppose I can carry you. But I don't have a fancy saddle like his, so take care you don't fall off."

Katrina extended her claws and held them up for him to see. "Once I lock these into your mangy hide you couldn't shake me off if you flew upside down." Then, putting on a wicked smile that showed her fangs, she sheathed her claws and stroked his feathered head. "But the Kitten accepts your gracious offer."

"Don't worry if she falls off," Chan added with a wink at his Fomorian friend. "She's a cat. She always lands on her head."

"Feet!" Katrina shot back, waving one clawed hand at the Dragon. "You overgrown lizard!"

Jake stepped forward for the first time and looked up at Chan. The silver scales of his Dragon-hide shirt shimmered with the red glow of the fire as he looked at each of his comrades, then at the Harpies, and then moved another step closer to Chan.

"You want to say something, Jake?" Chan said, encouraging him. "You're part of the team, so speak up."

The boy swallowed, then put his hands on his hips and spoke in a firm voice. "I think we should go now," he said. "If Valindar's such an unfriendly place, maybe we should get as far across it in the darkness as we can."

Morkir growled again. "The Man-child makes sense."

"My name is Jake," he answered curtly, turning toward the griffin. "And I'm not a child."

Morkir bowed his head to the ground, and then looked up again and answered with great seriousness. "Indeed, you're not. My apologies."

Chan sensed a certain unease between Jake and Morkir and chided himself for not recognizing it before. Though they harbored no obvious animosity for each other—at times Morkir seemed protective toward Jake—neither had yet forgotten that not so long ago Jake had dealt the blow that killed Morkir's brother, Gaunt.

"Put out the fire, then," Chan instructed. Though Jake was the youngest of them, his advice was sound, and Chan felt a deep pride in his human friend. He wondered why all humans couldn't be more like Jake, why Angmar and Degarm seemed always at war with Wyvernwood caught in the middle, and why Valindar apparently harbored such fear and distrust. What was the madness that infected their hearts?

But then he noted Morkir, a griffin, yet also a friend and ally, and he felt a brief shame for leaping to judgment. Wyvernwood was not exactly a land at peace these days. The griffins made war on the Dragons, enslaving other creatures to serve them and tend their nests. And he, himself, had led a battle force only months ago when an army of soldiers from Degarm tried to invade the forest.

Perhaps the Dragonkin and the races of Men were not so different. He thought about that for a moment and licked his lips as he stared westward once again. The idea disturbed him even as it offered a glimmer of hope.

The light died as Jake and Katrina, with the help of a pair of Harpies, scooped dirt on the fire. On a boulder nearby, Skymarin watched in silence while Morkir stretched and flexed his wings and paced in the deepening shadows. Everyone seemed suddenly tense, expectant. Even Electra dropped her voice to a whisper, as if worried that her words might carry down the mountain slopes and be heard in Valindar.

"In time you'll come to a river," she said, "wider than any you've ever seen that runs through fertile plains and woodlands as green and rich as your beloved forest. Once, we called it *the Flow of Dreams*." She looked wistful as she wrapped herself in her wings again. Her gaze seemed fixed, not so much on the west, as on the past. "But those were more romantic times before we fled to Wyvernwood. Who knows what it might be called now? When you find it, turn southward. If time has been kind to the land, and if luck is with you, you may find the Drake."

With the fire extinguished, Chan bent low to the ground so that Jake could mount into the saddle. While the boy fastened the numerous straps and buckles that secured him in place, Katrina balanced herself on Morkir's back. Despite her bravado, she looked nervous.

"Lord of Eagles," Chan said quietly to Skymarin, "Your eyes are sharp, and you should raise no fear in the hearts of Valindar if you're spotted."

"Skymarin the Scout, at your service," the eagle replied, spreading wings and taking to the air. "But watch it with that *raise no fear* crack!"

Chan watched Skymarin race away into the night, then glanced at his companions. Jake sat relaxed and ready in his buckles. Morkir and Katrina muttered to each other in barely audible tones as they waited at the edge of the tor. His heart began to beat faster, whether with excitement or dread he couldn't quite say.

Tranquility Tor. The Wall of the Worlds. He squeezed his eyes shut as a wave of emotion swept over him. From this point, his father had guided the migration into Wyvernwood, and to this very spot his father had often come for peace and meditation. The wind that blew across the peak whispered to him with Stormfire's voice, and Stormfire's presence permeated the air. He opened his eyes again, half believing in ghosts.

Electra drifted away to stand with her harpy sisters. Eddies of smoke from the dead campfire curled around them like gray veils, making them appear strange and mysterious as they stood together like stone sentinels. Indeed, they were sentinels against the world beyond the wall—the world into which Chan was leading his friends.

"Farewell, Electra," Chan said, raising one paw. "Old friend of my father."

Electra bowed her head, and then looked to him with a warning gleam in her hawk's eyes. "Remember, Son of Stormfire," she said. "The Glass Dragon contains a drop of magic. When you find it, be careful of what you may unleash."

Chan bowed his head in turn, promise enough to heed her words. Still, the Glass Dragon was only one of three talismans. Alone, how dangerous could it be? As if reading his thought, Electra shook her head, and then offered a departing wave. One after the other, the Harpies flew away down the eastward slopes and into the forest below.

Jake shifted impatiently, and the saddle creaked with a rough, yet softly musical sound. Chan knew the boy was cold; he could feel his shivering. Once away from the Imagination Mountains, he would have to fly lower where the air was warm. "Are you ready, young friend?" he said, craning his neck backward.

Gripping the saddle horn, Jake smiled and nodded. In a hushed tone, he began to sing:

> "Oh, the sky is wide and far,
> But the world is lit by moon and star!
> I feel the wind upon my face
> And yield to the unknown embrace
> Of things I have not seen,
> Places that I have not been!"

"That's beautiful," Katrina said, her eyes sparkling with surprise. "Almost like purring!"

Chan grinned, as touched by the song as Katrina had obviously been, but even more so by Jake's voice and the feeling it conveyed. "Where did you learn that?" he asked. "I've never heard it before."

"I don't know," Jake replied with an embarrassed shrug. "A little bird,

I think. I just heard it in the woods one day, and it came back to me now."

Morkir flexed his wings. "Well, it's appropriate," he said. "Now hold on, Kitten. Yeow!"

Katrina showed her fangs, grinning as she dug her claws into Morkir's shoulders. "Katrina," she corrected, "you flea-bitten example of anatomical confusion."

"You should talk!" Morkir leaped into the air, and it was Katrina's turn to shriek as her head snapped back and she fought for her balance. With a cat's grace and sureness she found it quickly and righted herself. Then, whipping the Griffin's flanks with her tail, she urged him on as they traded curses and name-calling into the night.

Chan cast a final look around at dark Wyvernwood and the starlit peaks of the mountains, then turned his face toward the wider world beyond, those *places where I've never been!* Jake's song echoed in his head. "Sing it again," he requested as he soared away from the tor on strong wings of scale and leather. "Sing, Dragon Rider."

"*Dragon Rider?*" Jake said with mocking innocence. "I don't think I know that one."

"Don't make me slap you with my tail."

Jake began to sing again. Across the peaks and down the mountainsides Chan flew with one eye on Morkir and Katrina ahead and the other on the distant Harpies who paced them for a time. His heart pounded harder, and now he knew the genuine thrill of anticipation. His home behind him at last, he thought of his brother and sister, Harrow and Luna, and wished that they were with him, too.

He flew across the last peak. Jake had stopped singing, and the harpies no longer followed. The Imagination Mountains seemed smaller to him on this side, less forbidding. He wondered at that.

The ground below leveled out, and he marveled. More forest on this side, too! The trees waved in the wind, welcoming him, and flocks of night birds rushed upward. He breathed deeply and opened his mouth for his first taste of Valindar.

Then, even through the night's blackness, the landscape ahead distorted strangely. He strained his far-seeing eyes, frowning, uncertain. Morkir apparently saw, too, and slowed his flight, allowing Chan to overtake him, and together they flew a little farther.

"What in the fires is it?" Morkir called.

Chan didn't answer at once. He'd seen something like it before on his brief adventure into Degarm, but not on such a scale. Towers, spires, and minarets, rooftops and ramparts and walls! Countless unnatural shapes and structures jutting up from the land! Curls of smoke! Dim lights glowing like baleful eyes through unshuttered windows! One dwelling, one building upon another as far as he could see, spreading like a stinking cancer.

"A city," he answered. "They call it a city."

11

THROUGHOUT THE NIGHT, the Dragon Harrow stood guard on the center lawn of Stronghold. With a watchful gaze he swept the skies and the surrounding forest while, grimly impatient, he thumped his tail on the ground and barely spoke to anyone. His mother, Sabu, also watched for a time, keeping her son company. Her calm presence soothed the fears of many of the other citizens, some of whom lingered outside their doors or in the streets, afraid to sleep.

At the canyon edge, Luna held council with Gregor, Bear Byron, and several Minotaurs and Satyrs. An angry-eyed red fox paced among the group, listening with pricked-up ears. Ariel stood to one side with her arms folded over her chest, watching the others with an intent expression as she monitored the progress of the moon through a growing band of clouds.

"We will *not* build a wall around Stronghold," Luna insisted, arguing with Bear Byron, who had proposed construction of a wooden barricade to protect the village. "First of all, it would never stop the griffins. With their strength, they'd easily rip it apart. Nor would it stop the crows, who would just fly over it."

"Any creature with wings would fly over it," Gregor agreed with a sage nod. He flexed his own small, white-feathered owl's wings. "That's half the population of Wyvernwood. At least."

"Second of all," Luna continued in a firm voice, "this entire forest is our home—all its trees and marshes and rivers and streams. It's wrong to seal ourselves off from it!"

The red fox stopped pacing and swished a bushy tail. "Luna's right! We sure as blazes shouldn't tear up the countryside with logging and tree-cutting to build something that wouldn't do us a bit of good!"

Bear Byron growled at the fox. "Well, jus' what do ye propose we should do, then? Stand 'ere an' take what comes? Some of us got families!"

Luna bent her ivory head low, and her voice conveyed authority. "We organize our defenses," she answered. "And we watch. One Dragon will stand guard over Stronghold at all times from now on while another patrols the skies." She turned her gaze directly on Bear Byron and the red fox. "Meanwhile, those of you with forest skills, particularly good night vision or sharp hearing, must organize patrols, too. If any unfriendly force approaches Stronghold, day or night, we can't be surprised again. With sufficient warning, nothing can stand against us."

One of the satyrs spoke up. A deep laceration marked his left cheek, and a cloth bandage encircled his head. One horn had been broken off at the scalp. "We didn't know the crows were unfriendly."

Ariel moved a step closer to the council. "We need to catch one of those birdies," she suggested. "I'd like to know why they attacked us!"

Immense wings fluttered suddenly in the darkness above them. A frightened gasp went up from the wounded satyr as he ducked and covered his head. The fox, rising on his hind legs, let out an excited bark. Bear Byron growled. Even Luna straightened as all eyes gazed upward.

"Phoebe!" someone shouted.

The crowd fell back to make room as the Last Phoenix spiraled down into their midst and crashed at Luna's feet. Her wings were badly damaged, and many of her feathers jutted at odd angles or were missing. A dark fluid leaked from her right eye and ran down in a thick stream toward her beak. Too weak to stand, she sprawled in the dust, and her chest labored as she struggled for each difficult breath.

At the shout of Phoebe's name other citizens of Stronghold rushed to join the circle. From the far side of the village, Harrow and Sabu came closer to see what all the excitement was about. Almost no one ever saw Phoebe except at sunset when she flew through the canyon to Stormfire's Point and then returned to her secret nest. Yet, here she was at night, injured, her beauty ravaged.

While the stunned villagers stood around, Gregor pushed through the crowd to offer his help. Half-maddened by her injuries, Phoebe beat her wings to keep him away, but the owlish Fomorian persisted. "Who did this?" he cried as he stroked her huge head and tried to calm her. "Who could dare to harm the Last Phoenix in the World?"

Luna pushed the crowd back with her wingtips and tail, and Phoebe's ragged breathing eased a little. "Speak to us, Phoebe," Luna said softly. "I promise you that someone will pay for this!"

The Last Phoenix turned one good eye up to the ivory Dragon. "Sweet Daughter of Stormfire," she said with dull recognition.

Another gasp went up from the villagers. Of all the creatures in Stronghold only Sabu and Ramoses, the oldest among them, had ever heard the Phoenix speak. Her voice made mellifluous music, sliding up and down scales that charmed the ear and entranced the senses. Yet, each word rang with clarity as though she was speaking, not to their ears, but to their minds.

"Black feathers! Black hearts!" Phoebe cried between painful breaths. "A murder of crows has murdered me!"

Luna bent lower, her eyes glittering with anger and worry as she put her face closer to Phoebe. "We know about the crows."

A sharp spasm shook Phoebe's body, and her wings twitched, knocking over a pair of Minotaurs that stood too close. Her good eye squeezed shut for a moment, then snapped wide again as she grew still again. "But white-oared ships! The graceful ships!" Her song changed, still eerie and beautiful, but full of pain. "Silent! Silent! Full of death!" The notes strained to a desperate pitch, and some of the villagers clapped hands to their ears. "The crows are black distraction! Killing, driving off sweet creatures near the river! Insuring you do not come there!" She shivered and flopped helplessly on the ground. "Bringing clawed destruction to my nest!"

Ariel could barely stand to watch. Every night since coming to Stronghold, she'd watched Phoebe's sunset ritual from the canyon rim. Nothing in all her young days, not all the wonders and thrills of the carnivals and circuses, had ever seemed more beautiful. Now the Phoenix's shaking and thrashing nearly broke her heart. Overcome, she shoved through the others, knelt down beside Gregor, and put her hand beside his on Phoebe's head.

"Don't talk anymore!" She glared in anger at Luna, then at the rest of the crowd until they fell silent. "Save your strength, Phoebe, and let Gregor help you! He knows herbs and salves that can help!" A Minotaur caught her shoulders and tried to pull her back. Ariel rose and turned just long enough to kick him in the shins before she threw herself down beside Gregor again. Tears filled her eyes and ran down her face as she squeezed her guardian's arm and urged him to do something!

Phoebe stopped thrashing, and her one good eye took on a dull twinkle as she twisted her head to regard the human child. Her great beak gaped, and a sigh escaped her lungs. Then with slow determination, she struggled to her feet and tried to spread her considerable wings. One of them drooped low from her shoulder, and torn feathers littered the dust.

"Bleakly sorry to frighten shining little girl," she apologized with a tilt of her head to Ariel. "Regret to bring such sparkling water from your pretty eyes." With a taloned foot, she retrieved one of her feathers from the ground and held it forth.

Harrow spoke over the assemblage. "That's a rare gift, Ariel."

"One to treasure," Sabu added.

Ariel accepted the feather and sniffed it as if it were a flower. It was as long as her arm and smelled like honey, but it shimmered like soft fire. Indeed, she would always treasure it, but her tears continued to flow. "Let us help!" she begged, reaching out to Phoebe again.

Phoebe opened her beak wide, the closest she came to smiling. "*Let us help!* No more important words in the world, little one. Sing them, and never forget."

The Last Phoenix grimaced, and her dark eyes flashed as she turned to Luna. "Black-hearted crows are allies with Degarm," she said, her breathing becoming difficult again. "While with rake-clawed treachery they diverted you, white-oared ships from the south sailed up the Blackwater River bound for unwary Angmar."

Bear Byron growled. "The back-door sneaks! They're going to attack!"

Phoebe ignored Bear Byron. "I tried to bring this desperate warning," she continued, "but falling, I failed—and failing, now I fall." Her good eye closed again. "On broken wing I sail the canyon way, draining blood, draining life." She turned slowly, growing weaker by the moment as she scanned the crowd. When her trembling legs gave out abruptly, she settled back in the dust. "Sabu!" she called. "Let me look on you, sweet Sabu!"

At the back of the gathering, black-scaled Sabu stretched out her neck to gaze down on the Last Phoenix in the World. "I'm here, Phoebe," she answered in a quivering voice.

"Sabu! Sabu! Hard and bright, you gleam like polished onyx." Phoebe's voice grew thinner. "But your heart was never hard to me. We are old, you and I. From far beyond the Imagination Mountains we came together, and now on wings of sorrow I fly beyond them once again." Her voice quivered and broke. "I barely remember my homeland, Sabu. I wonder if I can find it again."

A hush fell as the crowd parted to let Sabu lean closer. "I'll not forget that you came to Redclaw and helped me save Harrow from the griffins," Sabu promised.

Phoebe didn't answer. With her one good eye fixed on Sabu, she became still. No one moved. No one spoke. Then Ariel began to weep out loud, and someone behind her did, too. A whispering and murmuring spread through the village. Numbed with grief, the throng of villagers pressed closer, some holding and hugging. The red fox began a mournful keening.

The Last Phoenix in the World was dead.

"Let me go!" Ariel shouted, pushing Gregor away as he tried to comfort her. She wiped an arm over her face, drying her tears, and her expression turned ugly. "Let me go! I'll kill every crow in the world! Every last one of 'em, I swear!" Spinning around, she screamed at the crowd. "You just stood here like her dying was a sideshow! Well, the show's over! Are you just going to stand here and do nothing? "

She didn't wait for an answer. Shoving her way free, she ran through the streets and between the houses. Tears sprang into her eyes again, half blinding her, but this time they were tears of rage. She reached the edge of the forest and pushed into it, pausing only to unwrap the leather sling she wore around her wrist, the weapon Jake had given her. Between the gnarly roots of an old tree she found a rough stone and clutched it in one fist.

"I'll find her," Luna said. She was getting used to chasing after Ariel by now. She spread her wings, but before she took to the air her mother stopped her.

"Let her go," Sabu said, her voice crackling with seldom-used authority. "We've no time to waste on ill-tempered Man-children. If she learned nothing the first time she ran away, then maybe she'll benefit from a second expedition."

Gregor bristled, his owl feathers standing on end as he glared at Sabu. "That's harsh!" he objected.

"It's a harsh world, old Owl," Sabu shot back. "Safe in this refuge, many of us have forgotten that. Indeed, we've forgotten too many things!"

She pushed the crowd back with her wings, and when a minotaur tried furtively to pluck one of Phoebe's feathers, she sent him tumbling with the tip of her tail. "Get up, Fortunato!" she snapped at the minotaur. "Take your brothers and anyone else that will go with you. Gather all the wood you can carry. Enough for a pyre! Search Stronghold! Scour the woods! Find anything that will burn and bring it to the square as quickly as you can!"

Luna looked at Sabu as if her mother had gone mad. "What in all the flames are you doing?"

Sabu ignored her daughter as she addressed the rest of the villagers. "Tear down my longhouse," she ordered. "Dismantle it for its boards and logs. Every stick of my furniture, too—bring it all!. And the rest of you, everyone! If you've got chairs or tables to spare, bring them quickly!" She looked down at Phoebe's still form. The Last Phoenix might have been sitting on her nest, but her gaze was locked on some distant sunrise that no one else could see.

"If you loved this creature," Sabu cried, "then bring me wood!"

Fortunato the minotaur hesitated. Then, with a stern look he beckoned to his brothers and raced into the woods. As if jolted out of their shock, the rest of the village sprang into action, scattering into the forest and to all corners of Stronghold.

Only Gregor remained. In one fist, he clutched the feather that Ariel had dropped. He clenched his other fist angrily as he looked from Sabu to Luna and to nearby Harrow. "If anything happens to my little girl...!"

Ramoses soared suddenly over the canyon rim and landed next to Luna. "Nothing will happen to her," he told Gregor as he folded his blue wings. "She has a protector." Unsatisfied, the Fomorian raised a taloned finger to the old Dragon, but Ramoses interrupted him with a reassuring nod. "Make yourself useful, Gregor, and help us. We need to move Phoebe to the center of the square."

Sabu flexed her wings, and her silver eyes burned with worry and urgency as she looked at Ramoses. "You heard?"

"Sound carries very well into the canyon," the old Dragon answered. "I heard everything from my cave. Now let's move her. She's the last of her kind, and no effort must be spared."

Dragon's paws weren't made for carrying things, but Sabu and Ramoses, with Luna and Harrow, bent and lifted Phoebe's lifeless body. At first hesitant, Gregor caught the tip of one red wing and strained to help. Villagers were already piling wood and furniture in the square, but seeing what was happening, they ran to lend their hands and muscles, and a procession quickly formed to bear the Last Phoenix to her funeral place. Some picked up feathers from the ground as keepsakes and treasures, but under Sabu's stern gaze no one dared to dishonor the body, as Fortunato had tried to do.

They carried Phoebe to the center of the square, to the heart of Stronghold, and laid her gently down. The stacks and piles of wood grew higher. Sabu's house at the east side of the square came down swiftly, and its boards and logs were added to the pyre. Brush and kindling from the forest were tossed upon it. Doors and window shutters. Beds and chairs and footstools, all kinds of furniture. Some brought their dearest possessions if they would burn. That was the love of Stronghold for the Last Phoenix.

"Call every Dragon," Sabu told Ramoses. "Her fire must be brighter and hotter even than Stormfire's, and it must burn without faltering until the light of dawn." She looked at her children, Luna and Harrow. "I wish Chan were with us," she told them.

Luna frowned, only half-listening. She grieved for the Last Phoenix, but there was nothing more she could do that mattered. She worried about Ariel, alone in the dark forest, but other issues weighed on her mind as well. Those white-oared ships sailing upriver through the middle of Wyvernwood—if they succeeded in striking at Angmar, that nation would surely retaliate against both Wyvernwood and Degarm.

"I can't stay," she announced. Ignoring her mother's protests, she faced Harrow as she opened her wings wide. "Remember our agreement, Brother. Stronghold is yours to protect, but the forest is mine, and by all the fires I mean to protect it!"

The night breeze blew cool against her scales as she flew above the village and the trees and turned westward. Briefly, she searched the edges of the forest for any sign of Ariel, and detected some movement beneath a tangled canopy of leaves.

"Answer me now, child!" Luna called as she hovered over the spot. The ferocity in her voice surprised her, and she feared Ariel would misinterpret it. "You've only got one chance if you want to come along! Time is precious, and I won't wait!"

Not beneath the canopy, but a little farther ahead in a small clearing, Ariel waved a white-sleeved arm. "Here!" she answered. "Are you going to hunt the crows with me?"

The clearing was barely large enough to accommodate Luna, but she landed as carefully as she could. "I'm hunting far more treacherous game tonight," she said through tight lips. "If it's war you want, little soldier, then climb upon my neck and be quick."

Ariel wrapped her sling around her wrist and did as instructed, settling just behind Luna's head on the narrowest part of her ivory-scaled neck. Gripping tightly with her knees and bracing herself with her hands, she asked, "Where are we going?"

Luna didn't answer. *I'm a fool for taking her into danger,* she thought privately as she rose into the sky again, tearing leaves and branches away as she resumed her westward flight. But there wasn't time to turn back, and Ariel was, if nothing else, a child with courage. Luna felt her heart racing and sighed. *Perhaps in that regard she has something to teach me!*

The black forest rushed past beneath them as they flew together. Ariel's hair lashed straight out behind her, and her garments fluttered as she bent close against Luna's scales. Luna kept one eye turned upon her rider, grimly determining that soon Ariel would have a saddle of her own like the boy, Jake's.

At last she understood Chan's attraction for the human boy. She'd made fun of her brother, but she couldn't deny the joy she took in Ariel's company, or the growing bond she felt with her own rider.

Rider? She rolled her eyes in despair at the word. As if she were some beast of burden! And yet it seemed the right word. *Father,* she prayed with a soft sense of amusement, *forgive me!*

Luna poured on the speed, and they reached the Blackwater River in good time. The clouds broke overhead, and the moon shone down to dapple the flowing water with ripples of light.

"Hold tight," Luna instructed. As gently as she could, she dipped her left wing and turned northward.

"You're going after the ships," Ariel said, hugging Luna's neck as she remembered Phoebe's words. "*The white-oared ships, full of death.* Those would be soldiers!"

The banks of the river were unnaturally still. There should have been deer drinking from the water, beavers at work on their dams, serpents taking nocturnal swims. The trees seemed just as empty of birds, and even the insects were silent.

An unnatural hush hung over the forest. The crows had done a good job of spreading terror, and all to clear the river and let the soldiers slip past. She wondered what payment the crows had received. *Gold, no doubt,* she thought with growing anger. Crows loved gold.

"A lake!" Ariel called, pointing downward as they flew above the river.

"The Valley of Eight Winds," Luna explained. Her gaze roamed to the gentle hills surrounding the lake. There were still signs of ruins there, of the gigantic griffin nests that once had filled the valley and covered the hillsides before Harrow destroyed them. The wreckage had dammed the river for a time, filling the valley with water, changing the landscape, and the lake had remained.

"It looks strange in the moonlight," Ariel said in a quieter voice. "Kind of haunted."

Luna glanced down at the dark waters. Along the western shore, rotting brush and black, lifeless trees rose up from the lake, their stumps and roots submerged. The waves and ripples moved in an odd manner that caught her attention. She studied the signs for a long moment and then nodded to herself.

The wakes of passing ships.

At the far end of the lake, three warships battled against the current with banks of oars that struck the dark, sparkling surface in precise unison. Heavily loaded and sitting low in the water, they struggled northward at a slow pace. Swan-headed prows with painted eyes and gracefully arching necks cleaved the way. Sail-less masts stabbed skyward like spears.

In the moonlight, they were beautiful, and that made Luna angry. With a burst of energy, she surged ahead.

Ariel gave a sharp cry of surprise and hung on as tightly as she could. "I don't want to seem whiny and rude," she said, "but a little warning before you try to shake me off would go a long way toward improving relations between our species."

"Sorry!" Luna apologized. "Your human eyes don't see yet. But mine do!" She swooped low over the lake, cutting new wakes with the tip of her tail and the edges of her wings. "Jump off, Ariel. Swim to shore and wait for me to return. This is no safe business for you!"

"It's too late to get all parental and protective, Luna!" Ariel locked her arms and legs even more tightly around Luna's scaled neck. "I can see them, too, even in the dark!"

In the stern of the rearmost ship, sailors and soldiers keeping watch began to shout. An arrow zipped through the air past Luna's shoulder. The shot only fueled Luna's anger. "Mind your balance!" she called back to Ariel.

Rolling at a rightward angle, Luna overtook the rearmost ship on its starboard side. Stiffening her wing, she swept through the entire bank of oars, shattering them. Splinters and fragments flew over the water and up onto the deck, where wide-eyed soldiers too close to the rail screamed and covered their faces. The ship rocked under the impact, but Luna didn't stop.

"Are you still with me?" she called to Ariel as she bore down on the second ship.

"That was fantastic!" Ariel shouted in response. "Do it again!"

Luna swept higher into the air. As she sailed over the middle ship in the convoy, she flexed her tail like a whip and snapped its mast in half.

Timber and rigging ropes crashed onto the deck. "I hate to repeat myself," she said looking back with grim satisfaction.

In the stern of the leading ship, a score of archers rallied a defense, and a barrage of arrows shot upward. The arrows posed little threat to Luna, but mindful of Ariel, she swooped still higher. Then, arcing over the vessel, she turned and dropped low again to confront it head-on.

A loud voice on the deck shouted a series of commands. The oars rose and fell, rose and fell again, but in powerful backstrokes that halted the ship's forward advance. Around the rails, small fires suddenly ignited in black pots, and a helmeted figure climbed a narrow ladder to stand on a narrow platform atop the swan-headed prow.

Curious, Luna eyed the figure as she beat her wings and hovered over the river's mouth. Come what may, these three ships would never reach Angmar through Wyvernwood. On her father's name, she swore it.

The figure on the swan's head called out. "You're blocking my way, monster! Who are you? I know you have some name!"

Luna roared. Lifting her ivory head, she blasted a stream of fire skyward. On the deck, the sailors screamed and cowered, and she drew a cold pleasure from their evident fear. "I am my father's daughter!" she answered proudly. "Luna, sired by Stormfire!"

The figure hesitated before raising gloved hands to remove the helmet. Hair black as night blew long and free in the wind, and pale eyes gleamed with hatred.

"It's a woman!" Ariel gasped as she leaned down against Luna's neck. "The commander's a woman!"

"Well, we have that in common, then!" the commander sneered. "Isn't biology wonderful? I'm my father's daughter, too!" She drew the sword she wore on her hip and gestured with the blade. "Get out of my way, monster! My fight is with Angmar tonight, not with you. But touch my ships again, and you'll regret it!"

Luna stared in amazement, then laughed. Ariel laughed with her.

The commander glared at Ariel as she shook her head. "You should teach your human pet some manners!" she shouted. "She barks, but has no teeth."

Ariel bristled and leaned further outward to give the commander a better look. "How about if I come down there and sink my teeth into you? You're doing plenty of barking yourself!"

"Hush," Luna said quietly. Then she addressed the commander again. "I have teeth enough," she warned. "You and your crow allies have brought death and damage to this forest already. Still, I'll let you live if you turn back now. But mark me, and tell your masters! Degarm will never use this river, nor any pathway through Wyvernwood to conduct its war on Angmar!"

The commander brushed a windblown lock of hair back from her face. "Were you so stern and pure when Angmar sailed down and burned our cities?"

Luna winced. Indeed, Angmar had managed to sneak southward down the Blackwater some months before at the beginning of the war and set fire to one of Degarm's port cities. But occupied with the murder of Stormfire, the Dragonkin had barely been aware of the hostilities.

The commander waved her sword again. "For the last time, Dragon, get out of my way! I have a mission, and I mean to accomplish it! You can't stop me!" She tapped the rail of her platform with the flat of her blade. "Take a good look at my ships. See how low they sit in the water? The holds are filled with barrels of poison, enough to pollute Angmar beyond all salvation!" She raised the sword again and pointed it straight at Luna. "Consider that before you smash or burn us! That poison will flow into your own waters, and whatever damage the crows did will be as nothing!"

Luna roared and exhaled another blast of flame into the sky. The river turned red and sparkled in her firelight. On the decks of the ships, the soldiers shouted in fear again. Only the commander stood firm and unafraid.

Luna hesitated, suddenly uncertain. "Do your people have such a potent poison?" she whispered to Ariel. "Tell me truly."

Ariel spat before she answered. "She's bluffing! There's no such poison. The ships sit low because the holds are filled with weapons."

Luna thought as much and scowled. Stormfire's daughter was no fool to be tricked by a human! If she let these warships pass, then Angmar would certainly retaliate by sending their warships down the Blackwater. All of Wyvernwood would suffer if she let that happen.

"Enough of this!" the commander cried with an impatient wave of her hand. "Forward, Degarm! Work those oars!"

Luna steeled herself. "No! Turn back . . . !"

She didn't get a chance to finish her threat. The commander gestured with her sword, and a dark swarm of arrows flew through the air as half the crew snatched up their bows. Then a pair of huge fireballs *whoosh*ed upward, trailing smoke and stinking oil. "Catapults!" Ariel screamed as she pressed herself flat against Luna's neck.

One of the fireballs sailed well over Luna's head, but the other struck her right wing. Liquid flame splashed, and she watched in curious amusement for a moment as scale and leather appeared to burn. Neither fire nor heat could harm her, but startled by the way it clung, she felt a moment of panic and climbed into the sky.

With the way unblocked, the oarsmen struck water. The commander's ship leaped forward, and the middle ship followed it. The third ship, with only half as many oars to go around, strained against the current and lumbered after the other two.

In only a moment the oil on Luna's wing burned itself out. Enraged, Luna dived toward the limping third ship. In two swift passes she shattered the oars on both sides of the vessel and for good measure destroyed its mast with a flick of her tail.

On the prow of the lead ship, the commander screamed orders, and her men scrambled to reposition the catapults. The middle ship was already prepared and loaded. Another pair of fireballs streaked upward. Luna dodged them easily and glanced down. One missile splashed into the river, but the other hit the ground in a bright explosion. The forest was not thick around the Valley of Eight Winds, and she breathed a sigh of relief. That was something to thank the griffins for, because they had always used the available trees to build their nests. Now with even the nests gone, here was little chance of the flames spreading.

With another swift pass, she shattered the oars of the second ship, disabling it. "Stop this madness!" she shouted to the commander, as she flew ahead to block its progress again. "Pick up your countrymen and take them back to Degarm! I'll grant you safe passage! But you will not use this river to wage your war!"

The commander beckoned to one of her men, who passed her a bronze-tipped spear. Drawing back her arm, she flung it with all her might. The huge shaft tore into the leather of Luna's fire-blackened wing.

Luna shook the spear loose from her wing and breathed fire on the lead ship. She'd tried to reason with the humans! Even tried to show them mercy! But they'd answered with mindless violence. Arrows and more arrows! Spears and catapults and fire!

Well, she would show them fire!

On spare oars, the middle ship tried to flee, but in its rush to turn, it crashed into the floundering third ship. Timbers splintered. The hulls of both ships broke apart. Soldiers and sailors from all three ships jumped into the water. Some sank, weighted down by armor. Others swam for the shorelines.

"What does it take to teach you?" Luna screamed as she flew above them. "When will you learn to leave us alone?" Consumed by her anger and frustration, she fired the middle ship and then the third ship. Wreckage spread over the red lake. Fire and ash swirled, and smoke rolled into the sky.

On the eastern shore, a handful of soldiers scrambled out of the water, ran up the hillside, and over the summit. Luna thought of such men loose in Wyvernwood and flew after them.

"Please, Luna," Ariel said suddenly, her voice quivering with a strange note. "I—I don't think I can hold on any longer! Don't . . . ! Don't let me . . . fall!" With a soft sigh, she leaned sideways and slipped from her place on Luna's neck.

With strange grace, her arms and legs spread wide and hair billowing, Ariel seemed to float dream-like through space. Then, with a shock, she struck the lake and plunged beneath the waves.

Luna froze, staring in confusion. Then she cried out in despair as Ariel bobbed briefly to the surface again.

A feathered shaft sprouted from the child's back.

12

FARTHER UP THE COAST OF WYVERNWOOD, Marian stood on a rocky promontory and stared outward over the booming surf. Somewhere to the east beyond the high, tossing waves of the Windy Sea lay the green hills and mountains of Thursis. She reared in frustration and stamped her golden hooves on the hard stone as she cursed Ronaldo. That Dragon sorely tested her patience sometimes.

She uttered a fresh string of curses for Bumble, too. The little hummingbird was picking up too many of Ronaldo's bad habits lately, and they were turning into a pair of troublemakers. It would serve them right if she just retreated to her home in the Whispering Hills, found a nice bed of lemongrass, and forgot about them.

Unfortunately, even in Wyvernwood good friends were hard to come by for the Last Unicorn in the World. If she cursed Ronaldo and Bumble, it was only because she worried about what dangers they might be getting into without her. The Gray Dragon, she had to admit, wasn't the only one who sometimes felt overprotective. After all, she hadn't told him about the spider, Sinnobarre.

Drawing a deep breath, she tossed her mane and then fixed her gaze on the deep water. The crisp breeze gusted around her, and as the surf crashed on the rocks a cool salt spray caught the sunlight and filled the air with a sparkling. For an instant, Marian felt the crushing weight of her age. She squeezed her blue eyes shut and whinnied, but there was no pity or sadness in the sound. The sea answered, taunting her with its harsh sweep. She fell silent as she listened to the water's churn and swirl. Then, rearing high, she sang another wordless note, straining with all the power in her lungs to match her voice against the roar of the sea, pouring out her heart in a song of joy and laughter.

Why, she wasn't old at all in any way that mattered! She felt strong, young in mind and spirit, and filled with purpose. Opening her eyes, she smiled at the diamonds of light on the water and at the salt spray's scintillation. Rainbows of color flashed above the waves and rocks, seemed to dance around her golden horn. Her hide tingled with an almost electric excitement.

It was as if magic had returned to the world again!

The sea surged in foamy swirls around her front hooves and fetlocks as she moved forward a few paces and then stopped. With her forelegs in the water and her rear legs on land she stood balanced between two primal elements. The wind rose, whipping her mane and tail as she began to sing:

> "*Through the storm-tossed chilly sea,*
> *Hear my song and come to me!*
> *Keep the vow that once was spoken,*
> *Oath and promise still unbroken.*
> *Remember our immortal bond;*
> *Hear my song and please respond!*
> *Serpens Aqua is your name,*
> *And the ocean realm you claim.*
> *Hear my song, wherever you roam,*

And swiftly come across the foam!
Three times I call, as we agreed—
Answer in my time of need!"

She waited, watching the water seethe while the wind howled in her ears and the words of her song echoed deep within her mind. A second time she sang it, quieter this time, simply for the joy of singing. It had the rhythm and rhyme of a spell, and centuries had passed since she'd spoken anything like it. No true magic remained in the world, and yet she felt a thrill of half-remembered power that vibrated through her like weak lightning.

It was only the thrill of anticipation, she told herself. Not a true spell, not an actual summoning—just a call for help. But would it be heard? Would a promise made so long ago still be honored? She studied the waves and the rolling blue surface far away from shore for some sign. With a lift of her head she gazed toward Thursis, hoping for a glimpse of the fabled mountain peaks she knew were too far away.

Then, with a surge and rush, a wall of water shot up before her. Startled, Marian leaped back onto rocky soil, eyes flashing as she crashed her hooves on the earth and spun back toward the sea again.

A massive, sharply angular head rose up with the wall of water. Large, lidless black eyes glittered with ancient menace, nictitating as they focused on the promontory. Stretching its long and sinuous neck, it rose still higher. Seawater rolled off shimmering scales of green and gold; droplets flew from the golden dorsal fin that crested its skull and extended down its back, and from the numerous lateral fins along its sides. And still it rose, uncoiling, looming higher and higher.

Then, with a mighty yawn, it showed dripping fangs and rows of teeth. Without a speed that belied its size, it snapped its jaws and lunged. Heart pounding, Marian danced aside. Again, the creature lunged, breathing a potent miasma that stank of fish and seaweed. A scarlet tongue lashed across Marian's right shoulder. The Last Unicorn in the World leaped the other way and whirled about, shook her head, and brandished her horn to defend herself.

The sea serpent tensed to strike yet again. Then it hesitated. The great dorsal fin atop its head twitched. The fins along its sides fanned the air. Watery, nictitating eyes focused slowly on Marian as the huge neck bent with rubbery ease. Suddenly, it made a rattling sound not unlike a laugh.

"Mind your manners, you overgrown worm!" Marian warned as she backed a few cautious steps away. "Try to lick me again and I'll pierce your slimy tongue!"

The sea serpent yawned, exhaling another fetid breath. "That's fashionable," it answered. Its voice was a long unused rumbling hiss. It continued to stare, shaking its head as if in puzzlement, until gradually the light of full recognition brightened its eyes. "Bless my flippers!" it muttered. "I've grown so nearsighted I barely recognized you, Marian!"

Marian relaxed and paced forward until she stood under the creature's nose. "It's been a long time, Finback," she said. "I wasn't sure you'd come."

Finback nodded. "I'm a bit deaf, too," he said with a note of weary sadness. "Too much constant pressure on the eardrums in the deep depths where I spend most of my time these days. Not much point in coming to the surface anymore." Finback glanced skyward and winced. "Sunlight is so overrated." He slid back into the water, stretching the immense, unseen bulk of his body along the sandy bottom until only his head lay flat on the promontory. "Frankly, I wasn't sure who was calling me. *Serpens Aqua*! I haven't heard that name in . . . " He paused, leaving the sentence unfinished. The gills just behind his head opened and closed as he sighed. "Forgetful, too, I'm afraid."

Marian lowered her head and rubbed her cheek against Finback's scaled snout. "You didn't forget me, old friend," she told him. "And you didn't forget your promise."

Finback lifted his head to look around, then flattened on the promontory again. For a moment, he said nothing. He blinked twice, and thin tears started to ooze over his sea-green face to splash on the rocks. "The world has changed too much, Marian," he moaned. "I think I knew this coast once, but it's all so different! Why have you called me back?"

The despair in Finback's voice and his sudden tears stunned Marian, and she backed up a few paces. "I called because I needed you!" she answered. Yet now she heard the uncertainty in her own voice. Had she been wrong to invoke such an old friendship? She stared across the sea and thought of Ronaldo and Bumble. They were her friends, too. For their sakes, uncertain or not, she'd embarked on this course, and she had no choice but to pursue it. "You're the only one who can help me! I've got to get to Thursis!"

Finback's black eyes locked on Marian, and his tears stopped as abruptly as they had begun. "Thursis?" he said. "Ha—still the intrepid crusader you always were!"

Marian stamped her hooves in indignation. "I was never a crusader, intrepid or otherwise!" she snapped. "I'm just as reclusive and private as you are! Well, most of the time. But my friends are out there!"

Finback snorted. "And still the socialite party animal, I see." The spined crest on his head arched forward and then flattened. "What about Stormfire's edict? No Dragonkin to set foot or paw on that island."

Glaring, Marian became very still. "You were in trouble once, and I came to your aid," she said. "In return, you made a vow to me. I'm asking you to keep that promise now, Finback. Take me to Thursis!"

Finback gazed at her with a toothy frown. "That island's cursed, you know. It's always been a strange place. And the Mer-folk are beyond any help you could give 'em!"

Marian's blue eyes blazed. "Not the Mer-folk! I'm talking about my friends, Ronaldo and Bumble!" Then she shook her mane as Finback's words sank in. "What do you mean the Merfolk are beyond help?"

Finback leaned closer. The spined crest on his head sprang up stiffly again and he waved a pair of lateral fins. "They're belly-up!" he roared, blasting Marian with his breath. "Dead! Almost every one of 'em! Only a few got away, but they swam off to who-knows-what-ocean just as fast as their finny feet could propel 'em!" He hesitated as his crest flattened once more and his voice softened. "I saw a pair of 'em go by down the coast. That was some time ago—I'm not good at keeping track of time any-more. But they looked pretty sick, Marian."

Marian felt a stab of fear and an even greater sense of urgency. "You have to take me out there, Finback!" she pleaded. "It's too far for me to swim, and my friends could be facing greater danger than they know!"

Finback yawned and snapped his jaws shut. "It could be just as dan-gerous for you, little Unicorn," he warned. "Men control that island now, and on land or sea there's no more treacherous or conniving creature. They're like sharks, you know. All teeth, no brains, and pure predator!"

"I've a few teeth of my own," the Last Unicorn in the World reminded him in a voice turned cold, "and I've tasted their blood before—or have you forgotten the Dragon Wars? There's nothing you can tell me about the race of Man that I don't know, Finback."

Finback sighed, and his immense red tongue flicked out over the rocks and sand. His crest rose and fell. His smaller lateral fins twitched. "Swim out just a little way," he said finally. Then, arching his neck off the ground, he slipped back beneath the roiling waves.

Marian watched her friend depart as she steeled herself for what she had to do. Though she didn't mind a calm bath now and then, she hated swimming, particularly in tempestuous waters. Nevertheless, she leaped outward and plunged into the chilly deep. The incoming surf buffeted her; the waves washed over her head; a strong riptide tried to drag her under. Yet she fought her way through the swells, kicking with powerful strokes as she left the shore behind.

Finback's indistinct silhouette appeared suddenly beneath her, and without warning, she found herself lifted out of the sea as he surfaced. For a heart-stopping instant, she struggled to catch her balance on the slick scales of his broad back, and he helped, arching one smaller lateral fin upward to steady her as he stiffened the great golden dorsal fin to shelter her from the battering waves that might have washed her off.

"I've never lost a passenger yet!" he roared with a hint of amusement. "Actually, I've never *had* a passenger!"

Marian laughed. Her mane and tail whipped in the wind as the fine salt spray blew against her face. When she felt sure of her footing, she stood tall and proud, and lifted her head to marvel at a completely new experience. Finback swam with powerful grace across the glistening sea surface.

"This is amazing!" she cried as she gazed over his head toward the horizon.

"Got your sea legs yet?" Finback asked.

Marian's eyes narrowed with suspicion. Taking a wider stance, she adjusted her balance and braced herself for some trick, possibly a dunking. Finback wasn't above a little mischief, and he was in his element.

But mischief wasn't on his mind. Finback's muscles rippled, and his crest folded back. He surged through the water, pouring on the speed, cutting a frothing wake. Just ahead, a school of dolphins swimming southward took notice. Leaping and splashing, they changed course to race alongside for a short distance.

"Sea-mice!" Finback scoffed.

"Don't be such a grump!" Marian answered, watching the playful creatures as long as she could before they fell hopelessly behind. "They're beautiful!"

"You don't share the sea with 'em," Finback countered with a rumbling laugh. "They're vain, self-absorbed, smug. You know—a lot like unicorns used to be!"

Marian snorted. "It would be very impolitic to prick you with my fabulously lovely, not to mention very pointy horn right now." She started to say more, to make another joke. She liked Finback's deep laugh and she hadn't heard it for such a long, long time. But her joke died unspoken.

Just like unicorns used to be.

A strange, unfamiliar feeling crept over her. *Loneliness.* She must have felt it before, she told herself, but why couldn't she remember? There must have been a time when she missed her own kindred, when she wept for them, a shivery moment deep down inside when she realized that she was the Last. Why couldn't she remember?

Vague shadows began to stir in her mind. She knew the shapes—the Forgotten Others. White Unicorns with golden horns, like hers. Black unicorns with spikes as silvery as dew. Flaxen unicorns with horns of ivory. So many unicorns once, so beautiful and so powerful. So gone. So long gone. She should have made some effort before to remember them. They deserved that.

Marian lifted her face into the wind, letting the cold spray clear her mind as she breathed a wistful sigh. "Finback?" she said with quiet unease. "Are you alone, too? Are you the last?"

Finback slowed, lifted his head out of the water, and rolled one gleaming eye back toward her. For an embarrassed moment, Marian feared she might have offended, or worse, hurt her old friend.

"There are a few more," he answered. "Somewhere. I hear reports occasionally. Usually second-hand stories—someone who knows someone who claims to have seen . . . " He looked away as if something had caught his attention, yet he continued. "My kindred were never close. We never kept in touch. I live alone in the deep, offshore trenches where nobody visits and nobody bothers me. I sleep a lot, and I don't mind that."

Abruptly, Finback stopped talking and raised his head a little higher. He began to tread water with his lateral fins. His gills opened, closed. The spined dorsal fin expanded to its full golden height, and then folded almost flat.

"Ships," he announced.

Marian tensed, straining to see, but the waves were too high. "Are they sailing for Thursis?"

Finback nodded, then began to swim again. "Who are these friends of yours?" he called back.

"Ronaldo is a Dragon, and in Wyvernwood a very renowned artist," she answered with pride. "Bumble . . . well, Bumble's a hummingbird with an attitude."

"And you're a team," Finback observed with a note of mockery. "The Team Supreme, no doubt. The Terrible Trio." He gave a rumble that might have been a chuckle if his head had been above the water. "You always did make strange allies."

"And you're one of the strangest," Marian reminded him. "Now shut up and swim."

"The Dragon Rage?" Bumble protested as he flew circles around the Gray Dragon's head. "Well where does that leave me? You've got a scary new name, but Bumble is just Bumble! Or Bumble-bird when you're being patronizing!"

Ronaldo—*the Dragon Rage*—glared at the scurrying sailors in the encampment below and sneered as they readied their pathetic arsenals of arrows and spears and other useless weaponry. *Murderers, every one of them!* he thought with bitter resentment as he observed them from the mountaintop. They weren't worthy to stand on the same beaches as the mer-folk they'd destroyed!

"Get out of my way, Bumble," Ronaldo warned, in no mood for antics or games. When the little hummingbird circled past his face again, he filled his cheeks and blew a sharp puff of air that caught Bumble off-guard and sent him spinning beyond the mountain's edge.

"Blowhard!" Bumble cried in a hurt voice as he tumbled head-over-heels outward. Spreading his nimble wings, he righted himself and charged back toward the Gray Dragon. "That earns you another good kick in the eardrum! Right or left ear—take your pick!"

Ronaldo wasn't listening. Spreading his great wings, he leaned into space and sailed down the side of the mountain, following the path of ruin his landslide had caused. Amid the rock and stone and earth, his gaze fell on a large boulder. For an instant, he landed on top of it, dug his claws in, and clutched it with his hindmost legs. Then, with a furious beating of his wings, he lifted it from its bed of dirt and resumed his flight toward the beach encampment.

Flights of arrows fired in haste by nervous archers sang through the air, only to fall short. The sunlight glinted on points of iron and steel, but Ronaldo laughed with savage mirth. How had such weak creatures as these, he wondered, ever driven the Dragonkin into refuge?

He swooped upward, climbing higher and higher with his boulder until he reached the beach, and he laughed again as he watched the frightened and disorganized Men below swivel their necks and spin about to follow him with their gazes. Another volley of arrows launched skyward. Most of the shafts missed him by wide margins. The forceful downbeats of his wings sent the rest off-course.

Yet one shaft actually shot high and straight enough to shatter against his boulder. The arrow's point, or perhaps a jagged fragment of the shaft, struck him in the tender tissue between his claws where scales didn't grow and his leather wasn't quite so tough. Ronaldo roared—but not in pain. The tiny wound only served to increase his anger.

He circled the beach as he looked around for a target. It gave him cold amusement to watch their heads twist and twist and the men turn and turn like drunken dancers as they tried to follow him, tried to draw their bows, tried to get a bead on him. It would be fun to see if he could dizzy them enough to make them all fall over, but the boulder was actually getting heavy. He wasn't a griffin, after all, and even a Dragon had his limits.

A large tent on the inland edge of the beach where the sand met the forest seemed to serve as their armory. But where was the fun in collapsing a tent? He looked to the barracks, or what he guessed were barracks. Then he surveyed other structures: tool sheds, supply shacks, and along the border of the woods funny narrow dwellings with half-moons carved in the doors, whose purpose he couldn't guess.

None of those suited him. But something else caught his attention: a vessel further out in the harbor—a grand sailing ship with polished rails, gleaming decks, and a single tall mast with rigging that hummed as the wind blew through it. But more, the ship boasted an intricately carved prow fashioned in the shape of a Dragon's graceful neck, with a head and elaborate eyes painted in gold and outlined in silver. It seemed to glare with those eyes, and it nodded in challenge as it rode upon the waves.

As an artist he appreciated its beauty, yet there was more mockery in its design than the Dragon Rage could stand. Fire bubbled in his throat as he turned toward it, but he swallowed the flames. The ship would be too easy to burn; it would die too quickly!

The decks began to fill with Men as he approached it. More arrows raced upward followed by a barrage of spears. A few shafts clattered against his scales. He barely noticed.

"Wooden Dragon!" he shouted as he flew above the ship. "Show me your Dragon heart!"

Something on the broad foredeck near the carved prow burst into flame. Thick smoke and an oily smell surged upward in a cloud. Raucous shouts rose from the decks with the smoke and stench as a long wooden arm sprang forward to hurl its fistful of fire.

The blazing load rocketed past with a *whoosh!* The Dragon Rage fell silent and grim as he watched it go by, and then he turned his angry gaze back to the ship. So the mock-Dragon breathed fire, too, after a fashion. Was this supposed to instill fear? A Dragon approaching an enemy's shore, perhaps at night or at misty dawn, and appearing to breathe deadly fire would certainly confuse and intimidate.

The idea offended and sickened him. Had Angmar come to Thursis in this horrible impostor to breathe death? Had the innocent Mers understood the false threat? He recoiled at the thought. What if the Mers hadn't seen through it? What if in their last moments they'd been fooled and felt betrayed by the Dragonkin?

Ronaldo screamed and released his boulder. Straight and true it plummeted to strike at the abomination. Timbers shattered as the massive stone crashed through the deck. The mast tilted with a despairing groan, and then fell sideways through the starboard rails. Rigging ropes whipped about with deadly force, knocking men into the sea, and the Dragon-ship bucked as a geyser of water shot up through its center.

Most of the crew flung themselves overboard and swam for shore. For the moment, Ronaldo let them go. In rapt fascination, he watched a fluttering of red and gold cloth at the end of one of the tossing ropes. He knew fancy silk and finery when he saw it, even if he didn't know the arms and legs or the young face tangled in it.

With a hissing gurgle, the Dragon-ship began to sink. The sea churned. Wave after wave washed over its decks. On the shore the shouting grew louder, angrier. Arrows flew his way, rocks, hammers, refuse, anything that Men could throw. None of it posed a threat. None of it even came close. Ronaldo only had eyes for the brightly colored cloth and the struggling figure entrapped in its folds. The ship sank lower, lower, and then it was gone. At the end of the rope, the red cloth spread upon the surface of the water like a drop of blood. It lingered briefly before it, too, went down.

In triumph, the Dragon Rage blasted flame at the spot where the ship had been. Water boiled, and steam rose in wispy white clouds.

On the shore, the Men who had gathered to watch fell silent. Some, but not all, dropped their weapons. One by one or in small groups they began to scatter into the woods.

Across the harbor, the other Angmaran ships dropped oars and turned seaward as fast as they could go. The Dragon Rage dipped one wing and chased after the slowest vessel. Under his merciless breath its decks burst into flame, and the crackling drowned out the abrupt screams of its crew as they threw themselves into the water.

Ronaldo stared after the other ships. His great chest heaved, and the blood pounded in his veins. He wanted to pursue the rest of the ships, but instead he let them go. Let them carry the warning: Thursis no longer belonged to Angmar, nor would it ever again!

He flew slowly back to the island. Most of the Men remaining on the beach ran away when they saw him coming, but here and there a brave soul stood his ground. On the face of one, he noted an unexpected expression not unlike rapture or worship. In the eyes of another he observed anger and a rage not unlike his own.

Of all Men, that one he understood.

Ronaldo circled the beach one more time, then flew to the mountain peak where he had last seen Bumble. Although he regretted mistreating his little friend, his mind wasn't on the hummingbird. Settling to the ground and folding his wings, he thought of the Mers and the poisoned rivers. He still hadn't done enough to avenge them, but even an avenger had to rest. Closing his eyes, he began to weep.

A familiar humming interrupted him, and he opened one moist eye. As Bumble landed on Ronaldo's snout, he shouted proudly and thumped his chest with one small wingtip. "Rumble! That's my scary new name— I'm *Rumble!* What do you think?"

"Yes," Ronaldo answered quietly as he closed his eye again. "That's good."

Marian watched the small fleet of Angmaran ships with growing concern as Finback paced them at a distance. On the far horizon, a thin plume of dark smoke curled across the sky. Where there was smoke, there was fire, and she couldn't help thinking that where there was fire, there was Ronaldo.

"Maybe we should try to turn them back," Marian said. She'd become confident enough in her balance and footing to pace along Finback's spine.

The Sea Serpent gave a short, sharp roar. "I'm not afraid of battle," he answered, "but I'm not going into a fight in the middle of the sea while you're using me for a walking path. And don't underestimate the Angmarans. They'd put up a fight."

Marian snorted. "It would be brief."

Finback splashed her with a lateral fin. "If your horn was a snorkel, I might risk it."

Marian frowned. She was growing tired of overly protective friends— first Ronaldo, and now Finback—but she held her tongue and continued to watch the ships. Her eyes were sharp, and when the waves were low she could see the rows of Men pressed against the rails in the vessel's bow. The smoke had drawn their attention, too.

"More ships," Finback observed, "coming toward us this time."

Marian paced to a new position right behind Finback's head. "From the island? What in the world is happening there?" She stared toward the first group of ships they were pacing. "I don't think they've seen us yet, Finback. Can you drop behind them?"

"Is an eel slippery?" her comrade answered. "Am I not Serpens Aqua, King of the Sea?"

Marian tossed her soggy mane and snorted. "I was under the impression you'd abdicated your crown, Your Majesty."

"Sarcasm doesn't becomes you," Finback replied in a hurt tone. "Now stop prancing around like a four-legged ballerina in ill-fitting tights. Your rough hooves are making me itch."

The first fleet of ships surged toward the second group of oncoming vessels as Finback slowed his speed and carefully adjusted course. He sank a little lower in the water, too, putting his nose into the waves to reduce his profile. Marian smiled to herself. There was nothing she could do to hide. What would a sharp-eyed sailor think if he turned and saw her floating upon the sea?

She'd barely finished the thought before a high, distant shout went up. In the stern of the rearmost ship, a pair of sailors stood and pointed. Others quickly joined them. Finback slowed a little more. With his natural coloring and with the waves rolling around his flanks, he seemed almost invisible in the water, but there was no doubt that she'd been spotted.

The rearmost ship broke away from the others and turned with a lumbering effort. "Do you want me to smash it?" Finback asked.

Marian considered as she watched the ship's approach. "I don't know much about sailing ships," she answered. "Can you snap its rudder without destroying it and killing the crew? Drop me in the sea if you have to, and pick me up afterward. But I think we'd better try to keep them away from Thursis."

Keeping low in the water, Finback raced forward again. In the ship's bow, excited sailors lifted their weapons. Marian's heart pounded as she felt the wind rising on her face again. It felt cold this time, not at all refreshing. The first volley of arrows shot through the air like a swarm of black insects. A wave washed powerfully around her hooves. Making her own decision, Marian drew a deep breath and leaped into the sea.

Finback didn't slow and didn't glance back. For all their caustic banter, and for all the time that had passed since their last meeting, they knew each other, and they'd fought together in tougher times against tougher foes than these. The Last Unicorn in the World swam as hard as she could, fighting the swells and the icy water that filled her mouth and nose. Freed to act, Finback raised his great dorsal fin and charged, heedless of the tiny darts that rained down around him.

At the last possible instant before impact, the Sea Serpent rose up out of the waves, arching his body to reveal himself—Serpens Aqua in all his vast and terrifying glory! The sea churned. The Angmaran ship, dwarfed by the beast confronting it, pitched and rocked treacherously. Its crew recoiled from the rails and threw themselves down upon the decks, shouting and screaming.

Then Finback slipped back beneath the water, vanishing. For a moment, the Angmaran ship resettled itself. Frightened, wide-eyed Men ventured once more to the rails in dreadful anticipation.

Finback surfaced again, this time behind the ship. With the sun now at his back, his shadow spilled across the decks. The ship jerked to a stop, caught. A loud wooden groan sounded, and then the helpless ship lurched. Its bow rose up, exposing the forward hull. Men tumbled; cargo broke free and slid in all directions, and the bright sail whipped itself to shreds.

The ship crashed back into the water. Finback yawned, exposing fangs and teeth. "Abandon hope if you linger here!" he roared at the sailors on the decks. "Take your chances in the Windy Sea!"

The Angmarans didn't have to be warned twice. Wasting no time, they dived overboard from all sides of their ship, grabbing for crates and boxes, pieces of railing, any bit of wreckage or flotsam they found in the water with them. A desperate few swam after the rest of the fleet.

Finback surfaced again beneath Marian and lifted her to safety on his back. Half drowned and exhausted, she shivered and shook herself as she tried to catch her breath. "No witty greeting?" he asked. "No passionate outpouring of thanks?"

"Words fail me," she answered with a cough and sputter. "I think the Windy Sea is only half as full as it was before I jumped in."

With Marian rescued, Finback made once more for the now-abandoned vessel. The sailors in the water scrambled to get farther away. Marian observed them, noting the hate that shone through the fear on their faces. Ahead, the first fleet, now joined with the outbound ships, all turned to with a new sense of challenge.

"Your carriage, Milady," Finback said as he swam alongside the abandoned ship and arched his back so Marian could step onto the deck. "Wait here, please, while the hideous Sea Monster gets grim and grisly on some frail human skulls."

Marian's hooves clattered on the wooden deck as she pranced to the stern. "They actually called you a *monster*?"

"Imagine," Finback answered. His front lateral fins twitched in a semblance of a shrug. "They are such a rude race of creatures."

"And ugly, too," Marian agreed as she gazed toward a group of sailors in the water who were paddling farther and farther away. "But try to restrain yourself, Finback. Don't hurt them if you can avoid it. Just disable those ships."

Finback scoffed as he slipped back below the waves. "Don't distract me with talk of restraints. I haven't had this much fun in ages!"

Feeling useless and left behind, Marian watched her old friend charge toward the oncoming fleet. There was one thing she could do, though. Crates and boxes, boards and pieces of broken timber still littered the deck, and there were still Men struggling to stay afloat not far off. With her shoulders she pushed the larger pieces over the side. With hooves and nose, she nudged the smaller bits.

A few of the swimmers turned back toward the ship, thinking it safe with Finback gone, and catching hold of rigging that dangled over the side, they began to climb aboard. Marian ran along the rail, determined to stop them, kick them back into the sea if they persisted. But then, remembering the icy embrace of the waves and the sense of panic as the water filled her mouth and nose, she relented.

"Don't mistake mercy for weakness!" she warned as the first two stepped on board.

Shivering and wild-eyed, the two stared at her and looked for an instant as if they'd prefer to jump back into the sea. But one clutched the arm of the other for courage. "You can talk!" he shouted in disbelief.

Marian frowned and sneered. "I can even hold a conversation, and that's probably more than either of you can manage!"

The second man shot a look around at the weapons on the deck. "What kind of demon are you?" he demanded.

"The kind that can launch your butts back to Angmar if either of you make a grab for anything," she warned with a toss of her mane. "Now mind your manners! And tell any of your friends who wish to they can also come aboard. But trust me—try anything, and my Sea Serpent friend will be the least of your worries. I'm a unicorn on the edge!"

The two turned slowly. Keeping wary gazes on Marian, they beckoned to their comrades. Another pair scrambled up the rigging, and one immediately collapsed from cold and exhaustion.

"Help him, if that's in your nature," Marian told the dripping newcomer. To the others she added, "Get blankets, sheeting, or whatever will serve for warmth."

The first sailor glared and clenched his fists. "You destroy our ship, order us overboard into freezing waters, and now you expect us to believe you're concerned for our comfort?"

Marian paced closer to the angry sailor and bobbed her deadly horn up and down beneath his nose as she fixed him with a blue-eyed gaze. "The world is full of contradictions," she said. With a sudden movement of her left front hoof, she sent a dark-metal sword flying over the side and into the sea lest it tempt someone into rashness. "Take your race— you produce fine poetry, sculpture, and art, excel at architecture, build beautiful cities. Yet you're vicious, bloodthirsty, predators and killers, smugly determined to claim dominion over all other creatures. Nothing so distinguishes you as your wars, and nothing so defines you as destruction!"

The sailor drew back his shoulders with stubborn pride. "You're not so unskilled at destruction yourselves," he charged, pointing an accusing finger.

Marian glanced over her shoulder to follow his direction. Finback loomed over one of the ships of the fleet. "He's only disabling your ships," she answered in a cool tone. "If he had destruction in his heart, you wouldn't be standing here arguing with me, would you? Now help your friends."

Turning her back to the sailors, she returned to the stern of the damaged ship. Finback went about his task with swift efficiency, shattering rudders and tearing rigging. The fleet began to drift. Hulls scraped together, though none ruptured. Finback nudged the ones in danger of serious collision into safer courses.

He really was magnificent, Marian thought, with his emerald scales and golden fins and awesome size. Fearsome even to her, when she considered him in a certain way. But a *monster?* She nickered softly as she shook her head. Only a fool with no eye for beauty could consider him that.

But in these times, with the Age of Dragons fading, the world was full of fools. So much confusion. So much hatred. Maybe Finback was right. *The world has changed too much!* She wasn't sure she knew her place in it anymore. She wasn't even sure if a unicorn had a place in it.

With the Angmaran fleet in disarray, Finback swam back to her, and as he reared above the place where she stood on the deck he arched his spiny crest proudly. He barely spared a glance at the sailors cowering against the rails behind her. The afternoon sun glimmered on his sleek, wet form, and his fishy lips curled into a semblance of a grin.

"On to Thursis?" he said. "I'll tow, and you push."

"You tow," she countered, "and I'll stand here and admire your beautiful self."

Finback nodded. "Sounds fair, and surprisingly rational for a unicorn. Yes, I think I like that."

The ship lurched forward, then began to glide through the waves with Finback leading the way. On the decks of the disabled ships, sailors crowded the rails to watch the strange spectacle with unreadable expressions. An uneasy silence hung over the sea as even the wind grew still.

"You can jump now, if you want to," Marian said to the sailors she'd allowed on board. "I'm sure your captains will pick you up." But none of them moved. Huddled together, wrapped in found blankets and sipping flasks of water or wine, they observed her and watched Finback. Their eyes were wary, but for the moment empty of fear.

On the horizon, the mountain peaks of Thursis loomed. Marian stared ahead, searching for the source of the plume of smoke she'd seen earlier, but she spied nothing. A smell lingered in the air, though—a smell of death and burning.

As Finback towed the ship into the harbor, Marian scanned the beaches, noting the sheds and tents, the larger buildings, the mounds of timber and the fallen trees. Except for the flapping of tent fabric, nothing on the shoreline moved. On the mountainside, a deep brown scar drew her attention.

What have you done, Ronaldo? she thought with a nervous sense of dread as she turned her gaze upward toward the high peaks. She remembered the Angmaran ships fleeing the island, remembered the smoke, and sniffed the air again. *Death and burning.*

On the highest peak at the center of the island, a movement caught her eye. Gray wings, a shadow sailing against the sky, circling, slipping among the clouds.

The deck boards creaked as the sailors got to their feet and moved closer to Marian. She turned her head to look at them, but they were watching the shadow as it changed its course and flew down the mountainside. The fear had returned to their faces.

The ship came to a stop. The harbor had become too shallow for Finback. "I think we've found your friend," the Sea Serpent said in a low, rumbling voice.

The Last Unicorn in the World wasn't so sure.

13

"SURELY, THAT IS THE ARMPIT OF THE WORLD!" Morkir muttered as he stared toward the city. "At least, it stinks like one."

Chan agreed with his griffin companion. The pale moonlight shining down through the thin clouds above did nothing to favor the city. Indeed, the soft glow only highlighted the bleak outlines and improbable angles of the city's countless structures so that every edge appeared tinged, not with light, but with rime and ice.

Jake shook a finger at Morkir. "Don't you know anything about geography?" he chided with mock-seriousness. "I've told you before—*Degarm* is the armpit of the world!"

"Do we go around it?" Katrina called from the griffin's back. She looked doubtful as she scanned the dark horizon. "*Can* we go around it?"

A sharp eagle's cry pierced the night. A moment later, Skymarin came racing back toward them with wings spread wide and eyes gleaming. "We've been spotted," he announced. "I've never seen Men like these. They're horribly deformed!"

Chan observed Skymarin closely. He'd never seen the Lord of Eagles so agitated. "Deformed?"

Skymarin tilted his wings and wheeled about to fly side-by-side with

Chan. "Their eyes are as long as their arms! They stand atop their walls and do nothing but watch!"

Chan bit his Dragon lip as he studied the ground below. A short distance ahead he spied a hilltop where the trees were not too thick. "Let's grab some ground," he said to the others. Without waiting for agreement, he stiffened his wings and began a slow glide toward the summit.

Skymarin flew closer to Chan's left ear. "I feel in my feathers that the skies are not friendly to us."

"I feel it, too," Morkir said. "The wind currents on my wings vibrate with warning. We're not alone."

Chan stared toward the city's jagged silhouette and wondered why the mere sight of that place sent shivers up his spine. Some deep instinct cried out for him to avoid it, to turn around and flee, or to fly the widest possible course around its towers and stone walls. His heart quickened, and his throat tightened. Yet, at the same time, some strange curiosity compelled him. *The Book of Stormfire* contained no mention of this city, nor had Electra mentioned it.

It was new then, at least to the Dragonkin, unknown and never visited. Didn't that warrant a little investigation? But the hilltop was rushing up at him. He extended his claws, and then beat his wings powerfully to slow his flight. Mindful of Jake on his back, the son of Stormfire settled between a pair of tall pines and gripped the ground. Morkir landed nearby, but not with so much grace and care. Katrina pitched over his head with a snarl and rolled along the nettled earth like a furry ball before she struck a stout tree trunk.

Getting to her feet with a dizzy expression, she shook a fist at the griffin. "Your mother was a flying fish!" she hissed. "And your father was your mother's brother!"

Morkir yawned as he pressed one paw to his beak. "I love the way she talks," he said, although he didn't sound very convincing. "Remind me to catch a mouse and leave it in her nest."

"She doesn't have a nest," Jake reminded the griffin.

Morkir stared at Jake for a long moment, on the verge of saying something. But he seemed to think better of it, and only smirked before he turned away. "My apologies, Cat-girl," he said to Katrina. "I'm not used to this beast-of-burden act yet. Your weight threw off my balance, and I landed too hard."

"My weight?" Katrina shrieked, looking as if she'd rake his nose with her claws. "You fat sack of bones!"

From a branch in the top of the tallest pine, Skymarin interrupted with a short, high-pitched cry. "They're coming," he reported, his gaze fixed on the black cityscape in the distance.

"Hold tight, Jake," Chan warned. Then, rising on his hind legs, he stretched his neck as high as he could. The boy gave a whoop of surprise, but the saddle straps held him securely in place as Chan followed Skymarin's gaze.

Tiny shadows flashed across the moon, countless shapes, sleek and swift and menacing. Like knives they flew across the clouds and the thin, random patches of stars, coming straight for the hilltop.

"Your vision is matchless," Chan said to the Lord of Eagles. "Can you see what they are?"

"Falcons," Skymarin answered with a dreadful calm. "But I've never seen Falcons group in such numbers. It's unnatural."

Chan's heart quickened again as he bent low to the ground. "Get off," he told Jake, "but stay close to me. And Katrina, you stay close to Jake. If the falcons attack, I can shelter both of you with my wings, but strapped in the saddle he's just too exposed to sharp beaks and talons."

Jake wasted no time and swiftly unbuckled the saddle straps. When the last strap was undone, Katrina reached up to help him down. Stubborn and proud as always, Jake declined her hand and somersaulted over her head.

The furry Fomorian braced her hands on her hips and scowled. "Showoff!"

Jake seemed not to hear. Walking away a few paces, he stooped beneath another tree and picked up a thick branch in both hands. He swung it a couple of times, then looked back at Chan and said cryptically, "In Degarm, we played a game called *stick-ball.*"

"I know this game," Morkir said as he rose up on his hind legs and extended his claws. "But we call it *splatter-bird.* A most satisfying pastime."

Katrina turned up her nose. "You're sick," she said, but she strode toward another tree to find her own club. "How do I play this game?"

"Simple rules," Jake explained, showing her the proper stance and grip. "You swing the bat—you hit the bird."

Katrina made an experimental swing and nodded. "I can see the appeal." Then she made a face and stuck her tongue out at Morkir, who stood by grinning.

Chan rose up to his full height again. "They're almost upon us," Skymarin told him as he stood watching. Chan nodded without speaking. He could see the falcons plainly now and could hear the wind rushing through their feathers like a soft song. There were hundreds of them.

Abandoning his perch, Skymarin soared upward. Moonlight flashed on his wings as he spiraled higher and higher, farther and faster than the Falcons could climb. The sky was his element, and if he had to fight he would fight from there.

But the falcons showed no interest in the Lord of Eagles. Straight on to the hilltop they came, hitting the pines like a gentle storm. The branches shivered, and the needles rattled. Pinecones rained down.

Morkir roared a challenge as the trees filled with dark-winged shapes, and Katrina raised her stick.

The largest falcon settled on the tallest pine on the very branch Skymarin had vacated. Large round eyes fastened on Chan. Then the creature spread its wings, wrapped them slowly around itself, and bowed its head. "Welcome, O Dragon!" it said in a deep and formal voice. "Your kind hasn't been seen in Valindar for many generations. Yet we've been expecting you. Welcome, and thrice-welcome!"

"What kind of bird-brained trick is this?" Morkir shouted from the ground. "We've come a long way, and we're all a little tired, so let's get on with the fighting before my muscles cramp up!" He roared again and, holding up one paw, exposed his claws.

"Bird-brained trick?" The Falcon stared at Morkir with genuine surprise before it tilted its head and gave a hearty laugh. "Such an expression from one with a face as avian as my own!"

Chan frowned at Morkir and flexed one leathery wing in subtle warning. Jake understood and laid a calming hand on the griffin's head. Apparently, these falcons hadn't come for battle, and a good thing, too, for their numbers were great and their talons impressively sharp.

Yet there was something more that unsettled the Son of Stormfire. The trees were thick with falcons, yet they had not just settled down at random wherever a branch presented itself. They sat in ranks, unmoving and evenly spaced among the limbs—watchful with an admirable military precision, awaiting some command.

Prepared to fight, the falcons were choosing not to do so, and for the moment at least, that seemed the wisest course for Chan to follow as well. He turned his gaze back to the falcon leader and, extending one open paw, said, "We come in peace and with good will." He glanced around to judge the effect of his words on the other falcons.

"O Wise Dragon, you speak soothing and reassuring words." The falcon leader preened and fluffed his wings. "My name is Emissary, and I bring you an invitation from great Karnalis. He would be honored if you would visit him in Throom Odin."

Chan narrowed one curious eye. "Throom Odin?"

Emissary blinked as he tilted his head. Making a sweeping gesture with one wing, he explained. "The Living City," he said. "The beating heart of Valindar. Even in the dark of night you see it before you."

Morkir called upward. "This Karnalis is your king?" he said. "That's where we'll fight?"

Moonlight gleamed on Emissary's black feathers as he swiveled his head back and forth. "We have no king in Throom Odin, my raptor half-brother," he said to Morkir. "Karnalis is our Chief Critic."

Chan's ears pricked up, and he narrowed his other eye. Was that a hint of mockery or insult he heard in Emissary's voice, or just some odd falconish inflection he wasn't used to? He listened for some sound of restlessness from the rest of their hosts and watched them carefully. To the bird, they maintained their positions.

Emissary seemed not to notice Chan's reaction and continued on. "...Final Arbiter of all Things Beautiful and Brummagem. In matters of judgment and taste, we hold his word supreme."

Katrina rolled her eyes toward Jake and spoke just loudly enough for all to hear. "*Final Arbiter*, you say? Well, he can arbitrate this." She tapped her rump with one hand. "Let's skip the social call and just get on with..."

"Shut up," Jake said, cutting her off.

Katrina looked as if she'd been slapped. "What?"

Jake repeated, low-voiced and stern, without glancing at her. "Shut up. Now."

Katrina gaped, showing her fangs as she glared at the boy. The fur on her neck stood on end. Like any cat, she was quick to anger, quick to strike. Before she could make any regrettable move, however, Skymarin glided out of the darkness. Jake raised his arm, and the Lord of Eagles perched upon it.

Embarrassed by her impulsive behavior, Katrina relaxed her claws. The fur on her neck lay back down as she gazed at Jake, then Chan, then at the ground.

"Fascinating," Emissary said, breaking the uncomfortable silence. "The eagle and the Man-child share a bond."

"He's not a child," Morkir said with a wink before Jake could say it.

Grateful for Skymarin's swift intervention, Chan breathed a quiet sigh. The last thing he needed was trouble among his companions, but Jake had been right to interrupt Katrina before she said too much.

For the first time, as he studied the falcon leader and the great army at attention in the trees, he realized he and his friends were in hostile territory. The harpy Electra had tried to warn him, but he hadn't taken her words to heart. As a result, he found himself in an uncomfortable position.

He made a quick decision. "We'd be happy to accept the invitation of your Chief Critic, Karnalis," he said, inclining his head ever so slightly. "The Dragonkin are eager to forge new bonds of friendship with our neighbors."

Emissary's eyes glittered. "Then bonds will be forged," he answered with an unconcealed hint of amusement and menace. "If you will follow us to Throom Odin, we will make you comfortable and see to your needs."

Despite the danger, Chan hesitated, suspicious and unwilling to be pushed quite so easily. "Look for us at dawn," he said. "My friends need rest and a chance to freshen themselves." Emissary's talons tightened on his perch, and he swiveled one dark eye, but before the falcon could speak, Chan continued. "We wouldn't want to greet the Final Arbiter of all Things Beautiful and Brummagem looking less than our best, would we?"

Morkir called upward, lending his growly voice to Chan's. "First impressions are so important." He swept his gaze around the trees, taking in the nearest falcons. "Grand entrances and all that. I'm sure you understand."

It was the most insincere, subtly sarcastic speech Chan had ever heard from the Griffin. He marveled as he struggled to suppress a grin.

"You waste your breath addressing my troops," Emissary said to Morkir in a cool tone. "Only I, among all the falcons, may speak. Hence, my name."

Katrina looked up and chuckled. "I get it!" she said. "The emissary to the arbiter is the bird with the word? The hawk that can talk has a thing with the king?"

"There is no king," Morkir corrected.

Katrina looked crestfallen, then gave the griffin a mischievous wink and twirled her stick. "The Critic in the city holds the land in his hand while the bird with the word keeps an eye on the sky?"

Morkir looked thoughtful, and then nodded approval. 'It has rhythm," he said. "Yes, I think you've got it."

With one hand over her heart, she bowed.

"Enough!" Emissary displayed his wings and thrust out his feathered chest in obvious annoyance. "Come at dawn, then," he said to Chan. "I will inform the Chief Critic." Leaping from his perch, he glided on an impressive wingspan past Chan's head and called back. "My troops will wait a little way off to escort you when you're ready." Then he turned toward the city called Throom Odin. The trees shivered, and like a great black wave, his troops followed, but only Emissary flew high enough to ride the moonlight. The rest kept low and didn't go far.

"A narrow stream runs at the bottom of this hill," Skymarin informed them. He fixed his gaze on Katrina. "A drink and a bath would cool some of us down."

"I'm cool," she replied defensively. "I'm very cool. I just don't respond well when I'm told to shut up!"

"You were about to give away our mission," Morkir said, siding with Skymarin. "As far as anyone else is concerned, this is a social call. We're just a sociable bunch of misfits looking to be sociable."

Katrina frowned and looked to Chan for support. The Son of Stormfire bent his head close to the ground and spoke softly, aware that Emissary's falcon-troops were still nearby. "I'm afraid they're right, little Furball," he whispered to Katrina. "Never mention our purpose to anyone, and certainly never mention the talisman. Despite their manners, these falcons are not our friends, nor I suspect, are the people within this city. Be on your guard." Then he licked her with a thick, wet Dragontongue. "Gotcha!"

Katrina rolled head-over-heels backward and sprang to her feet with a lithe motion. Dirt and pieces of grass stuck to her orange-golden fur. In disgust, she flung her stick aside and rubbed brisk hands over herself. "Yuck! Now I really *do* need a bath!"

The others laughed as, together, they started down the hillside with Skymarin leading the way in a slow glide. Jake quickly stripped off his shirt and laved his face and chest with cool water. Katrina kneeled next to him and cupped water in her hands. Unable to resist the temptation, Morkir gave a low snigger and, brushing them both with one broad wing, toppled them headfirst into the drink.

Rising tall on his hind legs, he gave out with a raucous, leonine laugh. "Are you cooled off yet?" he asked as he watched the pair splutter and splash.

On silent wings, Skymarin hit the griffin from behind with just the right amount of force to unbalance him. With a wide-eyed yelp, Morkir hit the water as Jake and Katrina scrambled to dive out of his way.

"I'll pluck you bare for that, you old bird!" he roared as he stood up in the center of the stream. He gave a violent shiver, shaking water from his wings, but before he could chase Skymarin, Jake and Katrina piled on his back and neck.

"Now who needs to cool off?" Jake laughed.

Chan grinned to himself as he watched their play from the corner of one eye. Play was a good thing. It fostered teamwork and forged strong bonds, and he wished that he could stretch out on the bank and roll in the grass with his friends. Instead, he kept watch over them. But his mind was on the falcons, on the city called Throom Odin, and on its Chief Critic.

He couldn't explain the wave of misgivings that swept over him when he stared at the black architecture across the plain. Though the moonlight lit its angles and edges with an almost razor gleam, it shrank away from the darker places, and the stars that spangled the velvet night avoided its towers and rooftops. Throom Odin stood like an evil wall, like a barrier, to the rest of the world beyond.

A barrier against him, he realized. *Against all the Dragonkin and all the creatures of Wyvernwood.*

What was it that stood between his kindred and the race of Man? Was it hatred? Was it fear? Why wasn't there more in *The Book of Stormfire* about the origins of the ancient animosities that drove them apart? The Time of the Dragons was passing, and the Age of Man was just beginning—how many times had he heard that? It didn't seem enough of an explanation to him anymore. It didn't seem to explain anything at all.

He would go to Throom Odin. With open eyes and open heart, perhaps he could find the answers to his questions. There were things to learn behind those dark walls, and new experiences waiting.

Dawn found them all awake, bathed, rested, and ready. The cloudless sky was such an intense cobalt color that it almost shimmered, and a warm breeze blew as the sun climbed higher. It was in all regards a picture-perfect morning. In the rising sunlight, even Throom Odin seemed a little less menacing. All the light in the world, however, couldn't strip it of its mystery.

Chan drew his companions close together for final planning while a squadron of falcons circled high overhead. "I think our escort is getting impatient," he said with a grin to the others.

"Let them," Morkir chuckled after a quick upward glance. "If their leader, Karnalis, is pompous enough to style himself *Chief Critic*, then he must surely appreciate the importance of a fashionably late arrival."

"Put the stick down, little Furball," Chan said to Katrina. The feline Fomorian had just picked up her club and taken a practice swing. "We're not going in with weapons." Katrina gave a soft growl, but cast the stick aside.

Jake touched the leather sling bound around his wrist. It looked like a bracelet. "Not obvious ones," he murmured.

Chan nodded to Jake. "Make sure you sit up straight and stay in plain sight. You said it yourself—a human boy riding on my neck makes me look just a little less threatening." He bent down, and Jake climbed into the saddle. When the straps were fastened securely about his legs and thighs, Jake patted Chan's neck, and the Son of Stormfire rose to his full height.

"Best manners, everyone!" Chan reminded them. "No claws and no teeth. But keep your eyes open and your senses sharp. They don't trust us."

"We don't trust them, either," Katrina said, smiling and giving a mock-curtsey before she climbed upon Morkir's back. "There now," she added to Morkir. "Don't I make you look a little less frightening, too?"

"Sure," Morkir replied with a roll of his eyes. "What's frightening about a griffin and his housecat?"

Katrina shrieked and extended her claws.

"No claws and no teeth," Chan reminded. Then winking at Katrina, he added, "I can't stop you from twisting his ears off, though, but do it before we get to Throom Odin, and don't make him bleed on any carpets."

The Fomorian's eyes lit up with mischief, but Chan didn't waste any more time. He nodded to Skymarin, and the Lord of Eagles soared upward to meet their falcon escort. He was both scout and herald for their small fellowship. Then, spreading vast leather wings, Chan followed, ascending quickly and smiling with private satisfaction as the falcons raced to get out of his way. Morkir, with Katrina laughing on his back, rose to take position on his right side.

"Do you think Karnalis will be impressed?" Chan called back to Jake.

"He'll wet his pants, *Sumapai*." Jake laughed softly. With Chan's hearing, he knew he didn't have to raise his voice. "You not only breathe fire, you shine like a bolt of fire. All red and gold and orange—I wish you could see yourself just once with Man's eyes."

"*Sumapai?*" Chan said with some surprise. The word was Degarmian. He didn't know its meaning, but he hadn't missed the emotional nuance behind it. "You've never called me that. What does it mean?"

Jake shrugged and adjusted himself in the saddle as he leaned closer to Chan's neck. "Teacher, guide, guardian," he answered with a hint of embarrassment. "And more than that. More than brother. More than father. Much more than friend." He hesitated and straightened up a little. "I probably shouldn't have said it."

"I like it," Chan said truthfully, his heart swelling with pride and affection for Jake. "It must have a converse, though. How would you call your part in such a relationship?"

Again Jake hesitated and fidgeted. "I would be *Chokahai*," he answered at last. "Student and acolyte. More than brother. More than son."

Chan thought about that as he raced toward the walls of Throom

Odin. *Sumapai* and *Chokahai*. They described a relationship more personal than mere names, something that went beyond even kinship and blood-bonds. With a flash of insight, he remembered something Jake had only recently told him.

"Keven was your *Sumapai*," he said with gentle understanding. Keven, the sixth Man-child, Chan remembered. He'd been the oldest one—perhaps not a child at all—and he'd drowned to save Jake's life. There was much yet to learn about Keven, Chan suspected, and many stories yet to hear.

Jake's answer was heavy with barely contained sorrow. "It's not the custom in Degarm to speak much of the dead."

Chan shook his head, refusing to accept that answer. "You're Dragonkin now," he said with simple firmness.

Atop the walls of Throom Odin, strange lights began to wink and flash. Chan fell silent as he studied the action going on there and observed the red-cloaked Men scurrying about. Skymarin hadn't been exaggerating! Their eyes really were as long as their arms, so long they needed both hands to hold them up! The winking lights, he understood now, were the reflection and glinting of the sun as those huge, hideous eyes turned their way!

Whatever could have caused such massive disfigurement?

"Telescopes!" Jake exclaimed as they flew closer. "I've seen one before in the carnival—but only one! Never so many!"

"Telescopes?" Chan repeated. They were almost to the walls by now. Hundreds of Men, most in red cloaks and most with repulsively distended eyes, shouted and waved. Some held weapons, but others seemed unarmed or without obvious weaponry. Yet, to a man, they appeared enthusiastic and welcoming!

"Devices," Jake tried to explain. "Telescopes are tools. With them, a Man can see as far and as clearly as a Dragon." He held his hands up in front of one eye in exactly the manner of the Men below. "In the carnival, men could pay a small fee and use it to watch while women bathed in the nearby river, or sometimes to peek through a cottage window at the far end of town." He paused as he leaned down to observe the activity on the wall. All the telescopes focused on him, and a collective gasp went up as he waved. "It looks like these people have found an entirely new use for it."

A military use, Chan thought to himself.

The falcons closed ranks around Chan and his companions. There seemed to be more of them than before, and as Chan flew across the wall and into Throom Odin, Emissary flew up from the wall suddenly to meet him.

"Greetings again, Dragon," he screeched, "and greetings to your companions. As you can see from the crowds on the walls, the people of Valindar are eager for a glimpse of you, and they've prepared a welcome."

A tall minaret was in their flight path, and Emissary led the way in a wide circle around it, bringing them right back to the wall. "Then if you would not mind walking, follow me, please." The falcon leader didn't wait for an answer, but dove downward at a steep glide and into a wide street that stopped at an immense gate on the outside of the wall. In the middle of the dusty way, Emissary landed and gazed upward at Chan. Folding his wings over his chest, he leaned forward with great dignity and pressed his forehead to the dirt.

"Beware of Falcons that bow too deeply," Jake whispered to Chan.

The Son of Stormfire landed beside Emissary as an immense cheer went up from the crowds on the wall. A moment later, Morkir landed beside Chan, and Katrina dismounted to stand proudly beside the griffin.

Still in the saddle, Jake held out his arm, and Skymarin settled upon it. "We are five," Jake reported to Chan. "Present and accounted for."

Five against a numberless foe, Chan thought as he swept his gaze over the cheering crowds. His previous sense of unease returned, but with it came a new sense of excitement. He had not even entered the city yet, and he was already learning new things. *Telescopes!* How wonderful!

Emissary turned around and, with a sharp movement, snapped his wings open. Chan's heart lurched, and Katrina snarled, but it was only a signal to open the gate. With a noisy grind of gears and a cranking of chains, the portal swung ponderously open, two great wooden doors parting and drawing back.

From atop the walls, baskets of flower petals in all colors snowed down to carpet the street, and throngs of people lined the route, all throwing flowers. With easy grace, Emissary beat his wings and lifted into the air. With a short screech, Skymarin followed on wings even larger and more majestic than Emissary's.

Katrina looked at Chan, then, lifting her head high and arching her slender tail, she walked under the arch and through the open gate. Flower petals rained down upon her, some of them sticking to her fur. She held out her hands to catch a few.

Morkir followed her, roaring as he passed beneath the arch. The crowds fell silent for a moment, startled or perhaps even fearful to hear such a roar from an eagle-like beak. But he was half lion, too, at least in appearance, and they quickly grasped the fact, set aside their presumptions, and welcomed him with loud cheers.

But the loudest cheers were for the Dragon and his human rider. Chan ducked his head and folded his wings tightly against his body as he passed through the gate. Baskets and baskets of petals poured down upon them, an almost blinding torrent of soft, sweet smelling snow. Jake sputtered as he rubbed a hand over his face and tried to snatch at the petals that slipped down his neck and inside his shirt.

"A simple key to the city would have been sufficient," Chan muttered to Jake.

Jake's answer was a low grumble. "They'll probably dump a basket of those over your head, too."

The squadron of falcons flew overhead as the strange parade of visitors moved through the wide street and into the heart of Throom Odin itself. Everywhere, people cheered and waved, and not just from the sidewalks—they leaned from the windows, hung over the sides of the rooftops.

"This place stinks worse than any city I've ever been in," Jake said suddenly.

His words were like a splash of cold water in Chan's face. He'd gotten caught up in the cheering and the waving and the excitement of the procession. But now he looked closer, behind the smiles and the festivity.

The people didn't look healthy. They were thin, sometimes almost skeletal. Their red cloaks were often tattered, and the threadbare garments they wore beneath them looked like little more than rags. Their cheeks were leathery and sunken, and their eyes bulged above lipless mouths full of bad teeth.

There had been some hasty clean-up, but it didn't take much of a glance to note the refuse and filth that littered the streets and alleyways off the main thoroughfare. The flower petals couldn't hide it all. Nor could they hide the black stone rot and decay that marred many of the structures.

Chan sniffed and wrinkled his nose. With so many buildings and such tall ones, the wind couldn't get in to cleanse the place, and the rain only collected in stagnant ditches. The trash and the slops? Well, it was plain enough where those went.

"Remind Katrina to wash her feet," he whispered back to Jake.

Jake nodded. "I'll remind you, too."

The parade came to an end as they reached a vast square. Here at least there was a breath of wind, but it only bore the stench from other parts of the city. On the far side of the square rose a tall dais of black stone with a cascade of steps before it, and a great throne draped in silks and piled with pillows at its center.

A plump little gnome of a Man sat there eating with a large spoon from a bowl he balanced on one hand. His oiled beard hung down almost over the bowl's rim, and his long hair was tied back and braided with gold ribbons. The features of his face were all exaggerated with colorful paints, bright reds for his lips and cheeks, blue for his eyelids, and jet black for his high-arched eyebrows. He pretended not to notice the procession at all until it stopped at the bottom of the steps.

Emissary flew up to settle on the high back of the throne. He spoke a few inaudible words, and the Chief Critic of Throom Odin, Arbiter of All Things Beautiful and Brummagem finally looked up with his spoon halfway to his lips. Pausing to look at Chan, he smiled, and ate his spoonful, then set the bowl aside.

"Baby snakes," he announced as he wiped his lip with one red silk sleeve. "So tasty, and so good for you. Prepared in sunflower oil and lightly spiced, with a few pine nuts, and an ever so delicate broth to conceal the faint venom flavor . . . " He kissed his fingertips. "It's simply an indescribable pleasure. Four stars, really. You must try it sometime."

Chan allowed himself a private frown as Karnalis dipped a finger into the bowl and sucked the brothy tip. He had met so few Men in his lifetime, but he felt an instant dislike for the Chief Critic. There was a coldness in the Man's eyes, a cruel cunning that surpassed that of any creature he'd ever known.

"Let me down," Jake whispered. He was already unfastening the straps that held him in his saddle. Before Chan could protest, the boy slipped to the ground and took a position at Chan's side. He looked relaxed, stretching as if he was merely stiff from riding, but Chan knew Jake well enough to read the smaller, more subtle signs. When Skymarin gyred down and tried to land on Jake's arm, Jake feigned irritation and waved the eagle away.

"Baby snakes?" Chan said, turning his attention back to Karnalis. "I'm afraid they're not on my diet."

Karnalis arched an eyebrow and sat up with greater interest. "So, it's true! You really do talk!" He shot a look at Emissary on the back of his throne, then turned back to Chan. "You *are* one of the ancient Dragonkin that passed through here so many centuries ago!" The soup bowl clattered to the dais, spilling its contents around his slippered feet as he brushed it with a sleeve. He seemed not even to notice as he stared at Morkir and Katrina. "And these monsters? What are they?"

The scales on Chan's neck rankled. Leaning forward, he brought his face closer to the Chief Critic. It had the desired effect. Karnalis paled as he took a step backward, slipped in his soup and sprawled ungracefully across his pillows. When a wet stain seeped across the front of his garish trousers he quickly swept a corner of his cloak across his lap.

"I told you so," Jake muttered in a voice so low that only Chan could hear.

"They are my friends," came Chan's calm reply.

Emissary, still on his perch, gave a sharp screech. In response, four red-cloaked guards armed with bows and arrows rushed up the back side of the dais and surrounded the Chief Critic. Almost before they took their positions, four more rushed up behind them, armed with steel-tipped pikes. Overhead, the squadron of falcons dropped lower and flew watchful circles above the throngs.

Recovering himself, Karnalis waved a hand. The guards lowered their weapons and relaxed. The falcons climbed higher and then settled on the rooftops, evenly spacing themselves with the same military precision they'd exhibited before.

"I apologize for my lack of manners," the Chief Critic said to Chan. His tone wasn't very convincing, though; neither was his frown. He glanced up and waved his hand again. "It's the sky," he continued. "This dreadful shade of blue wears on my nerves. I'm afraid it's put me out of sorts."

With one eye on the guards, Chan dared a quick gaze skyward, but before he could say anything, Katrina called out. "Are you blind? That's a perfectly gorgeous sky! There's not a cloud at all"

Karnalis rose from his pillows again to give Katrina a smugly tolerant look. "That's exactly what's wrong with it," he explained as if he was a teacher speaking to a new pupil. "It lacks contrast and texture. The unadorned blue is so achingly bland that it strains the eye. Like a blank canvass, it offers nothing to stimulate or excite." He fanned his face with one hand and looked as if he might faint. "Such monotony taxes my sensibilities."

Chan drew back. It was difficult to hide his disdain for such an obnoxious little tyrant. *Snake-eater,* he thought. *That's not a far step from cannibalism for him.* "It must be hard being the Arbiter of All Things Beautiful," he said with false sympathy.

"And Brummagem," Karnalis reminded with an exasperated sigh. "There's so much gawd in this world, so much that is merely cheap and showy. Your colorful scales . . . " he paused and stroked his beard in a gesture of consideration, and Chan braced himself for another insult. "Those, however, are astonishing and beautiful. I approve with fullest enthusiasm, although you could use just a little more red among all that gold and orange. I love red, and I insist that all the people of Throom Odin wear it."

"He's breathless with delight to hear your opinion," Morkir growled. Stretching full-length on the ground next to Chan, he folded his wings and yawned as he rested his chin on his paws. "He's too modest to admit it, though, so I thought I'd speak for him."

The Chief Critic arched one eyebrow and put on an expression that could have conveyed either irritation or amusement. He swept his cloak back over one shoulder. Then, remembering the stain on his trousers, he covered himself again. He looked to Chan. "I can see you have a standard for choosing your friends."

Not a high standard or even a low standard, Chan noticed. Just *a standard.* Karnalis gave offense as much by what he didn't say as by what he did say.

"And now I understand your diet," Chan replied as he drew erect. He'd come to Throom Odin in the hope of learning something about the Race of Man, but he was finding that he didn't care much for the teacher. Stretching his neck high, he gazed down at Karnalis. The Chief Critic really was quite a small man. "It's fuel for the venom you spew."

The guards on the dais shifted in obvious discomfort and clutched their weapons. Emissary gave another screech. Along the rooftops, the falcon squadron fluttered their wings, but for the moment they kept their perches.

Karnalis sank back on his pillows as a slow grin spread over his chubby face. He pointed one slim finger at Chan. "You're an impudent monster," he said, "but you have a certain way with words, a gift for the perfect turn of phrase." He nodded as he turned the same finger on himself and tapped his chin. Then he pressed his palms together in restrained applause. "I appreciate that. It doesn't quite rise to poetry, but there's wit in it, and that's rare. I would as soon destroy a great work of art as destroy you, Dragon." He gave another sigh. "But by the ancient charge laid upon me and upon my fathers before me, I must do my duty."

Morkir growled as Karnalis raised both hands above his head. A loud clanking and groaning and grinding filled the air. On the rooftops above the square, huge wooden machines not unlike giant bows with giant arrows rolled into view, each one pushed and manned by a score of soldiers.

"Ballistas!" Jake cried as he shot a gaze at the huge weapons.

Behind Chan, from the far side of the square, came more grinding and groaning. The Son of Stormfire twisted his neck around to see. A different machine trundled into view, a wooden platform on wheels with two tall wooden pillars and a massive gleaming blade suspended between them. The pillars, Chan noticed, were ornately carved with all manners of Dragons, Wyrms, Wyverns, and Drakes, all superbly polished.

Morkir growled again. "I think it's time to engage in a little deconstructive criticism of our own!" he said, displaying his powerful wings as he glared around.

Chan wasn't so sure and didn't move except to study the rooftops. The strange weapons there—*ballistas*—concerned him. Ordinary arrows stood no chance against a Dragon's scales, but the missiles loaded on those machines were far larger even than spears or pikes. They looked deadly and fully able to penetrate even his scales.

Feigning a yawn, he looked to Karnalis again with a look of boredom. "Hasn't anyone ever told you it's rude to point? Especially with pointy sticks. I could take it personally." The flame bubbled in his throat. It would be very easy to toast the Chief Critic. He obviously deserved it. Yet Chan resisted the impulse, swallowed his flame, and instead belched only a puff of warm smoke through his nostrils as he issued a warning. "You wouldn't like me anymore if I took it personally."

Coughing delicately, Karnalis waved a hand to disperse the fumes, but a new sound drew Chan's attention. The ballistas on all four sides fired, launching their missiles across the square to the rooftops opposite. Lines of netting trailed behind each missile to form a swift web. Red-cloaked soldiers secured the lines while others reloaded and re-aimed the massive weapons.

"Finally!" Jake shouted, spinning around to glare at Chan. "You're caught, and I'm free!" He spun about again and raced halfway up the dais. "Your munificence!" he appealed to Karnalis. "These monsters have kept me prisoner for months. I beg you for protection and sanctuary! Don't let them take me away again!"

"Come on, boy!" the Chief Critic answered. He beckoned to two of his guards, who descended with swift steps to take Jake by his arms and hustle him to the top of the dais. "I'm sure we can find some position of service for a strapping youngster. Stand here by my side and see how we deal with monsters in Throom Odin."

"Be careful of that one!" Jake cried, pointing at Morkir as the griffin rose up on his hind legs and swelled his golden-furred chest. "He's strong, and he blames me for killing his brother!" He shrank behind the Chief Critic as if he was afraid Morkir might fly up and snatch him.

Dumbfounded, Chan stared at Jake. In doing so, he missed the soldiers in the crowd who had sneaked close. Throwing back their red cloaks, cloaks that every citizen seemed to wear, they unfurled nets, dozens of nets that flew toward the griffin, ensnared him and tangled his wings. More nets flew over Katrina. She snarled and kicked and slapped about with her claws, but a dozen swords suddenly pressed against her writhing form, and she grew still. Morkir was similarly surrounded.

Karnalis frowned, then flashed a look of pure exasperation. "Well, this is just disappointing!" he shouted, bracing his hands on his hips. "Where's the action? Where's the personal growth and character development? This entire encounter lacks the drama and suspense that I crave! It's all been too easy!" He scuffed one slippered foot on the dais stone, then began to pace. "It's your fault, Dragon!" he added, thrusting a finger at Chan.

"You haven't caught me yet," Chan reminded him. "I can shred your netting or burn through it." He gave a cold wink. "Come to think of it, I could do the same to you!"

Karnalis slapped his thighs. "Hah!" he answered, sitting back once more on his pillows. "Of course I've caught you! Are you a stupid Dragon? I've got your freakish friends at swords' point! And look over there!" He waved a hand toward the elaborate machine with the carved pillars and the blade. Lined up before it were twenty thin and sorry-looking townspeople stripped of their cloaks and all clothing, and behind them stood another twenty soldiers with swords at the throats of the naked twenty. "Wimps and sympathizers!" Karnalis continued. "Scum, who forgot the purpose for which this beautiful city was built! They wanted to welcome you truly! Let bygones be bygones, they urged!"

So there were a few examples of sanity in Throom Odin after all, Chan thought as he studied the sympathizers. But only twenty in the entire, seemingly endless city? "What do you want of me, you vile little toad?" he said over his shoulder to Karnalis.

The Chief Critic leaned forward on his throne. A hint of excitement crept into his voice. "I want you to walk over and stretch your neck between those pillars. Put your head under the blade. And please take care not to step on any of my subjects."

Chan faced the machine and drew a shallow breath. So Karnalis meant to behead him. He wondered how old the machine was, how long it had been waiting to taste Dragon's blood. The blade looked heavy enough to do the trick.

"If you hesitate," Karnalis continued, "my soldiers will kill your two friends. Then, if you continue to hesitate, I'll kill the sympathizers one at a time." He shrugged and even managed to look somewhat regretful. "It's all melodramatic, I know, but it's the purpose for which Throom Odin was founded: Destroy all monsters. When you crossed those mountains, you sealed your own fate. If it's any consolation, I promise to make the most splendid carpet from your hide."

Chan rolled his eyes. His mind raced, but in truth he couldn't see a clear way out. Jake's sudden betrayal stung, but he had Morkir and Katrina to think about, too. "Oh, I'm so consoled," he answered.

"*Sumapai*, did you say *consoled*?" Jake shouted from the right side of the throne. "Or did you say *boot sole*?"

Sumapai? Chan twisted around as Jake sprang into action. With a savage kick, the boy sent the nearest guard tumbling over the side of the high dais. In one smooth spinning motion, he struck the next with his fist, caught the front of his uniform, and flung him forward down the stairs. A pike whistled toward his head. Jake ducked the blow and cartwheeled over the throne.

As he flew upside-down over Karnalis, Emissary gave a loud screech, spread his wings, and leaped with his talons extended. In mid-flip, Jake shot out a hand and caught the falcon leader by one leg, and Emissary screeched a new note.

Landing on the other side of the throne, Jake swung the helpless falcon with all his strength, striking another guard. Feathers exploded, filling the air. In the confusion, Jake dropped the bird to seize a pike from the grip of a sputtering guard. Whirling it staff-like with expert skill, he struck again and knocked two more opponents off the dais.

Once more, he cartwheeled over the throne and a stupefied Chief Critic, and another kick sent yet another soldier over the side. Three guards remained. One of them rushed up and managed to wrap his arms around Jake.

"You've got him! You've got him!" Karnalis cried in red-faced excitement as he shot to his feet. "Don't hurt him, though! He's a magnificent little hunk of . . . !"

Giving no warning at all, Jake dropped to one knee and twisted. With a startled cry, the luckless guard lost his hold and flew over Jake's head to bounce and roll down the stairs and finally lie motionless at Chan's feet. Only two guards left, and one rushed up behind Jake to try his luck. Jake didn't even look as he snapped his elbow sharply back into the man's groin. Even Chan winced.

With an almost lazy grace, Jake backflipped over his crippled attacker and kicked the remaining guard down the rear stairs. Only the guard to whom he'd introduced his elbow remained, and he was on his knees clutching himself, wide-eyed and speechless with his cheeks puffed out. "Mind if I borrow your sword?" Jake asked politely as he reached beneath the poor man's red cloak and drew it from its sheath. The man shook his head before he crawled to the edge of the steps and slithered down head-first in a trail of thin vomit.

Chan gaped. The entire battle had happened with astounding swiftness. One boy against eight soldiers, and Jake wasn't even breathing hard.

"Now that's what I call King of the Hill!" Katrina shouted gleefully, heedless of the swords and the soldiers still menacing her.

The Chief Critic fanned himself breathlessly as Jake put the sword's point against his fat belly. "There's only one monster here, and it's you," he said. He extended one arm, and Skymarin landed on it. "Now let my friends go before I let some of those baby snakes out through your navel. And if I hear one twang from a ballista . . . " He inclined his head slightly and let the threat hang.

Karnalis hesitated, studying Jake's grim face. Then he waved a hand. The soldiers responded at once, stepping away from Morkir and Katrina. Morkir lurched to his feet and shredded the nets that covered him. "Now can we tear this Man-nest apart?" he said to Chan.

"No, but you can rip away the nets between us and the sky," the Dragon answered. "And then, if you really want to flex some muscles, smash the ballistas. But no more than that."

Katrina shrugged off the last of her nets. "He gets to have all the fun," she grumbled.

The falcon squadron no longer behaved like a squadron. With their leader injured or dead, they circled without purpose or remained trembling on their perches. Morkir scattered them as he went enthusiastically about his task.

Chan glanced toward the bladed machine. The sympathizers look back at him, but their expressions were confused, uncertain. If there was any hope for understanding between the Dragonkin and the land of Valindar, it probably lay with those twenty, but Chan wasn't sure what he could do for them. Would the Chief Critic let them live? Where could they go if they were freed from Throom Odin?

What a strange world this was, he thought to himself. Greeted with flowers and threats—what was he to make of it? He marveled at the contradictions as he turned his gaze on the bladed machine. Another contradiction—deadly, and yet it was also a fine piece of artwork, carved and polished and awesome.

Morkir, with his griffin strength, smashed the ballistas one by one and then returned to Chan's side. "Are you sure we can't rip the city apart? I feel like I still have some aggression to work off."

Chan shook his head as he stared around the square. Some of the citizens had run away, but to his surprise many still remained to see what would happen. The hungry ones, he realized. The hopeless ones who would have been happy to have even a bowl of snakes to eat.

"Look at them," he said to the griffin. "Do you really want to destroy their homes and what little they have? You've changed, my friend. Perhaps they can, too, in time."

"*Sumapai!*" Jake called from atop the dais where he still held Karnalis prisoner. Skymarin sat perched where Emissary had previously been on the back of the throne. "Are you enjoying your vacation in this scenic hotspot, or would you like to move on?"

Chan stretched his neck toward the dais. Karnalis, fearing he was going to be eaten, paled and threw himself back upon his throne and hugged a fat pillow while Jake climbed back into his saddle and fastened his leg-straps.

"You didn't fool me for a moment, you know," Chan said, "with that *Save me, your Munificence!* nonsense."

"I didn't have to fool you," Jake answered. Secure in his straps, he threw the sword down at Karnalis's feet. "I only had to fool the fool."

With Katrina on his back and wearing a bright red cloak, Morkir flew up to the top of the dais. "The sky is wide and far," he grumbled, but his meaning was clear.

Katrina rubbed a furred hand over the soft fabric of her new cloak. "And I'm really bored with where we are." She gave a short laugh. "But the shopping's not bad!"

"Then farewell to Throom Odin." Chan nodded to Skymarin, and the Lord of Eagles soared into the sky, leading the way. His thoughts turned once more to the Talisman, the Glass Dragon that they sought, and his heart began to race as he considered the adventure before them. "As for you, Karnalis," he continued, "I really don't care how you fare!"

Spreading his wings, he rose above the square. The wind felt fresh and free on his scaled face, and the strains of Jake's song echoed silently in his mind.

He felt like laughing.

14

WHILE THE PYRE IN THE CENTER OF STRONGHOLD continued to grow, Fortunato the Minotaur and his brothers stood by with burning torches awaiting a command from Sabu. With a nod, she gave it. The gathered citizens, some still grasping single, treasured phoenix feathers, fell silent. With immense dignity, Fortunato walked forward and thrust his torch as deeply into the pile as he could. His brothers did the same, moving to all sides of the great pyre, making sure that the wood ignited.

"Now stand back!" Sabu ordered when Fortunato and his brothers had done their part. "Everyone, enough ceremony! Stand back!" As the crowd fell away, she moved closer to Phoebe's pyre. Blue Ramoses moved to position himself on the opposite side while Harrow, Son of Stormfire took an honored place near the head of the last Phoenix. "Diana!" Sabu looked into the sky and summoned Ramoses cobalt daughter from among the ranks of Dragons flying overhead. "Since Luna has abandoned us, I ask you to take her place and be our fourth!"

With easy grace, Diana dropped to earth to stand at the foot of the pyre, but the look on her Dragon-face said she was not pleased. "Not even you, Sabu, has the right to speak ill of Luna!" Her silver eyes glared with anger as she spoke up for her friend. "Particularly to me. But I'll do my part."

Sabu snarled at Diana's impudence, and then turned her attention back to Phoebe's pyre. "Burn it!" she ordered. "Burn it, and don't stop until the flame dies in your throats!"

The torchfires were already beginning to spread through the wood, but their feeble, slow-flickering flames were swiftly engulfed in a violent conflagration as Sabu, Harrow, Ramoses, and Diana together breathed red-hot streams over Phoebe's pyre. Branches exploded under the sudden heat. Sparks shot into the dark sky, and citizens screamed in surprise and fright, throwing up their hands to protect their eyes and faces as a hot wave swept outward.

The four streams of fire blended into one blazing maelstrom. "Hotter!" Sabu cried, pausing just long enough to encourage the others. "This must be a fire like the world hasn't seen for centuries!" She opened her mouth, and the red flames she spat roared and crackled, strained toward blue, then white.

Ramoses, the oldest of all the surviving Dragonkin, faltered first. As his eyes unfocused and his flame failed, he lifted his head to draw a breath and tottered weakly backward.

Watchful Sabu noticed, and while Harrow and Diana continued, she paused and looked skyward again. "Fleer!" she called. "Replace Ramoses!" She stared at the old blue Dragon with kindness and gratitude. "You've done your part, Ramoses. Now rest and grow strong again. This fire must burn until dawn."

Nodding, Ramoses spread his wings and flew away to make room for emerald Fleer The green Dragon wasted no time with words, but opened his mouth wide and joined his fire with Harrow's and Diana's.

Sabu's heart pounded with furious pride as she observed the determination of the younger Dragons They didn't yet know what they were doing or why, but they sensed the importance and gave everything they had to give. *If only Chan was here,* she thought, *and if only Luna was here! If only . . .* She gave a sudden, choked cry as she thought a forbidden thought and remembered a forbidden memory. Then stubbornly, angrily, she thought it anyway. *If only all her children were with her now!*

But they weren't, and her flame faltered. With all her willpower and the last of her rapidly fading strength, she exhaled another blast and felt her fire dwindle to nothing. Her throat raw, she looked skyward again and spied Luna's sometime-mate. "Tiamat!" she shouted as she spread her wings and rose to surrender her place. "Tiamat, burn for two—Luna and you! Through dark of night til the sky turns blue! Engulf the pyre in Dragonfire!

Ruby Tiamat dived downward to take his turn. The fire reflected on his red scales, shimmered and danced on his powerful form until he looked himself like a pillar of flame. Snapping his wings wide, he lunged above the pyre and breathed potent destruction.

Almost in the same breath, Harrow and Diana failed. Sabu beckoned for them to join her in the sky. "Sakima! Kaos!" she called to another pair of Dragons. "Jade twins! From the green bowers of the Far East you came! You know my purpose! Breathe your flame!"

Harrow looked uncertain for a moment. Then, with stern concentration, he snapped his black wings wide. But the old wounds in the center of each pinion had not healed with the same black quality. The new tissue was pale, almost white, and the large scars shone like stars with radiating striations, as if they gave off light. With a savage cry, he leaped upward, following Diana, and for just a moment it seemed as if his wings would fail him. Then, with a powerful downbeat, Harrow soared!

"Well done, my good son!" Sabu cried, filled with joy to see Harrow whole once more. "Were we not in flight, I'd wrap my neck around yours and kiss you this night!" She directed her attention downward once more as the twins, Sakima and Kaos, joined their hottest fires with those of Fleer and Tiamat.

Harrow brushed one wingtip against his mother's wing. "What are we doing, Sabu?" he demanded. "We all loved Phoebe, but this pyre surpasses that of Stormfire, himself!"

"Your father, Stormfire, was a great leader of the Dragonkin," she answered. Then she paused, surprised by the depth of her bitterness and sarcasm. She softened, however, as she regarded the incredible blaze below. "But Phoebe is last of her kind, Harrow. The Last Phoenix in the World. Do you grasp the tragedy in that?"

Harrow hesitated, shocked by his mother's tone. Slowly, he nodded.

"Then hear me, my son," she said with the barest glance his way. The flames from below shimmered in the onyx blackness of her eyes and filled them with a frightening power. "It's a tragedy that need not be. Hear and remember always what you soon will see! The Dragon and the Phoenix have ever been—in more than name, we two are kin!"

She saw on her son's face that he didn't understand. Her rhymes and riddles made no sense to him. He even thought she might be mad—and perhaps she was! She heard again the anger in her voice that had so startled Harrow. *Stormfire was a great leader of the Dragonkin!*

Except he wasn't! To her, he was a monster, and this night she remembered why she'd refused to share his cave, why despair and sadness had kept her grounded and subdued for so long. *If you knew your father!* she thought. But Harrow didn't know him, not as she knew.

An explosion of wood below interrupted her memories and drew her attention back to Phoebe's pyre. Fleer coughed his last flame and flew away to make room for his replacement. Without waiting to be called, huge Paraclion took Fleer's place. His silver scales, like mirrors, caught the firelight and scattered it in rays that shot across Stronghold. Swelling his mighty chest and arching his neck, Paraclion joined his fire with the others'.

Sabu gazed eastward to the horizon. The first dim glow of coming dawn tinted the night and limned the leaves of the trees, but the sun was not yet in the sky. Something stirred within her, some awakening that brought both pain and ecstasy, and it was not done yet. Like the dawn, it rose out of blackness, growing stronger, brighter, taking form, until like some unfamiliar eye it stared back at her, and she saw. . . .

Herself.

Sabu, lost, but found.

"Hotter and hotter!" she cried, and as Tiamat faltered, she plunged down to take his place where she had stood before. Her wings snapped wide and her tail lashed behind her as she loomed above the pyre and let the flames lick and tongue her scaled face.

> *"Ancient Phoenix, hear our prayer*
> *As your spirit rides the air;*
> *Into heaven bear our songs!*
> *Find the ones we lost so long*
> *Ago. Seek them out and let them know—*
> *Bright as ash and ember,*
> *How we still remember*
> *Through the sorrow and regret,*
> *What the heart cannot forget!"*

With all her strength, Sabu poured forth her flame, and over the crackling rush she dreamed she heard Phoebe's voice and the song of the Last Phoenix in a sweeter time when the world was younger. Phoebe had been her friend once long ago, but out of grief and loneliness and loss,

Sabu had turned away, turned away from almost everyone and shut herself in her longhouse. Later, she would grieve again and weep for Phoebe. But not now. No, not now!

She faltered again, her fire failing her, and Snowsong descended to take her place. Sabu folded her wings this time and kept to the ground. Stronghold's citizens clustered around her as she backed away from Phoebe's pyre. The villagers looked tense and nervous. Though mesmerized by the soaring flames, they feared it. Their faces were sweating and reddened, and their pelts were singed. The leaves on the nearest trees were heat-shriveled, and the grass around the square was wilted, as were all the nearest flowerbeds and bushes.

"Beggin' pardon, Mother Sabu." Bear Brian stole up beside her and bowed his head as he spoke. "But what's it all about? Our homes are fair to burn if the wind shifts, what's left o' our homes, anyway. We give so much wood—our doors, our shutters, some of us even our porches an' stoops. An' we don't begrudge it none, cause we all loved our Phoebe. But it's got to mean somethin', cause we ain't never seen nothin' like this before!"

Sabu looked down at Bear Brian, then bent low and brought her Dragon face close to his. "That's because you're so young, Brian," she answered. "You've lived all your short lifetime in this forest. You never knew the lands beyond the Imagination Mountains or a time when magic flowed wild and free like rivers across the world."

She glanced toward the east again as she answered Bear Brian. The horizon had segued from black to purple to plum. The first rays of the sun were barely visible through the trees. Still, it's brightening light had not reached Stronghold's square. "Stand by me and watch," she continued in a voice filled with expectation. "And soon you'll see a sight not seen in Wyvernwood before!"

Bear Brian pressed his paws together as his large brown eyes moistened. "Can ye not tell a poor ol' bear, Mother?" he said. "Can ye not tell us all? We hear the hope in yer voice, an' we could all use a little hope right now, an' some understandin', too"

"Wait," Sabu urged with new gentleness as she stared into the fire. "Watch!"

Sakima and Kaos surrendered their posts to Maximor and Starfinder. Then Tiamat returned to take Paraclion's place. *So few of us remain,* Sabu thought to herself. She studied the skies and the Dragons circling over-head. Once, the skies were full of Dragons. *Our Age has passed, and we will pass, and none will remember that we ever were.* Perfectly still, yet aware of the villagers watching her and her Dragonkin watching her as well, she gazed into the fire and saw visions from days gone by, faces of friends dimly remembered, of battles and happier times.

Of Dragon-children.

At last the sun touched the tops of the trees, and light poured forth like a slow-spreading stain from the edge of the woods, across the village, to the edge of the square. "Watch now!" Sabu urged as sunlight touched Dragonfire. "Watch, and tell me there's no magic left in the world!"

Ramoses landed behind her on the canyon rim, and the Dragon Diana landed beside him. As if acting on some forgotten instinct, all the Dragons descended, landing where they could find room on the rim, around the village, or at the forest edge.

On Phoebe's funeral pyre, sunlight and Dragonfire intermixed and churned. Red flames turned blue, then white, and the crackling rose to a deafening rush and roar. Ash and sparks swirled and funneled straight up to wink starlike in the night and disappear.

A soft and solemn sound came from the canyon rim, and all eyes turned briefly toward Ramoses as the old Dragon began to sing. No words to his song, just vocalizations and hums in strange keys and sooth-ing rhythms. Sabu knew the song—it was very old, older even than

Wyvernwood itself—and she joined her voice to his as she had joined her fire to his before. Then Diana surprised her, for she knew the song, too. One by one, the Dragons picked it up as well. On the far side of the pyre, Sabu looked at Harrow, and he looked back. She never loved him more or felt more proud of him.

Then she couldn't see him at all.

Phoebe's pyre exploded in a tempest of flame and light. A collective gasp went up from the villagers, and many cringed away, covering their eyes. But the Dragonkin continued to sing, and Bear Brian called out. "Don't hide!" he shouted fiercely. "Mother Sabu says to open yer eyes and see a piece o' the old world! Look, I tell ye!"

They straightened and looked, stepped as close as they dared and stared deep into the fire, though it hurt their eyes. Some, particularly the musically gifted Satyrs, even picked up the Dragons' song and did their best to merge their voices into it.

In the very heart of the blaze, something moved, a shape barely perceptible through the white brightness of the shifting, dancing flames. The fire seemed to swirl around it, form it and caress it. Within that white heat it lifted a slender head and displayed wings of fire and flame.

"It's Phoebe!" someone shouted, and others took it up. "She's alive! Rising from the flames! From her own ashes!" Unable to contain their excitement, the villagers cheered, and hugged each other. Some even knelt down and wept for joy.

The shape at the center of the fire lifted its head higher and gave a piercing screech.

A second shivering screech answered.

Deep within the flames, another shape moved, as large and as awesome as its twin. As the first one had, it lifted its head and drew breath, inhaling the flames as if they were life. Stretching, testing its new form, it arched its wings high. Without distinct outlines, it was impossible to tell where bird and fire separated. The flames danced wildly, and the birds writhed with the miracle of birth.

The villagers had fallen silent, expectant. "There's two!" Bear Brian murmured in wonder. "Two Phoebes!"

Sabu used her tail to draw some of the villagers closer. They had watched. Now it was time to learn. "That is not Phoebe," she told them. "Phoebe is dead." The joy on their faces turned to confusion. They stared at the shapes and back at Sabu. "Every Phoenix, from the point of maturity, carries within themselves one egg. But this egg can't be hatched like a normal egg."

Only in the throes of death could a Phoenix fertilize its one egg, and if it died alone its egg died with it shortly after. But the Dragon and the Phoenix shared a bond. Although any fire might cremate the parent, only Dragonfire could incubate the egg through one long night and give it life.

It wasn't efficient. It was one of the great, mysteries of nature that one species should be so dependent upon another.

And here is another mystery! Sabu thought as she marveled at the sight of Phoebe's twins. *No, not a mystery—a miracle!*

One after the other, the new-born birds rose from the flames, ready to fly, eager to test their wings and explore the world. With a shimmer of red and gold plumage, they turned toward the sun, and side by side they flew away.

The startled villagers called after them, but Sabu shook her head. Now she could grieve for Phoebe, but there would be tears of joy, too. "They'll be back," she said.

The pyre quickly dwindled to sparkling ash. As the morning continued to brighten, the villager drifted off to home and bed, and most of the Dragons to their caves. It would take a lot of work to restore the square to its former condition. The verdant grass that once grew there would probably never grow again.

Standing watch over the smoke and ash, Sabu glanced toward the bare foundation of her longhouse and laughed to herself. She felt young again and powerful. Yet, at the same time she felt as if she'd just fulfilled her purpose.

She didn't know what to do.

Harrow landed beside her and displayed his scarred wings. *Not scarred,* she told herself as she looked at him. *Artful. His wings are full of stars.* "Harrow," she said, "Starflyer."

"I don't need a new name," Harrow answered quietly. He stared toward the sun and the east. "I'm thinking of Phoebe. She never spoke of it, but I know she was lonely." Sabu could only nod. In her heart, she knew it, too. "It must be terrible to be the last," he continued in a soft voice. "I'm glad that these two will have each other."

"Castor," she said as she thumped the ground with her tail. "And Pollux. I've already named them." She shrugged her Dragon shoulders.

"You seem to be in a naming mood." Harrow winked and gave her a nudge. "I like those. I certainly like them better than Starflyer."

The breeze blew little eddies among the gray ash. Though the ground still gave off heat, not so much as a spark remained. "I'm glad that I have you," she said, nudging him back. *And Chan and Luna, too, wherever they are.*

15

LUNA CALLED ARIEL'S NAME OVER AND OVER AGAIN, Dragon tears spilling from her eyes as she flew in frantic circles over the spot where her young rider had fallen. The ripples still marked the exact place, and yet she spied no sign of the child! She gazed toward the shore, hoping Ariel had managed to swim there, but it was false hope.

The red glare from the burning Degarm ships spread across the water like a bloodstain, and thick smoke drifted over the waves. The bobbing debris confused her. Desperately, she darted past broken planks and shattered crates, praying to find Ariel clinging to something. But that hope proved as empty as the shoreline!

She blamed herself! What foolish compulsion had made her bring a child into a battle zone? "Ariel!" she screamed. Out of rage, she struck the surface with her tail, using all her force. Flotsam shot into the air, riding the monumental splash, and rained down again to be swept downstream by the powerful current.

The current!

Snatching at a faint new hope, Luna turned and flew at her greatest speed, watching the river as she skimmed its surface, studying the banks on either shore. The waves gleamed with strange black oil that exuded a sweet odor like lavender and dill. Yet Luna pushed it from her mind. Nothing mattered in the black, wet night but to find her wounded friend!

But it soon became clear that Ariel had not been swept downstream, and Stormfire's daughter raced back again, guided by the flickering light of the still-burning ships. She cursed herself again, and she cursed Degarm, then Angmar, too. Damn them and their war! Why couldn't the race of Man just leave the Dragonkin alone? Why couldn't they leave Wyvernwood in peace?

What would she have to do to just make them stop?

Drawing a mighty breath, she exhaled fire, hoping that in its brief light she might spy Ariel. The child had been in the water so long, if she was still in the water at all. The fleeting glimpse of the evil arrow in the little girl's back haunted and angered her. On outspread wings, she glided over the one remaining ship that, though it burned, still floated. There was no sign in the water of the sailors that crewed the vessel, but it didn't matter to her. The ship was the symbol of all she hated now.

"Murderers and monsters!" she cried.

Using her tail as a great club, she smashed the dying vessel into flaming kindling, hastening its demise, killing it with an unbridled savagery, and when the deed was done she shot a look around for a man—just one man—to whom she might do the same. She thought of the female captain and gave a roar that echoed across the lake and down the river. If Ariel was gone, at least she had taken one foe with her!

But to Luna that offered no comfort. She began to weep again as despair filled her heart. *If Ariel was gone. . . .* How would she explain it to little Pear? To the boys, Markham and Trevor? To Gregor and Carola or to anyone in Stronghold? Ariel couldn't be gone! She just couldn't be! In desperation she flew up and down the length of the lake again and back and forth across it, skimming the waves, searching the banks.

But it was no use. Exhausted, she finally landed on the eastern shore and cried with great, wracking sobs. Never had she known such bleak despondency, such hopelessness, not even when her father, Stormfire, had died. The loss of Ariel seemed greater somehow, a deeper wound, for the little girl had been her responsibility, and Luna had failed her.

> *"Hush, my little one,*
> *Don't you cry.*
> *The moon will find us*
> *By and by.*
> *Close your eyes;*
> *Don't make a peep.*
> *The stars will guard us*
> *While we sleep."*

Luna opened one eye and wiped away a few of her tears with a paw as she listened. The night grew still again, except for the soft lapping of the waves. What song was that? Where had it come from? Had she heard it at all or just imagined it?

> *"Pirate ships*
> *Are pretty and bold,*
> *With chests of jewels,*
> *Coins, and gold.*
> *But all that wonder*
> *Has no charms*
> *Compared to the treasure*
> *In my arms!"*

"Who's there?" Luna called, her voice little more than a harsh, strained whisper. She had no doubt now. It wasn't the lapping waves or the wind on the water, but a song as sweet as any she'd ever heard, a lullaby coming from. . . . She couldn't tell from where. From everywhere, it seemed, and from nowhere. Looking up and down the shore, she called again, "Who's there? Who's singing that song?" Then a dark suspicion crossed her mind, and she snarled. "If you're one of the sailors, then I'll find you and grind you into the mud!"

> "Gentle dreams
> Will fill your sleep,
> Dragon dreams,
> So soft and deep.
> Go to sleep,
> My precious child.
> I'll sleep beside you
> In a while."

The strains of the song and the easy voice of the singer melted Luna's anger. It was no soldier, no sailor, singing. It was a mother somewhere in the darkness rocking and reassuring her child, calming and lulling it.

The song stopped, or at least the words stopped. But the melody continued as a peaceful humming for some moments. Luna half rose, stretching out her neck. Even the river seemed to have grown placid. Not a burning splinter remained, and the wisps of smoke that lingered seemed almost to waltz upon the water.

The night was silent once again, but still she looked and looked for the singer.

A voice spoke close by. "Looked for, I cannot be found, Daughter of Stormfire." A pebble dropped into the water with a quiet splash right in front of Luna, catching her attention. The voice spoke again. "Watched for, I will not be seen."

Luna closed her eyes and tilted her ivory-scaled head ever so slightly. A Dragon's hearing was also very sharp, but she detected no footsteps, no rustle of garments, not even a breath—only the water, and the wind, and the sound of her own heartbeat in her ears. "I prefer your songs to riddles," she said, but not unkindly. For the moment, it didn't matter who the mother was or where she was, or even that she seemed to know Luna's name. Luna welcomed her company. Drawing a deep breath, she sighed. "It was most unfair of you to sing so sweetly for I've lost a friend tonight."

"What one loses another may find," the mother answered. Though soft-spoken, her voice was as deep and rich and soothing as her song. "Ariel is here with me."

A susurrus of sound, a troubled respiration, touched Luna's ear and caused her to turn her head. She opened her eyes, and the darkness at her feet seemed to part like a veil. A tall, thin figure stood at the water's edge beside her, almost completely concealed in a voluminous cloak and hood. Yet even through such robes she possessed an air of femininity and grace and confidence.

With gentle, loving care she held Ariel cradled in her arms.

Luna didn't question how this strange woman had managed to creep up beside her. Perhaps she'd been there all along, hidden somehow from Luna's Dragon senses. How that could be, she didn't know. Nothing seemed to make sense at the moment.

All that mattered to her was Ariel. "Is she all right?" she whispered, bending and bringing her face close to the ground. She shot a glance at the woman, hoping for a look of reassurance, and was startled to see nothing but blackness inside the enfolding hood. "Is she alive?"

The hood moved up and down—a nod. "No and yes," the woman answered. She hugged Ariel, pressing the little girl's head to her shoulder, rocking her with a delicate strength. Luna noted the woman's hands, the slim fingers gnarled with age.

"My name is Agriope," the woman said, anticipating Luna's next question. She seemed to look down at Ariel again and to press her hidden face to the child's pale cheek. "She sleeps now," Agriope explained. "I removed the arrow, but the shaft struck deeply. . . . "

"I searched and searched . . . !" Luna interrupted.

Agriope was as quick to interrupt. "She'll die unless you act, Daughter of Stormfire."

Luna arched her neck and snapped her wings wide "Unless I act?" she cried as her eyes filled with tears again. "My actions got her shot! She's hurt because of me!"

Agriope shook her head. "All possible roads have brought Ariel to this place at this moment," she said quietly. Then she looked up, revealing just a hint of a wrinkled chin in the starlight. "But you stand at a crossroads, Luna, Stormfire's daughter. You must make a choice."

Luna wiped her tears with a paw. "A choice?"

Agriope shifted Ariel's limp form, nestling the sleeping girl's head to her breast as she stroked and rocked and brushed back a lock of hair. Blood and brown mud caked the old hand. Ariel's blood. "To let this child die, or risk your own life to save her. And I cannot see the outcome."

Luna's pulse quickened. Whatever the risk, she'd do anything to save Ariel. She didn't understand the power of the bond she felt with the little acrobat, but she couldn't deny it, and if she understood nothing else—if Stormfire had taught her nothing else—she understood responsibility.

And yet, could she trust a woman who wouldn't show her face? Agriope spoke as if she could see the future.

Again, Agriope anticipated Luna. "I know your doubts," she said. With exquisite gentleness, she knelt and eased Ariel down onto the grassy bank. Ariel moaned, and a look of dulled pain turned up the corners of her small mouth, but she didn't wake. Agriope brushed a fingertip over Ariel's temple and pushed back another lock of hair before she rose again and reached into a pocket of her cloak. "Take this," she said, extending an object to Luna.

Bending low again, Luna reached out. A Dragon's paw wasn't made for holding delicate things, but she pinched the small mirror between her claws and held it tight. What she saw brought a small gasp—her own ivory face, golden eyes that sparkled even in the darkness, a sleek nose and proud, almost horn-like ears. She'd seen herself in clear water before and in polished bits of metal. But she'd never seen herself so clearly.

"You want to know who I am," Agriope said, "and *what* I am. Then use the mirror, Luna, and look at my reflection." Raising both gnarly hands, she slipped the hood away from her face and head. "But do not look at me directly."

With an uncertain sense of dread, Luna angled the mirror and gasped. The mirror slipped from her grasp, struck the ground, broke.

Agriope pulled her hood back into place and looked away. "Now you know that I have many eyes," she said. "And each pair sees the different roads that lie before us."

Luna swallowed, her mind still recoiling from the vision she had seen, from the improbable horror. That seething, writhing mass! She squeezed her eyes shut and swallowed again. "What about my road?" she asked. "You said I had a choice. What do I have to do to save Ariel?"

Agriope knelt down again, and then sat and lifted Ariel's head into her lap. "I've packed her wound with herbs and with the mud of Wyvernwood," she answered. "But she's beyond my medicines. Yet if you have courage then there's one hope."

"Anything!" Luna said. "Tell me!"

Agriope swept a hand over the grass and found a shard of the broken mirror. With great care she tore strips of cloth from her cloak, and then twisted and twisted them into one fine cord as she spoke. "Deep in the bowels of Redclaw you'll find what she needs." Around and around the sharp corners of the mirror she wrapped her cord. "My mirror will guide you." She held up the ends of the cord. The shard gleamed like a medallion full of starlight, and the ends of the cord were long enough to encircle Luna's neck.

But Luna hesitated. "Redclaw?" The word came out as a hiss. "My brother, Harrow, nearly died at Redclaw! The Griffinkin have claimed it as their fortress!"

"Nevertheless, it's there you'll find Ariel's only hope." She tied the ends of the cord together and offered it to Luna. "Indeed, the only hope for many of us."

A shift in the starlight, perhaps a wisp of cloud passing by, caused the lake surface to glimmer. It drew Luna's attention. For a long moment, she gazed outward, uncertain of what she saw—dots of silveriness here and there, not gleams of light, not wave caps

Fish. Hundreds of dead fish, rising to the surface, riding the current to the shorelines, sliding downstream. Luna's heart lurched as she remembered the female captain's threat and the strange oil she'd noticed with the faint scents like lavender and dill. That same sweet odor still lingered in the air, not lavender and dill at all really, something unfamiliar—and deadly.

Poison in the water, in the Blackwater River, the main artery of Wyvernwood! Luna's jaw gaped, and she wrapped her wings around herself to ward off the chill that shivered through her. It didn't help. "It's my fault!" she breathed, barely able to speak the words. "If I hadn't stopped them. . . .!"

Then, Luna raised her head and roared. The chill she felt turned hot, and despair gave way to rage.

It wasn't her fault!

A dead fish bobbed on a wave and rode up onto the shoreline at her feet. Its round, glassy eye fixed on her, and in its lifeless gaze she found a small measure of absolution. She'd stopped the Degarm vessels to prevent them from using Wyvernwood as a route to war. If she hadn't acted, they would have continued into Angmar and dumped their evil cargo there, but the poisons still would have made their way back down the Blackwater River and into Wyvernwood.

She roared again. The poison had a sweet scent, almost an enticing one. It would spread down the river, into the branches and tributaries. The citizens of the forest would come to drink—and die. In time, the poison would dilute and weaken. But how long would that take? How many would be lost?

She owed Agriope an apology, for when she saw the woman's reflection her first thought had been, *horror*! Yet through Agriope's outward appearance kindness and compassion still shone. Here, in the Blackwater River, was true horror—a pollution that would destroy the land and those who lived in it.

Ariel had said Degarm had no such poisons, but Ariel was a child.

"I'll go to Redclaw," Luna declared. "If there's any hope there, any remedy at all, I'll tear the place down stone by stone to find it and bring it back! But tell me, Agriope, what I'm looking for?"

But the old woman didn't answer. Luna looked down at the spot where Agriope had been, but she was gone, and so was Ariel. From a distance, somewhere and nowhere, she heard the faint humming of a familiar melody, and then a few snippets of words.

> *"Hush, my little one,*
> *Don't you cry.*
> *The moon will find us*
> *By and by."*

Luna remembered her own face, ivory and pale, in Agriope's mirror. "I'm that moon," she whispered, "and I will find you soon. I promise!" She picked up the mirror shard and the coil of cord that Agriope had left lying on the grass and slipped it over her head and around her neck. She didn't know what she was looking for, but the shard would be her guide. Agriope had said so, and that was enough.

With grim determination, she silently spread her wings and flew into the sky. Redclaw lay north and east of the Blackwater River near the border with Angmar. With or without the shard, she knew the way. She scanned the horizon and spied a lone owl on a late-hour nocturnal hunt. Dawn was not far off; it's timid light was just beginning to peek above the rim of the world.

What would Angmar think, she wondered as she raced above the forest, if they knew how she'd saved them?

Harrow hadn't visited Ramoses in his cave for a long time, but though it was well into the morning hour it didn't surprise him to find the old blue Dragon still awake and pouring over his books. "Sabu has taken Stormfire's cave for her own and settled in," he said. Ramoses barely looked up and nodded, and then returned to his texts.

The first-hatched son of Stormfire studied his old teacher in the flickering light from the hearth. The blue scales were fading, losing their color, and they grew thin in places across his Dragon shoulders. He hadn't thought of Ramoses as his teacher in years, but he'd known the old Dragon all of his life, and a sudden surprising wave of affection washed over Harrow.

"What are you reading?" he asked.

Ramoses seemed not to hear, but then he folded his paws across the pages of the large bound book on his desk and gazed at Harrow. He blinked as if to focus his eyes, and then he beckoned Harrow closer. "The very earliest entries in the *Book of Stormfire*," he answered. "I'm troubled by some passages."

There were many books on the shelves in Ramoses cave, but only the volumes that made up the *Book of Stormfire* seemed to interest him these days. He read from them constantly, made new notes in the margins, and added new pages. They represented his life's work, he said, for he'd dedicated himself to recording the deeds and words and thoughts of the Dragonkin's greatest leader.

Harrow approached the desk and leaned closer. The fireplace cast a reddish-yellow light that wavered over the scrawling black handwriting that covered the pages. In that soft shimmer, the words and sentences seemed to move and shift. It was an amusing illusion.

Then Harrow leaned closer still. "I've never seen these pages!" he murmured. "The writing isn't even yours! It's barely legible!"

"This is your father's own hand," Ramoses explained. "At first, he tried to set down this history himself, but his claws were large and strong and clumsy." He glanced at Harrow and rolled one eye with a hint of embarrassment. "So I took the pen for him and wrote what he dictated." He fell silent as he looked at the scrawl and seemed to forget that Harrow was still there.

Harrow's heart swelled as he stared at the script—his father's own writing! What a treasure! He longed to run his claw over it, to trace the loops and swirls, to follow the undisciplined patterns, but when he reached out Ramoses brushed his paw away.

"So what is the passage that troubles you?" Harrow asked with poorly concealed disappointment.

The old Dragon frowned. Leaning back on his haunches, he scratched the tip of his nose with one claw and sighed. "These talismans," he said after a pause. "Your father rarely spoke of them, and so little is known directly."

"I read what was in the books with Chan and Luna," Harrow reminded him, nodding. It was true there hadn't been a lot of information, but they'd gleaned what they could.

"I thought these older notes and scribblings might shed more light," Ramoses continued. "I've been pouring over them since Chan left." He tapped the page and turned the book toward Harrow. "I found this."

Harrow frowned at the mention of Chan's name. He wasn't jealous of his brother, but it was he, not Chan, who should have undertaken the search for the first talisman. His injured wings were healing and growing stronger everyday, and he'd secretly dreamed of making a journey some-day into the west.

He squinted as he studied the writing, and then turned the book back toward Ramoses. "I can't read any of this," he said with some irritation. "My father was leader, but apparently not much of a writer."

"He was a fine writer," Ramoses shot back defensively. "You've read his poetry." But then he relented and tapped the page again. "It was his pen-manship that blew cold ashes."

Chuckling, Harrow straightened and glanced around the cave. He felt tired after the events of the long night, but also restless. Something nagged at him, some unexplainable prickling sensation in his wings that made no sense. He dismissed it as part of the healing process and pushed it to the back of his mind.

"So did you find anything, Old Lizard?" he asked, prodding Ramoses. "You can read it. What's it say?"

A long moment passed with the gentle crackling from the fireplace the only sound. Ramoses sat perfectly still, head down above the book. Har-row pursed his Dragon lips and thumped his tail lightly on the cave floor.

Thinking Ramoses had fallen asleep, he started to nudge his elder.

Then Ramoses licked the tip of one claw and turned one page. "Here," he said quietly. He read:

> *"One will be sought;*
> *One will be given;*
> *One will be found without looking.*

"Riddles!" Harrow scowled. He hated riddles. "Are you sure it refers to the talismans?"

Setting a maple leaf on the page to mark his place, Ramoses gently closed the book. "I'm not sure of anything," he answered as he rubbed his eyes. "Even your father's choice of verbs confounds me. Is it *will* be sought or *must* be sought? *Will* be given or *must be given*? Do these lines even refer to the talismans?" He slammed his paw down upon the book's cover with enough force to shake the desk. "Confound it!"

"There are three talismans," Harrow said, trying to calm Ramoses. He wondered where his daughter, Diana, was and why she wasn't here to insist he go to bed, but he'd keep the old Dragon company a while longer and perhaps see to that task himself. "And three of us. Maybe Chan shouldn't have gone looking for these things alone."

Ramoses shot him a sly look. "You don't fool me, Harrow Stormfire-son. You've got your wings back now, and you're just looking for an excuse to go off on another adventure of your own. Redclaw taught you nothing!" He froze as if stunned by his own vehemence. Then he rubbed his eyes again. "I'm sorry," he said. "I'm tired and worried—and I shouldn't be." Forcing a Dragon smile, he looked up. "Did you see, Harrow? Phoebe's children! Two! Do you believe in omens, Harrow?"

Harrow stared at Ramoses. He was the oldest surviving Dragon, older than Sabu, older than Stormfire, and looking at him, Harrow couldn't shake the sudden terrible feeling that the old blue Dragon's time was near. The Age of Dragons was passing, and it was taking Ramoses with it.

"I've heard of omens, "Harrow answered cautiously, "but there's no more magic in the world. You've told me so, yourself."

Slowly, Ramoses shook his head and stared toward the sunlight beyond the mouth of his cave. "I was wrong," he whispered. He turned away from Harrow, his one-time student. "Now leave me, please. Sleep steals upon me."

Harrow watched as Ramoses crawled into the corner of the cave where he made his bed. The old one lay down with his golden eyes open, focused on the shelves and shelves of books that lined his walls. After a few more moments, those eyes closed. Ramoses let out a gentle snore and with it a gray puff of smoke from his nostrils.

Sleep well, Harrow wished his teacher. *May youthful dreams fill your head, and may you know that you're loved by all of us.*

He left Ramoses then and, and stretching wide his healing wings, glided away from the cave and outward over the canyon. The wind rushed beneath his wings and against his face, a delicious sensation that made him glad to be a Dragon. Yet still he felt the prickling.

Something was wrong. How he knew, he couldn't say, but the same wind that heartened him also whispered *danger* in his ears. He gazed around, taking note of a pair of Dragons, Diana and Fleer, flying guard over Stronghold.

Then down the canyon, flying as fast as its small, feathered wings could carry it, came an owl. With a sharp screech it strafed his nose, then plummeted toward the shore of the Echo Rush below and landed on the sandy beach. Harrow dived after it.

"Wise old bird!" Harrow called as he settled in the sand close by. "You fly like a rabbit in a windstorm! Your talons nearly raked my tender snout!"

The owl took a step, faltered, and flopped over on its side from exhaustion. "Doooon't drink!" he hooted. Pain filled his voice, and something more—fear. "The water! Doooon't drink!"

Harrow frowned. "What are you hooting about, you crazy bird? What do you mean, *don't drink*? What about the water?" Without waiting for an answer from the weary fowl, Harrow dipped his paw in the water of the Echo Rush and flicked the red tip of his tongue over it. "There's nothing wrong with the water!"

"Sooooon!" the owl answered as it struggled upright again. "In all the rivers, all the streams. Downward it comes on current and wave. Dead fish everywhere. In Grendleton are dead Wyrms because they drank! Deer and moose, dead from their morning quaff! Birds dead from bathing! Snakes, crawfish, water striders!" He shrugged and rolled his large, round eyes. "But who-who-who cares about water striders?"

Bending closer, Harrow lifted the owl on a wingtip so he could look the little fellow in the eye. If what he said was true, this owl was a hero. "You raced here to bring us this news?"

The owl shrugged again. "Well, no-no-no," he admitted. "I hurried to bring news of beloved Luna, Stormfire's daughter. No-no-no Dragon so lovely as Luna! Precious and beautiful is Luna! She makes my heart pound!" He blinked, rolled his eyes, and fluffed his wings to shake the sand from them. "But this wise bird thought you should know-know-know about the water, too-too-too!"

Harrow growled, wondering how much of the owl's story to believe and how much was a bird's over-excited imagination. Clearly, though, he'd seen something to cause him fright.

Suddenly, the scales on his neck rose, and he felt that irritating prickling he been feeling all morning. "What about my sister?" he demanded. "Where's Luna?"

"Too-too-too terrible to tell!" the owl answered. "Swift as a shooting star she flies, and straight her course for Griffinhold!"

"Griffinhold?" Harrow shouted. "Do you mean Redclaw?"

The owl shrugged and blinked its gimbal-eyes. "You say tomato, and I say tomahto."

Tossing the owl into the air, Harrow gave a violent roar and shot skyward. Up over the canyon rim he rose, flashing past the rooftops of Stronghold and the startled citizens below. Diana and Fleer glanced his way, but he wasted no time explaining.

Now he knew the cause of the prickling in his wings. He twisted his head from one side to the other, glaring at the white star-shaped scars where stakes the size of tree trunks had pinned him to the earth. All the shock and pain, the bitter memories, rushed back upon him, but he only used it to drive himself faster.

No matter what, he wouldn't let the same thing happen to his sister!

16

FROM HIS HIGH MOUNTAIN PERCH, Ronaldo spied the oncoming ship and took to the air with an angry snarl. In the woods below the mountain slope, watchful Angmaran sailors with their eyes ever on the sky quickly scattered and hid themselves beneath trees and under bushes. If they truly thought they could hide from him, then they were fools, but he would deal with them later.

He glided down the slope and toward the beach. Only then, did he notice something strange about the approaching ship. He might have flown straight out to the vessel and destroyed it anyway. He was determined to wreck and burn all Angmaran ships that passed near Thursis. Yet on a whim, he climbed higher to observe this one. He could smash it at his leisure.

As he reached the apex of his climb, he looked down again. The vast blue sea rolled beneath him, and as he twisted his neck around to locate the oncoming ship fire welled in his throat. He wondered if its crew had seen him yet, and he considered announcing himself with a fiery blast.

But then Ronaldo swallowed his fire. Tilting his wings and banking on the wind, he stared downward again and squinted in surprise at what he saw. *There was something strange about the approaching ship!* Though the wind was against it, still it advanced at a rapid pace. Stranger yet, it sliced through the water on neither sail, nor oar.

A harder look revealed the reason why. Ronaldo caught his breath. In all his life he'd never seen a creature like the one that towed the ship. All green and golden in the sparkling sunlit sea, it seemed almost invisible at certain angles, and its sleekly rippling form mimicked the very motion of the waves as it plunged ahead.

Whatever it was, the creature was magnificent. Its scales, though brightly colored, were not unlike his own. Even the shape of its head and the features of its face screamed *Dragon*! It belonged to the sea, and he to the air, and yet he sensed a kinship with it immediately—a cousin found!

It would make a splendid ally against the might of Angmar!

He tilted his wings again, changed course, and put the sun at his back. His distorted shadow flashed over the white sand beach, over the foamy surf, and all along the water's edge. Like a faithful dark companion it paced him. Adjusting his position to the sun, he sent his shadow out across the bay like a messenger to greet his newfound Dragonkin.

Then, beating his wings, he pulled up sharply in midair and changed his course again. Once more he looked over his shoulder and downward, and on the ship's deck in its bow, he saw he—*Marian*!

She'd found a way to Thursis after all, and more swiftly than he'd thought possible even for her. Resourceful Marian! He smiled to himself. Now that he'd secured the island and made it safe he was quite glad to see her.

The ship slipped into the bay. Heavy chains clanked, and a large anchor made a splash. Looking past Marian, Ronaldo searched the rest of the deck and scowled at the sight of four Angmarans near the rails. *Four more vermin to infest my island*, he thought. He'd take care of them all soon enough, and then he'd set about cleansing Thursis and healing it again.

Another splash drew his attention as he banked yet again. This time, he spread his wings wide and, making a shallow descent, glided toward the beach. Marian, having abandoned the ship's deck, swam with a powerful effort through the waves. The sunlight shone like fire on her golden horn as she achieved the shore, walked up onto the sand, and shook the water from her gleaming white coat.

Ronaldo's shadow rippled over the place where she stood as he landed. "I didn't expect to see you so soon!" he called with a Dragon-grin. The grin quickly faded as she spun to face him.

"You fatherless son of a nightcrawling earthworm!" she snorted. "You spawn of a prematurely hatched egg! In all your Dragon years you haven't seen the day you can outwit me, and there's no place in the world you can go where I can't follow!" Tossing her wet mane, she flung saltwater droplets in his face. "You left me!"

Stung by the anger of his friend, Ronaldo hesitated. His jaw gaped, and he licked his lips. He'd never seen Marian so angry, nor had he seen such a dangerous look in her blue eyes. Then his gaze narrowed as he felt his own anger rise. "I protected you," he answered.

She shot a look at the wrecked camp further up the beach. "And who protected you, Ronaldo?"

The Gray Dragon bristled. "Don't call me by that name," he warned.

Marian gave a short laugh and kicked at the sand. "Fine!" she said. "Right now I have a whole wide range of names to call you!"

Ronaldo dug his claws into the sand and turned his head away and gazed over the harbor as Marian recited a list of colorful nomenclature. There was no sign of the green and gold creature that had towed the Angmaran ship, and he frowned in disappointment, but in its bow he spied the four sailors he'd noticed before. They were watching him, talking among themselves, and pointing.

He couldn't guess what arrangement Marian had made with Angmar to convince them to ferry her to Thursis, but the very presence of an Angmaran ship in his bay offended him. Marian wasn't yet aware of how they'd murdered the Mers and poisoned the island, so he could forgive her rudeness, but that ship and those Men were a different matter.

With a powerful beat of his wings, Ronaldo rose into the air. Sand whipped around Marian, and she averted her head from the worst of it. "Come back here!" she demanded. "Where are you going?"

"To spit fire in the face of my enemy," Ronaldo answered as he turned toward the anchored vessel. He smiled grimly to himself as he watched the four sailors stumble back from the railing. He circled the crippled ship once and drew a deep breath. Fire churned in his throat.

Marian ran down to the water's edge and reared. "Finback!" she cried. "Stop him!"

Without warning, the green and golden Finback shot up out of the sea right beneath Ronaldo. The ship pitched from side to side, sending the four sailors sprawling, and still the creature rose, all head and impossibly long neck, faster than Ronaldo could react. Its hard snout struck him in the chest with the force of a battering ram, knocking him higher into the air and away from the ship.

Stunned, Ronaldo fell toward the sea, but he recovered before he hit the water, spread his wings and swerved back into the sky. The creature called Finback glared at him with a challenging look, and Ronaldo glared back. With an angry roar, he let loose a blast of flame.

With astonishing grace and speed, Finback slipped back into the sea, and Ronaldo's blast shot harmlessly over his green-scaled head. But an instant later, he shot upward again. Silvery eyes flashing, he opened his mouth and unleashed a powerful spray of water that smashed the Gray Dragon from the sky.

Ronaldo hit the waves on his back, sputtering as he struggled to orient himself and take to the sky again, but before he could rise coil after green-scaled coil wrapped around him, trapping his wings, pinning him. With another roar, he opened his mouth and prepared to burn Finback, but Finback shot another forceful spray straight down his throat.

Ronaldo reeled, choking and unable to draw breath as his foe contracted his coils and squeezed him. With his talons, he tried to rake Finback, but already he felt his strength ebbing, and Finback's scales were as tough as his own or any Dragon's. On the edge of consciousness, beaten for the first time in his life, he felt himself dragged through the water and finally deposited on the sandy beach.

Finback had released him, and he drew labored breaths, but he lacked the strength yet to rise. Marian appeared near his head. "Ronaldo?" she said. Her concern sounded genuine.

"Rage," he gasped. "The Dragon Rage."

Marian looked askance. "Whatever," she answered. "What have you done here?"

Ronaldo, called Rage, drew a painful breath and sat up on his haunches with his tail curled around his legs. "What have I done?" he answered bitterly. "Look around, Unicorn. This is Thursis—have you seen a single Mer?" He glared at Marian and flexed one wing experimentally. "We thought Angmar had imprisoned them. But they've murdered them, everyone. Poisoned the rivers. The entire island is slowly dying!"

From the water at the edge of the shore, Finback raised his great head. "Your friend may be right," the Sea Serpent said as he studied Ronaldo. "I told you the Mers I saw were sick."

Marian paced back and forth in agitation. Ronaldo watched her, feeling somewhat foolish, but unwilling to admit it. He cast a suspicious glance at Finback, too, unable quite to accept that the creature had defeated him with such ease. No, not defeated—humiliated.

"We'll search every crevice and cranny of this place before we leap to any more conclusions," Marian finally announced. "Finback, scour the sea around the island. But bring those four sailors on the ship ashore first. Ronaldo and I. . . . "

"Rage," Ronaldo corrected.

"Whatever," Marian repeated with a roll of her eyes. "We'll turn this island upside-down and shake it until all its secrets fall out. And now I've got one more question." She trained a hard blue gaze on the Gray Dragon. "Where's Bumble?"

Ronaldo—Rage—looked startled, then thought for a moment. He rubbed his chin with one paw as he tried to remember when he'd last seen the little hummingbird. "I don't know," he admitted.

Marian muttered and mumbled in an unpleasant tone.

"What's that?" the Gray Dragon asked with a puzzled look.

Finback shook his head and gave a wink. "The lost language of Unicorns," he said. "I think she just found it again."

Ronaldo studied the Sea Serpent with a sidewise glance. Though he still wasn't happy about losing a fight, he felt again the strange sense of kinship with Finback. "If you ask me," he said, "I think it should stay lost."

Finback twitched his whiskers, then with a flip of his golden dorsal crest, he slipped back into the sea. Ronaldo—Rage—feeling stronger, rose to stand and stretched his wings.

"Walk with me," Marian said in a gentler voice, "or take to the sky. But if you ever try to leave me behind again, I'll put my horn up your. . . . "

"I love you, too," he interrupted. He thumped his tail in the sand, and dropping to all fours, he started inland with a determined stride. "And from now on, I'll remember that you don't need anybody's protection."

"Yea, though I walk through the Valley of Death," Marian muttered as she caught up to him and took a place at his side, "I will fear no evil, for I am the meanest. . . . "

"Unicorn in the valley," Ronaldo finished for her. And he almost believed it was true. He knew Marian was old—older than Stormfire—and she'd been places and seen things in the world that he didn't even know about. Finback, for instance. He watched her from the corner of his eye as they left the beach and entered the forest.

He should have realized it before. Nothing survived as long as she had by being delicate. Maybe it was time he stopped trying to protect her and started learning from her, instead.

An arrow zipped past Marian's head, under Ronaldo's nose, and *thunked* into a tree. The last Unicorn in the World stopped, turned her head, and stared. In the bushes a short distance away, a nervous archer slowly rose with another shaft nocked and ready to fire.

"There's no way off this island, young man," she said in a cool, calm voice, "unless I let you off. Now put your weapon down and smile like you were my best friend—before I make you eat it."

The archer turned pale. His fingers trembled on his bowstring, and the arrow fell out of his grip. He didn't try to retrieve it or even seem to notice. His lips quivered, twitched, and struggled to turn up at the corners. Then, throwing his bow down, he turned and ran away.

Ronaldo sneered and shook his head. "How did they ever drive us into Wyvernwood?"

Marian gave him a long look before she resumed walking. "Even a lone wolf with teeth and claws will run away sometimes," she answered. "But in a pack, they're ferocious. Humans are like that, too. Never forget it."

At the first clearing, Ronaldo stood and spread his wings. "We'll cover more ground if I take to the air," he said. "But I can tell you what you're going to find—nothing. I've already searched. The Mers are dead."

"Search again now that you're calmer," Marian told him. She paused in the clearing, sniffed, and looked from side to side. "Angmar took this island months ago, but they haven't established much of a foothold."

Ronaldo frowned as he flew upward. In the far distance, swimming at the edge of the island, he spied Finback conducting his part of the search. He looked toward the ground. Marian was a white speck moving at an easy lope beneath the dense trees, only sometimes visible. Twisting his neck around, he observed the crippled ship at anchor in the bay. He still wanted to smash it, but for the moment at least he controlled his impulses. There would be time later when he'd learned from Marian.

Throughout the long night and through much of the day, he'd sat on Thursis's highest peak and, looking down on the destruction he'd caused, he'd contemplated many things. Some of those thoughts would be blasphemous in Wyvernwood, where questioning the wisdom of the Dragon Stormfire simply wasn't done. Still, he couldn't help but wonder if leading the Dragonkin into Wyvernwood had really been the best course.

Had they really found a refuge from a hostile world? Or had they built themselves a trap?

Maybe, despite the danger, it would have been better to have remained in the outer world and fought for their place in it.

These thoughts ran through his mind again as he flew back and forth across Thursis, up and down its rivers, and along its numerous streams. *Who am I to question the wisdom of Great Stormfire?* He asked himself. But then he asked, *Who do I have to be?*

The sun was beginning to set lower in the west, and its fading light ignited the sky like a Dragon's breath. He hadn't seen Marian for a while, he realized, nor had he seen Finback. Still, he continued to search, finding a measure of troubled peace in the wind against his face and in his solitude. He'd ever been a hermit and a recluse.

He found himself over the island's principle river once again. He'd skimmed it one end to the other several times already. Maybe it was some stubborn glimmer of hope that brought him back to it each time. Weren't the odd temple-like structures that dotted its banks proof of its importance to the Mers? If any of them survived, he reasoned, sooner or later they would turn up here to worship or pray or whatever Mers did.

But they wouldn't come by way of the river. That way meant death to all creatures. Even in the air, his sensitive nose could detect the faint, but now-familiar odor of the poison, the sweet herbal perfume of it, like honey and lavender. He licked his lips, and for the first time in two days, felt his own growing thirst. A Dragon didn't need much water.

The slow thought came to him as the sun went down. *I'm a fool.*

A Dragon didn't need much water. *But Men did.*

The thought disturbed him so much that he landed immediately in the first clearing he saw, a cultivated meadow of wildflowers not far from the river, now thick with weeds. With wings folded, he lashed his tail and paced back and forth. With the Mers gone it didn't seem to matter if he destroyed a garden or a meadow. He needed to think!

Or maybe he'd thought enough.

What he needed was an answer—an answer that only a Man could provide.

The sun had long ago slipped below the mountains that spined the island, and a purple gloom colored the sky. In the east, the first bright star, Rono, shone brightly, but advancing clouds promised soon to eclipse its light. Ronaldo flew upward on wings that beat as swiftly as his heart.

Over the mountains, he soared with the wind cold and sobering on his face. Then past the peak where for a night and most of a day he had contemplated the world and his place in it. Finally, down the long scar his landslide had made, over the forest treetops, and to the beach where the wreckage of the Angmaran camp lay strewn.

Finback's green and golden head glimmered at the water's edge. With his chin resting on the sand and his eyes closed, he seemed almost asleep, but as Ronaldo landed, the Sea Serpent opened one eye, and the crest on the top of his head stiffened.

"You look relaxed, Cousin," Ronaldo said.

"I could say the same for you, Cousin," Finback answered. He opened his other eye and directed it toward the forest further down the shoreline. "A few of the little beggars tried to slip out to the ship a while ago. I thought I'd just lie here and remind them how nice those woods really are." He blinked. "Not that I'd know, never having set foot on dry land."

Ronaldo stared down the beach. If there were Men hidden in the woods there, they were hidden well. "You have feet?" he asked in a conversational tone.

Finback yawned. "Toes, too," he answered. "But they've shriveled up like prunes. When you're in water as long as I've been, it's a problem."

Ronaldo studied the Sea Serpent for a long moment. He'd already noted a similarity in the shape of Finback's head and facial features. Now he observed his crest and what he could see of his dorsal fin. They reminded Ronaldo somehow of his own wings. "Speaking of feet," he said at last, "I'm afraid we got off on a wrong one."

Finback twitched a whisker. "Don't mention it," he said. "Good days and bad days, we all have them. Besides, you're right about the river. It's been poisoned. What did you say your name was again?"

The Gray Dragon thought for a moment as he watched the lone ship bobbing at anchor in the bay. "Rage," he answered, lifting his head a bit higher. "To them and all the world." But then he added, "Privately, though, you can call me Ronaldo."

"A stage name," Finback said. He drew a breath, and the crest atop his head stiffened and relaxed. "I have one, too. *Serpens Aqua.*" He blinked. "If I had shoulders, I'd probably shrug. You mind keeping watch a moment? My gills are getting dry."

"No problem, Cousin."

Finback slipped back into the sea, leaving only the slightest imprint on the sand where his chin had rested. The surf made a gentle rush as it hurried to fill it, and the grains of sand shifted and stirred. As Ronaldo watched the imprint vanish he had the strangest vision of Finback, or Finback's kindred, crawling up out of the sea, moving onto the shore, changing, and becoming—Dragons.

He rubbed a paw over his chin. Then he rubbed his eyes and blinked. What an unlikely idea!

Alone again, he remembered the problem that had drawn him back so swiftly to this place on the beach. He gazed over the rubble of smashed barracks and armories, the shattered timber, the charred ruins of tents and buildings he couldn't identify. He'd really done a good job. Not a crate or a barrel remained intact as far as he could see.

Dropping down onto all fours, he walked a little further down the beach and stared into the forest. He smiled to himself. They were hidden well, like little nervous mice, but not well enough. There were probably others scattered around the island by now, but any of these would probably have the answer he sought.

He tried not to sound too intimidating. "Come out!" he called. "Come out! Don't be afraid! I won't . . . !"

"Don't be afraid?" Marian came trotting through the sand from the opposite end of the beach. "Oh, that's reassuring! You've smashed their camp, burned their ships, killed who knows how many of them, and you tell them *don't be afraid*?"

Ronaldo looked at Marian and frowned. "You know, for a unicorn you can be a real nag."

Her tail whipped across her rump, a sure sign of agitation. "Play with the Humans later," she said impatiently. "I need you to come with me now. I think I've found something."

His ears pricked up. "Something to do with the Mers?"

Marian stamped one hoof. "No. It's. . . . "

"Then this is more important," Ronaldo said. "Finback brought those four sailors from your ship ashore, and I'll bet they're still close by. They trust you."

Marian stamped her other hoof. Then, she hesitated. "Well, maybe. . . ."

"Call them," Ronaldo insisted in a loud voice. He wanted the Men in the woods to hear. "Tell them I need to talk to one of them. Any of them. All of them. And after we talk, they can swim out to that ship and sail away, and I'll leave them alone."

"They can't do that." Marian dropped her voice to a whisper.

Ronaldo looked at her and squeezed one eye shut. "What?"

"They can't sail away," she whispered. "The rudder's smashed."

Ronaldo dropped his voice to a whisper, too. "Well, they can row away! Or Finback can tow them home! Just tell them!"

Marian drew a deep breath and then sighed. "Drag yourself back up the beach then, and give me a little room to work. This may take a moment, because they all think you're going to eat them."

Ronaldo moved back up the beach and waited. Thinking it might be a friendly gesture, he pushed some pieces of broken lumber into a pile and breathed on it. Everyone liked a good fire on the beach, didn't they?

"Maybe we should sing some songs?" Back from the depths, Finback lay at the edge of the surf, his large eyes shining. "I know some good ones. *Buffalo gals, won't you come out tonight!*"

"Please!" Ronaldo snapped. "I hate Fomorian music."

Marian came back up the beach at an easy pace. A single Man walked beside her, but his eyes glittered with distrust, and he kept one hand on the sword he wore at his belt. Halfway up the beach, his step faltered as he gazed at Ronaldo. Then, swallowing, he found his courage and came on.

"This man's name is Piper," she informed Ronaldo. "He was second-in-command of the fleet harbored here until you killed his superior. So he figures he owes you a favor and has agreed to talk. If you don't eat him, of course."

Pressing his paws together, Ronaldo inclined his head in a semblance of a bow. "I am the Dragon Rage," he said, ignoring Marian's disdainful look. "Tell me, Piper, how long has it been since you or your men had a drink? What are you doing for water?"

The Man called Piper shifted uneasily, but he let go of his sword. "Well, not since you attacked . . . I mean, not since you came here." He looked up questioningly and seemed to search for the right word. "Not since you came here, Sir? And we're a might thirsty bunch, I don't mind admitting, what with all the water barrels smashed and not a safe drop on the island!"

Marian backed up a step and gave Ronaldo a hard look. "They were having to ship drinking water in?"

Ronaldo closed his eyes. He had a vaguely sick feeling in his gut. "It worried at me all afternoon, after you pointed out that Angmar hadn't established much of a foothold here, but I couldn't quite put my claw on it until I began to get thirsty, too." Opening his eyes, he bent and brought his face close to Piper. The little Man stood his ground, though his knees were shaking like holiday noisemakers. "You didn't poison the river, did you?"

Piper's eyes grew wide and his face turned bright red. "Us, Sir? Damnation, no!" He drew back his shoulders proudly, but then thought better of it, and slumped again. "We took the island, all right, and we drove some of those creepy, fish-folks away. But it was Degarm that sneaked in here almost as soon as we took it, and they poisoned damn near everything to keep us from making any use of it!"

He waved his arm around at what was left of the camp and put on a look of complete disgust. "No water to drink unless we brought it in. And with no game, nothing but rations to eat! We weren't sure enough about the sea-fish to even try those!" He turned quickly to Finback. "Begging your pardon, Sir!"

He turned back to Ronaldo and Marian. Maybe it was his nerves, but once he'd started talking, he couldn't seem to quit. "Why, this is about all we managed to do here in the better part of three months! Now, if I'd been put in charge. . . ." He stopped suddenly, looking like a Man who'd said too much.

Ronaldo drew a deep breath and let it out slowly, aware of the way that Marian was watching him. Even she half expected him to eat the shivering figure that stood with his hand folded before him. What a ridiculous idea.

"Degarm poisoned the river to keep Angmar from building an effective base here," Ronaldo said coldly. "A base from which Angmar would have attacked Degarm. As a result, the Merfolk are dead and this island is ruined." He hesitated, struggling with the urge to flex just one wing and slap Piper into the middle of the bay. He clenched his teeth as he spoke again. "There's one ship out in the bay. Get your comrades on it, and get away from here as fast as you can—any way you can. And never set foot on Thursis again."

Piper hesitated. Squeezing his eyes tightly shut, he folded his hands and dropped to his knees. "Begging your pardon, Sir!" he managed through chattering teeth. "But—but we can't go home! That fancy ship that looked like a dragon that you sank and sent to Deadland? That was the private ship of Prince Shepar, himself, Sir—King Kilraen's only son. And Shepar went down with it. Kilraen's not going to look kindly on us at all for living while his son's picking fishbones out of his butt for the rest of eternity!"

Ronaldo remembered the intricate, dragon-styled vessel and the figure clad in red silks that had gone down with such poetic grace in its rigging. He couldn't quite bring himself to feel guilty. Nor could he find another drop of mercy. He glared at Piper. "I'm giving you your lives!" he roared. "Don't waste my time with your problems. If that ship is still in the bay at dawn, I'll burn it like I burned the others."

Piper shot a look at Marian, and then realizing he'd get no more help from her, he turned and ran back down the beach. At the edge of the woods, he stopped long enough to wave an arm and beckon to his fellows before he jumped into the bay and began to swim for the ship. The other Men poured out of the trees and quickly followed.

Marian stamped her hooves and shook her mane. "Well, that was diplomatic!" she said, as impatient as before. "Now will you come with me?

He shot a glance toward Finback. The Sea Serpent's eyes were closed, and he seemed asleep again. "What's one more problem to cope with?" he said. "Lead on."

"It's on the far side of the mountains," she explained quickly. "Not far from the river, but not close to it, either, so stay close!"

Without waiting, Marian turned about and raced into the woods. Ronaldo, called Rage, spread his wings and followed, skimming the treetops to keep her in sight. Powerful and lithe and untiring, she ran among the trees, swerved around obstacles, leaped crevices and gullies. Up the mountainside she sped, sure-footed, and with a purpose and determination that stirred Ronaldo's admiration as it stirred his curiosity.

As they crossed the mountains, Rono shone down with a bright glow. He gazed toward the dark, liquid ribbon that was the river, but Marian swerved away from it as she reached the mountain's base, taking a parallel course, instead.

What in all the fires has she found? Ronaldo thought to himself. At the next instant, the answer came to him. *Bumble!*

He'd been so wrapped up in his thoughts and his anger that he hadn't

given the little hummingbird much thought. Thursis was full of mead-
ows and gardens, and he'd assumed Bumble was taking advantage of
them. But he scowled as he remembered how rude he'd been and how
he'd treated a friend that had come so far with him.

Suddenly, Marian disappeared on the ground. Lost in thought again,
Ronaldo sailed right by before he noticed that she was gone. Dipping a
wing, he wheeled around and retraced his course and found the Last
Unicorn in the World waiting for him.

He expected petulance. Instead, she wore an expression of excitement!

He descended carefully. There was no good place for a dragon to land
without damaging the trees, so folding his wings at the last moment, he
grabbed a piece of the hillside nearby. It was a rough way to land, but
he'd made worse. On all fours and hugging the ground, he moved down
the grassy slope, around an outcropping of boulders and through a copse
of trees until he reached Marian.

At her back was a deep niche in the stone face of the hill. Not a cave,
just a deep impression. Four white-stone columns stood recessed into it.
It resembled closely the smaller temple structures the Mers had erected
along the river, but this one was larger and far older. The columns were
marred with stone rot at their bases, and honeysuckle vines had grown
upon them, making a nearly perfect camouflage—for anyone but Bumble.

The little hummingbird clung unmoving to one of the vines with his
gaze fixed on a spot high in the niche. "I found him like this!" Marian
explained. "He hasn't moved, not even to dip his beak in the blossoms as
far as I can tell. He just stares at something up there." She pranced among
the columns, her hooves striking on a moss-covered stone floor. "Ronaldo, or Rage, or whoever you are now," she continued without sarcasm,
wide-eyed and almost breathless. "I feel something, too! Something. . . .
I can't describe it!"

Ronaldo brought his face close to Bumble. His diminutive friend didn't react, but Ronaldo could see the way his small talons gripped the vine on which he perched, and he noted the barely perceptible tremor that shook the tiny feathers. "Bumble-bird?" he whispered. "Speak to me."

To his startlement, Bumble swiveled his head sharply and stared straight back. "*One has been found without looking*," he said in his small voice. He returned his gaze back to whatever spot held it.

Marian came for a closer look at Bumble. "He's always been the weirdest of us," she muttered. Then she turned to gaze upward, too.

Ronaldo wasn't sure what Bumble meant, and he was even less sure of what Marian was feeling. But curiosity couldn't be put aside. Rising up straight and tall, he squeezed between the columns and peered into the niche's deepest shadows. After a brief search he found a split in the old stone, a deep recess. Cautiously, he pushed a claw into the opening. Then two claws.

"A diamond!" he exclaimed, drawing his paw out and holding his treasure up to his eyes. "An immense diamond!" The jewel was as large as an apple and cut into perfect facets. When he blew the dust and dirt from it, it caught Rono's glow and hurled the light back in shimmering colorful beams that shattered on the niche rock and spread down the hillside.

Mesmerized by its beauty, Ronaldo brought it even closer to his eyes and gazed deeply into it. "Oh!" he gasped. "Oh!"

"What?" Marian demanded, unusually short on clever words. "What?"

Bumble flew suddenly up and perched on top of Ronaldo's head, tiny wings humming, freed from whatever force had held him. "One was found without looking!" he sang like a parrot. "One was found without looking! Awk!"

"I see you're not the only one suffering an identity crisis," Marian said to Ronaldo.

Ronaldo barely heard. The beams of light danced on his face and in his eyes as he turned the jewel around and around between his claws. "I see . . . I see . . . !" He paused and licked his dry lips, feeling his thirst has he never had before. "Inside . . . a Dragon! It's a diamond Dragon!"

Marian reared up as high as she could for a better look, then settled down again. "It's more than that," she said, her voice thick with wary awe as she backed up a step. "It's magic."

17

LIKE A BLACK CANCER GROWING ON THE EARTH, Throom Odin seemed to spread as far as Chan could see. Its countless senses-confusing structures, most seemingly built from dark wood or black stone, leaned at improbable angles, sometimes appearing to prop and support other structures. As far as Chan could tell, no corner was quite square, no window or door quite rectangular, no street ever straight.

From some parts of the city, arrows and larger missiles launched upward as he passed, but none came close. He considered swooping down and smashing some of the ballistas he spied mounted on rooftops, but he resisted that impulse. Nothing else mattered to him, except to get away from Throom Odin and its strange people and continue with his quest.

"Not everyone down there hates us," Jake said, leaning forward in his saddle as he pointed toward the ground.

Chan found it hard to set aside his doubts, though he wanted that to be true. Yes, there were weapons on the rooftops. However, on other rooftops and in some of the streets he saw crowds of people cheering and waving colorful banners. Their enthusiasm seemed genuine, but he couldn't forget the crowds at the gate with their baskets of flower petals and the *greeting* that followed.

Putting on a burst of speed, he climbed higher in the sky. *Safety in alti-*

tude, he reasoned, and from his improved vantage point, at last he saw the western edge of Throom Odin. There seemed to be no wall on the western border. The city just dwindled away like a tired and purposeless thing in that direction.

The crowds in the streets below had thinned, but the people turned out again when Morkir, with Katrina on his back, dropped lower and skimmed their rooftops. With impressive skill he dodged the towers and taller structures that sprang up in his flight path, and when clearance allowed he descended into the streets themselves, raising squeals of glee and shrieks of terror from the citizens as he shot by.

Katrina particularly seemed to relish the attention. As she and Morkir raced above the heads of the people, she called to them and waved her red cloak. Chan smiled a little as he watched. It was all a party to Katrina, and for the moment she was a Guest of Honor. If he worried about her safety, he didn't begrudge her a moment in the spotlight. Even for a Fomorian, she'd always been a little bit different, and she'd never quite found her place in Stronghold.

When they reached the edge of Throom Odin and the last vestiges of the city vanished behind them, Chan breathed a sigh of relief. Such a strange and confusing place, he thought to himself, nothing at all like the tranquil and ordered life of Wyvernwood. He gazed down at the dirty river that meandered across the countryside just beyond the city, with its brown water and potent stink, and he thought of the clear sweetness of Wyvernwood's Blackwater River. For a brief moment, he felt a stab of sympathy, and even sadness, for the people of Throom Odin and Valindar.

Morkir soared up beside him as they crossed the river and took his usual place at Chan's left side. Chan turned his head ever so slightly to regard Morkir, who still wore a look of thoughtful sullenness, and he grinned. "Grand-stander!"

The golden Griffin didn't respond at once. His gaze seemed distant, but not exactly on the horizon. "I wanted a closer look," he said finally. "Not at the leaders or the soldiers. Just at the ordinary meat."

"Speaking of meat," Katrina shouted as she wrapped herself in her fluttering cloak and stared back toward the river, "I could eat a fat carp!"

"Back in the mountains," Jake said without looking at the cat-girl, "I had a pouch with some sandwiches and cookies, but someone helped themselves while I was asleep."

Rubbing a paw over her nose, Katrina looked away and found something interesting in the opposite direction.

Chan sighed and stared forward. He knew Jake had to be just as hungry as Katrina. "Let's find a cleaner river or lake," he suggested. "This one doesn't stimulate my appetite."

The sun reached noon and then began its slow descent toward the flat horizon. With Throom Odin far behind, the countryside of Valindar began to change. Small forests—though nothing so grand as Wyvern-wood —dotted the broad steppes, and here and there thickets of grasses grew so tall even a Dragon could get lost in them. Isolated trees in strange shapes and with unusual leaves grew lonely and apart from everything else, and flowers with bright yellow blossoms grew almost as tall as the trees. It was a stark landscape, and yet a beautiful one. Chan noted how the blue sky seemed to hang low and stretch on forever. A Dragon could get as lost in such a sky as in the high grasses below.

Skymarin appeared like a feathered bolt suddenly at Chan's right side. "A village to the south," he reported. "Not large. No threat."

Chan nodded, glad to see the Lord of Eagles. He feared that Skymarin was taking his role as scout just a little too seriously, vanishing without warning for long periods of time, to return at unexpected moments. Still, in one respect it was welcome news. "Lead us," he instructed.

Skymarin twisted his head to look at Chan. "Did someone shoot an arrow through your common sense?" he asked. "Or was it just a rock upside your head when you weren't looking?"

"You said there was no threat," he reminded the Lord of Eagles. Chan wasn't at all enthusiastic about another encounter with the locals, but he had Jake to think about, and Katrina, too. In fact, it was midafternoon, and everyone could use a rest. "The boy's hungry," he continued. "Let's feed him something besides raw lake fish."

Jake leaned close and patted Chan's neck. "As long as you're around," he said, "I never have to eat raw fish. You can roast it for me."

With a look of resignation, Skymarin dipped one wing and changed course. "Here we go again!" he grumbled as the wind rustled through his feathers. "But just remember this old saying we Eagles have: *Fool me once, shame on me! But fool me twice, I'll rip your eyes out and feed 'em to your grandmothers!*"

Morkir came around on Chan's wingtip as they followed Skymarin. "There's diplomacy in this Eagle-saying," he murmured. Then, after a pause, he continued. "Let's land and walk into this village," he suggested. "My wings are tired, and maybe we'll look a little less monsterish to our hosts. Particularly if we want to find food—nothing spoils the soup like a frightened cook."

Chan regarded his Griffin comrade with growing respect. Not so long ago, he'd been *Mad Morkir*, a prince of the Griffin nests, scourge of Wyvernwood, and a force of terror and destruction. But Morkir had changed.

"Down then," he agreed. "Jake and Katrina can carry us for a while."

Katrina stuck out her tongue. "How about if we just drag you by your tails?"

Chan called out to Skymarin and then descended to the ground. His claws found purchase in soft, rich soil in a place where the grasses were not too high. With a rush of feathers, Morkir landed beside him, and

Katrina sprang off his back with a lithe movement. With a little effort, Jake slipped out of his saddle and eased himself to the ground. He rubbed his buttocks. "Everything's gone numb," he grumbled good-naturedly.

It wasn't far to the village, and it was good to walk for a change. Skymarin flew ahead, but stayed within sight. Katrina, always playful and full of energy, prowled the grasses off to one side, batting at flowers and chasing the mice she found there. Jake, too, seemed to need a little time alone, and he walked ahead of Chan and Morkir.

"There's something I need to know," Morkir said in a low, serious voice when no one else was within earshot. He hesitated and looked away before he turned back to Chan. "And I need to know the truth. Were you going to put your head under that blade for us?"

The question hit Chan like a stone. In the back of his mind he'd been asking himself the same question all day, and he'd been avoiding the answer. The farther he got from Throom Odin, the more it all seemed like a bad dream or a nightmare. But through the nightmare, that blade still shone like a razor's gleam.

He stopped walking, and Morkir stopped. "I don't know," he answered, and immediately as he looked at Jake's back up ahead he knew he'd lied.

Morkir knew it, too. The Griffin rose up on his hind legs to stare at him with a veiled expression. Then, without another word, he dropped to all fours again, folded his wings over his back, and continued walking.

They didn't go far before the tall grasses became cornfields and beanfields, and a little farther still they found a clear stream cutting across their way. By the time Chan and Morkir caught up, Jake and Katrina were washing their feet and splashing their faces. Katrina made a swipe with her claws at a fish and knocked it up onto the opposite bank where she pounced on it and bit the poor creature nearly in half.

"Barbarian!" Skymarin said as he landed close by.

Katrina stuck her tongue out. "Oh, like you've never eaten a raw fish!"

The Lord of Eagles fluttered his wings in indignation. "Yes—but I share!"

Breaking the fish in half with a sharp twist, she tossed the smaller piece to Skymarin, who swallowed it in a single gulp. Turning his back to the bloody feeding, Jake struggled not to make a face as he slipped back into his undershirt and then his outer shirt of ivory Dragon scales.

Chan watched as he dressed, and he felt the first stab of homesickness. He hadn't been gone long enough to feel that way, he told himself. And yet the scaled shirt still bore faint traces of Luna's scent. It keenly reminded him of his sister and brother, of all his friends back home, and he couldn't help but wonder what they were doing while he was off having adventures.

Bending his head, he drank a little water. A few shady trees grew on either side of the stream. None of them were nearly as majestic as Wyvernwood's trees, but still he thought it would be nice to lie down and take a nap beneath their branches or just stare up through the rustling leaves and watch the sky.

"Hello?"

Jake's soft greeting drew Chan's attention back from such thoughts. Lifting his head, he gazed across the water into the round faces of two wide-eyed little boys, no more than Pear's age, he guessed, with fishing poles over their shoulders and buckets in hand. They stared from hiding amid the cornstalks that grew close to the stream, afraid either to advance or run or make any move at all.

Smiling, Jake sat down on the bank not far from them. "What are your names?" he asked.

The two boys looked at each other, then at Katrina nearby, and then at Morkir on the opposite bank. Lastly, they stared at Chan. Then, throwing down their fishing poles and buckets, they turned at the same time and ran back into the cornfield. The crunching crash and the noisy shaking of the stalks followed them.

Katrina picked up one of the buckets and thrust in a paw. "Worms!" she exclaimed. She thrust a handful into her mouth and offered the bucket to the others. When everyone declined, she shrugged.

"Stop it." Jake snatched the bucket from her and recovered the second bucket, too. Then, picking up the fishing poles he told the others. "We'll take these with us into the village and return them as peace offerings. It'll show we mean no harm to anyone."

Morkir dipped his beak into the stream and took a final drink before he waded to the other side. There, he paused. "I'm having a harder and harder time seeing you as a mere carnival tumbler," he said as he shook the water from his paws. Without waiting for a reply he started through the cornfield.

Katrina snatched one of the buckets back, and one of the fishing poles, too. Then, turning up her nose, she followed Morkir. With a soft rush of feathers, Skymarin took off.

"I don't think Morkir likes me," Jake said when they were alone.

Lifting his tail high and folding his wings tightly, Chan straddled the stream. "I don't know if he likes you," he answered truthfully. "But he respects you. For a Griffin, that means a lot."

Shouldering the fishing pole and swinging the bucket he carried, Jake started through the cornfield, following the path that Morkir had made, which was in truth the same path the two boys had made, only wider. Chan came last, doing as little damage to the stalks as possible. The corn that grew over the heads of his companions barely came up to his knees, and far ahead he spied the village that was their destination.

At the edge of the cornfield, the villagers were waiting.

"How nice!" Katrina said as she emerged from among the stalks right behind Morkir. She extended her claws as she regarded the pitchforks and rakes and hoes, the hammers, and skillets and butcher knives. "Another reception committee. It must be a Valindar tradition."

"Spunky bunch," Morkir commented.

"Let me handle this," Jake said, taking a step forward with the bucket and pole.

But before he took a second step, the villagers brandished their makeshift weapons and charged forward with a raucous shouting. The looks on their faces were startling mixtures of fear and anger and determination. But to Chan, they only looked small and silly with their garden tools and kitchen utensils. With a shrug of his wings, taking care not to ignite their fields or their homes, he raised his head and exhaled a red blast skyward.

The villagers spun about, practically trampling each other, as they withdrew to their previous line. There, still clinging to their weapons, they glared nervously and muttered among themselves.

"We only ask for food for young friend!" Chan called in a loud voice. Gesturing with a paw, he indicated Jake. "And the chance to return these items which your children dropped. We didn't mean to scare them, and we don't mean to scare you!" He flexed his wings and folded them again. "Is there no hospitality at all in Valindar?"

The villagers resumed their muttering, and the one bearded Man with a leather apron over his hairy bare chest stepped forward. "Who're you callin' scared, Monster?" he demanded as he brandished his hammer. He glanced back over his shoulder at his anxious neighbors, then regarded Chan once more. "As long as it's none of us ye're lookin' to eat, I guess we can spare a little nourishment." He waved his hammer again. "But mind yer manners, an' don't step on nothin' we'll have to rebuild! Ye've already made chop out of some of the crop with yer big gallopin' feet!"

"Paws," Morkir corrected. "Dragons don't have feet."

The burly Man glared uncertainly at Morkir. "An' that goes for yer friends, too!" he added. "Ye're a peculiar bunch, an' I'm not too convinced even the boy is really just a boy! So you jus' wait right here an' watch yer step around us!"

Chan sat back on his haunches at the edge of the cornfield, doing his best not to crush anymore of the crop than he already had. Morkir stretched out on the ground, cat-like, and folded his paws under his chin, watching carefully while Jake and Katrina together walked just a few steps forward and placed the fishing poles and buckets of bait on the ground. As they retreated, the two boys pushed between the adults to run forward and claim their stuff. One ran immediately back, but the other stopped and set his bucket and pole back down again.

A black-dressed Woman with a worried face and a garden rake called to the boy, but with cautious steps, he walked toward Katrina and reached out a tentative hand to touch her orange-striped fur.

One by one, the other villagers walked slowly forward for a closer look as their fear dissolved. With a gentle word of warning so that he didn't startle anyone, Jake held out an ivory-scaled arm, and Skymarin sailed down to perch upon it. The villagers gasped with surprise and awe and pressed around to see the Lord of Eagles.

"Say something for them, Skymarin," Chan urged.

The Lord of Eagles swiveled his head and raised his tail feathers to flash his nether region at Chan. "Polly wanna cracker?" he said with some irritation. "What am I? A circus performer? That's Jake's job!"

The villagers gasped again, and then laughed.

A group of Men brought a wooden table, and others followed with trays of fruits and vegetables. Some children paraded out of the village with platters piled with sliced bread, cheeses, and bean curd. Some Women brought pitchers of water and milk, pies, and cookies. Some other Men made a large circle of stones and filled it with logs and kindling and invited Chan to do the honors. With a careful exhalation he ignited it, raising a chorus of laughter and applause.

An impromptu party began. While a few Men stood back with wary expressions, most of the villagers gave in to their curiosity. They wanted to feel Chan's scales, touch Katrina's fur and tail, and stroke Morkir's wings. The Griffin lay patiently still and let their hosts have their way with him. It was an astounding sight that Chan would never forget.

Jake wasn't immune from their curiosity, either. They poked and prodded him, reassuring themselves that he was, indeed, a Human boy, and they asked him all sorts of questions as they fed him hot steamed fish and corn-on-the-cob from the fire. In fact, everyone ate his or her fill, villagers and guests alike.

In a rare moment when neither Chan nor Morkir were surrounded, and when both their bellies were full, the Griffin spoke to Chan quietly again. "I have another question," he asked with a distant look in his eyes. Something had been on his mind all day, Chan knew, and he had a feeling Morkir was coming around to it.

"How does it make you feel," he asked, "when someone calls you *Son of Stormfire?*"

Chan squeezed one eye shut and regarded Morkir with the other. He wasn't sure what he'd been expecting, but that question wasn't it. But he closed both eyes and thought for a moment before answering. "Pride," he said, with memories of his father drifting through his mind. "Love and warmth." The corners of his lips turned up in a tight Dragon smile. "And a little emptiness, because he's gone."

Morkir regarded him with a strange look. "I envy you," he admitted. "Someone called me *Son of Gorganar* once, but I didn't feel any of that. I only felt . . . ," he closed his eyes as he tried to express himself. "Revulsion."

Chan blinked, unsure of what he should say. "Gorganar was. . . ."

"A monster," Morkir interrupted. "Some of us really are. I've come to accept that." He put his chin back on his paws, but though he looked at ease, his lionine tail twitched slowly back and forth. "It's not what I want to be," he continued, "but in Wyvernwood, I'll always be *Morkir, Son of Gorganar*. So I'm not going on with you, Chan."

Chan arched his wings, drawing the attention of the villagers and his comrades. Quickly, he smiled again and tried to look relaxed. "I need you!" he said from the corner of his mouth.

Morkir gave a faint shake of his head. "No, you don't. I'm going to stay here for a little while if these villagers will allow me, and try to learn from them. Then, I'm going back to Throom Odin. I think I can do some good there." He closed his eyes again, and his tail became still. "And maybe after a while everyone will forget that I'm the *Son of Gorganar*, and I can just be Morkir—whoever Morkir is."

"Just don't think you're going anywhere without me, you big flea-trap." Neither of them had heard Katrina slip up from behind them or even seen her slip away from the party. She touched Chan's paw as she turned an earnest face up to him. "I knew from the moment I left Stronghold that I wouldn't be going back. Following you just gave me the reason to leave and the courage I'd always lacked. But without Morkir, I'll only slow you down now." Turning away from Chan, she reached out and stroked the Griffin's spine. "Throom Odin was a *real* party. What do you say we go pay the Chief Critic another visit and make him wet his pants again?"

Chan felt a deep sadness as Morkir and Katrina agreed. The small fellowship that had left Wyvernwood together was breaking up to go separate ways. In a short time, he'd gotten very used to their company, to Katrina's endless banter and Morkir's sarcasm. Without them, the unknown road ahead seemed gloomier and more foreboding.

The party suddenly felt depressing, and plenty of daylight still remained. He called to Jake. "We've come to a crossroads," In as few words as possible, hiding his emotion, he explained things to his young rider. "You can make a choice, too." he finished.

Jake looked perplexed, then hurt. He tried to smile as he shook his head. "*Sumapai*, there's no more choice for me. I made my choice the first time we flew across the stars together. Don't you want me to come with you?"

Chan bent low to the ground and put his face close to Jake's. It made more sense to leave the boy here among his own kind. The village seemed a nice place, and despite rough appearances, the citizens had good hearts. It certainly would be safer for Jake. Still, his heart ached at the thought of leaving Jake behind.

"Indeed, *Chokahai*," he said, "that would be my choice."

The hurt vanished from Jake's face, and he grinned. Then, with a lithe movement, dashing past Chan's head, he sprang into the saddle and wasted no time securing the straps around his legs. Chan waited patiently, filled with a quiet joy, knowing that of all the choices still ahead, this choice was right. For him, there would never be a question of leaving Jake behind again.

The villagers, realizing that something was up, began to drift closer again. "So that's the way it is, eh?" The burly Man who had first confronted them came right up to Chan's nose. "Eat an' run?"

"Not for all of us," Morkir answered with a nod to Chan. It was as close as he'd come to a farewell, but it was enough. "I think I'd like to try a piece of pie. I've never tasted pie before."

Katrina walked forward and planted a kiss on Chan's nose. "Once in a while," she whispered, "when the full moon rises and the wind is warm, sit back and purr—and think of me."

"Little Furball." Chan worked to swallow the lump in his throat. "Once in a while when the dawn is breaking and the world seems sad, look to the east, to the mountains—and you'll always remember where home is."

"Will I, Chan?" she answered, and hidden in that gentle question lurked just a hint of fear and doubt. "The point of your quest is to find a new home for the Dragonkin. I won't know where it is."

Skymarin settled on Jake's shoulder. The Lord of Eagles had made his choice, too.

There was no more to say, and to linger any more would have only led to sadness. Chan thanked the villagers and took one final look around. Without actually entering the village itself, he felt he'd learned more about the Race of Man than he'd learned in all of sprawling Throom Odin. One of the villager children ran forward and tossed a pouch of sandwiches and cookies up to Jake, and he slipped it over his shoulder.

"Try not to lose that one," Katrina said with a wink and a wave as she wrapped herself in her red cloak and backed away to stand beside Morkir. The Griffin looked up. His face was stained with blueberries.

Skymarin took off, and spreading his leather wings to their full, impressive span, the Son of Stormfire followed. "*Chokahai!*" he called back to his rider. "Sing the song again!" And Jake began to sing. *Oh, the sky is wide and far. . . .*

They were three now, eagle, boy and dragon, and Wyvernwood seemed farther away than Chan could imagine. Yet, as he gazed downward, he remembered that he was retracing history. The Dragonkin had crossed through Valindar. Their pawprints were in the soil right beside the prints of Man. Their blood enriched the soil as much as Man's. A thought flashed through his mind as he soared above the rolling hills and grasslands toward the gradually setting sun.

He wasn't leaving home. He was returning home.

There were other towns and villages in Valindar, and some lay directly in his path. As he passed above those he spread his wings wide and blasted clouds of fire to let them know that at least one Dragon still remained. What must the world have been like when the sky was filled with Dragons?

The sun descended, and for a short time the rim of the world shimmered in a blaze of fire and color, revealing mountains sharper than any Chan had ever seen. Straight for those wicked peaks he flew, as fire and color faded and stars began to shine. But long before he reached them, a gleam of silvery darkness caught his eye, a river wide, and stretching long as he could see across the land.

A river called *The Flow of Dreams*.

18

NO DRAGON IN ALL OF WYVERNWOOD could match Luna's speed, and with Ariel's life at stake, she wasted no time. Across the vast forest she flew with the moon on her wings and her own dark shadow chasing after. Birds at rest in the branches shot upward and scattered across the sky, startled by her sudden passage. On the ground, meandering deer paused in their nocturnal foraging to look up, and choruses of wolves fell silent.

In the distance, moonlight limned the towers of Redclaw, but before she reached her destination, a pair of Griffins, gliding low over the tree-tops, rose up to intercept her. Luna charged between them, smashing the nearest one out of her way with a powerful downbeat of her left wing while his smarter companion swerved to avoid the same treatment.

Talons stabbed into her tail before she got past. Clinging to her with a Griffin's strength, her foe spread his wings wide to slow her down as he dug his claws still deeper into her flesh. The first Griffin shot up from the trees with vengeance in his eyes to rejoin the fight. Luna twisted in midair. Curling her head toward her tail, she slashed at the face of the Griffin clinging to her. Blood splattered, and the creature let out a scream that was more Eagle than Lion. Still, he held on, and Luna struck him again, knocking him away and freeing herself just as his partner hit her from the side.

Talons scraped on her scales, and a razor sharp beak stabbed at her shoulder. Luna beat at her attacker with her tail, fighting panic and trying to keep her head. She beat her wings frantically as she tried to stay aloft. The Griffin's wings thrashed against hers. Feathers filled the air. Then, changing her strategy, Luna folded her wings. Like a stone, she fell toward the trees. The Griffin beat his wings in furious desperation in an attempt to support them both. Not even his strength could accomplish that. With an angry roar, he released his grip and dived aside.

Twisting like a cat as the ground rushed up at her, Luna spread her wings at the last possible instant. Branches and leaves on the tallest trees exploded as she skimmed through the foliage. Two shadows raced beside her—the Griffins pursuing just above, waiting for their next chance to strike.

Flexing her claws, Luna growled to herself. With new determination, she swooped upward and turned to meet her foes. *Stupid beasts*! she thought as she turned to meet their attack. One of them should have flown to Redclaw for help. They were going to need it!

In mid-flight, they rushed her. With a powerful beat of her wings, Luna shot above them. Reaching out with her hind legs as she rose, she dug her Dragon-claws deep into the Griffin's lionine backs and slammed her foes together. Feathers flew, and the Griffin's screamed in pain. Before they could recover and use their strength to free themselves, she swooped low again and dragged them through the treetops. Branches snapped—but not so loudly as Griffin wings! High into the night she climbed again with her writhing burdens, high and higher. Then, with all her might, she flung them earthward!

She didn't wait to watch the impact. With an angry snarl, pulse pounding, she turned once more toward Redclaw. Her wounds stung, but they were not too deep, and best of all she had won the fight without using fire. With any luck, the Griffin fortress was not yet warned of her coming. She felt for the mirror in its cord around her neck to reassure herself it was still there. It would guide her, Agriope had said.

Hold on, Ariel! she prayed.

Far ahead, another pair of Griffins soared across her field of vision without seeing her. The cowards always flew in twos or threes, she thought coldly, or in groups. It didn't matter. Nothing would stop her from finding what she sought. Aware of the moon at her back and its penchant for glittering on her ivory scales, she dropped low to skim the treetops again.

The Griffins were patrolling, she realized as she watched their flight, and she wondered at that because it wasn't Griffin behavior. What made Minhep take such precautions? She thought suddenly of Stronghold and nodded to herself. Minhep was allied with Angmar. Had the Crows, the allies of Degarm, dared to attack Redclaw, too? It made her task a little tougher if the Griffins were on guard.

But only a little tougher. Still determined not to use her fire, she folded her wings and dropped through the trees to the ground. With a quick look around, she found a proper tree, snapped its trunk, and with swift slashes of her claws she stripped away its limbs. With her new weapon clutched between her forepaws, she rose into the sky again, climbing as fast and as high as she could until her shadow on the trees could not be seen.

She spied the Griffin patrol again and flew straight for them. Too late, they saw her coming. With surprise on her side, she swung her club downward, breaking a wing, and the injured Griffin fell in a crazy spiral, howling as he crashed in the forest. His partner, stunned to find himself alone with an angry Dragon, raised his paws in a weak-hearted defense. Luna's club struck solidly across his muscled stomach, then down upon his feathered Eagle's head. Still conscious, but barely in control of himself, he dived after his partner to hide.

Alone in the sky again, Luna scanned the horizons. Though the moon still shone, dawn wasn't far off. Unless their patterns had radically changed, most of the Griffins would still be asleep. Bending her wings and alert for any more patrols, she resumed her course for Redclaw.

As she raced to battle, Luna considered the cool night and the beauty of the waxing moon in the star-dappled sky. The treetops waving in the wind seemed to hail her, and the breeze played lullabies in her ears. Her thoughts churned, and yet she felt so focused and so strong.

I am Stormfire's Daughter, she thought to herself as she approached the Griffin fortress. But then, her eyes narrowed to concentrated slits. She drew a deep breath, swelling her chest, as she stretched her wings and began a long glide to her destination. "No," she corrected, embracing a new realization. "I am the Dragon Luna, and I stand in no one's shadow anymore—not even his."

The towers of Redclaw loomed upward like a gray hand in the moonlight. In daylight, the stones that made the fortress and its walls possessed a dull red color, lending the ancient place its name. No one knew or remembered who had built it, for it had been here when the Dragonkin came to Wyvernwood. But Angmar had restored it and given it to their allies. Redclaw was the Griffins' price for betraying the Dragonkin.

The land around the fortress's perimeter had been cleared and the forest pushed back, and the ground between the new forest edge and the wall was planted with stout black stakes. Flying high again, Luna studied the fortress, noting the small number of guards that prowled atop the wall, the pair inside the main gate, and the lone watcher perched on the pinnacle of Redclaw's highest tower.

Again she touched Agriope's mirror-medallion. The shard caught the moonlight as she lifted it with a claw, but in its polished surface, that moonlight bore a strange blue tint. What was she to make of that, or of the fact that she couldn't see her own reflection there at all?

Everything was mystery and puzzles, she thought with a frown, and Agriope most of all. All Luna could do for now was trust—and act.

As silently as her leather wings allowed, she slipped through the air toward the watcher on the tower, and such was her luck that the creature, bored by his lonely task, had fallen fast asleep. Only when Luna was upon him, did he snap his eyes wide and look up in surprise.

"Go back to sleep," Luna whispered as she swung her club and struck the Griffin in the jaw beneath his beak. His eyes glazed instantly, but as he started to topple from his perch, Luna caught him with one hind leg and set his limp form in a corner. Still unseen, she took his place and spread her wings to their fullest. Four Griffins on the wall, and two more by the gate. There had to be more asleep within the towers. "Come out, come out, wherever you are," she murmured.

Raising her head, she announced herself with a shining blast of fire that lit the courtyard, the top of the wall, and the edge of the woods beyond. As the startled Griffins all looked up, she roared.

"Minhep!" she shouted. "Wake up, you miserable old cat-bird! I've come a long way to see your ugly puss!"

One of the Griffin guards on the wall leaped into the air and flew straight for her with claws extended. With yawning beak, he let go a fierce roar. Luna almost grinned in appreciation at such a rare act of courage from a Griffin, but before he got too close, she unleashed another fiery bolt over the attacker's head. Still, the heat singed his wings. Quickly turning tail, he returned to his post.

Diving from the top of the tower with her club, Luna took a new position on the wall just above the gate. The pair of Griffins on duty there ran to the center of the courtyard, and the guards on the wall jumped down to join them. *Fools!* she thought with a shake of her head. She might have incinerated them all, so closely did they stand together.

A pair of oaken double doors at the base of the tallest tower swung open. Minhep, now the Griffin leader after Gaunt and Gorganar, paced out on all fours. He wore a gold coronet around his Eagle's brow, and a short blue cape over his lion's back, arranged carefully so it didn't interfere with his white-feathered wings.

He looked at Luna warily. "Brainless Dragon, did you come to fight?"

Luna chuckled softly. "No, you half-starved fleabag," she answered. "I came to trade insults. You look silly in that outfit. Gifts from your Angmar masters?"

Minhep fixed his gaze upon her, and she saw the treachery he was contemplating. "I think you need a backrub like the one we gave your brother. Come down, and we'll take care of that."

Luna felt a flash of anger at Minhep's mention of Harrow. Just outside these walls, the Griffins had pinned her brother to the earth by his wings and tortured him. They wouldn't get the chance to do the same to her.

"There is something within these walls I need," she admitted. She watched the Griffins in the courtyard carefully, and with her ears she listened for things she couldn't see. Still, she clung to one small hope that she could avoid trouble. The Dragonkin and the Griffinkin had not always been enemies. "A child's life hangs in the balance, Minhep. If there can be peace between us for one hour, we need not fight this time."

Minhep regarded Luna for a long moment. Luna knew a stall when she saw it, and with her Dragon hearing she noted the soft pad of Griffin paws outside the walls and the easy whisper of the wind in feathered wings. "Indeed, a child's life hangs in the balance!" Minhep cried, his expression turning angry. "Bring me the man-child that took Gaunt's life, and then, Luna, I'll give you anything!" He shook one lion's paw.

It must have been a signal. While Minhep held her attention, other Griffin forces had slipped through back doors and back gateways to sneak up on her. Without moving from her place, she turned her head and blew a cloud of fire that scattered the foes assembling overhead. Feathered wings burst into flame, and lion fur smoked. Griffin screams echoed into the woods.

"Idiots!" Minhep roared. "She one lone female!"

Luna spun about and hurled her club like a spear straight for the Griffin leader. "With Dragons as with so many others!" she answered as Minhep flung himself aside. "The female is the deadliest of the species!"

Another Griffin attacked her from her left flank. Spreading her wings, she leaped into the air and snatched him in mid-flight. "This for my brother, Harrow!" she shouted as she flung the Griffin down upon one of the stakes outside the wall.

From opposite sides two more came at her. One, she knocked out of the air with a flip of her tail. She caught the other with her teeth, sank her fangs deep into his throat, and hurled him at the Griffin leader. "I'll tear this fortress stone from stone to get what I want, Minhep!" she warned.

Picking up the coronet, which had fallen from his head, Minhep flew into the air. "Didn't Harrow try that once?" he laughed. "Is there some competition between Stormfire's children that I can exploit?" Swooping across the courtyard, he seized up a rain barrel. "You shouldn't have come here, Luna," he cried as he flung the barrel. "You won't be leaving!"

The Griffin's hit her from all sides. With beaks and talons, they tore at her scaled hide. She beat her wings with furious energy, rising in the sky, diving and slamming through their ranks. When they tried to grab her, to pull her down, she burned them with her fire. Blood ran down her scaled face—hers or Griffin blood, she couldn't tell.

The battle carried her to the top of a tower, and five griffins flew at her with rage in their eyes. Luna's claws dug into stone. Ripping great chunks free, she flung up a barrage that scattered the five and sent them howling. Two more rushed at her from behind. Luna turned. A breath of fire, and they plummeted like shooting stars.

Lined up on the wall, Minhep's Griffins regrouped. As she had used stones against some of them, now one of them flung a stone. With Griffin strength, it zipped through the air to strike her in the head. For a moment, she reeled and started to topple from the tower, but she caught herself. It was enough of a distraction, though, for two to get above her with nets. That was how they caught her brother!

She could burn the nets, burn every Griffin that stood in her way. But how much time was left? She shot a glance to the east where dawn was breaking, where fingers of light were pushing back the stars. How much time was left for Ariel?

With his Griffins on the wall, Minhep shouted. "Bring her down! We'll crack her skull the same way we cracked her father's, and make stew out of her! Then, when our bellies are full, on to Stronghold! We'll make them all regret this night, and Wyvernwood will be ours!" A great cheer went up from the Griffinkin.

It was short-lived.

Over the tops of the trees, a great black Dragon sailed, blasting fire. The wooden stakes outside the wall erupted, becoming pillars of flame, and the Griffins turned to quiver and stare. The newcomer hovered above them, and the red firelight reflected fiercely on the white stars in the centers of his wings.

"Harrow!" Luna cried. She looked up long enough to blast fire at the net-bearing Griffins overhead, then dived down toward the courtyard. Before she reached it, Harrow breathed fire upon the wall. Too late, Minhep reacted, spreading his wings and leaping upward directly into the heart of Harrow's blast.

With another leader dead, the Griffinkin lost heart. For a moment, they stared at each other in stunned silence. Then, one by one, or in twos and threes, they took off in different directions, some toward Angmar, some toward the dawn, some following the retreat of night. But none flew south toward Stronghold.

Luna circled above the fortress, making sure they were gone before she folded her wings and settled down in the courtyard. Harrow landed on the wall, then sprang down beside her. "Since when did you become the suicidal lunatic in the family?" he demanded. While he waited for an answer, he kicked at a scorched ring of metal near his foot—Minhep's coronet.

"Don't act so surprised," she told him. "Luna—lunatic. Think of it as prophecy. All fortune in a word." She raised a paw to Agriope's mirror medallion, and a chill ran down her spine. "It's gone!" she cried.

Harrow's eyes narrowed. "What's gone?"

"A shard of a mirror!" she answered as she looked around. "Wrapped in a cord! I've got to find it! Ariel's life depends on it!"

Harrow folded his wings tightly as he regarded his sister. "You really are a lunatic, and a raving one at that!"

There wasn't time to explain. Luna wasn't sure how she knew, but unless she found the mirror shard and whatever it was supposed to guide her to by daylight, it would be too late. She remembered her brief glimpse of Agriope's face. It wasn't a face that ever knew the sun!

"Help me find it!" she insisted as she searched the courtyard, then the top of the wall and beyond it. Flying upward again, she searched the towers, not one of them, but all of them. Harrow, too, caught up by her desperation, began to search. Luna began to despair. It was just a mirror, a delicate piece of glass. If she'd dropped it, it could be in countless pieces!

"Luna!" Harrow called suddenly from the center of the courtyard. He pointed upward. "What's that?"

Halfway up the side of one of the towers, something glimmered. Luna approached it carefully. "It's the mirror!" she called to Harrow. The cord had come untied and fallen from her neck during the battle. In falling, it had caught on the outer molding of a window shutter. Only a miracle had kept it from shattering.

Luna feared it would take another miracle to retrieve it, for the shard hung precariously. Her claws weren't made for delicate grasping. She might drop the mirror again. Nor could she get close enough to it without her wings generating wind, which might dislodge it.

There was nothing to do but try. As carefully as she could, she reached out, but her lightest touch sent it falling through space. Luna gave a choked shout.

Below her, Harrow reached out with cupped paws and caught the shard. "Not bad!" he said, as he held the mirror up to his face. "Not bad at all."

A soft voice spoke from the shadows at the base of the tower. "Never put too much value on appearance. What is ugly on the inside can be beautiful on the outside, and what ugly on the outside may yet be beautiful."

Folding her wings, Luna landed beside her brother. She knew that voice! "Agriope!"

The old woman, still concealed in her robes and hood, stepped to the edge of the shadows, but no further. Ariel still rested in her arms as if weightless.

"Is she alive?" Harrow asked in a quiet voice.

Luna had a different question. Even after her glimpse beneath Agriope's hood, the mystery surrounding the old woman eluded her. She was frightening and soothing at the same time. Alien, yet embracing. Dangerous, and yet she inspired trust. Even in Harrow, apparently. Luna spread her wings to deepen the shadows around Agriope. "How did you get here?" she asked in nervous wonder. "All the way from the Blackwater River without wing?"

Agriope's hood turned ever so slightly upward, but not enough to reveal her face. "Am I without wings?" she asked with just a hint of mischief. "Now bring the shard, child, and follow me."

It took Luna aback to be called *child*. She and Harrow exchanged quick glances as Agriope, still bearing Ariel, moved from one shadow to the next toward the oaken doors of the tallest tower. With a surety of step, she went inside as if she'd done it many times before.

Luna, however, was not so sure.

"Think of it as a cave," Agriope called from within, "but keep your head down!"

Luna folded her wings tightly upon her back. She disdained the undignified position of walking on all fours like a common animal, so crouching as low as she could, she struggled through the doorway and found herself in a long corridor with arching ceilings. The stink of Griffin nearly overpowered her.

A robed arm beckoned from the far end of the corridor where another pair of large wooden doors opened, and Luna followed as Agriope disappeared through them. Luna's claws scraped on smooth stone tiles as she made her way. When she squeezed through the second set of doors, she found herself in a vast, dark chamber. "This was Gaunt's throne room," she whispered. Morkir had told her about it.

"Use your claws to tear through the floor, Luna," Agriope instructed. She was standing at the far side of the chamber and gently rocking Ariel. "There's a cave beneath this place. Redclaw was never anything more than a marker."

Ariel hesitated. A marker for what? "Shouldn't Harrow . . . ?"

Agriope shook her hooded head. "Harrow was tested," she answered. "And failed. Look at the shard you hold."

Luna gazed at the piece of mirror she held in one paw. It glowed with a pure blue light like nothing she had ever seen. She stared at it for a long moment, tilting it one way and then the other. The light remained unchanging. "Is this magic?" she whispered? She shook her head. "There isn't any magic left in the world."

Agriope didn't answer.

The chamber was high enough for her to stand a little. Setting the shard aside, Luna hooked her claws under the floor stones and tore them away. Beneath them, she found another layer of stones, older and less smooth, pitted by time. From the corner of her eye, she noticed the shard again, and its glow was an even deeper shade of blue. She tore away the second layer of stones, making a deep hole in the center of the chamber. Indeed, the walls of the chamber seemed almost to have disappeared and the ceiling to have receded, until she worked in a darkness lit only by the shard.

Beneath the last layer of stone, she found only earth. "Strike it with a hard blow," Agriope instructed.

Luna raised her paw high and struck the earth. Like punching through a crust, the earth gave way. Without waiting for instruction, she struck again and again, enlarging her hole, and with each blow the shard glowed brighter and brighter. When the hole was large enough, she knew what she had to do next. Yet she hesitated.

"What did you mean when you said Harrow was tested and failed?"

Agriope came to the edge of the hole with Ariel, and finding some steps in the darkness, began to descend. "Your brother came to this place with hatred and revenge in his heart," she answered. "You risked your life to come here for love."

Luna thought about that. It didn't seem fair to her somehow, but there wasn't time to think about it if Ariel's life was still at stake. Was Ariel's life still at stake? She caught her breath suddenly as fear clutched her heart, and picking up the shard again, she followed Agriope down into the earth.

The cavern was deep and cold, but dry with room enough for Luna to stand if she wished, but she continued on all fours. The shard in her paw pulsed with a deep cobalt glow, then slowly faded away. "It was only a key," Agriope said, "to the treasure awaiting you."

At the farthest end of the cavern, another soft light began to glow, a gentle rainbow radiance, crimson at its heart. With Agriope at her side, Luna approached it, and spears of light touched the cavern walls, the ceiling, igniting mineral streaks and the natural crystals embedded in the stalactites and stalagmites.

To one side, lay a flat stone with a stone pillow. Agriope placed Ariel upon it. "This is where I've slept for longer than even I know," she said with a note of wistfulness as she took the shard from Luna, "and where I'll sleep again shortly."

Luna blinked, because the shard seemed to be a complete mirror again. "I don't understand."

Agriope pointed. "Go toward the light."

Squeezing one eye shut, Luna gave Agriope a look. "That's never a good idea." But she went, advancing slowly, filled with a sense of wonder because the light seemed to dance on her ivory scales, to make her part of it. It tingled and tickled until she almost laughed.

Then, on a pedestal of stone that might once have been a natural stalagmite, she saw the source and caught her breath again. It called to her, for it knew her name. And she reached out to touch it, but drew back her hand, knowing on some instinctive level that it wasn't time.

It was a red jewel of improbable size, mounted in an upright ring of exquisitely carved ivory dragons. Agriope picked it up in both her hands. "*One must be given*," she said as she offered it to Luna. "This is the Heart of All Dragons. I've guarded it since Stormfire placed it in my keeping for one of his children."

Luna's heart felt like it would burst with joy. This was one of the talismans! "But what about Ariel?" she said. "Will the talisman heal her?"

The light coruscated over Luna's paws, rose twining and writhing up her legs. Luna's eyes widened, not with fear, but with amazement as the light spread like warm fire over her chest scales and entered her body. Then, the light in the jewel began to ebb and fade until only a soft crimson glow remained.

"You're the talisman now," Agriope said. "The essence of the Heart of all Dragons is love."

Luna hesitated, and felt a brief sadness, for suddenly she understood why she, not Harrow, had been given this gift. "But what about Ariel?" she persisted. "Is she alive at all?"

Agriope led her back to the little girl's side. "She has a fate and a destiny," Agriope explained as she stroked a tender finger along Ariel's cheek, "to die and be reborn in the elements, to be the bridge between old worlds and new. She will take my power, Luna, and she will take my place."

Luna frowned and set the talisman at the foot of the stone bed. Now she didn't understand. Ariel seemed so still and cold, as if she was already dead.

Agriope seemed to know her thoughts. "She died in the air when the arrow struck her, and the water cradled her when she fell. I packed her wound with the mud of Wyvernwood. She is already of three elements, Luna. And as you love her, you know what you must do."

Air, water, earth . . .

Luna recoiled. "You're mad!" she hissed. "I can't!"

And yet, she knew she had to. Agriope looked up and slowly pushed back her hood. "I'm old, Luna. Far too old. Ariel will care for the forest now. She will be its spirit and its protector, and because she's of the new world, she'll see all roads without this hideous visage."

Luna squeezed her eyes shut, and then opened them slowly. There was no need to fear Agriope, or to shrink from her. "What's ugly on the outside may yet be beautiful," she said. "I heard that once. I won't forget it."

While her resolve was still strong, she bathed Ariel in a stream of fire. The flames crackled over her clothing, consuming them, but they kissed her flesh, breathed new life into her small body. Luna watched in dreadful fascination, yet filled with hope and love. Her rider, her friend, would never be hers again.

When the flames flickered out, Ariel drew a soft breath and yawned. Her features composed themselves into an expression of peace as she turned over on her side and folded her hands under her head.

"We'll sleep together for a little while," Agriope said as she pulled her hood up again, "and then I'll teach her what she needs to know." She voiced a gentle yawn of her own and added, "It'll be easier now without a house full of Griffins overhead."

With both joy and sadness, Luna made her way through the cavern and up into the tower's throne room. There, she pushed the stone and rubble over the hole she'd made, sealing the chamber beneath once more.

Harrow still waited for her outside. She twined her long neck around his, embracing him as best a Dragon can. She had so much to tell, but one thing of most importance. "I love you," she said.

He untangled himself and took a step backward. "You really are a lunatic," he answered. But there was at least a hint of pleasure in it.

There was hope for him yet.

19

CHAN GLIDED SLOWLY ACROSS THE WIDE, MAJESTIC RIVER. Its waters glimmered in the last of the sunset as it ran with deceptive, serpentine grace between banks that were lined with sweeping forests of cottonwoods and willow trees. The branches waved, and leaves of green and gold and silver shivered in an easy breeze. The air was alive with colorful birds and swarms of insects.

Beyond the Flow of Dreams lay Asgalun, already deep in the shadows of night. Its distant mountains loomed black and sharp as broken teeth, and the final vestiges of sunlight vanished behind them as if swallowed by some fearsome maw. The forests that grew thick in the rich soil near the riverbanks thinned out as Chan continued westward, and the landscape turned strange. The slightest wind raised veils of ash and dust. The few misshapen trees seemed to lift their feeble limbs in surrender or in appeals for help.

These were the Haunted Lands where fierce battles had been fought by forces and powers beyond Chan's comprehension and with weapons unremembered. He shuddered as he looked around. As far as he could see the land was the same, and he couldn't resist the thought that by crossing the Flow of Dreams he'd entered another world. Even the air in the sky through which he flew reeked of an older Age.

Jake had been silent for a long time, but finally he spoke up. "Electra said we should follow the river southward," he reminded in a guarded tone.

Heeding Jake's admonition, Chan dipped one wing and turned back toward the Flow of Dreams. Soon enough they would have to cross the wasteland, but for a while they could rest beside the river and refresh themselves. As he turned, he gazed to the south, hoping for a glimpse of the unusual mountain formation called *the Drake*, but darkness and distance defeated his Dragon sight.

Returning to the river, Chan settled in a clearing near the water's edge. Jake unfastened his straps, and dropped out of the saddle onto the spongy earth. For long moments, he stood rubbing feeling back into his thighs, then he began foraging and groping about for pieces of driftwood and kindling. He wanted a fire, and in very little time he set a small pile of wood on the bank for Chan to ignite.

With the fire going, Chan stretched out on the grass and closed one eye while Jake sat near the warmth and munched a sandwich and a cookie from his new pouch. He chewed carefully, slowly, taking his time with his meal as he watched the flickering fireglow dancing on the water. When he'd swallowed the last bite, he drew his knees up to his chest and wrapped his arms around them. In a soft, weary voice he chanted as he glanced skyward.

> *"I spy! I spy!*
> *Way up in the velvet sky,*
> *The first star of night I see"!*

He didn't finish the familiar children's verse, and his voice trailed off across the wide water.

Chan gazed upward with his one open eye. Bright Rono shimmered like a jewel just above the eastern horizon, like a talisman with its own special power to draw the eye. He wondered if any of his friends in Wyvernwood were watching it. He wondered if Morkir and Katrina were watching. "Now your wish will come to be," he said, completing the verse for Jake.

Without rising, Jake twisted around. The firelight lent a red blush to his young cheeks as he forced a smile, but shadows masked the rest of his face. "I wish that the Time of Dragons would never pass." He turned his back to Chan again and, with a sudden flip of his wrist, he skipped a stone over the water. *Plink! Plink! Plink!*

Chan smiled as he listened to the sound. Apparently Jake had picked up more than wood in his foraging.

A familiar screech in the darkness above announced Skymarin's approach. The Lord of Eagles had left them at the river to do some exploring of his own. "It's strange and troubling," he said as he perched on a nearby tree branch, "how so few creatures on this side of the Imagination Mountains are able to converse. It's as if they've lost the ability to express themselves." He swiveled his head from Chan, to Jake, and back to Chan. "It makes a traveler feel lonely."

"None of the animals in Degarm can talk," Jake told him. "Or if they do, they only talk to themselves." Folding his hands under his head, he lay back on the grass in the fire's warmth. "Look!" he said, pointing upward. "A shooting star!"

Chan and Skymarin both looked, but the heavens were still. "That's the trouble with shooting stars!" the Lord of Eagles grumbled. "They come and go so quickly with barely time to make their acquaintance!"

Jake didn't answer. The boy seemed to have fallen asleep almost instantly without even removing his pouch, or his boots, or his shirt of ivory Dragon scales. His face turned toward the fire as his slender body relaxed and his mouth opened.

"I could drop a fish in that hole," Skymarin commented with amusement.

Chan grinned. "Bugs are more fun," he said. "Big black beetles, especially. But unless he starts to snore, just let him rest." He stretched his wings and then folded them and curled his sinuous tail around to rest his chin on its tip. "I'm going to do the same," he announced. "Good night, Skymarin."

Yet, he didn't fall asleep at once. The gently rushing water and the rustling leaves filled his ears with a pleasant harmony. The campfire crackled and popped. Insects chirped. He gazed up at Rono again and at all the other stars spangling the night. All the smells of the woods wafted over him—the moist earth, the grass, the bark, the river, and the smoke from the fire. He savored them all, opening his senses to the world around him, knowing he might not have such a quiet moment again.

The savage screeching of the Lord of Eagles woke him, and mingled with that, other screams that chilled Chan's Dragon blood. Snapping his eyes open, he stared toward the riverbank where Skymarin fought some dripping, half-scaled shapes. Locking his talons deep into flesh, the fearless bird stabbed over and over with his beak at something's face and eyes. He beat his wings furiously, and blood flew everywhere.

Two more dripping shapes reached for Jake as the boy sat up. He kicked at one, but it caught his ankle and tried to drag him toward the river. Before Jake could react, the other one grabbed his arms.

Then, one of the attackers, seeing Chan for the first time as he arched his wings and rose, glared with slittted yellow eyes and gave a sharp hiss that revealed needle fangs. Folds of pale skin on either side of its bald head and neck flared in warning. It pointed a thin, rubbery finger at Chan, then running back to the river, dived in and disappeared. It companion followed it.

Realizing that the attack was over, Skymarin stopped fighting and flew to his branch. He puffed out his red-stained chest with pride and glared as the third, badly shape staggered toward the water and fell in.

Leaping up, Jake seized a brand from the fire and backed away from the river. "I thought I was having a nightmare!" he said.

Skymarin swiveled his head and winked at the boy. "The nightmares nearly had you!" he said. Then with a more serious expression, he looked to Chan. "I've never seen Fomorians like those! And what are they doing so far from Wyvernwood?"

Careful to avoid the fire, Chan walked to the edge of the water and looked up and down the bank. Their visitors were gone without leaving trace or trail. "They weren't Fomorians," he said. "They were Nagas. Ancient snake-creatures—cobras, actually—older even than Dragons. There's a chapter on them in *The Book of Stormfire*, but it says *they're* supposed to be extinct."

"They didn't feel extinct to me!" Jake answered as he waved his brand around. He was still jittery and pale from his brush with the Nagas. "They touched me, *Sumapai*! I feel like my skin's crawling!"

According to the chapter, the Nagas had that effect on almost all creatures. They sparked an almost instinctive repulsion. No need to tell Jake that now, though. Chan stared into the depths of the river, then up and down the banks again, and into the forest darkness as he wondered how many of the Nagas still lived. A few? Hundreds? More?

He sniffed the air. "I think they're gone, " he said,

But Jake wasn't ready for reassurances. "That's a great idea," he answered as he threw his brand into the water and watched it sizzle out. "I vote for being gone, too!"

"Not until I've had a chance to bathe," Skymarin insisted. Flying down to the water's edge, he began to wash his talons and clean his bloody wings. "All this filth in my feathers throws off my balance."

"Fine, but just remember," Jake said, seeming to calm a little, "if you feel a little nibble at your toes, it might not be fish."

A soft splash sounded upriver, but the Lord of Eagles seemed unconcerned. Chan stretched his long neck over the water and looked around again. This time he saw them, saw their yellow eyes gleaming with dull animosity. The Nagas were gathering on the shoreline, hiding among the trees at the river's edge while others undulated slowly just off shore, watching.

He said nothing to Jake about the danger, but with the tip of one wing he scooped water onto the fire. The coals hissed, and smoke swirled. The small clearing, which had seemed so warm and pleasant, filled with shadows and an eerie gloom lit only by a moon that hid its face behind the trees.

He turned back to Jake and bent his head low. "I'm in the mood for a little night-flying," he said. "Mount up, and let's see where the wind takes us."

Scaled hand shot out of the water, grasping for Skymarin. With a screech, the Lord of Eagle beat his wings and soared upward. At almost the same instant a dozen Nagas charged out of the forest. Jake gave a scream as two of the creatures came straight for him, but despite his fear, he caught their outstretched arms and, falling suddenly to his back, flung them over his head.

Before the agile boy could rise, the rest of the Nagas ran forward. "Stay down!" Chan warned, and with a swing of his powerful tail, he scattered their attackers. Two more Nagas rose out of the river. Gleaming wetly, they charged ashore.

Skymarin dived down from his perch with talons reaching, and one of the Nagas screamed. The other came on, and Jake leaped up again. Seizing a half-burned branch from the dead fire, he swung it with all his young might and knocked the Naga back into the river. Another tackled

Jake from the side and bore him down. Folds of skin flared out like a hood, and fangs flashed.

They seemed intent on the boy! Unable to use his fire in such a confined place, Chan lunged forward to pluck the Naga off Jake with his claws. Roaring in anger, he hurled the cobra-man across the treetops. But an unexpected weight landed on his neck as another Naga sprang up. He felt the scrape of fangs against his scales and almost laughed. He shook his head, but somehow the tenacious creature hung on.

Jake sang out. "Chan, hold still!" A brief whir filled the clearing, and a stone zipped through the air. The Naga on Chan's neck shrieked and tumbled to the ground. With his sling at the ready, Jake drew another stone from his pouch. With a rapid flip of his wrist he let the missile go, and another Naga just rising from the river, screamed. "I've found a whole new meaning to *rolling snake-eyes!*" he shouted over his shoulder to Chan.

"They think you're the number one item on their breakfast menu!" the Son of Stormfire answered as he swung his tail again as another group of Nagas rushed out of the woods.

"If they'll take a bite of you, they'll take a bite of anything!" Jake shot back. Raising an ivory-scaled arm, he gave a sharp whistle.

Relinquishing his grip on a Naga's face, Skymarin flashed to Jake's side. His talons and beak dripped blood. "Those things taste like . . . !"

Jake cut him off. "Don't say it!"

Chan stretched out his neck again. "Anybody want to stick around?"

Skymarin spread his wings and took off again, climbing high into the night as Jake jumped up, caught the saddle and swung into place. Shoving the sling deep into his pouch, he grabbed the saddle horn with both hands. "Go!" he urged.

Mindful that Jake hadn't wasted time strapping himself in, Chan spread his wings and flew into the air as smoothly as he could. Out over the broad river he sailed before he banked southward with Skymarin leading the way. The moon, almost full now, glimmered on the rippling surface as they followed the river's course. With one keen eye directed downward, he scoured the banks for signs of more Nagas. *Ramoses will have to rewrite the chapter on these cobra-creatures*, he thought to himself as he flew onward.

Working carefully, Jake began to fasten his straps, and with that done, he wound his sling around his wrist again until it looked once more like a harmless bracelet. Chan pursed his Dragon-lips in a thoughtful expression. *Slings, arrows, telescopes, ballistas, that strange beheading blade in Throom Odin*—he had to give credit to the Race of Man—Humans, as Jake called them. They were inventive, even clever.

A munching, chewing sound caused Chan to twist his head back. Jake grinned around a mouthful of cookies. "All that exercise gave me an appetite," he explained, spewing crumbs as he spoke, but in the rush of their flight, the crumbs flew backward to speckle his face.

"I'm sure we could have stayed for dinner," Chan answered.

Jake shuddered as he pushed another bite of cookie into his mouth. "Everyone wants to eat me!" he complained as he chewed. "The Griffins, the Nagas. . . . "

The Son of Stormfire chuckled. "They don't appreciate how tough you are."

The moon continued its journey across the night sky. Falling silent, Chan paid more and more attention to the western horizon as he sought for a mountain formation that resembled a Dragon. The forests along the riverbanks began to thin, especially on the side that was Asgalun, and soon rugged cliffs rose up, instead. He saw no sign of Nagas, nor any other life, not even birds.

The land possessed a pallid grayness that might have been caused by the moonglow, although most likely it was the same ash and dust he'd seen before. This far south, thick clouds of fog drifted over the river, filled the rocky gorges, and spread outward in wisps and vapors. The few solitary trees that he could see looked black and barren, more like trees in the dead of winter than in summer.

Asgalun looked scorched, and not just by Dragonfire.

Skymarin voiced a short cry and darted suddenly across his path. In his role as team scout again, he'd been flying farther inland, exploring and searching on his own. The Lord of Eagles shot past and then wheeled about to take a place near Chan's left wing.

"Polly wanna cracker?" Jake held out the remains of a cookie in good-natured teasing.

Skymarin pretended not to hear. With the wind sweeping through his feathers, he called to Chan. "Our journey's end lies this way." Dipping a wing, he angled off to the southwest.

With a frown, Chan pursued the Lord of Eagles. "Electra said to follow the Flow of Dreams!"

"Three hundred years is a long time, Son of Stormfire," Skymarin reminded without looking back. "Past these cliffs the river changes course. If you follow it, you'll never find your mountains. But the old bed lies this way. Trust me."

"You've always had my trust, old friend," Chan answered.

Side by side, they turned away from the river to sail above the gray, moonlit cliffs. Over rolling hills they flew, and through misty valleys that should have been lush with vegetation, but weren't. Gliding low to the ground as he followed the Lord of Eagles, Chan studied the signs he knew to watch for. Skymarin's matchless vision could not be doubted, though, and the Eagle raced ahead with crisp precision, sure of his destination.

When the land flattened out once more, he saw at last the ancient riverbed, the wide cuts and deep channels in the ground that erosion tried but failed to hide. To the east, the Flow of Dreams in its new course couldn't be seen, but when he looked to the west neither did he see Electra's mountains.

Strapped and secure in his saddle, Jake had fallen asleep. Moonlight shimmered on the ivory scales of his shirt, and the wind whipped his hair. Though his hands were locked upon the saddle horn, his eyes were closed tight. "Sleep well, *Chokahai*," Chan whispered with a backward glance. "Wherever your dreams flow, may they be sweet."

With a soft warning screech, Skymarin dived toward a tall, dead tree that rose like an ominous emblem on the old riverbed. Perched on one of the barren limbs, he swiveled his head to look westward. Not wishing to wake his rider with a sudden plummet, Chan flew on, losing altitude gradually as he gently circled back. With utmost care, he settled to the ground beside the tree. "Lord of Eagles, why have we stopped?" he asked in a low voice.

Skymarin rolled one toward Jake. "I thought the boy could use a pee-break," he answered with just a hint of mirth. "In truth, my wings are not as strong as yours, Son of Stormfire. I've reached my limit."

"You have no limit, Skymarin," Chan said, though in his heart he heard the sorrow and fatigue in the old bird's voice. "You've flown farther and faster than any Eagle."

Skymarin bowed his head at the compliment, but then he looked westward again. "This tree marks a point as surely as if someone had planted it for the purpose," he continued. "You can't see it yet, but I can—three mountains, the middle one cragged and taller than the other two. Before this point or past it, they're mountains like any others. But viewed from here, from this very angle, they suggest an image, the unmistakable shape of a Dragon."

Chan strained to see. A Dragon's eyes were good even in the dark of night, but no such image presented itself, nor did he see any mountains. "I'll wait here with you until sunrise," he said.

"No, Chan." He sounded tired, but there was no weakness in his voice. "Your destiny waits there, and you should never make destiny wait longer than necessary. Fly with the moon straight west, and trust your senses."

With great effort and eyes dull with pain, Skymarin flew to a higher branch to look Chan in the eyes. "Son of Stormfire, do you feel it?" he said. "Your father stood here where you're standing now. The ground vibrates with his presence!"

Awakened by the voices, Jake sat up in the saddle and rubbed his eyes. "Where are we?" he asked.

"The Dragonkin with all the fabulous races fought their last great battle here against the Race of Man. An ancient Age ended at this place!" Skymarin stretched his feathered pinions wide and then wrapped them around himself. "We stand on history, Chan. And if I don't make it home to Wyvernwood, the flight was worth it."

"What's he talking about, *Sumapai?*" Shifting uncomfortably in the saddle, Jake shot a look at Skymarin. "Of course you're going to make it back home! You'll make it if I have to carry you in my arms! Tell him, Chan!"

Chan didn't answer at once for he was lost in visions. With narrowed eyes he turned his head from side to side. The clash and clangor of battle filled his ears as ghostly warriors fought. Dragons filled the skies as far as he could see, with Griffins, Rocs and Harpies, too. The roars of ancient Manticores tore across the fields while Minotaurs beat bloody drums and Wyrms and Satyrs screamed, and one lone white Unicorn trumpeted commands.

And in the raging tumult Men screamed, too, their high-pitched voices distinct and unmistakable!

Everywhere he looked, the fertile ground ran red, and crimson streams ran down the riverbanks to stain the Flow of Dreams with nightmare.

The gasping breaths, the death rattles, the pleas, the prayers—he heard them all. Then something more that froze his heart —the angry song of sorcery! The smell of magic filled his head, mingled with the death-stink, as the sky flashed, but not with lightning. His eyes burned! His scales itched and tingled in the savage storm of spells, in the crackling, electrifying horror of their power! The heavens churned! The earth bucked and twisted! Such unbridled, unrelenting fury!

It could only have one end.

All magic drained. Life drained. The land drained.

Chan sank to his knees, and then to all fours, as the visions ceased. With uncontrollable bitterness and grief he wept, devoured by sights and memories not his own. Asgalun had been waiting for him, waiting for a Child of Stormfire, to tell its tale as no book or scroll could tell it. *Waiting—like a trap.*

Throwing back his head, Chan howled in pain and stared toward the west. He could feel the talisman now. Its power throbbed across the Haunted Lands. It waited for him, too.

"*Chokahai*," he said to Jake, "get on." The boy had jumped out of the saddle to stand trembling and wide-eyed by the boll of Skymarin's tree, but when Chan bent down, his rider swung into the saddle again without a word or hesitation. To Skymarin, he said, "Rest, Lord of Eagles. It's almost done."

Rising into the sky again, he looked about to see the ghosts of countless Dragons flying with him, escorting and guiding him. He didn't need the moon or sun to find his way. He followed where his kindred led. He felt their eyes upon him as he flew, sensed their curiosity about his rider

He's one of us, he told them. *He has a Dragon soul.*

His kin accepted that.

The moonlight limned three mountains in the distance, one tall with two smaller on its flanks. Like a Dragon's shadow it rose up from the plain. *The Drake*, Electra called it, not knowing if the talisman waited there, or if it only marked the way.

But Chan knew.

With the ghosts of his kindred chasing, he flew around the slopes and peaks. Then, high up on a precipice with barely room to land, he spied a cave where one more ghost awaited. "Go inside and bring out what you find," he said to Jake as he settled down. "You've earned the honor." *I'll wait here*, he added silently, *and have a conversation with my father.*

Ignoring the height and the dangerous winds, Jake jumped from the saddle. For only a moment, he stared at the gaping blackness before him where not even the moonlight penetrated. Then, with a lift of his head he entered the cave.

"You thought there was no magic left," he said to his father. "Did you know that Asgalun, itself, would trick you?"

Saying nothing, Stormfire looked down, and then flew away on wings of ghost-fire.

A moment later, Jake emerged from the cave. "One will be sought," he murmured, extending his hands. Cupped in his palms he held an exquisite crystal figurine—the Glass Dragon. Though its eyes shone in the moonlight, its wings were caked with gray dust and ash.

"It needs some cleaning," Jake said. "Who were you talking to?"

Chan glanced skyward. The ghosts of his kindred were gone. "Guard that well," he said with a nod toward the talisman. "It's yours to carry until we get back to Wyvernwood."

Jake's face lit up. "We're going home?"

Chan smiled as he bent low so his rider could mount. "We're going home."

EPILOGUE

"AND THEY DID GET BACK HOME, DIDN'T THEY?" Puck said with a yawn. Turning on his side, he scratched the golden scales on his belly and looked at his mother. He could barely keep his eyes open. After all, he'd had a big day.

"Of course," Marina answered as she closed the book and balanced it on her knee. "Even Skymarin. Heroes always get back home eventually, and the ones who found the talismans were true heroes."

Puck's tail thumped the floor as he rolled over on his stomach. "Not always!" he protested. "Morkir and Katrina were heroes, too, but they didn't come home!"

Marina set the book aside and rocked herself as she gazed into the fireplace. "That's true," she answered slowly, "but they found new homes for themselves, and that's really what they were looking for—not the talismans, but their places in the world." A wistful smile turned up the corners of her Dragon lips. "Sooner or later, that's a quest we all undertake, and when we find that, it's worth more than all the magic in the world."

With a soft sigh, Marina rose and put the book on the shelf in its proper place among the other books. She didn't really think of them as *her* books. She was only their guardian and caretaker. Someday they would belong to Puck, just as they had belonged to other guardians and caretakers before her.

"When the three talismans were united," Puck said thoughtfully, "how long did it take to . . . ?"

Marina interrupted her Dragon-son with sly shake of her head. "That's enough storytelling for tonight," she said.

With an insistent frown, Puck thumped the floor again. "But when Rage went to Stronghold . . . !"

Marina pressed a claw to her lips to hush Puck's questions. If she left him hungry enough for the answers, he'd come back for another story. Or maybe he'd show more interest in the books and decide to read for himself. "Go to bed now," she told him. "You'll need rest for all the adventures you've got planned for tomorrow."

Rolling over on his back, Puck folded his paws on his chest and stared at the cave's ceiling. Going to bed was always the last thing he wanted to do. "I don't have any adventures planned," he said, yawning for a second time.

"At your age, you've always got adventures planned," Marina countered with a hidden grin.

Reluctantly, Puck got up and headed for bed. For just a moment, he lingered near the bookshelves, and his gaze roamed over some of the titles. The light from the fireplace glimmered on his scales, lending him a reddish sheen that rippled when he moved. *Almost like flame,* Marina thought. *That's how Chan looked.*

"Tomorrow night," she promised. "After dinner, if you like, we'll read about Ronaldo. . . ."

"Rage!" Puck corrected. "He chose that name, and I like it, too."

"Pish," Marina said with a stern look. She turned away to admire the paintings that decorated the walls of her home. They were among her most cherished possessions, and every one of them bore the same artist's signature. "Nobody ever called him that with a straight face, except a few weak-kneed Humans who didn't know any better. Certainly not his rothers. *Ronaldo* was a perfectly good name, and a very honored one!"

Puck's shoulders slumped, but he planted a kiss on his mother's cheek as he went to his bed. She grinned again at the way he pouted.

Alone, she cast another look at the book she'd just read to her son and lightly touched its spine. The story didn't end there, of course. No good story ever ended between two covers. The questions still on Puck's mind, though, were not the ones that intrigued her. She knew the answers to his questions.

Agriope had given Ariel a mirror—not the same mirror that Luna broke, but a different mirror, which she had left in Carola's home. What had become of it? The answer to that mystery, she knew, lay somewhere in one of the books she had not yet read. Even a grownup Dragon had to have something to look forward to.

With Puck in bed, she went to her door and looked out at the night. The wind was warm and carried the scent of the flowers in her garden. Rono shone brightly, and the crescent moon made a pleasant smile in the western sky.

"Marian?" she whispered as she took a step past the door and out into her yard. "Are you there?" She listened, hearing only the wind and the chirping insects. "Ariel?" Then she laughed softly at herself.

Grownups need adventures, too, she thought to herself, *even if they're only small adventures.* She pulled the door to her cave gently closed and turned to face the sky again. She hadn't flown in a long time, a very long time, but the stars were magical tonight, each a talisman unique and twinkling, and the wind called her name. *Just once around the hill, she decided, or maybe a little farther.*

Her silver wings caught the moonglow as she rose, and every ghost in Wyvernwood turned out to see Marina's shadow.